THE DEEP BREATH

—— A Paladin's Tale ——

DR. ANTHONY G. JOHNSON

Order this book online at www.trafford.com
or email orders@trafford.com

Most Trafford titles are also available at major online book retailers.

Printed in the United States of America.

ISBN: 978-1-4907-4252-6 (sc)
ISBN: 978-1-4907-4251-9 (e)

Trafford rev. 09/17/2014

 www.trafford.com

North America & international
toll-free: 1 888 232 4444 (USA & Canada)
fax: 812 355 4082

PREFACE

Blood always has distinctive smell and sound when it has been spilled especially when it drips from metal. A cold breeze rushed through the building. All the warriors and the hostages heard it; a sadistic giggle. Then they heard this eerie whistle. It was a familiar tune that had an ominous tone; normally a person doesn't whistle a children's song at a time like this. Rock a Bye Baby was the song for those lucky enough to survive this day, which would never have the same meaning again. *He has come*, Petamauck thought. The only way that this does not turn into a complete tragedy was if the marauder was sent to negotiate. Yeah, that will *never* happen.

The members of the Paladin Liberation Party, the warriors that had sworn allegiance to Petamauck, were certain that even if the monster was called, they could stop it. The feeling was that there was no way that it could kill all of them. Some were of the thinking that if he was called, his love and admiration for his mentor would cause him to hesitate, if not join their cause. This is a level of danger that none of these proud warriors have ever known. Never has a group of warriors of the Order ever faced an enemy so overwhelmingly committed to ending their lives. Paladins are trained to be fearless in the face of certain death. The question now is how to deal with certain death from someone that even more fearless and resolute than they are? The screams heard from these proud warriors werebeyond nerve rattling; the blood curdling screams. In his entire career, Petamauck had never heard one of his comrades' scream in terror; until now.

The hostages were afraid also but that should be expected, but not my own warriors, Petamauck pondered. Captain Voss had decreed that it wouldn't reach this hall, but that was not true; because he was already there. The noises were beyond anything that the hostages had ever imagined. These sounds were similar to a butcher carving up pieces of beef or pork; accept the stock was coming from his fellow Paladins who were unlucky enough to have crossed the monster this evening.

Petamauck knew that his death was coming soon and there was nothing that he could do about it. It couldn't be bargained with and it couldn't be reasoned with. He had always heard of the screams that usually followed when the monster was near, but never pointed in his direction. It is said that no one has ever crossed the monster and lived. Outside of the hall doors, you could hear the bones being broken and bodies being ripped apart, as well as blood being spilled. A cold chill went up his spine. Voss screamed and then nothing but another song being whistled. The little girl with gray-eyes said it best, **"Mommy is this what death sounds like?"** You could hear the blood dripping from his toys as it walked; and then that awful melody. They say that when you are about to die, every breath is labored, but also a sense of peace occurs. In this room, the despot felt a sense of calm, but God it is cold in here; so hard to breathe. And then the monster kicked in the door with this huge smile on his face; a spook story made real.

CHAPTER 1

Today Is A Good Day To Die!!!!

"**It has been a good day!!!**" exclaimed the madman. This is truly a day of days: one of the most accomplished members of the Paladin Order has not only gone rouge, but he has brought the Mu Star system down to its knees. The planet Mu-Prime was one of the most visually stunning planets within the Terran Alliance. Its shimmering blue-green skies have been darkened by the black smoke, fire, and ash. The beautiful capital city of this great planet, Axum, a testament to both artistic and scientific excellence has been essentially torn asunder by the destructive treachery of the once respected and revered warrior. Petamauck, the greatest teacher of logic and reason within the Order of Paladins has chosen to devolve into madness based upon the thought process that his actions are not only considered right, but also necessary to ensure peace throughout the quadrant.

There are twelve planets within this binary star system, with more than 350 billion inhabitants. This entire way of life for these peaceful and hardworking people has literally been ground to a halt, as this would be despot has taken control of the capital planet and has dared anyone who considers himself/herself brave enough to challenge him and his followers to a fight to the death. He has most of the leadership of the system, including the family of the system's Regis, under his domain.

For 899 hours, the capital planet has been under his rule. His minions have destroyed most of the planet's defensive infrastructure and has also killed most of the elite guard that has been assigned to protect the Regis; the star system's Senate, as well as the Religious and Cultural community. Outside of Representative Mathias, who was on a diplomatic assignment, Petamauck has everyone and everything that he needs to continue a prolonged siege and force his opposition to any terms he deems sufficient. Right now in the capital city, it is quiet, save a couple of explosions here and there; brave soldiers and normal citizens have continued in vain to keep fighting. Hoping against hope, that someone will come to aid them in this disparate hour. The explosions are becoming fewer and fewer as these rebels are being captured or being killed as the hours go by.

"Are you ready to bow and swear loyalty to the Paladin Liberation Party or are you ready to die for standing against us?" sneered the captain. **"It is okay to cry and beg for mercy for you and the terrorist that you serve. Are you ready to confess your treason? Speak!"** The commanding officer was a proud and confident member of the Paladin Liberation Party; she was a former member of the Terran Navy, now aligned with the bold and visionary leader of the party, Petamauck. The "terrorist" are actually nothing of the sort; they are children who have been forced into a violent, bloody conflict by former Terran Alliance soldiers who now believe it is their right to govern over their home system and are prepared to kill to make their point both simple and plain. The leader of the freedom fighters for planet Mu is only 19 years old, a former student who decided to take a stand against those that took what did not belong to them. This group of dissenting soldiers believes that their charge gives them the right to take liberty from others under the banner of freedom from the Terran Alliance.

The resistance leader, Nasir Sodiq, was prepared to die. He was not a man of tremendous stature; the leader was so young that his facial hair had barely begun to grow in. At first the citizens were intrigued when Petamauck and his troops came to Mu promising an opportunity to be rid of the oppressive nature of the Terran Alliance and their overseers, the Inter Galactic Federation. The young leader was one of the few who would stand against the rhetoric; he could read between the lines and through all the lies. At first, Nasir wanted to engage in a debate with Petamauck over liberty and free will. That was before the young orator's parent's had been murdered. At that point, he knew that there was no turning back. Even though he was no soldier, he knew that he had to fight against the occupation of his home solar system. He went underground, knowing that his defiance would certainly mean death but he was okay with this proposition. The freedom of his people is worth fighting for. That freedom is worth dying for.

The young commanding officer was going to be executed when the PLP troops had caught up with him. With his forces dwindling and hope dissipating, he planned a last desperate attempt to assassinate Petamauck and failed; now he was theirs. Nasir Sodiq, a criminal in some circles and a hero in others, was going to be executed by firing squad for crimes against liberty. *What a joke*, thought the warrior. Nasir was not some well-trained soldier, he was a student. He wanted to become a cleric and now because of the madness of Petamauck and his minions, he is going to die. He will never have children, he will never no true love; he will never get a chance to become a great contributor to society. His father and mother would never get a chance to see him grow up; they were taken away from him. All of his loved ones had suffered at the hands of these so called patriots. All of that has been taken away from him and countless others for a cause that is not their own.

Whether he wanted it or not, he became the symbol of hope for his planet. He led a campaign of both optimism and strength. Many of the freedom fighters were prepared to fight and die by his side. The head of the PLP, Petamauck, even admired this young man. Like many of the citizens of Mu, he had never even been out of his own star system; Nasir wanted to go to the University of Kumasi, located in the Eden system, when his primary studies were over. His mother and father dreamed of him being a great teacher of love and logic; it happened, but not in the way that he originally conceived. Before this set of circumstances, he had always wanted to meet the great and wise Petamauck. He heard that the leader of this campaign had graduated from the same university; not exactly a ringing endorsement at this point.

The captain had thousands of people standing there to watch this punishment of the would-be freedom fighter. Sodiq is not alone; more than 1,300 people, none being older than thirty were all about to be terminated. Their deaths would serve as an example of what will happen to all who stand in the way of liberty and progress. It is ironic because there is nothing virtuous about the actions of the captain and her troops. Captain Pax Voss was beautiful; she had a regality that belied her current behavior. The young commander finally did speak to her, knowing that his words would one day ring true. Her death and the death of all of the would-be liberators was inevitability.

"I have nothing left to say. I will not kneel to this man, you or anyone else in your cause. You believe that you are serving a just cause huh? You are nothing. You don't deserve to say that you defend the innocent and helpless; you should be protecting us, but I do not

fear death because I know where we are going. I believe that very soon we will be able to continue our debate over liberty and free will." The captain then halted the execution. She was so beautiful, so seductive, and powerful. She walked up to the commander and kissed him sweetly. She whispered to Sodiq. **"So you think that I will die soon? Just who is going to be my executioner? This is just the beginning. No one will stand against us."** At this point, another officer hit Nasirin his ribs, shattering his left side. Then Voss smiled and nodded her head as five other officers began to pummel the young leader as his fellow citizens watched as he was bloodied.

A funny thing happened, while Sodiq had been bloodied, his spirit remained unbowed. Coughing blood and choking, he was able to gather enough strength to make one final statement, standing in defiance of the bullies. He smiled. **"My dear captain, you think that I am your problem? That's funny. We were just trying to prove that righteous shall not be forsaken. An angel will come for us when this is over; I am at peace with who I am and what I have done. The question is do you have the same level of comfort?I also know that someone will come for all of you as well. I don't know his name; even if I did, I would dare not speak it. But he will come for you soon. You are all dead. You just don't know it yet."** With that last statement, the alluring captain kissed him, then she stabbed the man-child, and he fell. Once she walked out of the way, the rest of the young dissenters were cut to shreds. Her commanding officer was watching the melee; she walked up to the leader, a powerful and wise man, and kissed him passionately. She smiled. **"This is a good start."**

Every hour that goes by only further strengthens Petamauck and his follower's resolve that they are serving a just cause. An entire attack force of more than fifty star destroyers and countless star fighters have been razed surrounding the planet. Three dozen star cruisers have arrived from the Terran Alliance Armada to witness the carnage that this rouge Paladin has caused and considering the abilities of the madman and his followers, no invasion force seems to be able to break their defenses.

One massive ship has emerged from the compacted formation to move forward and assume the position of command. Even for a Colonial-Class star cruiser, it is considered enormous. It is more than seven thousand meters long and has a level of firepower that strikes fear into the hearts of any opposition foolish enough to challenge it. The Alpha

Centauri is a legend among friend and foe, its accomplishments far too numerous to mention. If there is a problem, the Centauri and its crew are usually sent to resolve it. This colossal dreadnaught's main energy turrets are now pointed at a friend, prepared to destroy this entire planet if necessary. The orders were simple: stop Petamauck and do it as efficiently as necessary. If the leadership of this system cannot be saved, destroy the entire planet. This is not the *last* resort, but the *only* resort. It is an ironic twist of fate that the Alpha Centauri would be sent, because this vessel is the very one that the Paladin and Teacher, Petamauck actually served. He served as the Centari's commanding bridge officer and tactician. His chair, his laugh, and his experience are sorely missed during a time of crisis; he is the cunning foe instead the virtuous leader he had been known as.

The bridge, however, is busy none the less. Instructions are being shouted and repeated and various officers are moving quickly and with purpose. All of these men and women are preparing for the deep breath. If the order is given, the crew of this great ship will go into action and will kill a valued and trusted friend, not to mention countless innocent people. Petamauck hasn't just trained most of the officer core of this ship, but he has trained many commanding officers throughout the Terran Alliance. It is a surreal environment, knowing that in a few tense moments, the entire course of the Terran Alliance could be changed forever.

There are 13 star systems associated with the Alliance. This could not be happening at a worse time for humanity, as their application for full entrance into the Inter-Galactic Federation (IGF) is about to be reviewed. The most beloved and respected Terran Chancellor, Alron Kush, has recently died and all Hell has broken loose. Since Kush's demise, there has been one crisis within the Alliance after another. This is the worst of worse case scenarios. At a time when unity is most needed within the leadership ranks of humanity, it is as if the very fabric of the Terran Alliance is coming apart at the seams. Under most circumstances, the Order of Paladins would be thought of as a beacon of hope and a pillar of stability. Unfortunately, Petamauck and his minions have chosen to try and break the Alliance in half.

Petamauck is leading this rogue faction of Paladins, who believe that history will judge them as heroes and liberators; to the masses, he is a madman who is in command of a brutal, yet cowardly menagerie. His group of seceding patriots has always believed that humanity does not need the IGF and that Terrans are being forced into joining a conflict that has nothing to do with them. That their benefactors, the Rioans, are forcing them to make good onIGF obligations; the 11 trillion Terrans should not be coerced to fight in a war created with a race of people that they have never seen. That from time to time, the river of liberty must be replenished by the blood of patriots. From time to time, bloodshed is a necessary component of diplomacy. None of that matters at this point, if the order has been given, 22 billion humans, the population of planet Mu Prime, will be wiped out.

Strategically, this star system is one of the most important, because it is in the region that is closest to the IGF territorial border. Petamauck'stroops began the conflict by attacking an IGF space station, destroying more than 20 star ships and killing more than nine million people, including more than two hundred thousand humans. He then retreated to the Mu system, which in turn the leader and his followers have overtaken the government. The IGF has sent fifteen Colonial-Class battle cruisers in an observation capacity only. If it were up to the Federation Military leadership, they would have handled the Paladin situation a long time ago; blood for blood. This is a dicey situation because the Federation and the Alliance are allies; no matter how destructive the situation, cooler heads on both sides realize that cooperation is far more important than potentially an all out incursion. The only ship that will be acting at the present will be the Centauri.

The leader of the Terrans, Alron Driax, has been on the capital planet, Eden, desperately trying to negotiate a diplomatic resolution so that the IGF and Terran Alliance can continue peaceful coexistence. She knows that time is running out. Every tactical offensive that has been attempted has not only failed, but failed horribly; and all the Terrans have been witness to both Petamauck's resolve and also listen to his rhetoric. Each failure by her military forces further reinforces the Paladin Liberation's position that she is in over her head as leader of the Alliance. Driax, the novice, has decided that it is time to have her most dangerous weapon at her disposal to be activated. She has been backed into a corner and has no other choice. God help them.

The most dangerous weapon that is at the disposal of the Terran Alliance or the IGF is not the Alpha Centauri however, that is merely the transport. The most dangerous weapon in the quadrant is a Paladin.

Not just *any* Paladin, but *the* Paladin. The top of the food chain; the best trained, most resolute, and most intelligent, he is the very best at the very worst. Even the most dangerous of all foes, the warriors from the Great Void, the Dark-Siders, have a healthy respect, if not fear of this combatant. The Alpha, as he is known, comes from the oldest planet of humanity, Terra or as the natives call it, Earth. He goes by the name of Cain; Commander Gaius Nicolas Cain. However, those within the IGF refer to him by his official title, *Khan Antonius.* Antonius is the most recent and some believe that will eventually become the greatest general in the history of the Inter Galactic Federation; the Alpha Paladin. For those who are unlucky to cross him, he has but one title that matters, *executioner.*

On the Alpha Centauri Bridge, the one remaining leader of Mu, Senator Mathias, is in consult with ChancellorDriax and standing beside him is a stunning brunette. Even in her battle uniform, her figure cuts a silhouette that makes her male officers sometimes blush; beautiful and powerful. She is the acting commander of the Alpha Centauri, since the normal Bridge commander is playing the role of madman oppressor for this evening. She is a hybrid, with Danyzer, the great Rioan general, as her father and Aya, an influential Terran senator within the IGF, is her mother. In her father's native language, her name would be unpronounceable to humans, so she merely goes by the initials, AC. Her codename is *The Weapon Maker*, but she is much more than that. She is a strategist and time traveler, not an immortal, but those abilities make her virtually eternal though. AC is considered a wise and valuable counselor in times of crisis and this time is no different. In one hour, the bombardment of an innocent planet will commence. On the capital planet of the Mu Star System, Mu Prime, billions of lives will be lost if something is not done about this madman, who has also been a dear friend to all who stand against him at this time. Bigger issues will persist, lines will be drawn. This is a potentially quadrant altering event; many of the Alliance's remaining citizens' spirits will be crushed. Even though many desperate circumstances may have led up to this point, it will be difficult to fully explain to the rest of the citizens that an entire planet had to be sacrificed. Confidence will be shaken to say the least in the capabilities of the new Chancellor; is this action the first of many other destructive decisions? Could these actions lead to secession of other human systems from the Alliance? The whole of the Terran Alliance and for that matter, the entire quadrant could be at risk. In one hour, the Terran Alliance could become just a memory.

One of the most trusted officers of the Centauri, Captain Sayied Faris, has begun to make a report on battle preparations. **"Everything is moving according to schedule Chancellor. Bombardment will commence within the hour unless otherwise specified,"** the officer replied. **"However, I must inform you that he is on the ground; just received a communication 90 seconds ago."** A puzzled look moved over both Mathias and Driax's faces. Frantically, the Terran leader inquired, **"what? He's there? I thought that he was on the ship!!! What is he doing?"** The commanding officer replied calmly, **"he is waiting for your orders. You said to commence attacks within the hour. The commander will ensure that those orders are carried out. None of them will leave the planet alive."** The remaining leader of the Mu star system interjected, **"Where is he? How far away from the Regis and the representatives is he? Can the Commander reach them? We must give him the opportunity. If the Major is right, he can stop them all before a more drastic action has to take place Chancellor. We must give Commander Cain time to try."** Driax's face immediately reddened.

Of all the issues that Alron Driax had to deal with during the first period of her ascension to the post of chancellor, Commander Nicolas Cain is easily the most difficult for her to comprehend. Her most impressive and unpredictable asset is at her disposal but this situation is complicated. Cain was loyal to the previous chancellor and he was also considered the closest friend to the leader of the PLP. He has recently returned from a secret mission from deep space and he has never interacted with her. This is a serious problem for her. All eyes, both friend and foe, are watching her actions.

The Chancellor has her allies, the IGF, demanding that she send Antonius to deal with the situation on Mu while her Terran Alliance advisors are against it stating that no one is certain of his political affiliations. She has no idea which way he is leaning. Commander Cain ordered Petamauck to be her counsel and the indirect results of that order was the creation of the Paladin Liberation Party. No political leader within the Terran Alliance has any idea of the foundation of this coup was the result of Petamauck's background intelligence report or whether this was the result of something far more sinister.

This was the opportunity that she had hoped for, but also was weary of. Cain might be the only person that could avoid a genocidal scenario, but she was apprehensive about using him. Alron Driax had so many factions trying to advise her to keep the Blood Knights out of this situation but she has no choice. The Paladins that compose the bulk of the PLP are among the most well prepared and well accomplished of the Order. These men and women have also been decimating the Alliance Naval Fleet. Several military officials have suggested that they reach some compromise with them because the Terran Alliance is being embarrassed by such a small force. No other Paladin Operations groups have been charged with dealing with the PLP because there is no guarantee that those warriors won't support Petamauck's position.

This is the chancellor's first military command decision; she had only been in charge less than one galactic rotation. The only member of the Terran leadership who had ever had direct contact with Cain was Alron Kush and he was recently assassinated. All the Regents, Clerics, and the Economic Guild were interested in her leadership skills, in particularly how the newest Alron would deal with Cain. She is the youngest Chancellor on record, while Kush was the oldest. She was certain that he was on her side because the Alpha Centauri and its crew were apparently still loyal to the Alliance. Cain only believes in total annihilation of the enemy; collateral damage means little to him. He is a problem solver and his primary problem is killing all of the Alliance's enemies. Besides, how could he reach the capital building in under an hour?

This Cain situation could be considered delicate to say the least. AlronDriax was a junior member of the Chancellor's cabinet. Kush didn't even take her on the diplomatic mission that ended in the demise of him and the rest of the senior staff. She wasn't involved in neither military or diplomatic affairs before this responsibility had been thrust upon her. She had little to no experience in dealing with the military arm of the Terran Alliance, much less the Paladins. She had never even seen Cain; as a matter of fact, no one in the current Legislative arm of the Terran government had. Everyone who had been familiar with him had been executed. The newest of the remaining leaders didn't even believe that he existed, that he was some spook story made up by the government to explain circumstances that they didn't want to explain. Commander Cain was an especially difficult situation because Kush was the only person that he answered to. Cain and the Centauri had been in another vicinity of the quadrant dealing with another conflict; he and Alron Driax had never spoken.

The mighty Khan had been considered a wild card throughout this entire situation because of his relationship with Petamauck. Antonius and Petamauck are especially close; Petamauck helped train him and considered Nick like a brother. Those who were in the know commented that Nick may have been the greatest student that the Order of Paladins has ever produced. Several members of the executive leadership were nervous about the Paladin uprising because Cain could easily be standing at his mentor's side. If Cain decides to take up Petamauck's charge, there would literally be nothing that anyone is this part of the universe could do to stop them. This concern about Cain's position had been enough of a deterrent to keep the Centauri out of the conflict until now. Cain's presence is the primary reason why the Federation hasn't approved deadly retaliatory measures; it is unknown how he'd respond. Whatever position that Cain takes, the crew of the Alpha Centauri will certainly follow. In one fell swoop, the young chancellor could forfeit her greatest military assets and witness the demise of her beloved Terran Alliance.

The intelligence report suggested that at least one hundred fifty Paladins were on the planet's surface. However, there were at least 30 Paladins within the capital building. The fear was that these forces would be able to overwhelm Cain and he would not be able to complete the task set forth by the Chancellor. After hearing about the number of Paladins on the surface, the Chancellor and Mathias began to discuss with Faris and AC what their other options were. It was believed by the politicians and clerics that thirty Paladins were impossible for a soldier even of Cain's ability. The leadership of the Terran Alliance was certain not even Cain could deal with these foes; after all, it wasn't like these warriors who served Petamauck weren't up to par. They were either Paladins or members of the elite Terran Special Forces as well. Besides there was no guarantee to the Terran leadership that Cain would not follow his friend and abandon the Alliance. Obviously, these leaders didn't know about the Khan's devotion to the Cause.

Negotiations of some kind of peaceful solution seemed to be a reasonable course of action. One potential option was for the Terran Alliance to cede their proprietorship of the Mu Star System and anyone who was prepared to leave the Alliance for their control was more than welcome to do so. The Chancellor quickly dismissed that idea. She was certain that if these soldiers realized that the Alliance would give in to their demands so easily, it would be open season. Every group of dissenters and rival systems would be trying to take a piece of the Alliance until there was nothing left. As far as the new Alron was concerned, negotiation from a position of weakness was totally out of the question. What was her most pressing concern was trying to stop the IGF from entering the fray to assist in the cleanup of the Terran Alliance's mess. As she was trying to address this crisis, her subordinates also wanted to observe how she deals with the Cain issue; he was ready to go to work.

The Federation had already given their marching orders to Cain; kill everyone who was responsible for the space station's destruction. That included Petamauck and Voss; those were the primary instigators. Senator Aya said that negotiations would continue between the IGF and the Alliance, but the command was given to slaughter the PLP. Nick was trying to wait until he received the go ahead from his Terran superiors; they were stalling. He had been monitoring the negotiations between both the Terran Alliance and also the PLP. This action went against the code of the Alpha; he does not negotiate. Cain was tired of listening; he had heard enough talking. It was time for the Alpha Paladin to exchange unpleasantries with his former comrades.

The Terran career politicians had no idea about the true abilities of this deadly operator. Very few had ever been exposed to Cain in general; his unit and his ship were considered the deep space operatives of the Alliance; they spent more time in Federation space than they did in Terran space. They had never been called to deal with domestic issues, until now. Not only was he inside the city, he was already *inside the capital building*. Finally after tiring of the diatribe between his superiors the Paladin finally spoke. **"Mistress, I am ready to strike without a moment's hesitation or an ounce of regret. I serve you and am at the service of the Terran Alliance and the IGF; that hasn't changed. They have crossed the line, simple and plain. My weapons are loaded and my blade is sharpened. I have already incapacitated the guards below the primary levels. I will slaughter them or anyone else who would dare cross you my sweet Alron. You can send the rest of the troops in whenever you get ready; it won't matter though. I promise you that there will be nothing left but the broken and dismembered bodies**

of your enemies. Just say the word; I am your blade. You have my answer. Petamauck is a dead man. Today is a good day to die."

Nicolas was born in Barstow, California to Humanities Professor Dr. Antoine Cain and Professor of Woman's studies, Dr. E. E. Cain. He was given up for adoption right after he was born. The day of his birth was an especially sad one. On that day, his father had been executed by rebels who had accused him of being a spy; in reality, he was delivering supplies to refugees from the civil war in his native country. His father died in the service of the very people that he was attempting to aid and his mother died during child birth, many of the doctors felt it was from a broken heart over her lover being killed because of what she felt was a senseless conflict.

His paternal grandparents decided against raising him because they didn't feel prepared to handle another child. They were already taking care of too many children in their orphanage. His maternal grandparents did not want him either. Their belief was that he was a child of death; his parents were dead before he was but a few moments old. Even though she had been adopted, his mother's parents felt the sting of her loss. His mother was their only child, but her death was so traumatic his grandfather decided that he would be too much of a reminder of their child's demise. Both sides of his family had mutually decided that theywanted no contact with him; ever. His first experience of death and loss was the first moments of his life and it would be a sign of things to come.

After being placed in a foster agency, he was sent to live with some foster parents who had a pristine reputation. Unfortunately, it was a farce. His foster parents turned out to be sadists of the highest degree. He had four foster brothers and sisters and he was the youngest. They were all being abused by cruel caregivers. He was beaten constantly physically and emotionally, constantly being told that his parents' death was his fault by his foster mother and he was physically abused by his foster father, who beat him with belts, broomsticks, and also burned him with an iron. His foster sister, Maya, was also abused; not just physically, but also sexually. After she turned 15, their foster father took a keen interest in her sexual "development." After a particularly brutal attack, Nicolas had enough of their abuse. At 6 years old, his second meeting with death had occurred.

With uncommon focus and resolve, he poisoned his foster mother and then framed his foster father. He blamed his foster mother for creating an environment in which depravity was acceptable. He blamed his foster father for existing. She needed to die, but he needed to *suffer*. With an intellect far beyond his age and a purposeful mindset of someone much older, he set about a plan in motion that not only dispatched his enemies but also liberated his siblings. Even as his foster mother was being put in a gurney and his foster father in the back of a police car, the night filled with his cowardly shrieks that it was that demon infested child, Nicolas. Nicolas gleefully waved good-bye.

Unfortunately, his luck did not change much for the better. The aftermath of the incident led the state of California to remove Nicolas from his "sister," which led to him feeling a sense of both loss and abandonment. The injuries were too much for her overcome and she eventually died from the abuse; he felt he hadn't acted quickly enough. Even though she was older than him, he still felt responsible for her. He vowed that he would never be too late in acting again. Eventually, he was placed in another foster care facility that once again had its share of problems. This time it was not from the parents but from one of the other foster children.

Freddie, an older boy, had been bullying the other kids in the facility. He was older, almost 15, and a lot stronger than the others. He has been abused physically and sexually, and felt it his right to inflict pain upon others. Freddie never tested Nick though; he always said that there was more wrong with Nick than anyone else at the home. It was something about Nick's eyes; they were always cold and dark, as if nothing was there. Sean was older than Nick, but he felt as if Nick was older because he was developmentally delayed. Freddie tried to rape Sean one night and Nick decided it was time to act. In an act of brutality that was beyond the comprehension of the normal 9 year old, much less a grown man, he stopped the offense from occurring. He broke a broomstick in half the week before and had begun sharpening it. By the time that Freddie had attacked Sean, he was ready. The fifteen year old was disemboweled by a child who should have been playing with toys. After the incident, Nick looked at the rest of his roommates and simply said **"shhh."**

All of the other boys understood the message. Freddie had raped at least three other boys before Nick had been placed at that facility and their care givers told them to suck it up and stop being punks. Freddie had beaten up Rondell in the shower because he tried to stand up to him. He was half of Freddie's size, but he decided that he would not be sexually assaulted that evening. His reward was a concussion, two cracked ribs, and then being punished by the staff for causing such a ruckus; that he should have kept his mouth shut. Cain decided that Freddie had lived long enough. Nicolas had also been siphoning cleaning products so that when the time was right, he could clean up the mess that was made by Freddie's timelypassing.

Rondell was the closest thing that Nick had to a friend in the center. Everyone else was completely freaked out. The boys' concern was not that Nick had killed Freddie, but rather how he killed him. It was both clean and quiet; no one heard a thing. These boys were not well educated in anything but violence. They knew that most forms of violence were predicated on rage. This death was brought about from a different place. Nick used intellect. That was something that none of them were used to. It leads to an entirely different set of questions.

Did Freddie deserve to die? For most of them, the answer was yes; of course. While they were relieved that their tormentor got his, there was another question. Was Nick actually more dangerous than Freddie? Was the murderer *worse* than the rapist? What do the victims do when your bully has just gotten beaten up by someone else? What if the new bully wants more lunch money? Nick's actions presented an entirely different set of problems; a potentially worse set of problems.

When the boys looked at Freddie's body, they realized that Nick could do this to anyone of them if he chooses to do so. They were all disturbed at the competency that he possessed. Many of them had seen violence growing up; it was a way of life, but this was different. Nick wasn't noisy or cruel, but rather he was so cool and meticulous. Nick was actually *skilled* at killing. The rest of the boys considered him a different kind of evil; a worse kind. Was Nick the new Lord of The Flies? Rondell asked him if he felt killing Freddie was the right thing to do. To which Nick replied, **"No it wasn't the *right* thing to do. But it was the *best* thing to do. What were you going to do? Tell the guards? I am going to sleep."** Rondell then asked how he planned on sleeping after doing such a horrible thing. Nick then smiled and yawned. **"Like a baby."** That night, Nick giggled in his sleep.

The next day, the facility workers had discovered the pristine environment save one corpse. The other boys were so relieved that they said nothing, except for Sean. Not realizing he had indicated that his tiny protector was the one that had killed his oppressor, he thought he had done the right thing by telling the truth about the actions that had taken place. All the other boys in the home were afraid that when Nick found out, he was going to kill Sean too; Rondell told them that there was nothing to fear though. That isn't how Nick's mind works. There was no reason to kill the boy that he protected. When Nicolas did find out, he was not angry at Sean, but he reserved his anger for those he felt that had failed them all; the staff.

The facility was full of either under qualified or outright sadistic people who were posing as role models for the boys. In the fifty years that Our Lady of The Rose had been in existence, it had developed a terrifying reputation as a place where little boys go in and hardened criminals leave whenever they get out. For sport, the men that worked there would place boys in a cage and tell them to fight and if they didn't, then all the boys would be beaten severely. This type of savagery created predators like Freddie. It created victims like Sean. For Cain, he felt that it was time to put OLTR out of business.

By the time that the staff had discovered those horrifying events by this small child, Nicolas had already hatched a plan to make the staff liable for their lack of accountability and inaction. He tearfully confessed to the killing of Freddie to the police and made an impassioned plea to remove him before he was forced to kill again. In an incredible acting job, he intimated that he was only mocking something he saw on television and that the staff would laugh at Freddie while beat and sodomized the children. He had even jabbed himself with the very weapon he used to deal death to the tormentor.

By the time the smoke had cleared, all of his enemies had been dealt justice. But it was at a great cost. The district attorney wanted to prosecute, but the case was thrown out because he was only nine years old. Besides he was already in a group home, there wasn't any other place to put him. Nick didn't care; his life sucked anyway. He knew that the likelihood of him ever getting out of the penal system was small, if impossible. No one was willing to adopt him, not after being allegedly involved in at least two murders before the age of 10. Even if he was convicted of killing Freddie but he didn't care as long as those who had done evil would, even if that meant himself.

Over the next several years, Nicolas has been both the abused and also the vigilante. Several terrible incidents that resembled both his foster mother's and Freddie's death seemed to occur wherever he lived. No one could ever prove his involvement, but the coincidence was too great to ignore either. He was delivering his own version of swift justice all the while reading and learning as much as he could get his hands on within the juvenile justice system. The pattern was consistently elegant; a tormentor, whoever it was, was always dealt a deadly hand whenever this boy lived there. Children at other facilities used to threaten their oppressors by saying that Nick was coming to get them. This child, barely in his teens, could evoke that kind of fear.

Nick was not a sloppy killer, but rather a subtle and unpredictable operative. Intellect, not brute strength was his primary asset. The youngster favored misdirection, but he had no qualms about brutality if it was the most efficient way to achieve his goals. He read the entire library on the human anatomy on the internet, learning about every vital organ and system within the human body. He learned seven different disciplines of martial arts just by reading the instruction books, usually taking one day to understand the techniques and less than one week to master them. He read the Bible, Art of War, The Assassin's Creed, Tolstoy, several books on economics, eastern and western medicine, and psychology, in particularly panic and phobias, and also several hundred novels and narratives, usually with themes of redemption or revenge; those documents became instrumental in him being able to focus his body, stimulate his mind, and develop his own code of honor and truth.

By the time Nicolas was 15, he had been a ward of the state of California his entire life, and it was time for a hearing to decide whether he could be released. Unfortunately, there was no place for him. The foster care system argued that it did not possess the resources to accommodate him nor was there anyone willing to adopt such an obviously disturbed child. He had been designated as both a sociopath and also someone who might actually have had the *highest* IQ score on record. In actuality, the score was not reflective of what it could actually be because the IQ has inherited limitations; apparently Nick's mind was beyond the scope of the test.

The last four psychiatrists who were designated to work with him either quit the profession or developed mental health diagnosis themselves. The mental health community designated him too dangerous to work with. He was deemed too treacherous to ever be let out of the penal system by several talented attorneys who feared for the society at large. Nicolas, after taking a month to read *every* law book on civil commitment ever written had an even more compelling brief than the state's application. The head of the Stanford Law School later commented that his brief was the best legal document he had ever seen. The governor was so flustered by the fact that a minor not only represented himself and had such a compelling brief on habeas corpus, he ordered the state's attorney general to try the case herself. The judge, citing the brilliance of Nick's abilities, said that while his application of the law was considered more than accurate, the fact that he had been accused of killing at least *nineteen people* before the age of 12 was too compelling to ignore.

At this point, a chance encounter occurred in Nicolas Cain's seemingly miserable existence. Dr. Peter A. McNamara, a renowned English Psychologist had stepped forward at the trial. He said that while the United States had not the means to address the various problems and also inherit abilities of this extraordinary young man, his private hospital and orphanage did have the facilities that such a gifted and disturbed young person did need. The Attorney General, Jean Wilcox, for the state of California was hesitant to consider a solution such as the one being presented. However Dr. McNamara, not being a man to mince words pointed out that Nicolas would likely not stop with this ruling and could get this overturned in either the 9th Circuit Court or even the Supreme Court easily. Nick was petitioning for emancipation from the state; that meant that he would be *free*.

There were some serious concerns over Nick's situation. Was society at large better served with Cain behind bars even if there was no legal way to keep him there? Since no one had ever proven that he was involved in any crime, what was going to stop the case from being overturned? Furthermore how would it look that she lost to a fifteen year old? When stating the obvious, Nicolas then giggled. Not a sadistic giggle of a monster, but that of child who had heard his first dirty joke. Many of the staff who were at the trial commented that it was the first time they had ever heard Nick laugh. At this point, the judge looked at Nicolas Cain really for the first time.

Even at a young age, he was intimidating. He was already more than six feet tall and almost 190 muscular pounds, but that wasn't the intimidating part. He had these piercing eyes; that made you think he knew what you were thinking and could change your mind from the inside. But then he smiled at the judge. Not a sadistic grin or smirk, but a genuine smile. A smile that belied hope and possibility, not to mention the fact that Dr. McNamara was correct, he *could* get out. Perhaps a person as smart as the good doctor could actually help this child was actually a possible outcome. Looking at his case history and the abuses he has both seen and suffered, coupled with the fact that everyone who he had allegedly attacked was a potential abuser, could it have been possible that there was something both redeemable and noble about this child, who had no family? Hell he could be someone else's, some other country's, hell some other *continent's* problem. It might take some creative adoption on the state's part, but why not? *He could get out and then be pissed at all of us.*

Whether it was the fact that Dr. McNamara lived in England or the fact that Nicolas Cain would not be in the United States was the greater appeal to all the parties involved was irrelevant. An emergency adoption was implemented and fast-tracked through the proper channels. Attorney General Wilcox was intrigued by Dr. McNamara's motives for this brilliant and seemingly nonstandard individual but it didn't matter anymore. The fact remained that not only was Nicolas Cain the smartest offender she had ever encountered, he was also the *smartest attorney she had ever encountered.* Maybe that quack from England could do something, but either way he was out of the state and the country and hopefully, he would never return.

As soon as he was within the care of Dr. Peter Anderson McNamara and heading away from the state of California and the United States of America, he remarked in a mild yet cross tone, **"what took you so long?"** McNamara responded that he had to find him without alarming their enemies that he was trapped on Earth as a child instead of the powerful, full born Paladin that he had become. An accident in his time displacement training had sent him too far into the past, with Nicolas Cain experiencing childbirth, the pain of his sister being taken away and several abuses and fights that he did not want to experience in the first place much less for a second time.

As they left the States, the Gulf Stream private plane converted into its actual form, a Delta Wing Fighter, far more advanced than any Earthling or Terran had ever been exposed to. As they returned to their battle fortress cruiser, The Alpha Centauri, a female voice reported that all preparations had been made and all repairs had been completed and that the accidental time displacement would *not* happen again. Upon entering the massive dreadnaught, a stunning brunette with grey eyes and jet black hair emerges. A kiss is planted on Nicolas' left cheek and the stunner replied **"I am so sorry Commander. I forgot how cute you used to be."** The youth snarled, **"I hated it when you did that when I was a kid and the second time around hasn't made it better."**

The Chancellor realized that she needed to choose her words carefully. If he finds it necessary, Cain will destroy everything and spare no one. As far he is concerned the line had been crossed and inequities needed to be rectified. Killing Paladins, especially during these tense times would still be difficult to navigate; however, these men and women have already killed countless innocents. As far as Nick was concerned, when these people took up arms against their Alliance brethren and Federation allies had forfeited the right to live any longer than it will take for him to kill every last one of them. A lesson had to be taught and Nick would be the instructor for the evening.

This was an even more difficult situation because Driax had to trust that Cain would only kill those he felt were responsible and not go too far. The Rioan General Danyzer had warned Driax that she had to be specific or Nick may be left to his own interpretation of how to handle these circumstances. The Federation didn't care as long as Petamauck and Voss were both extinct. Cain spoke to his new leader in a sarcastic yet joyful tone. **"My sweet Alron, you should have called for me first; this would have been over a long time ago. Management is your thing; cleaning up messes is mine. I don't pontificate; I never negotiate. It is my job to *act*. Never doubt my commitment to you or the Cause. All you have to do is say it and they will die. Some will die quickly, but all will die violently; especially Petamauck. He knew better. I am but a tool; you have to make the choice. Go on and make the command, *you know that you want to*. Blood has a distinctive smell when it is spilled, especially when it has been heated due to a gun blast or when cold metal touches it. I wish you were here to witness your servant in person my Chancellor."**

Still, this is Driax's first conversation with the most dangerous Paladin in the history of the Order. If the chancellor is concerned or alarmed at the glee with which her servant speaks, she does not let on to him. There is an audience that she must perform for also. She knows that if this goes wrong, such as Cain accidentally killing a hostage, it could set back the Terran Alliance for generations to come. Not to mention the fact that the IGF is also intently watching how this scenario will unfold. Kush was deeply respected, while Driax is an unknown. Of all the chancellors who have commanded this noble warrior, he loved Kush the most. However, considering Petamauck's actions, she felt it better to dance with the devil she knew versus the one she did not.

Driax was uncertain if her servant was baiting her into allowing him to kill the others or daring her to make a command judgment. The chancellor, knowing that the rest of her subordinates may not fully trust her judgment, chose to follow her conscious, **"Commander, obliterate the PLP!!!! Your orders are the same, kill them all!!! No one is above the law!!! The Terran Alliance bows to no one!! Make Voss suffer. Hear me clearly my wonderful monster;** *kill every single one of them.* **Happy Hunting!!"**

Driax spoke with an authority that was consistent with her position as chancellor. After all, she was Cain's *boss*. The Alpha Paladin was delighted; he was waiting on her to command him to do what he is the best at. Cain's confidence in his superior's resolve was well-placed. Then he giggled, he actually giggled. AC closed her eyes; every time she has heard that sound from Cain, destruction usually follows.

He responded with glee, **"Hahaha!!! That's all I needed to know my dear Chancellor. Petamauck and his crew have fucked with democracy for the last time. It is time for the hunters to become the hunted. Sayied, 15 minutes. The defenses are down. Don't worry AC, they used to be comrades; I will kill them quickly. But Voss has it coming. I hope you enjoy the extravaganza."** Everyone on board the Alpha Centauri as well as the Chancellor and her staff on Eden all watched the "extravaganza" that Commander Nicolas Cain then put on.

These actions that are currently taking place is something that hasn't occurred in a long time. Ever since the Blood Knights became his permanent crew of the Alpha Centauri, Cain has never gone into a crisis situation alone. This set of circumstances is different however. Cain believes that this action is necessary because of the targets that he has to eliminate. He couldn't fathom a scenario where he would ask his fellow Knights to dispatch the PLP. Many of them had been close comrades and colleagues; people that many have served with or went to the academy with. Nick couldn't risk one of his troops hesitating because of a familiarity with the enemy. It was unfair and he considered it his burden. Petamauck served under him and he felt like everything that had happened was under his watch. As far as Nick is concerned leadership is never about ability, but rather it is about responsibility. No other Paladin would pay for Petamauck's madness with blood. Only the PLP who crossed Cain would die this evening.

Nick had already taken out the guards in the lower levels of the facility. He didn't want to make too much noise so he did it the old fashion way, in hand to hand combat. Five guards were stationed at the west basin of the tower. He used an Ocularian assassination technique; he hit them in power points on their bodies that made their brains explode. This method was clean and silent; no one heard a thing. On the east basin, he used an aerosol poison, killing them all instantly. The fourteen guards were killed so quickly that the monitors could not actually record what happened; they literally fell dead. *The warm up is over*, pondered the monster. *God, this is going to be fun.*

Commander Nicolas Cain, the Alpha Paladin, began to arm himself for battle. To incapacitate the guards below the main hall didn't take long, but to take out the Paladins was going to be a tad more difficult. He changed into his combat uniform; he was armed to the teeth. Cain put on his body armor for his chest and arms, with special compartments for his acid grenades and knives. Then he put several magazines for both his pulse rifle and also his mini-Gatling guns in his jacket pocket. He then grabbed his favorite weapon, a Japanese Katana. A slow smile crossed his handsome face. It was now time for the warrior to misbehave.

In the primary chamber, Petamauck looks at the faces of all the hostages. He sees the fear and anger that they have for him. *They will all see that we are right soon*, he thought. One of the elders spits on the floor when Petamauck looks at him, a sign of the ultimate disrespect from someone who is native to the Mu Star System. One of Petamauck's subordinates smacks him with the end of his rifle. The architect of the PLP glared at the soldier but he knew that this was the path that they had all chosen. But the leader is determined to see this through to the end. Lord Petamauck had more pressing concerns; *Nick will be here soon*, he reflected. He knows that it is a matter of time before the Alpha Paladin decides to show up and when he does, the greatest teacher of logic and reason in the history of the Terran Alliance will have to be at his very best. He knows that he has a small window to try to convince Cain that his point of view is the right one.

In Petamauck's mind, this entire situation has escalated far out of control. It was his intention to lead a peaceful secession from the Alliance, but instead it has devolved into bloody standoff. His troops are barely able to contain their bloodlust and thirst for power. Mu is one of the solar systems with the most natural resources in the quadrant and also has access to some of the most powerful weapons in the Terran Navy. Petamauck had no idea it was going to turn into a defined military campaign so quickly. Captain Luke Tobias led the force that destroyed Space Station *Charity* in IGF territory; Tobias knew more than 200,000 humans were there and he didn't care. The PLP strike force led by the captain considered it an imperative that they show the Alliance and Federation that they meant business.

Despite the madness, Petamauck's plan hasn't gone completely astray. His core belief is still that Driax is too young and inexperienced to be Chancellor; her response on the complicated battle efforts has strengthened this position. Even with an entire squadron of Paladins, along with a legion of Alliance troops at his disposal, he knows that the force they have is not strong enough to deal with the Alpha Centauri or the Alpha Paladin. He knows what his subordinates don't; Cain will kill every last one of them if he needs to. Or if they are lucky, he won't order the Centauri to decimate most of, if not the entire planet. This whole campaign hinges on Lord Petamauck's ability to reason with Nick and hope that he sees it their way. If not, there is a strong possibility that the campaign of 899 hours never reaches nine hundred.

One of Petamauck's most trusted commanders, Saul Aaqil, has just made a disturbing report for the leader. **"Greetings my lord, nearly every group has reported no activity but the guards at the west basin haven't checked in yet. I have sent some guards from the northern section to check it out."** Petamauck turned his back to Aaqil and sighed. He closed his eyes and replied, **"Don't bother; they are already dead. He is here for us. Tell Marcus, Cyril, and Luke to not engage until they have more help. Three will not be enough."** Pax Voss, a beautiful yet deadly operative from Aquilonia responded to Petamauck commands. **"Sir, if he is here, Cain has made his choice. He has decided to be against us. I think it's time for us to deal with him. We are all Paladins; there is no way he could be *that* good. There is no way he could be *that* deadly. I say it is time to deal with Cain once and for all. We must remain vigilant my lord. Cain will give no quarter, neither can we."**

There it was; the name that Sodiq dared not to mention. The name that many had been told was the deadliest of the deadliest. One of the rumors about Cain was that he had a death list or what he affectionately called "the shit list". It had been said that the list never long and that everyone who has ever been on it has been killed by Cain or the warriors under his command. Many within the PLP have never heard any of this because these are stories within the IGF or deep space territories. Mu is the system closest to the IGF territory. Many of the stories about Cain were related to his Federation title and not his Paladin designation. Most of the Terran Alliance had never had correspondence with their IGF brethren; they had no idea of the carnage that Nick had done to enemies of the Federation.

The only thing that most of the Paladins know about him is that he works with the deep space unit. No one within the bulk of the PLP really knows much about him except for Petamauck. They knew that their leader was a man who only seemed to fear one thing and that was Commander Cain himself. Many of the PLP's key stakeholders were not convinced that Cain should be held in the same regard that their leader had for Cain and that it would be a matter of time before they proved once and for all that their power was absolute. It is especially frustrating to Captain Voss, because she is certain that the stories that have been spoken about this particular Paladin are just that; stories. In her mind, any of the fellow Paladins have just as impressive a combat record as Cain, but what she doesn't know is that most of Nick's record is sealed. She believes that they are following a righteous cause and that her friend, Petamauck is a just leader.

There were eight Paladins in the foyer, all ready to fight to the death. These warriors, some of whom had been fighting for hundreds of Earth years and had been considered masters of several disciplines of death, all fell. These warriors surrounded the mighty Paladin. He cracked his knuckles; then he smiled and pulled out his sword. Many of these warriors had been some of the most accomplished in the Order of Paladins. All of them had been waiting for this moment; this type of combat is the only way to prove who was superior. This could get ugly, really ugly. Nick smiled and said sweetly to his former allies. **"My primary assignment is Petamauck and Voss; you aren't important. I don't actually *need* to kill you; I am going to do it just for the *fun* of it. This is not going to go well for any of you. You can stand down**

**or I will put you down; permanently. This can be the easy way or the
hard way. Make a decision. Let your next move be your best move."**

The apex predator was no longer trying his best to be polite. These
warriors had no idea what kind of peril they were truly in. Next thing
these proud Paladins knew, they were all screaming in agony. With blood
gushing from several different directions, Nick admired his work and
said sweetly, **"I love it when they choose the hard way."** The main
conference room was filled with sounds that they had never heard from
some of their fellow comrades. Many of these warriors had served in
countless campaigns and the words such as please, stop, and mercy, was
all foreign to them; until now. It was as if Nick was sending a message
to not only the Paladins there, but all the Paladins throughout the order.
Going against the Chancellor would *not* be tolerated.

Petamauck could tell from the swiftness of the deaths that Cain had
no desire at all to end this standoff peacefully. Voss was still of the belief
that this situation could be salvaged, but that wasn't going to happen. The
hostages in the main room, especially the older planetary senator who
had been hit with a rifle earlier knew that their time of liberation was at
hand. He smiled at Petamauck. The head of the PLP knew what all of the
hostages knew; Cain would take no prisoners. Mercy was not coming.
Death was at Petamauck's door and Hell followed him. Several of the
key leaders of the Paladin Liberation Party were preparing for one last,
desperate stand against Cain. They were all on borrowed time.

As Nick was in route to the adjacent conference foyer, nine of the
original members of the party went into the room with their bladed
weapons already drawn and ready for use. These warriors were considered
master swordsmen and had the honor of being their leader's personal
bodyguards. As far as the Alpha was concerned, they were merely targets.
He entered the conference room and smiled. He slipped his katana
from its sheath. They looked at him and he looked back. They began
to surround the mighty warrior; the devoted followers of Petamauck
saw that Cain did not mind being outnumbered. What was even more
disturbing was that he didn't even mind being out flanked. There was
a specific training that Cain had received from the IGF that had tactics
designated for close quarter combat at which he is acutely proficient.

Cain smiled at his prey and finally spoke. **"Hi Luke, you've been a
very naughty boy. You have been taking these people's lunch money.
I think that it's about time to end this little camping trip. Don't**

worry; I'll be quick." This was going to be an especially pleasurable experience for Cain because Luke was the captain who led the *Charity* Massacre. *Now I can get him out of the way,* thought the executioner. Tobias ran at Cain in full sprint and Nick turned his back towards him. In an instant of blinding speed, Cain turned around quickly, cut both of the captain's arms at the wrists, and tripped Tobias as he ran past him, shattering his right ankle in three places. As the captain screamed, the Alpha grabbed his head and snapped his neck in a single motion. Perfect. Nick then threw the captain's corpse to the floor, the master assassin then smiled at the remaining troops and said simply, "**next.**" All the remaining troops rushed him at the same time, with curses and battle cries; Cain yawned. The next sounds heard throughout the facility were blood gushing, ear piercing shrieks, and flesh being carved up.

The Apex Predator still hadn't entered the main conference room. He turned the lights off in the foyer. The main door opened slowly. A sound filled the room; an earpiercing cackle. Then all the sudden, objects that sounded like balls were being sent into the conference room; he rolled the head of Captain Luke Tobias, the commander of the space station massacre, along with the heads of several of his former comrades. Then the only other sound was an eerie whisper. **"I'm waiting Pax; time to dance."** She screamed and called him a bastard. She was angry and unfocused; the perfect target. At this point, Petamauck knew that she was going to go out there, into Nick's domain. It would not be pretty.

For the PLP's staunchest supporter, Captain Pax Voss, Cain saved a special destruction. There had always been a certain tension between Cain and Voss; she had always felt he was both violent and far too secretive. She also knew of the relationship that he had with both Danyzer and the Commandant; it always made her feel uncomfortable. When the captain tried to give him star fighter combat training, the novice defeated her in less than three minutes. Voss had been considered the fleet's top fighter pilot before Nick arrived. He defeated Erik the Red in hand to hand combat and had been considered equal of Petamauck in logic and reason. These new realities had occurred far too quickly for Voss' taste.

Erik was okay with the fact that Nick's abilities were far superior; Voss and Petamauck were not. Pax was angry when she found out that the Alpha Centauri not only was created with Rioan technology, but also that Cain was the hand-picked commanding officer. Captain Voss was also angry when she found out that Cain picked AC instead of her for the crew of the Alpha Centauri. She resented the fact that he had a special unit for deep space and also had intelligence that she would never be privy to. Furthermore, she was also angry because Cain was the one officer that her seductive charms never worked on. He always said that she was just cute; nothing more. He always believed that AC was far more stunning and neither could touch Quenas. For a woman of Pax's ego, it was a shattering understatement. She hasn't like him since then.

As she entered the room, Voss saw the dismembered comrades in arms. Nick blew a kiss at her and spoke sarcastically. **"Hello pretty girl. You know you want a piece of *this*."** The beautiful captain cursed at him. She was unfocused. She angrily reached for her weapon, but it was too late. Nick sliced all of her fingers off her body. **"Am I *still* overrated?"** the apex predator inquired. He then kicked Voss in both of her knees at once, rupturing both of her patella tendons. The Alpha then punched her in the face, shattering her nasal cavity and finally burned her eyes with an acid grenade. As she shrieked in agony, cursing the name of Nicolas Cain, he stabbed her in the mouth with a pen. Gleefully, he snorted, **"You always did talk too much Voss."** At this point, all the hostages in the conference room heard the screams of these deadly warriors. Then they all heard the bones being broken and then for the first time in many of their lives, they smelled the combination of steel, burning flesh, and blood.

For the first time since the siege began, Lord Petamauck, would-be liberator showed doubt. He was no longer as resolute; he knew for the first time that his former student, a man that he trained with and fought beside was now there to kill *him*. He had always fought side by side this monster, this man. It was an eerie feeling to hear the monster whistle as he worked; he was actually enjoying killing these people. *No wonder he is called a worse kind of evil,* thought the despot. Panic had really sunk in. What could he do? He knew that Nick would not stop; he would not negotiate. Nick liked to say that a Paladin's job was to protect democracy, not practice it.

As Cain kicked in the door, one last Paladin follower attacked him. It was a feeble attempt by Petamauck's last guardian. With an attack similar to the one that liberated Sean many years ago, in one killing stroke, he disemboweled the final foil. Now, standing before Petamauck was his executioner. The predator was pleased; he has found his prey. *Oh God, what have I done,* thought the former ally turned target. Petamauck did the only thing that a warrior reduced to cowardice could do; he grabbed the nearest child and fled.

The Regis of Mu and her cabinet had been set free, but her child, Kima, a beautiful nine year old girl with gray eyes, had been taken. Cain's warriors, the Blood Knights, with Representative Mathias in tow, had arrived to secure the area. All the troops found were hostages and dismembered bodies. Just as Cain had promised, the situation had been resolved before AC and Mathias had arrived. The remaining leadersof the PLP were singing a different tune by the time AC and Faris had arrived. The followers of the pseudo despot who were lucky to have their lives surrendered without a fight. Many of these mighty warriors had never known fear until they had crossed paths with the Alpha Paladin.

The remaining warriors of the PLP had decided that engaging with Cain was not a good idea. Many had been stationed all across the planet and had seen the monster at work on the primary leadership of their cause. They saw a man completely slaughter the most skilled warriors within the party. Several later commented that Cain was the deadliest man they had ever seen and were certain that he was going to kill all of them. Before witnessing Cain's ability, many hoped to test his mettle. Second-in command Pax Voss was one of the main agitators of this action; claiming that Nick's skills had to be overrated; there was no way one marauder could kill so many Paladins. Obviously, she was gravely mistaken.

Then these warriors saw a creature that could dance between sanity and madness. He was so hideous, so powerful, yet breathtaking; it was a symphony of death by a conductor of exquisite yet lethal dexterity. Cain is spine tinglingly effective and deliciously efficient. If anything, Nick's reputation had been woefully *underreported*; had many of them known that he was the genuine article; this coup may have never had so much support. Very few in the Alliance had any idea of just how powerful Cain might truly be. It was not enough that he defeated them; he wanted everyone to realize that crossing him would be a life ending experience.

It had been proven that day that there were two classes of Paladin; *Cain and everyone else.* No one wondered why only Khan Antonius was sent any longer. These mighty warriors went from being insulted to a sense of relief in the 15 minutes it took the Alpha to kill *45 Paladins.* The question was what was primary reason for many of these warriors changing their position? The answer was that they never crossed Cain. All of the remaining troops realized that the only reason they were alive was because they were not at the capitol building. This thought process was *definitely* on their minds.

As Cain pursued his prey, the Regis pondered whether Cain would care more about killing Petamauck than saving Kima. AC, the gray-eyed stunner, softly replied to her **"your daughter is now the safest person on this planet. She will not have one hair misplaced."** Cain finally reached his foe, which was standing on the edge of the roof of the capital building. Knowing their history, Petamauck tried to reason with Nicolas, rationalizing that his position was correct and that humanity was being played. That Driax was not a worthy successor to Kush. **"I can see that you are not in the listening mood but try to hear me out. I wouldn't have taken this position unless I was certain that it was the right one. I love my people; I am only doing what I know in my heart to be the right thing. Why can't you see it from my, from our point of view? You haven't spent any time with Driax; she is a child. What I am doing is for the good of all people; she is over matched. I am asking you to consider the circumstances."**

Cain saw that he was holding the daughter of the Regis in front of himself, using her as a potential shield. He put his sword and his guns on the roof of the building. Petamauck knows his brother well. The PLP leader is aware that just because Cain put his primary weapons down didn't mean that he wasn't armed. This was the bad time; Petamauckknew his words had fallen on deaf ears. Clapping his hands andsmirking, Nicolas responded, **"You've been practicing this speech haven't you? Did you practice it with Voss? I had no idea that she was *that* good. How interesting. Oh I'm sorry, are you finished? Allow me to retort. You act as if you don't know me? I *never* negotiate. The only reason you aren't dead already is because Alron Driax hadn't called me sooner. You have some nerve to think that you are *that* important; so disappointing. You knew better."**

At this point, Cain began to move towards Petamauck only for one last PLP soldier to appear in a desperate attempt to kill him. The warrior leaped from the top of the roof, with sword in hand, trying to surprise Nick from behind. As he jumped, the beautiful girl screamed, **"look out!"** At the last second, Nick turned and caught him in midflight by his throat. Cain then quickly crushed the combatant's hyoid bone, while

Petamauck cut him across his left eye socket. As he was being cut, the Alpha kicked Petamauck in the ribs, cracking four of them. The force of the blow knocked the leader back nearly 5 meters and Cain was able retreat with the child around the side of the building.

Petamauck began shooting his gun at his former protégé, who was trying to shield the child from the blasts. Kima smiled at Nick as the blasts were flying over his head. He smiled and said that they would be fine. She kissed his cut and it stopped bleeding. She simply replied, **"I know. You're cute. What is your name?"** Cain smiled at Kima; she had immediately won his heart on the spot. **"My name is Antonius. But people call me Nick."** She smiled at him; she was comfortable with the chaos because he was with her. **"That's funny. Ant? An-tone? Never mind. I can't say that first name. I am going to call you Nicky."** The monster smiled at his newest little friend. **"Nicky huh? Yeah, I like that."** Their first encounter was pleasant enough. Even with Petamauck trying to blow Cain's head off.

Back to the matter at hand, it was time for Lord Petamauck to die. Cain didn't want to scare Kima, but the Lord of the PLP was in need of being sent to the after-life. Cain pondered how he would kill him and then figured it out. Nick then looked at the beautifullittle girl, who was the spitting image of her mother. He winked at her and said confidently, **"Hey you with the face, do you want to see a magic trick?"** She nodded her head. He said quietly, **"don't tell anyone okay?"** Then it happened.

The monster then ran at Petamauck in a full sprint, he moved so quickly it was as if the blasts were too slow to actually touch him. He then performed a summersault and landed so hard that the roof where Petamauck was standing flew up in the air almost ten meters. Cain then leaped almost the same distance while pulling out a pulsation grenade set for seismic. Cain then kicked Petamauck under his chin in a forward flipping motion, while placing the grenade in his uniform. Nick landed, grabbed Kima, pressed the button activating the grenade and then used his coat to shield her from the blast. Petamauck was literally shaken to death. His organs exploded and made a tremendous mess. Kima yawned and then quietly said, **"Do it again. Do it again!!!"**

Petamauck and his followers had created a tremendous amount of unrest in the 899 hours they occupied the planet Mu. Many good people had been displaced and a civil war almost broke out. However, all had been averted. The most dangerous weapon at the disposal of the Terran Alliance had been activated and he did the job he was trained to do. As the Regent of Mu spoke to the people of the system, Chancellor Driax reassured all the Terran Leadership that peace has been restored. This had been the first time that many of the new Leadership had ever witnessed Nick in action. Needless to say, these people were more than just disturbed. They were outright terrified.

Regent Fuentes asked the new chancellor if she approved of the "extravaganza" that Nick had put on. His words implied that Cain's efforts were borderline sadistic; Driax was not in agreement with that sentiment. Now that Cain had shown loyalty to her, it was time to repay his good faith. She answered the question with unwavering authority. **"Yes, these actions were horrific;** *Petamauck's* **actions were horrific. Maybe you weren't paying attention, but** *Petamauck* **created this set of circumstances. Everything that Commander Cain did was a direct response to what the PLP had done. This was** *our* **mess;** *my* **Janitor cleaned it up. The Alpha did what he was trained to do; protect the innocent and terminate the wicked. The question is why the other Paladins felt that a coup against the Alliance seemed logical? That is the query that should be pondered."**

Another debate was happening among the newly formed cabinet; what to do about the Paladins. Chancellor Driax said that she would leave that to the Paladins themselves. On one hand, it seemed like a tactically risky proposition, but on the other, it could be considered tactically shrewd. She correctly deduced that the Paladins were embarrassed by the behavior of their fellow Paladins and they were of the belief that things needed to change. The Order suggested it themselves, much to her delight. It was probably time for more transparency in the Paladin process; because of the actions of the previous 899 hours, Driax would have the leverage to press for a more streamlined development process. Furthermore, she had the trust of the Alpha Paladin and that might be her greatest advantage. Kush told Nick that if the situation went bad before his death, his final standing order with Cain was to make sure that Driax was fully supported. She would be good for the future of the Terran Alliance was what Kush told him; Driax has done nothing to shake Cain's belief in that sentiment.

All the while, a lonely warrior stands on top of the now repaired capital building, mourning his beloved friend and all the comrades in arms who had to be dispatched to ensure that fragile peace could exist for just a little while longer. He wanted no medals for his work, no songs of valor either. He took a small token of appreciation, a friendship bracelet by a beautiful little girl. Her name was Kima and she is absolutely beautiful. She had only one request and that was that this powerful man of immense abilities would allow the scar that he earned saving her and her family to remain. **"It's because you look handsome Nicky!!"** Kima replied. *Oh God, she's got me,* he mused. For the first time that day, he laughed.

AC, his beautiful second in command came to the roof to spend time with Nick. Usually when a loved one has died, he likes to spend time alone with his thoughts about that person. This is a bittersweet day because Cain's target and his lost loved one were the same person. Petamauck was the one who found him on Earth so many years ago. He was his dear friend, second on command of the Centauri and one of his best teachers. AC knew that he was angry and hurt, but she was uncertain if he was angrier than he was more hurt. He didn't look at her as he spoke, she could feel the rage in his words. **"Fucking Paladin Liberation Party. *Amateurs.* It would have been more interesting if the Oculari had tried this instead."** then kissed his cheek, which he always said that he hated, but secretly loved, and said, **"time to go home Antonius."**

On planet Eden, two powerful women were having a quiet chat. One was the new chancellor, Alron Driax and the other was the dominant senator, Aya, who just happened to be both AC's mother and Danyzer's wife. Right now, she had another duty: advisor to Driax. Aya is one of the few Terran senators within the IGF; her understanding of the quadrant's political landscape is always a valuable asset to the Terran Alliance Chancellor. Her expertise is especially vital at this point because Driax is the least trained and youngest Alron is the history of the Alliance. Lady Aya has an incredible influence over both the Terran Alliance and also the IGF. If there was anyone who could help the young chancellor get through this incredibly rough adjustment period, it would be her. It also helps Driax to know that she has a strong connection to the Alpha Paladin.

Aya sips her mint tea and speaks casually to the newest and youngest Alron. **"What did I tell you Chancellor? Does he love his job or *does he love his job*? Petamauck, Voss, and Aquil were all the epitome of pompous jack asses; that's why he had to obliterate all** of them. **Commander Cain had to make sure that everyone knows that crossing you will lead to a violent death. I told you that you should have called him as soon as Petamauck acted up. The Paladin Liberation Party my ass. I only wish that Nick was really pissed; he was just annoyed. You want to know what's really funny? What you saw was the *extent* of his mercy. I can't wait until you see him when he has time to really go to work on someone. He *loved* Petamauck; I cannot imagine what terrible things he is going to do to Atlas."** Driax spoke in a consolatory tone. **"Yes Lady Aya, you were right. And you are saying that the Alpha Paladin will do that anytime I need him to? No hesitation? No mercy?"**

The Federation senator realizes that a great many things have been laid at the feet of her young colleague. *My God, she is only a baby*, thought the venerable senator. It is of no consequence though; this is a job that Driax must hit the ground running. The new chancellor's learning curve will be a steep one indeed. At this point, Aya realizes that she hasn't done her homework assignment yet. **"Alron, you haven't read the file on Cain have you? You need to read that before you talk to him face to face. My husband just gave him his next assignment; you have time to prepare for your first meeting. Might I suggest after the festival on Mu? I can't stress the imperative of your preparation for that first official meeting enough. You want to know why Kush loved Cain so much? Because your predecessor was prepared to meet him. He learned about Cain before he ever spoke to him. Trust me that will go a long way with the Alpha. Chancellor Kush reading Antonius' file was the thing that saved their relationship before it began. Most of the leadership that has had initial difficulties with Cain has been primarily because they didn't learn anything about him before they met. He is indeed a monster, but he is *your servant*. He is also an honorable being; I love him dearly. I know that you are overwhelmed, but please don't make the same mistakes that many of your predecessors did. Make Nick important to you. All you have to do is ask him and he will do it. For the love of God, please let him love you. He is your best asset; he will be your best friend. *Even better than me*."**

Two figures were watching the actions of the Alpha Paladin from afar and had very different emotional responses to what they had been witness to. One of them was in his chambers watching Cain dismantle the Paladin Liberation Party one at a time; he was enamored by how Cain took glee in the physical destruction of one Pax Voss. She had always said to anyone that would listen that there was no way that Cain could actually be *that* good. Captain Voss once served with Lt. Colonel Elisma and believed that she was without peer in the Paladin ranks. She felt that there was no way that anyone was ever in her former comrade's league. Apparently that is not the case. Nick is beyond Elisma in every way. The man cackled with joy whenever he saw the display of power and dexterity that Cain produced.

The second figure was the Rioan General, Danyzer. He was more than concerned with what he saw. Plus he was annoyed at the fact the second, unknown figure kept rewinding the same part. He snapped, **"Stop showing that dammit! This is your fault. He is not supposed to be *this* good. I should have known that you would not be capable of keeping your word. What did you do to him?"** The second figure, the man in the shadows smiled and kept laughing. **"It wasn't what I did *to* him; it was what I did *for* him. Hypocrisy doesn't suit you Danyzer. Where was your moral indignation at what he did to the Unori? Hm, I wonder where was your outrage then? You really want to know what I did to him? I stopped holding him back. I cannot wait to see what he does next. He has a shit list in his head of who is going to pay. You are just nervous because you are not certain if you are on it or not."**

Danyzer knew that what the unknown figure had said was correct. He was concerned that Cain may one day decide that he has lived long enough. One day, he figured that Antonius would no longer consider him an asset, but rather a liability. Today is not that day. The mighty general sighed. **"And you are not? There are too many unknowns. What if we were wrong?"** The second figure replied with glee. **"Wrong? This is the most right thing that we have ever done. Besides, he loves me. Still, he loved Petamauck and look what he did to him; his dedication to the Cause surpasses even ours. Even if it is my time to die, I have lived longer than I probably should have. Now that I think of it, you have lived longer than you probably should have also. Remember, *I know what you did*. You have far more blood on your hands than I do; and that is truly saying something. I can't wait to see what he does to him. He is so creative, isn't he? Cain is going to kill him in the most exquisite method. I wonder how? It is inevitability, you should accept it."**

Antonius and Petamauck's actions carried deep ramifications throughout this entire region of space. Even though these actions were between Terrans, the IGF observed these actions and considered these events detrimental to these two parties working together. The IGF is still upset about the fact that a Terran of the highest order led a rather large faction of Paladins in a conspiracy laden revolt against the Terran Alliance. It took a great deal of negotiating between the last Chancellor, Alron Kush, and the IGF representatives to even get the Federation to even consider the Terran Alliance. The Federation General, Danyzer, was also instrumental in these negotiations. Kush died before the negotiations could be completed; Driax must now continue this negotiation. Danyzer's daughter, AC, serves Khan Antonius and is a Paladin herself, which indirectly help matters. Furthermore Antonius' actions kept the circumstances from exacerbating and his charge to lead the IGF into war with the Dark-Siders does carry significant weight. However, Petamauck's actions have created a tremendous setback. Much larger problems are on the horizon.

Officer's Log: Faris, Sayied

Operational Officer's Log: I love going to graduation. It is like a new opportunity for hope and redemption. Look at them, they are so eager to take on the universe. They've been told that they are the best of the best. So young, so fresh, and oh so sweet; they have no idea what their lives will be like after the ceremony and pageantry is over. Then the moment happens. All the playtime will be over when my master walks into facility. Right. About. Now.

A hush had taken over the room of excited graduates of the Paladin Academy. The rookies always think that they can handle anything or anyone until *he* shows up. Then the man walked into the room. He is my commander; he is my friend; he is my brother. They had never seen him, only heard about him. There he stands, the real deal; Commander Gaius Nicolas Cain. Cain walked onto the graduation platform. Even though this is supposed to be a festive occasion, he is still in his full combat uniform. That says everything about him.

The troops recognized that he was relatively tall, but he was not the giant that he has sometimes been referred to. For many of them, this will be the first and only encounter with the Alpha Paladin; he is not known for being involved in small talk. He didn't smile, he barely looked at them. Only Nick can render an entire crowd by silent and still like this. There were more than five thousand new Paladins who recently graduated from the Paladin Academy. The new head of Paladin Academy walked into the room with AC following behind him, with Chancellor Driax's personal aide and her security detail also trailing the two veteran leaders. Cain was looking at these new warriors over to see if there was a reason for him to select any of them. The Chancellor thought it was probably best for Nick to select his troops before everyone else does. The main reason is that we have an assignment and are about to head out into Federation territory. We don't have time to waste.

The graduates don't realize that the Blood Knights are the smallest military unit within the Terran Alliance. For as much as they think they know, they really don't know anything. Boss doesn't like adding new troops because our assignments tend to be the most emotionally taxing. Our unit is for the most committed. Every time the Knights enter into a conflict, we are usually vastly outnumbered. But that isn't the difficult part for newcomers; the biggest adjustment is dealing with the pace of our lives. When you are assigned to the Blood Knights, you literally could be I the middle of a fire fight within an hour of the ceremony being completed. You just have to get used to it. I remember when Lance and Nathan graduated. Hell, we were on the way to shit on the Dec'lense in less than 20 minutes after they were initiated; those were the days. *This is just how we get down.*

No other assignments are as demanding as oursand no other commanding officer's expectations within the IGF and Terran Alliance are even close in comparison. He is the most intelligent officer in the fleet and expects his warriors to be beyond reproach; no matter the task set before them, they will find a way to complete it. No matter the personal loss or safety to themselves. The Knights will never retreat and they will never surrender. We have to learn to operate at one speed; *his speed.* The Cause matters more than anything; but you have to be ready to die for it and for each other. Cain, after looking over their faces, decides to speak.

"I am Commander Cain. First off, congratulations for completing such a difficult task; you will be needed throughout the Terran Alliance and occasionally, the IGF as well. However, our profile is a *little* different. You see, we are the unit that goes everywhere. We don't negotiate, we don't bargain, we kill everyone and everything that is deemed a threat to the Alliance and its interest. Most of the time, we have no help either. It is possible that every time that we go out on assignment that you may never return alive. There will be no songs of your heroism or glory. No one within the general populace or for the most part, your fellow Paladins will ever know what you did. We are the people that the Chancellor sends to solve problems. We will be cruel and do horrible things to the enemies that we face; we will wipe out entire races if necessary. We are the spook stories that everyone, including your fellow man, actually fears. I promise you that once you join these ranks, the only thing that I can guarantee is that at some point you will face death. At some point in our future together, we will face an enemy that we cannot defeat, and we will fight and die anyway. Our job is to protect the innocent, the helpless, and to destroy the wicked. There

is nothing heroic about it. The universe is a dirty place. We are the Terran Alliance and the IGF's *Janitors*, we clean up evil."

There was nothing inspirational or glorious about what he said. No thoughts or words were spoken of honor or adventure. This was as intense as any training assignment that any of the recent graduates of the order have ever had. Here's the question: can you keep up with the Alpha Paladin? Why would you even want to? That is not an activity for the meek of heart. No one ever wants to talk to you after you become a Blood Knight; everyone looks at you differently. People that were in the academy with you stop being friends. Most of the people that have been with Nick awhile never get promoted to anything else. We aren't usually good for anything else after you've been a Janitor that long. You become unplugged, detached from the very kingdom that you are sworn to protect. You become a secret, but secrets have costs; they aren't free.

One of my old girlfriends saw me once after an assignment out in the deep. She walked right past me in the market and didn't recognize me. It didn't seem that long to me, but I knew that it was a lifetime ago. I mean she kind of recognized me, but her husband and grandchildren made her hurry on. We are shadows in the backs of minds; passing thoughts in a person's history. That's when I figured out what being a *Janitor* meant. Being a Blood Knight scares everyone that knew you before. I can't really say that I blame them. It is something about our eyes; everyone says that when you spend enough time with us, the eyes always seem a little colder. A little bit darker. This is true, because we stare into the face of death; *all the time*. This is what some of them have to look forward to.

Cain is not one for witty banter; he never uses any more words than he has to, but the message is very clear. The Blood Knights are the *hit squad* of the Terran Alliance, plain and simple. Blood Knights don't go to diplomatic functions and we don't do interviews; most of the people that we protect don't even know that we exist. Commander Cain *likes* it that way. Boss looked at the shocked faces of the new graduates and then selected 10 out of the five thousand. Kima and Kira were among those chosen. Paul, I am so sorry.

I could tell some of them were relieved that he didn't pick them. There was one girl; Emily I think is her name. I have no idea why he picked her; I thought he picked the guy next to her. Whatever his reason, we will find out soon, because we are about to do some really heavy shit. Nick doesn't paint a pretty picture of the life of a Paladin; he doesn't paint a pretty picture of anything. He then left the facility. The ten warriors that had been chosen were following behind him, knowing that following him would mean certain death. But they will soon realize that all death is certain, but with Cain, you will take a lot of people with you before you go.

Kima and Kira are so gorgeous! AC's kids; damn, I am getting old! Those were the main reasons that we showed up. I can't even imagine what she is thinking right now. We've talked about it before, but really? Nick had to pick them. Even if he hadn't thought of it initially, Lady Aya would have complained until he did. Sometimes, I forget how crazy AC's mother can be. She actually wanted her grand-kids with us. AC is only half Terran; I think that her mother is even more Rioan than her father. She may be crazier than Nick and that is truly saying something. I know that Boss can't wait to get Kira out in the field. Word is that she is really something. That she is almost *Elisma* good. We shall see soon enough.

One new graduate had a question for the Commander. It never fails. There is always one dummy that is too smart for his own good. His classmates tried to stop him, but he insisted on being heard. He inquired as to why the commander didn't try to talk to the rogue Paladins out of their goal of conquest when they staged a coup under the leadership of Petamauck. He also inquired was it necessary to have to kill so many Paladins to ensure peace. Normally Nick doesn't answer stupid questions, especially those questions that are steeped in condescension. I remember that kid; I think his specialty was counter intelligence. God, he wasn't that bright. He'll probably be an Admiral in a year or two. Was he doing that because Cain felt it was the simplest course of action or was there some darker reason?

For a moment, I could tell that Nick thought of making an example of the young warrior. A while back, some prick tried to test him. Fucker had the nerve to mock the Oculari; I guess he didn't know they are *anywhere* and *everywhere*. That still brings me chills; it was so fast and precise. That cadet was so lucky that he wasn't killed. Nick only fractured his forearm; Sho Uchida never made that mistake again. Every time Nick sees him, he rubs Sho's forearm. That's what he thinks of as a funny joke. It's an inside thing. Only the Janitors know what Nick is doing when he does that in public. Sho always either gives Cain a dirty look or he curses at Cain when we are not in mixed company. It cracks Nick up every time.

I knew that Nick was thinking of something similar, but changed his mind. We don't have time to mess around; there is a new addition to the *shit* list. That kid was so stupid; he was lucky. Nicolas looked at him and said coldly that if a Paladin has broken their oath to the protection of the innocent and helpless, then the logical conclusion was that the day they cross Cain would most assuredly be their last day of their life. Then Nick stared a hole through the youngster's soul. He sheepishly turned away. Like I said, he was stupid. Like I said, he was lucky.

As is customary with the entrance into the Blood Knights, the Chancellor's aide has the opportunity to see Nick pick his new troops and then it is noted in the archival log the names of those individuals. After that, their names are stricken from the regular records of the Paladin order. The reason being is that almost all of the activities of this unit are clandestine. The leadership of the Terran Alliance, from the Regents, the clerics, to the majority of the military will never have direct knowledge of these deadly practitioners again. If one person dies during an incursion, the Knights will mourn them and their names will be placed in the public archives as missing in action. Make no mistake, if that a Knight dies, whoever did that deed will not have long to gloat over their apparent success.

Chapter 2

Greetings and Blessings

More than twenty rotations have passed since the Mu incident. There are still a lot of hurt feelings and mistrust between the Paladins, the Terran Alliance, and also the IGF. However, circumstances are about to occur that will bond all of these groups in a manner that will shape the future of this quadrant of the universe, almost 28 million light years, for the immediate future. Commander Nicolas Cain, also known as Khan Antonius, and his acolytes, the Blood Knights aka *The Janitors*, will be crucial to the new future of all these intersecting groups. For all parties concerned, there could be no better choice for the troubles that lay ahead.

It is a festive occasion on planet Arcadia. It is the time of the spring festival. The skies are clear, the southern breeze is welcomed. It is a warm 90 degrees and the twin sunsare shining, a perfect day for the Festival of Champions. This festival is similar to a college graduation mixed with the Olympic ceremonies of the ancient past of the home world, Earth. It is also a time of renewal, because the mightiest warriors of the Terran Alliance, the Paladins are graduating another class. It is a day of days; the most important of all Terrans, from the Terran Senate, the clerics, and the Economic Guild, as well as the current Chancellor of all 11 trillion humans has arrived. More importantly, representatives of the IGF as an example of good will and friendship have also arrived for this special day. In the time since the incident, relations between the two groups have been frosty, but because of the bravery of several Terrans besides the Alpha Centauri, negotiations have resumed. This is an important memorial.

The mutual enemies of free peoples of this quadrant, the Dark-Siders, are on the move; whatever issues that exist between the Terrans and the Federation pales in comparison to the issues that their mutual folly represent. Four rotations ago, planet Nhirada, one of the most important diplomatic and economic strongholds of the Inter Galactic Federation, had come upon attack by the Dark-Sider Armada. It was a relatively small fleet, about 400 cruisers. The IGF fleet sent to stop them was completely destroyed. For the IGF, loosing Nhirada was not an acceptable option. Only one Terran battleship, the Polaris, was in proximity to the planet.

The Polaris, a cruiser with a contingent of less than six hundred, went to their aid without hesitation. Even as the massive Colonial Class ships of the IGF were outmatched by the siders, the captain, Paul Darius, had decided to act anyway. The captain was the former helmsman for the Alpha Centauri before being promoted to his current position. Thecaptain was not just a Paladin; he's a superior navigator and battle strategist. Darius had been long considered a tactical genius and his actions against a vastly superior numbered fleet of Dark-Siders did nothing but enhance that reputation.

The ship was able to hold off several of the sider's fleet; until finally being damaged beyond repair. In an act of true heroism, he crashed the Polaris right into the flag ship of the Dark-Sider fleet. By these desperate actions, it bought the Nhiradians time; the IGF were finally able to send reinforcements. The star system was saved. Those actions began to thaw the frost between the Terran Alliance and the IGF; coupled with the fact that Centauri lead a fleet of Terran/IGF warships on a search and destroy mission on the Dark-Siders that resulted in the destruction of more than 2 thousand Dark-Sider star ships.

There is another reason for the festive atmosphere on this day. Two of the most beloved young people in the region, the twin daughters of the Regis of Mu, Kima and Kira, completed their training for the Paladin Order. News such as this always has a positive energy. In the time that has passed between the Mu Incident, no new Paladins had been created. The reason given was that a new training regime had to be created and the chancellor, Alron Driax, decided that a more stream-lined training system had to occur. The process, which had been kept behind closed doors for eight thousand Earth years, had to be changed. One new requirement of all the Paladins was the secondary discipline that each of these warriors had to be well versed in. So that these warriors had a deeper investment in humanity, not only did these men and women have instruction in war/death, but also a field that pertained to the development or sustaining of life. This process met with resistance from the older members of the Paladin Order, but when the Alpha Paladin,

Nicolas Cain, agreed that changes needed to occur, many of them reluctantly signed on for this.

The Paladin training had long been a secret. It had been more than eight thousand rotations ago since the first Paladins been created. The Rioans had long been the protectors of the Inter Galactic Federation and all of its allies but the prolonged conflicts with among others the Kurgax, the Hunians, the Ikog, and the Dark-Siders had vastly depleted their ranks. The humans were considered a viable replacement for the Rioans as a military force because of their adaptability and proficiency in war. However, even the best of the humans could not best many of the potential foes of the Terran Alliance and the IGF. The Paladin solution became the option of choice.

The origins of the Paladins had been dubious at best. Seven thousand warriors underwent the physiological and combat training to become the newest and deadliest warriors of the quadrant. The process worked *too* well. Many of these warriors became psychotic; unable to distinguish between an act of protection versus simple, sadistic murder. In the beginning, the Paladins were almost as dangerous as their foes. In some cases, they were worse than their opposition.

Over the next few eons, the process of the physical training had been modified and with the wisdom of SaintThomas, the addition of *The Cause* was indoctrinated into the Paladin training process. The Cause is defined as simply that these men and women were tools of God; they would fight for those who couldn't fight for themselves. It is *never* about us, but that it is *always* about God. These warriors became legendary throughout the quadrant, able to subdue even the strongest and deadliest of foes.

The incident on Mu however, had eroded the trust of both the IGF and the Alliance. Petamauck had not only shaken the Paladins to their very core but also betrayed the confidence that both the Federation and Alliance had in them. If it were not for the actions of the Alpha Paladin, civil war could have easily broken out and the 30 million light years of space controlled by the Federation and Alliance could have been drastically changed. Chancellor Driax said that major changes had to occur to the Paladin training process so that these issues never happened again. For starters, these warriors would be kept a longer period of time and a secondary discipline would be taught to them to ensure that these warriors had a stake in something besides death and destruction.

The Paladins are trained under the harshest of conditions. They are constantly tested in combat situations; their minds are under constant attack as well. These men and women's very souls are constantly at war; giving them instruction in the killing arts, philosophy, quantum principles, star fighter combat, politics, as well as theology. These men and women know that countless lives depend on their ability to keep their wits when everything around them is in constant chaos. The ability to concentrate under these incredibly harsh conditions as well as the ability to not squander hope in spite of all that they have seen or had to do arealso key essentials in the development of a Paladin.

The Paladins decided it was time to start over; back to the basics. The integration of all these new realities was incorporated into the training of these newest warriors. The 5,000 new graduates of the academy had spent almost ten rotations working on their craft. Even though several had participated in missions before their actual graduation, they were constantly tested and monitored to ensure that the warriors were of the highest quality. Many of these warriors will be integrated into other aspects of the military instead of acting as if these warriors were not a part of the military. These warriors would be placed within the leadership hierarchies of the Alliance, many were either assigned the rank of Ensign, Chief, or Captain. The most selective unit within the Alliance Military would be Commander Cain's unit, *The Janitors*. The Janitors are the deep space clandestine unit of the Alliance. No one wants to hang out with that unit; it's far too dangerous.

In order for the training for this newest collection of warriors to be complete, they were in need of a new primary teacher. An educator whose knowledge and wisdom would be above reproach; who had been humbled by their own mistakes and could be an example of the power of second chance; someone who had to earn the respect and trust of his fellow Paladin, as well as the trust of the Terran Alliance once again. AC, the wise and beautiful second in command of the Alpha Centauri made the suggestion of the new head of the Paladin Academy.

When she made her suggestion, it was immediately questioned and also heavily scrutinized. Erik the Red, one of the oldest and most powerful members of the Paladin order suggested that she was under the influence of evil forces when he heard her suggestion. Nya the Brave also was against AC's suggestion. Chancellor Driax however was intrigued. She believed that AC's choice was an inspired one. The Head of Paladin

Academy should be someone who has fallen and now has rehabilitated himself. Who better to speak to value of humility, charity, and second chances? Even though she was not a Paladin herself, the chancellor had developed a reputation as a smooth negotiator and a balanced leader. The members of the Terran Military had come to trust her judgment as well as the Economic Guild, and maybe most importantly, she had earned the loyalty of a certain Alpha Paladin, which might have been her best trump card.

As the crowd of more than 2 million gathered in the famed Arcadian Courtyard, a feeling of great excitement came over the crowd. The Chancellor, a master orator, had command of the Courtyard, the Planet, and the Quadrant, as all the Terran Alliance who could not attend had been were tuned in via teleconference feed. 11 trillion humans and countless other races had been waiting for this day. "**Greetings and blessings to all; we have much to celebrate today!!!! It is my pleasure and privilege to welcome you to the Terran Peace Festival. We come together as one people to celebrate the wonderful opportunity to share our charity and remember the sacrifices made by so many so that we can exist here and be citizens of the Universe. If it had not been for those sacrifices and lessons learned none of us would be here today.**"

While the crowd cheered for the chancellor's words, off in the distance two figures stand on top of a massive, Colonial-Class battle fortress floating on top of the ocean. Both of these figures cut stunning silhouettes; one a stunning feminine form, the other a striking male figure. AC, Cain's right hand, stood beside him. Her raven hair blowing against the blue-green ocean's breeze, tears were slowing rolling down her cheeks. She is after all, a proud mother. Her twin daughters, Kira and Kima, have achieved a monumental goal. To become Paladins, guardians of the Terrans and all the innocent peoples of this universe. Their lives will never be the same. To devote one's life to the protection and development of another is the charge of all these powerful and devoted people. "**Their father would have been proud. I am so proud of them. And I am so proud of their father also; their instructor did such a wonderful job. Look at the results of his labor. I told you that this was and will always be the right decision,**" she spoke softly. "**I know that this isn't your normal thing, but could you at least *act* like this moment moves you. Not too much to ask is it?**"

The Alpha Paladin, possibly the most dangerous Terran in the history of humanity looked at his second in command. He realized that if he didn't say something deep and heartfelt, AC would badger him until he did. *Dammit*, he thought. There is nothing that he could do about it. AC does not play fair; even when he was younger, she would do this to him. Make him feel things; Nick always hated that, but he always loved that. Instead of some deep words, Cain put AC's arm inside of his and she leaned her head against his shoulder. She smiled and said sweetly, **"thank you. I knew you felt the same way."** She knows that Cain will always display his affections for her through deeds, not words. The Centauri's second in command always hated that, but she always loved that.

AC was among the first people to ever show Nick unconditional love, affection and kindness, but he was not ready to receive it when she started working with him. He was both indignant and lethal when they were first introduced to each other. Even though he was not necessarily kind to her, Cain deeply respected AC as an important asset in his life. Over time, he slowly came to realize that she was more than just an asset, but was also a dear loved one. In time, the youthful assassin learned how to relay those feelings for his dear friend.

Their relationship was awkward at first because she didn't really understand him at all. This was hard for her to understand in the beginning why he was reluctant to allow her into his heart. At first AC thought it was because of his Ocularian conditioning, but that wasn't the reason. Petamauck told her that the only loved ones in his life, especially his sister, had died. To make Cain more comfortable with his new surroundings, she colored her black hair red. Maya and Wilcox were the only people who were kind to him; they were both redheads. Cain liked that, but he never told her. Many have commented that comparing Nick between then and now is literally like night and day. Talking was not his strong suit back then. Much like his Ocularian comrades, he usually communicated everything with his eyes or his actions. Even though he is far more verbal now, the Alpha Paladin still believes in the adage of actions speaking louder than words

There was another reason that AC was particularly emotional about this set of circumstances. Her fiancé was Captain Paul Darius. They fell in love while he was the helmsman of the Centauri. He was also considered a close friend of Nick and was the executive officer of the ship. This was before the Centauri become the flag ship of the Alliance and Federation. When Paul was given command of the Polaris, AC was torn about what to do. Was she going to go with her future husband or would she stay with Cain? Nick told her that she was free to make her own choice, which he would support whatever decision that she had to make. Nick said sweetly to his dear friends, **"Whatever decision that you make will be the right one. Good travels my friends."** Another set of circumstances created a greater dilemma for the Paladin officer.

AC and Paul found out that they were expecting twins not long after Paul was given command of the Polaris. The Rioans have a custom that if both the man and woman are both soldiers, the woman will select a foster mother for her children so that she can continue her duty. This is in part because the Rioans are a warrior race. Children are a necessity for the population to continue. Service always trumps everything in their society. Female Rioans by nature are always sworn to duty; children are not usually a thought. If a Rioan is pregnant, she gives the child up and continues to serve her expected charge.

Paul was upset that she wanted to continue her duty. They had a huge fight. He reminded her that she is a human also and humans understand the value of parents raising their children. This angered AC; she stated to her fiancé that if he didn't understand why she had to continue to serve, then he didn't understand her at all. His beloved AC was a warrior when they met and she was a warrior still; anything else was absurd. She may be of Rioan and Terran heritage, but she has been raised Rioan ever since she chose a life of service. How dare Paul believe otherwise? The wedding was off.

AC went to talk to her mother about the decisions that she had recently made. She was torn about her break-up and more importantly she was concerned about where she should continue to serve the Alliance and the Federation. AC knows that she is child of two worlds. Her mother has always made her feel that being a child of hybrid heritage was always a positive asset. Was she making the right choice? **"Mother, I am giving the girls to Maia; they will have a good life on Mu. But I don't think that I can go with Paul. I belong with Nick. He is the best leader in the entire fleet, but a part of me still loves Paul."** Her mother kissed AC on her forehead. **"Child, what does your heart tell you to do? I know what your father would say; he grows weary of you always being in such dangers. You know what Paul would say. You even know what I think. The question is whether your sense of the**

Cause is above your love for your dearest Paul. You know what Nick will do without you, don't you? You know that this circumstance doesn't just affect you. You remember why you were assigned to the Blood Knights? Your primary duty is to stop Nick from being *himself.* Khan Antonius had *one bad day* and one trillion people died. Imagine if he has *two bad days?*"

AC smiled and kissed her mother. She knew what she had to do. AC's primary duty was to always keep humanity relevant in the thinking of the crew of the Alpha Centauri. AC taught him how to care and also to invest; she taught him how to be human. She is the primary reason that Antonius at least *considers* collateral damage. This is the deadliest unit within either the Alliance or the Federation. They destroy everything in their path. Once it is decided that the Centauri is tasked with an assignment, there is one conclusion. Furthermore, the Alpha Centauri is a deep space battle cruiser. They stay gone until the job is complete. AC is also the Teran Alliance Liaison Officer within the Federation; she has many different duties because of both her Paladin designation and also her Rioan heritage. She loves being all those things; it gives her a sense of both purpose and perspective. That is a lot to give up for love.

Nick stayed out of the set of circumstances that was destroying their relationship. It wasn't that he didn't care, it was the fact he didn't *care*. In the world of Cain and the Blood Knights, there was a constant battle. There would always be a maniacal despot or tyrant that needed to be disposed of. The commander had more pressing concerns than his friends' fraying affiliation. An incident in the Potamian Galaxy had been called to his attention; the Knights had been given a deep space tasker. AC had the twins and then gave them delivered to her friend Maia Quintus, the future Regent of Mu, as her chosen mother for the girls. As was custom, AC recovered for a short period of time and then she was ready to return to her assigned duties. She only named her children; she never saw them after that.

It is not that Rioan women don't love their children. In fact, it is quite the opposite. Once a Rioan female emotionally bonds with her child, the women are not always objective and can become incredibly territorial, which can be a hindrance to doing their assigned duties. This one of the primary reasons that these warriors give their children up so early because that level of bias makes it difficult to complete their assigned duties. Rioans believe in giving up anything and everything for their loved ones. They believe that those being warriors make their children's lives safer. Humans always have an issue with that particular sentiment. Paul was furious, but he respected the Rioan custom. In part because he knew that AC didn't care and Aya cared less than AC did.

Captain Darius also knew Nick; he doesn't get involved with his crew's personal crisis. Once a member of the crew has a family issue, the commander will give them all the time needed to resolve that issue. Once a person has returned to the Centauri, total focus is required because of the level of danger that the crew will be in. Paul knew that his commander had given them enough time to deal with their issues and now it was time hunt down the wicked. Cain was the one who delivered the twins to Maia. Life goes on for the Centauri; Petamauck was promoted to executive officer and Faris was promoted to helmsman. Captain Darius went on to his ship, fully expecting AC to report to the Polaris for duty. A funny thing happened, she didn't show up.

As Nick and the Centauri crew were preparing to enter deep space, something unexpected occurred. As instructions were being shouted and repeated, a familiar voice repeated Petamauck's instructions. AC showed up and took her place on the ship. Petamauck and Faris were among all the bridge officers looking blankly at her. She snapped, **"Is there a problem? All systems are reading green Commander. Mr. Faris, do we need an invitation?"** AC stood next to the commanding officer of the Alpha Centauri; never looking at her, he folded his arms, smirked and said whimsically, **"you're late."** The mighty Terran warship raced off into the dark cold. Darius and AC never spoke again.

After the chancellor concluded her speech, she introduced the Head of Paladin Academy. His salt and pepper hair, cut in a Caesar, just like his ancestors, was cropped perfectly. He had briskness to his steps but also a humility that made him endearing. His fellow Paladins, his students and all those in attendance had their eyes focused on him. The leader was both confident and humble; charamismatic and cool. He understood the responsibility and felt at ease in front of them. Much like the younger version of himself, the one that was filled with arrogance and madness, he is a secure orator, able to sway countless masses with the sound and balance of his words. Those words gave function to actions that might have one day destroyed the Terran Alliance, until his closest friend and former student killed him.

Peter Anderson McNamara is the Earth alias for the greatest teacher of Logic and Reason in the Terran Alliance. His actual name is Petamauck. He was dispatched by General Danyzer to retrieve Cain when he was a teenager on Earth. Nicolas was full of potential, power, and also an incredible amount of rage. Cain had been wreaking havoc throughout the foster care system in California as well as causing several psychiatrists to either quit the profession or becoming patients themselves. Petamauck was able to help him focus his incredible mind and point his hostility in a positive direction. As he was being trained by Paladins, it became apparent that even for a Paladin, Nick was something to behold. The guru and apprentice spent many nights just talking about liberty and free will; it was important that Cain become a balanced human, not just a highly skilled assassin.

Since he born under the Riddle of the Sphinx, Petamauck was given another chance at life, but not as a young man. Even though he made a terrible choice, he was still needed. He has finally reached middle age, more than nine hundred Earth Years old. He is still Petamauck; but a much older, a much wiser and definitely more humble version of his former self. He spoke. **"Peace and blessings to all free people of this quadrant. I am humbled by the words of the chancellor and also by the life I have been given. I hope to become the man that all of you may one day forgive and accept. I strive everyday to become worthy of the second chance that God has bestowed upon me. To my friends who stood up for me when I gave them no reason to do so, and to those that I wronged in my former life, my deepest apologies. This is truly a day of joy and remembrance. The children that the families gave me to watch and nurture are now the Paladins that I return to you in this time of need. They are ready for duty, ready to serve, and if necessary, ready to die for the Cause."**

On planet Acre, the capital planet of the IGF, Danyzer is pacing back and forth, pondering the set of circumstances that has recently occurred on Arcadia. This reality still leaves him flustered. Petamauck's previous transgressions cost him several friends; it is difficult to think that he is in charge of training new warriors. The general is still angry that his grandchildren have been trained by Petamauck and even angrier that it was his daughter's suggestion that they were trained by him. *Why didn't Nick put a stop to this*, he fumed. The Commandant was standing by him, with a smug grin on his face. Aya just contacted him via vid-link. **"Husband,** this is such a beautiful event. I still don't understand why you didn't come. What is this; why are you frowning darling? Why are you angry?" Danyzer didn't get a chance to speak. "He is mad because Antonius allowed Petamauck to be in charge of the Academy. Your dearest husband is still under the impression that this was Nick's decision. You never told him huh?" At this point Danyzer yells in anger; he hates when they know something that he doesn't. "Told me what?! You know I *hate* when you do that. If it wasn't Nick's decision to make Petamauck the Head of the Academy, then whose was it?" The senator smiled at her mate. "It was *mine*. I had the deciding vote. It was tied and I was tie breaker. Nick just made sure that there would be no sass or back talk after the decision was made. There was some resistance to the choice but he made sure that it didn't get that far."

At this point, Danyzer was almost afraid to know what Aya meant by that statement, but as usual, he had to know what happened. He sighed deeply. "So what did he do?" The Ocularian Commandant, the one who was responsible for Cain being so deadly responded with glee. "Oh you are going to love this story. Don't forget my favorite part Aya." Before she could speak, the general snapped again. "How do you know what happened? Did Nick tell you?" The venerable mentor responded. "I am the head of the Oculari. Stop acting as if you don't know what that means. You know that I don't have to *be there* in order *to be there*. Stop interrupting." Aya smiled. "Thank you my dear, sweet friend. Well Onera started bitching about the decision. AC said that the decision was made. That she didn't have to discuss the issue any further. He wouldn't drop it and said something under his breath. I think he called her a bitch and you know what happened next." Danyzer's eyes got bigger. "He didn't."

The teacher knows his student. Nick doesn't handle disrespect very well. Once a decision is made there is nothing left to discuss. Certainly no back talk once a Federation Senator or a superior officer has given final word on a discussion. This is the bad time. Aya continued gleefully. "Yeah he did. Right in front of us. Snatched his eyeball out. Antonius never even raised his voice. Then he said 'what did she say? Say something else cute, and I will dislocate your shoulder; and that's just to start. Apologize and *maybe* I will put your eye back in the socket; she's waiting.' We were just sitting there in shock; he is *everywhere* and he is *anywhere*. My friend, you have taught him so

well. It was the most impressive action that I have ever seen. None of us even knew that he was in the room; he was there the entire time. God, I love watching my Nicky work."

Petamauck's words were beautiful and wise. However, he didn't know that those words would also turn prophetic. As he was about to announce the new Paladins for the quadrant to meet and become proud of, a hissing noise become so shrill that it could no longer be ignored. A series of explosions was so forceful that panic had taken hold of the crowd. A ship that had IGF clearance but was not an IGF craft had begun attacking Cyprus, the fourth moon of planet Arcadia. Much like the Trojan Horse, the Dark-Siders sprang from the fake ship and attacked. This was significant because it was where the ship building yard of the battle fortress cruisers of the Terran Alliance was happening at the same an attack from the crowd had also occurred. As the carnage and panic had occurred, a sense of fear raced through the Terran Alliance. Not sense the Mu incident had such fear been felt.

The military group that had been put in charge of protecting this event primarily was the Terran Defense Command Special Forces. These troops usually were responsible for any event that the Chancellor or any members of the cabinet or local leadership were going to be involved in. These soldiers were some of the best trained in the Alliance Military. Their reputation had taken a hit as of late because of what happened both in the Mu System and what had happened to Alron Kush and the Alliance Cabinet more than twenty rotations ago. In less than one galactic rotation, the Chancellor had been murdered and the Paladins waged a hostile takeover attempt led by Petamauck to control the Alliance. These warriors, while brave and resolute were no match for the forces that murdered Kush or the Paladins who nearly destabilized the entire quadrant. If it were not for the actions of the Blood Knights, this particular date in history would have had an entirely different meaning.

Once the siders began to attack, the Special Forces began to rebuild their reputation with the valor that they had been known for. Even though there were Paladins at the event, their energies were being directed towards the problems on Cyprus. Furthermore, the Blood Knights were not equipped for close quarter combat with the siders with civilians in harm's way; collateral damage means little to nothing to them. The paladins who served Cain were primarily a deep space unit; their weapons and tactics were not suitable for Terran planetary combat.

This knowledge was primarily why when Cain attacked on Mu that the leadership was so worried initially about the potential for damage. The special forces would have to protect the citizens effectively if there was to be a victory that day. Fortunately for all, there was a unit that was up to the almost impossible task of protecting the Chancellor despite incredible odds stacked against them. Redemption seemed to be the theme of the day and these monsters had crossed the wrong humans on the worst day ever.

For many of the citizens of the Terran Alliance, this was the first time that any had ever seen the enemy known only as the siders. These monsters usually were either ground drones that looked liked humanoids or they were sky drones that looked like star fighters. These creatures had black and silver metallic looking skin that was created from some unknown material in this part of the universe. The ground troops were usually 2.75 to 3.25 meters in height. They had arms and legs and were extremely agile; resembling large primates, these creatures moved like primates and usually attacked in packs. For the average citizens in either the Federation or the Alliance, these monsters were terrifying, always heavily armored with metallic fangs and claws as well as powerful hand weapons. They didn't speak in any known language; their auditory communication sounded more like wolves growling.

For a group of warriors like the Paladins, these creatures were not that tough. Nick liked to say that they were big and stupid; that being said, Cain also believes that the only thing more dangerous than one dummy was two dummies. However, the sheer numbers of monsters per incursions, usually ranging in the six figure range, make them a difficult opponent. When coupled with the fact that these monsters also seemed to disregard their own individual existence, these foes were difficult to fight to say the least. The best way to beat them was to try and take them out as quickly as possible. Fortunately for the people in attendance, destroying Dark-Sider drones was a specialty of the Order of Paladins.

The fighter drone ships were equally frightening. These ships looked like vampire bats moving against the night sky. All of these ships would be traveling at high speed all in the same direction, all at once. It could be an extremely unnerving sight to someone who has never seen them attack before. Horror stories were devoted to the fear that the siders had created throughout much of this part of the universe. One of the primary reasons that the Federation and the Alliance collaboration is so important was because these warriors of Terran blood were the only people left in the star cluster who were able to stand up to the might of the Dark-Sider war machine. Usually when the siders began attacking, they will not stop their assault until your entire system has been destroyed. Under Cain's leadership however, the siders have been routinely defeated. In actuality, they have not just been defeated, these monsters have been slaughtered.

It is not that the Dark-Siders haven't been defeated before; Danyzer led a campaign against them in the past, but the unintended consequences were almost more destructive than the actual combat. The price of those victories were far too great. Under Commander Nicolas Cain, the results have always been far more tactical and successful. These flying monsters also attack in waves, hoping to outlast their prey's resources and overwhelm them. This is usually an unsuccessful strategy against the Paladins, in particularly the Blood Knights. The weaponry used by the Blood Knights is far too destructive; this knowledge is why the Federation covets them so much. No one else in the quadrant has as deadly a military force at their disposal.

Most of the Alliance military personnel had begun trying to hold the line against the foot drone attack. Many of the two million civilians had been rushed to safety, but a group of forty thousand people, human and Federation members that had been stranded behind the lines that had been drawn. Erik the Red, one of the most accomplished and deadly warriors in the Order took charge of the situation. He needed two dozen Paladins to aid him in the quest to eliminate the infestation of sider drones in the capital suite. He and Petamauck knew that the military personnel, while formidable, would not be able to hold the drones off for long and all those innocent people would die.

Erik looked at his old friend and smiled. Red picked up his huge broad swords and grabbed his massive hand cannon. He yelped out a Neo Carthaginian battle cry and took off running. *He never waits,* thought Petamauck. The head of the Paladin Academy smiled to himself. He picked up his double swords and linked them together; *time for the old man to lead the babies,* he thought. Petamauck called forth the recent graduates of the Paladin academy and spoke to them with deep urgency. **"The innocent are in danger. You are not going to just stand here are you? Today is a good day to die!!!"** In that instant, all five thousand of the new Paladins immediately prepared to attack, battle units formed, and instructions were carried out. The drones will wish that they hadn't chosen this day to invade Terran territory. Erik the Red took off after the siders on foot with twenty other warriors, including Petamauck in pursuit of their adversaries. Predators that have now become prey.

The siders were taking the Alliance Special Forces unit assigned as security for the event completely apart. One small unit of 11 soldiers, led by Captain Alexander Cormier took the responsibility of protecting the Chancellor. Cormier was from Arkadelphia, as were all of his unit. They were not going to let the Chancellor die without a fight. He radioed frantically to anyone who would listen while he and his unit were pinned down in front of the suite. **"Is anyone out there? We are taking heavy fire near Chancellor Driax's suite. We will not let them have her!! But we are going to need some help with the clean up."** A voice answered the call. **"This is Faris. Hold out Captain. Janitors are on the way."** This made Cormier feel better for a moment. Then he resumed unpleasantries with the drones attacking his forward position. One of his trusted corporals, Aaron Marez asked why that made him feel better. Janitors wouldn't help the situation, they needed Paladins. Cormier between throwing his grenades replied that Janitors clean up evil. They just needed to concentrate on not letting anyone else in that room.

As these men and women tried desperately to keep the leadership safe, behind the two thousand kilo steel door a conversation was taking place. It was an odd time to have a negotiation, but for those who were familiar with Chancellor Alron Driax, she revels in these chaotic situations to press her advantage. **"Senator Ruquxa, I would like to say that the Terran Alliance would very much like to be a part of the IGF, but only under the right circumstances. As you can see, our military is not only brave, but well prepared. What do you think?"** Flustered, the IGF representative asked how she could consider continuing negotiations at a time like this. The senator inquired, **"what if they get in?"** To which the Chancellor smiled and continued sipping on her mint tea, **"*They won't.*"** This type of steely calm is exactly why Cain trusts his boss.

At this point, it was time for these foe disguised as friend to learn what fear really was. The bridge commander of the Alpha Centauri, Sayied Farris, smiled and said to the crew, **"light them up! They're out of their minds!!! The Dark-Siders thought we were going to just to sit back and take it? Close their eyes. Permanently."** At this time, five dozen delta wing raptors, the deadliest fighter ships ever conceived by

Terran or Rioan technology, had emerged from the hull of the Centauri. All of the fighters had pilots save one. This star-fighter was a predator in every way. The weapons systems and powerful engines seemed to growl. There was something both beautiful and frightening about this craft, just as there was something beautiful and menacing about its pilot.

Wing Alpha, a black and red dragon-like menace was in hover mode, waiting on its master to command it to do horrible things to its enemy. The two figures that were standing on top of the Centauri would now depart. The man would head straight to Cyprus to wipe out the attack on the depot, while the woman was charged with the destruction of the folly that was creating chaos on the ground. The celebration would have to be delayed. **"See you AC in a little bit, leave none alive. Yeah I haven't forgotten; I will take you and Kima when this is over. Once you are done, meet us at Cyprus,"** said the Alpha. **"Oh yeah, one more thing,"** he uttered. **"Tell Kira to meet me at Cyprus, if she's ready."** *Oh shit it's already begun*, AC thought to herself. Kira was considered the best pilot and deadliest Paladin amongst the new class. Cain is interested in putting her reputation to the test.

Nicolas then took off in a dead sprint towards the edge of the Centauri. He then leaped off the ship and landed in the cockpit of the Delta Winged Raptor. As he landed into the cockpit, his battle uniform converted into space ready apparel. Cain smiled and spoke to his companion, **"hey baby, did you miss me?"** The ship seemed to purr like a kitten. AC, watching this affectionate display, for a split second almost seemed jealous. The only thing that he didn't have was his helmet; almost on cue, a compartment opened and his helmet, scared from countless battles appeared. He smiled, **"Thanks girl, it's time to go to work."** Much like the Alpha Paladin, it is truly one of a kind. After putting on his helmet, his brain was then linked up with multiple operating systems of his ship. Considering the enormous power of his brain, the computer would be lucky to keep up. The systems linked together with Cain's incredible senses. The cockpit then sealed him inside much like a cocoon. Wing Alpha was now complete; an exquisite tool of mass destruction.

The stories of the pilot and his ship are legendary throughout the Federation. Many have cowered in fear at the prospect of Cain and Wing Alpha being sent on its task. This star fighter is the *ruler* of the intergalactic habitat; it has no natural predators. Before Cain, no one had ever truly mastered the vessel so its most deadly potential was never realized. That is until Antonius claimed it as his own. The irony was that his "baby", Wing Alpha, is actually older than he is. AC, who was the project manager for the raptors, often lamented that Wing Alpha, should have *never* been built. Before Cain took ownership, everyone who had attempted to control this ship had died or gone mad. But for the Alpha Paladin, it is a perfect fit. Nick said his prayers for the safety of his warriors and success of the mission. Then he took off into the endless night.

Captain Cormier was losing troops and retreating back to the base of the blast door. **"Here is where we make our final stand. Help is coming, but we have to wait them out."** At this point, he had only three troops left. They made a promise to both God and each other that the Chancellor would not have one hair misplaced. Even if it meant their deaths, the Alliance Leader would be safe. Cormier's best friend, Major Kelton Trammell was in charge of the contingent that lost Chancellor Kush; he was not going to let his best friend down. It always stayed with him that he couldn't be there; the only reason that Cormier is in this position currently is because Trammell was murdered with Kush. If not for Trammell's death, he would have been following instead of leading. He was going to honor his best friend by rectifying that inequity today. He was not a Paladin, he and his troops were not super warriors; they are just dedicated and well prepared. Just like the crew of the Polaris.

Another twenty drones entered the room and another twenty drones had been cut down. Driax will not be harmed. It was that simple. The trooper to his left had just been shot in the arm, she needed medical attention. Sergeant Major Cara Subramaniam put her gun in the other hand. She smiled and said, **"Don't worry Captain, I am a lefty now."** *Shit, where is our backup*, thought the brave commanding officer. The Alliance military unit lead by Cormier were finally overrun by the sheer number of drones that had attacked the Chancellor's suite. The Special Forces unit was able to hold them off in another incredible display of bravery; 11 troops held more than one thousand sider drones away from the intended target of Chancellor Driax and the IGF representatives

Erik and his small rescue unit had arrived just in time to stop a potential disaster and they were not in a forgiving mood. Then all of the sudden, the growls had become squeals. The Paladins had arrived just in time. **"What took you so long?"** The senior Paladin replied, **"I am so sorry sir. We got hung up at the base of the building. This will** *never* **happen again.**" Erik was the superior officer, but he understood the heightened anxiety that the Special Forces had been under. They had fought with the boogeyman and emerged victorious. Men like Erik and Nick recognize and honor bravery, especially when someone has survived through their faith. The Cause always matters the most. Cormier and his troops were worthy of that respect today.

As Nicolas and the rest of the Blood Knights went to Cyprus, the mighty Alpha Centauri went to quash the Dark-Siders who were attacking the festival. The sider ships that were hovering above the chaos below were destroyed with surgical precision. Because of the circumstances of being on a planet with civilians, AC and Faris had several scores of the Blood Knights attack the siders on hover boards. In order for the siders to not hear their impending demise, Faris had the Knights use older weapons technology; bows and arrows. By the time the sider drones became aware of the threat, it was too late.

The new Paladins, lead by their headmaster Petamauck, continued slaughtering their enemies on the ground. Little did the Dark-Sider leadership know that these new Paladins were in many ways deadlier than the old guard. Two of the new Paladins followed behind one of the oldest. Erik the Red gave orders for Kira and Shiro to attack from the flanks and he would attack from the middle. Shiro used his knives to shred the drones; Kira shot the primary enemies with her hand cannon. The pawns did not have a chance. No to be outdone, Erik then dispatched the final two enemies with his bare hands; he is a brawler through and through. Before the final enemy could be crushed another Paladin entered the room. Nari the Wise is the best interrogator in the order. He is also a telepath; he needed to read the mind of one of the primary Dark-Siders.

Much like game of chess, the Dark-Siders use their pawns as expendable assets. Their leaders actually know the plan; however, when cornered, the leaders will execute themselves before their plan can be found out. Considering the vastness of their race, losing a few thousand per incursion is not significant. As Nari moved in, a green mist emerged from the primary drone. It was a poison. Nari was paralyzed by it; Kira, not one to take chances, shot and killed the primary. Nari's probe of the primary proved successful; the plot was to kill Driax and the IGF representative during all the bedlam.

As order was being restored on Arcadia, the fight was just beginning on Cyprus. Seventy thousand sider drones had emerged from the moon.

At that instant, Nathan the Magnificent, Cain's second in command, spoke over the intercom, almost laughing. **"Boss this is going to be a piece of cake. Don't the siders know by now not to fuck with the Knights? This doesn't make sense."** The commander responds, **"oh yes it does. Very cute. Stay sharp boys and girls. Don't use the good stuff. Just Blasters."** Most of the Blood Knights battle mecha was too destructive to be used in closed, populated environments; the blasters would do just fine. Just before the carnage was about to be begin, Major Faris had an announcement over the comlink. **"Remember today's theme, mercy first!!!"** this got a laugh out of the Alpha. **"Just kidding Boss."**

The best of the worst, the Blood Knights, began to take the siders apart. The mantel was the same, no prisoners, no mercy. As the raptors began to destroy the drones of the Dark-Siders, a lone ship that was just out of the line of sight of the attack was recording the attack patterns of the Blood Knights. At that point, a missile was fired upon its port side, severely damaging it. Another raptor had come from the planet. It was Kira, following the orders of her commander to enter the fight once the planet was secure. As the Dark-Sider command ship escaped further destruction, she then entered the fighting with the drones. *Target practice,* she thought. Noticing that Magnificent and the others were just using blasters, she did the same.

Of the seventy thousand drones, she destroyed more than 1,400 of them. Impressive considering how late she began the skirmish. Once the last drone was finished, it was time to go home. **"Nice work everyone, head back to the Centauri for repairs, Nathan don't forget it's your turn to cook. Don't make that shit you made last time either. I HATE eggs,"** said the Commander laughing. In fact, everyone but Kira laughed; it was an inside thing. **"Come to think of it, don't bother; you only know how to make crappy food! By the way Kira, can you cook?"** It is tradition that on a successful mission that the Knights eat together, even though many are awful cooks. Kira has earned their respect today.

Once the Knights returned from the encounter, an assessment had to be done of what was lost and also what was gained. The drones had been destroyed in space, Cyprus had been saved. All the leadership had been protected, no harm, save a few bumps and bruises had befallen them as well. For a confrontation from the most feared enemies of all the free people of this sector, all in all it was not that bad. That is what worried Commander Nicolas Cain. This was a lot of trouble, the siders had traveled a great distance to in essence waste the time of such a deadly and proficient foe like the Alliance.

The warriors that had been trained by Cain's dear friend, Petamauck had shown themselves approved. Several of these new warriors would now be integrated into the various operation units; Deep Space, Espionage, Tactical Operations, and Planetary Defense are amongst the choicest assignments. The most selective program for the Paladins has an interesting codename: *Janitors*. This is the codename for The Blood Knights, the clandestine search and destroy unit of the Terran Alliance. Of all the five thousand graduates, the Knights would only take 10. Chancellor Driax, a leader who has the ability to turn a negative into a positive, used the day's events to assure both the IGF and the Terran Alliance that their futures were in capable hands. Furthermore, Kira is a good cook. *Good to know*, thought the Khan; *good to know*.

Chancellor Driax used the potential cataclysm to reinforce the Alliance position to the IGF. The bravery of Captain Cormier and his troops were lauded throughout both the Terran Alliance and also the Federation territories. These soldiers, in particularly the Captain felt vindicated because of their ability to protect the Chancellor while being overrun by the siders. Demons were exorcised by these actions because of what happened to Kush and the cabinet. Their bravery would be listed along with the crew of the Polaris. They would forever be known as the *Arkadelphia Eleven*. Nicolas in particular was honored to meet them because of how much he valued Kush and how much he has come to value Driax. Somewhere Kush was smiling at what had transpired.

Petamauck and Nicolas, old adversaries, but even older friends finally got a chance to speak face to face. In the twenty rotations since the Mu incident, neither had seen each other. This wasn't because Cain was avoiding his mentor, but rather because something was more pressing to him. Cain was certain that AC and the Chancellor were correct in their assessment that Petamauck was the right person for the Paladin Academy. The thing was that he didn't need to talk to Petamauck; Cain has this incredible ability to accept and forgive. There was nothing for him to say. When Aya asked him about it, the response was typical Nick. **"He made a mistake and paid for it. If God can forgive, so can I. We need him; that's why he was returned. He will be better than before; much more asset than liability."**

The previous difficulty for Petamauck was that even though he was the greatest teacher of logic and reason that humanity had to offer, Nicolas Cain's intellect far surpassed his own. He and Nick would occasionally have disagreements on how to handle Paladin affairs in part because of the capacity of Cain's understanding. Nicolas understood issues and problems on a level that even Petamauck could not fathom. The teacher had been surpassed by the student, even though the pupil was too humble to ever show up his mentor. Even during the coup, Nick was relatively polite to his teacher. Compared to how his fellow usurpers were dispatched, Petamauck got off light. The first time that Petamauck was certain that no Paladin was in Nick's league was during the Mu incident. Now that small tidbit has been resolved, these two dear and trusting friends are free to resume their baseline duties of making the universe a better place.

It was important for Petamauck to let Nick know how much he appreciated him and their friendship. Petamauck was disappointed in his actions, but he wanted to atone for his failings. Furthermore, he wanted to earn Nick's love and trust again. The problem was that as far as Nick was concerned, it was a dead issue. There was nothing to forgive. Petamauck was determined to make amends. He not only strived to train great warriors, but also great thinkers; it was imperative to him that Nick knew that he was deeply regretful. Petamauck knows that Cain never holds a grudge, much less judge's people's actions. Nick always said he didn't have a right to. When the humbled leader saw his commander, he immediately bowed as a symbol of deference. Cain wouldn't allow this action to continue. He smiled and hugged his dear friend. Nicolas put his left hand on his friend's right shoulder, in typical fashion responded in few words, **"No need. You had me at greetings and blessings. We are brothers, both in arms and blood. That will never change."**

As the great star ship, the Alpha Centauri, readied preparations to launch into space, to chase after their quarry, a meeting between the chancellor, Erik the Red, AC, Petamauck, and Nicolas Cain occurred. AC and Cain were on the ship, while the rest were still on the planet. The newest set of Paladin recruits were on their way to Arcadia, while Erik was preparing to escort Driax back to planet Eden. In the mean time, the Centauri was preparing to hunt down the Dark-Siders and anyone who might have aided them. All knew that a disaster had been averted; this could not happen again.

As this group of intelligent and capable individuals' converse, a thought crosses Cain's brilliant mind. *They were testing us*, he figured. As he began to speak, another thought entered his mind but he didn't put it there. *You are right Nicky,* said the voice in his head. He smiled because he knew who it was speaking to him. Turns out, his dear Kima, a Paladin assigned to his command, is a telepath. She is connected to him, just as she was when she was a kid. He knows that the fight for the future of all humanity is linked to the future of all free people's of this quadrant, all 80 Octodecillion sentient beings. He is going to need all the help that he can get for this fight. Thanks to Petamauck, reinforcements have come at the right time.

CHAPTER 3

The Lonely Joy

After the incident in the Arcadian system, the Terran Alliance has been shaken to its core. The actions of the Alliance military, in particular the Paladins, turned potential calamity into triumph. The IGF representatives were witness to the bravery and sacrifice that humanity displayed. After a short period of deliberation between the IGF admittance council, the Terran Alliance was given a provisional acceptance in the Inter-Galactic Alliance. Full admission was based on one small, but incredibly vital detail: the size of the Terran Alliance.

Is the Alliance a government numbering twelve star systems with 11 trillion humans or was it thirteen star systems with Earth being the final system? Because of the complications of those circumstances, the IGF is giving the Terrans one Earth year to resolve this conflict amongst its people. The mightiest warship in the known universe, the Alpha Centauri, was commencing with final preparations to hunt down the Dark-Sider Armada that attacked planet Arcadia. Commander Nicolas Cain had decided that answers for this incident need to be given; when he has questions, he always gets answers.

On planet Arcadia, the reconstruction of the famed Arcadian Courtyard was nearly completed. Fortunately, the Dark-Sider attack was limited to just this area of the planet. Most of the most beautiful artistic works are held on this planet and within this system; damage to the museum would have been a terrible loss. In the capital city of Arkadelphia, the First Museum of Antiquity possessed some of the most exquisite works of art by human hands. While the majority of the crew of the Centauri are readying final preparations for their search and destroy mission, three members of the crew, AC the Weapon Maker, Dr. Kima Darius, and a certain Alpha Paladin are taking in the sights. These two beautiful and influential women are dragging Commander Nicolas Cain, kicking and screaming to the museum. It was the last chance for a long while that they would have to see something that all could agree was beautiful.

"Why are you dragging me to this place? I have stuff to do. We are leaving in two days. I don't want to leave anything to chance," the commander groaned. **"Just because your child is with you doesn't mean that I am afraid of you woman!!!"** The gray-eyed stunners both looked at him and laughed. Whenever Cain snaps like that, the rest of the universe is nervous about the potential destruction. These two women have little fear because they have leverage over him though. He hates mushy stuff, but at this point, the most dangerous Terran in the universe is at the mercy of AC and her beautiful daughter.

Too make matters worse, Kima made Nick hold her hand, just like when she was a kid. AC thought that was the cutest thing that Cain is being so affectionate (at least for him.) He did not have a chance. **"A promise is a promise. You said that after the ceremony that we could go anywhere that I wanted to and this is where we are going!!! Just because the siders attacked us doesn't mean you get to squirm out of this,"** the beautiful mother quipped. **"Besides, Sayied doesn't need you. It's not like he is new to preparations. We have done it without you before. Stop stalling and take us to the museum Nicky!!!"** *Once again AC is cheating*, Cain thought to himself. At this point, Kima giggled. Nicolas was unsure if that was because she read his mind or because she thinks that the most deadly warrior in the Order was being punked by her mother. AC's obligations to the Cause are legendary within the Terran Alliance. Only when Nick was with Kima, was he truly able to appreciate the depth of AC's sacrifice.

Kima was at ease with the situation; she was re-united both with her 'big brother' and her mother. She is her mother's daughter, in her looks, outlook, and also her ability to get to Antonius. Even with the circumstances that had recently occurred and the impending uncertainty of chasing down a Dark-Sider armada, she was remarkably upbeat. She was different than Kira. Kira would have hated going to a museum and can often seem moody, accept when it is time to fight. Kima likes to hug, while Kira likes to empty her gun. Fortunately, Nick is familiar with both of the twins' tactics.

In their own way, the sisters are just alike though. When the raven-manned twin first saw Cain after all those years at the Academy, she gave him a huge hug and kiss when he walked into the command center. Kima was the only person in the room so Nick's reputation hadn't been affected in any way. He was incredibly happy to see her also, he was also impressed with her ability to sneak up on him. That rarely happens; her clandestine abilities are considered first rate. For an instant, he thought about not adding her to the Janitors, but that was a passing thought.

The first time he saw Kira, she had turned off all the lights in the room and attempted to strike Nick in the dark. They spared for 10 minutes before he finally disarmed her. When he was about to go in for the killing stroke, she kissed him on the cheek. He then remembered Kira was dear to him; it was the only thing that kept her alive. Cain couldn't wait to get her into the field.

As the three Paladins walked around the great museum, a sense of the moment also crossed AC's mind. *I am so proud of my daughters*, she pondered. These two impressive women have made her feel that those sacrifices have not been in vain. There were many things that AC missed out on with them, but she is deeply appreciative of the fact that the Cause has not been lost upon them. They were in their teens when the Regis told them of their true heritage and who their mother was. Thank God Nicolas came to Mu when he did or Kima would not have even been here today. He does have a wonderful sense of timing and AC was happy to know that Kima got to him when he first met her. Nicolas is always nice to children, but he can sometimes be *scary*. His first encounter with her daughter was when he killed at least fifteen other Paladins. The fact that even in the midst of such a destructive and devastating first impression, Kima still saw the nobility, the humanity of Cain. That is vital.

It was also important to AC that her daughters were also dedicated to the Cause on the same level that she was. She felt that this should be a gradual process of introduction; that her girls should have the opportunity to be children. As they were growing up, their foster parents tried to get them involved various cultured activities, but that path just didn't take. The twins had that fire in their blood just like the rest of the family.

Kira and Kima went about it differently, but both have the deep felt desire to serve others in a mighty way. Both of the sisters are different yet alike. Kira always wanted to push herself, both physically and mentally as far as she could go and then go further. Kima was interested in serving others less fortunate than she was. They are definitely the children of

AC and Paul; when their foster parents revealed who their parents were, neither was moved. Both understood the circumstances for one reason: *because they already knew.*

AC's mother, Aya, was the keynote speaker at a conference that they attended when they were children. When she saw the girls for the first time, she just couldn't take it any longer. It didn't make sense to her to withhold the truth and then try to reveal it later. *That's what a human would do*, she mused. *She must get that from her father.* Aya revealed that they were her grandchildren while they were at the conference; they were much younger than AC had wanted them to be to learn about their heritage. It was time for them to get ready to join the family business. Their grand-mother had explained to them that the Cause was why their mother had to give them up and when it was time, she planned to re-enter their lives and they would all serve the Alpha Paladin. This was their destiny. As far as Aya was concerned, AC's plan was taking too long. It was better to accept it and embrace this reality.

Both of the emerging warriors did just that. Over the course of their instructional development, the Oculari would abscond with the twins from time to time so that they could spend time with their grandmother, grandfather, and their "uncle OC." The girls had trouble saying Ocularian Commandant, so they shortened it; many of the family still uses that as a term of endearment. It was important for them to understand who they are. AC wanted to wait until they were older, but the senator was having none of that. It was better for them to grow up with this reality. OC helped them deceive their instructors and their foster parents.

It was important to AC that they were told these facts gradually, but she was overruled by Granny Aya. *There would be no sissies in this family*, she mused. They were Rioans first and foremost; duty matters more than anything. There was no room for selfishness or weakness in this family. Kima has a future as a healer, while Kira has a future as a commander. The sisters had perfect synergy; opposites in the right proportion. Just as Aya wanted it. The matriarch wasn't a Rioan, but she may well be the toughest of them all.

What AC also never knew was that Nick had also spent time a great deal of time with her children. Nick was Kira's original combat instructor. He taught her most of what she knows about combat. If it were up to Kira, she would have joined the Oculari instead of the

Dr. Anthony G. Johnson

Paladins, but Nick expressively forbids it. Both Danzyer and OC knew that Kira being in the Killing Academy would have put every other Oculari in danger. So much as a *scratch* on Kira's face would have angered Cain to the point that he might have killed *every* Oculari in the Federation.

It's one thing for everyone to deceive AC, but it is something else entirely to disobey one of Nick's marching orders. Not even the Commandant or even Aya would be so bold. Cain doesn't show it, but in many ways he loves Kira even more than he loves Kima; he is deeply concerned about her well-being. Nick said that Kira enjoyed fighting and killing *too* much; Oculari are tasked with completing complicated objectives that may require the sacrifice of their fellow agent. Leaving someone behind because it is the best way to meet their objective doesn't compute to her. Her intensity and loyalty can get in the way of the main objective and that would violate the Ocularian Covenant. His statement seemed ironic; he never said that he didn't think that she couldn't handle it, but no one was willing to broach the subject either. He once said that he had other plans for the ivory manned Darius twin; everyone has been too afraid to ask what those plans are.

Kira is a great warrior and outside of him, could be considered the deadliest warrior in the Terran Alliance. He is so confident in her abilities that he almost never holds back when he trains with her. She is the only Paladin that Cain has ever personally trained in hand to hand combat. Kira frequently practices combat techniques with Cain; she knows more about hand to hand combat than any other human besides him. That doesn't mean that she is close to him, but rather it places emphasis on how far Cain is above the other Paladins. Kira has a huge crush on Cain and she tends to become annoyed when others comment on how handsome Nick is. She hopes that Cain will look at her as a potential mate but at this point it is a slim chance for one reason; she isn't a redhead.

In Nick's mind, if one of the twins should go to the Killing Academy, it would be Kima. He believes that she had the necessary temperament to complete the long, dark road. Quiet as its kept, Cain actually knows the truth: Kira possesses tremendous ability, but Kima is actually the more gifted of the two. Some of skills that an Ocularian Operative has to be trained in, she actually already possesses. She can be efficient and cool-headed, the most important traits of an operative. That being said, Kima had shown no interest in that path and Cain wouldn't try to influence to go in that direction either. He loves the fact that she is walking joy; she looks forward to everyday as a gift from God. Kima constantly makes Nick talk to her about the places he has been, while Kira spends most of her time trying to find a way to beat Nick in a fight. AC and Paul's oldest daughter is an excellent student, adaptive and vicious; eventually she will make a great commander. Nick believes a great Paladin would probably make an awful Oculari and vice versa. Cain also believes that a vicious soldier doesn't have the discipline of a cool headed assassin. Kira has done nothing to change his assessment.

Kima always wants to know what Nick is feeling; she wants him to share things and on rare occasions, he does; but only with her. Because of Cain's peculiar ways, Kima might have been the most spoiled girl in the quadrant. When she was a kid, Nick would often take Kima to his favorite places. She is one of the few people who knowwhere Nick's favorite places of refuge are; not even AC knows where all of those hiding places are located. She has gone with him to see the fire falls of Volcandahar, he took her shark riding on Xanic, and he even took her to his favorite place to go fishing. It is a secret planet that only fourteen people know the actual location; when he doesn't want to be bothered, Nick goes there.

If anything were to happen to AC, she knows that Kima will take care of him. Nicolas has so many responsibilities, both home and away, he can sometimes become *too focused* on the objective. AC knows that when provoked, he is capable of rage that goes *beyond* madness. No one within the Federation or the Alliance really looks after Nick the way that AC does as far as she is concerned. For AC, this is a tremendous source of frustration. Nick is not just a tool; he is a person. The Commandant, her mother and father, and every one of the Chancellors seem to forget that point. *Nicky was so sick when Petamauck and I found him*, she remembered. *I just wanted to comfort him; it took him years before he would let me even touch him.* It had been 10 Earth years before he let her into his personal space. The first time that she tried to kiss Nick, he was so shocked that he grabbed his gun and was ready to shoot AC. It took another ten years before she did it again. Nick always frowns when AC is looking at him after she kisses him, but when she turns away; he is always smiling after she does it.

Cain's history is rife with sorrow and pain; he channels that sorrow and pain into deadly tools of his trade. Many of the leaders of both the Alliance and the Federation consider him merely a necessary, deadly asset; AC thinks that particular assessment is far too narrow. AC is still angry that the Ocularians had him for as long as they did; Nick became even deadlier than before. *He can be so warm, but is so cold*, she thought. Kima can make sure that he retains his humanity and Sayied will always make him laugh. The psychoanalysts always report that Cain is the one person within the Paladins who actually *enjoys* his work; that is of great concern to AC.

I worry about him so much, she thought. As far as AC is concerned, too much has been asked of Nicolas already. He would tell her that she worries too much and he is often right in his assessment. Nick always says that God never puts more on a human than they can bare; his favorite human prophet was said to have been in seclusion for forty days and nights being tempted by the devil and didn't fold; he admired that. To Nick, that always gives him a sense of both purpose and perspective.

At this moment, Kima comes upon a picture that really moves her to the point of tears. **"This is incredible**," the shocked stunner uttered. **"Look at it Nicky!! Mother, who did this?"** At this point in the museum, the two female Paladins have come upon the pencil section of the museum, never noticing Cain isn't with them. It is a picture of both Kima and Nicolas; except it is when she was a younger child. The picture had incredible clarity and was with intimate detail, every curve, the sweat, the blood, and also the joy in both of their faces of overcoming such a dramatic set of circumstances. AC remembered that day fondly; the day that Nicolas gave both the Regis and AC their daughter back. It was as if a person used a computer to graft an image from their memories.

The night before, Nick was in one of the fiercest battles he has ever had. A warrior of his renown had faced several enemies from all over the universe and stared them down without flinching. His opposition at present was far more determined. His beloved was still pissed at him for leaving. She thought that they would have a chance to spend time together during the festival and now he is telling her that he has to go; possibly forever. Arielle was still angry with the damnable misery of the situation. Terrans like Arielle grow up in one solar system. A human's anatomy has to be restructured in order to handle deep space travel. Time works differently in various solar systems; this fact makes a human's circadian rhythms work differently depending on the star system that person is from.

Most humans rarely leave their own solar systems for an extended period without having this procedure. If a Terran's physiology hasn't been altered for those purposes, space travel is relatively limited. Even with the velocities that star ships can travel, the typical Terran body is still far too frail for the immense distances. Arielle has not known her dearest Gaius for a long period of time but she would love to give her body and soul completely to him. He knows that is unfair. The Janitors normally travel a *minimum* of 425 thousand light-years on deep space operations; no one goes where they go.

The radiant red head stands her ground about this point; she demands to go with him. **"Baby, I don't care. I don't care where you have to go; I want to be by your side. Ever since you told me the truth about being in the military I have wanted to go with you. I don't care about anything else. You don't have the right to decide for me."** Her eyes were red with anger, despair, and fear of a future without him. Nick spoke with passion and pain in his words. **"I know. I wish that you could come with me, but I cannot let you go. There is the military and then there is what I do; my unit is the deep space unit. Where I am going, you cannot come. It's time for me to do what I do best. Even if you could physically take the trip, you would be in danger the entire time. The risk is too great."** His Scarlet Carson responded painfully. **"You lie!!! How many times has this happened Nick? This is why I never wanted to get involved with a military man. I know what the Navy does; there are civilian positions that I could take. We can make this work; I know that we can! How many times are you going to not let anyone love you? You are not just good at bad things. You have a choice; look at what you did after just one lesson baby. Just one. You have so much more to give than just death; you have so much more to be. *You* have a *choice*."** She cried and hit him in his chest, desperate to reach him on a level that would change his mind. But she knew that it was not working.

She sat in his lap and sobbed. She hit him in his chest. She hugged him tightly, squeezing as if she would die if she let him go. It was a passion that he wanted, but knew that he couldn't reciprocate. His touch was light, gentle, and also detached. If he acted on what his heart desired, the universe would be jeopardy. He spoke with all the pain and joy that he could truly muster. Nick has had lovers since Quenas, but no one has ever touched him like Arielle has. A scarlet carson is the rarest of red roses in the universe; you can only find them on one planet in the quadrant. A Carson is that exquisite and rare; that is what she is to him.

It wasn't that she wasn't reaching him. The fact was that she *had reached* him; he contemplated for a moment that staying with her was what he truly desired. For one minute, he was torn about what to do. Should he embrace this choice of his heart or remain the cool-headed assassin that he was purposely trained for. For a man with his brain capacity, *one minute* is a long time to think about anything. She had reached Nick on a level that no one else had save one person. Nick's wife had died in service of the Cause. Those who were in the know were aware of the fact that Cain can love someone deeply. He loves Arielle at this level. He is also aware that his obligations will not allow him to put her above the needs of so many people. It was a dream. But it was a *good* dream. His personal desires were not worth the safety and protection of the entire quadrant. Not even Arielle was worth that price. She would never know the conflict that his love for her created or the damage that love could have indirectly wrought on the Virgo Super Cluster. He snapped out of it and told her what he needed to say.

He lifted her chin and kissed her. He spoke quietly. **"You don't understand. I am not in the Navy; my unit is classified. No one even knows that we *exist*. Technically, *I don't exist*. You once asked about my family and I didn't answer you. Well, that's because *I don't have one*. The stars of my birth are different than yours; I wasn't even born here in this part of the quadrant. I was a man when I finally saw what my parents looked like. I don't have a home either; except for my starship. My life is different from anything that you could imagine. If it were up to me, then you wouldn't come with me; I would stay with you. But it isn't up to me. I can't put my desires ahead of the needs of so many."** She looked at him, even with her eyes puffy from her hard tears, she was still a beauty.

She kissed him and leaned her head against his chest. **"I knew when you told me that this day would come; just not so damn soon. I am so sorry; I need to not be angry with God, but I am jealous. I am selfish, I want you all for myself and I know now that it can't happen. We can never be can we?"** Nick smiled and looked at her and spoke as if she was the only women in the entire universe. **"I am lucky to have been with you as long as I have. Being loved by you is worth a lifetime."**

The curator, Arielle Star-Fire, a radiant red-headed woman with alluring features walked up on the stunned mother and daughter. **"Magnificent isn't it?"** the statuesque woman asked. **"He was my greatest student, only needed to teach him one lesson. The next day he did this. He called it 'The Lonely Joy.' In fact, it is a shame that he doesn't have time to do more work. He has several pieces hanging in the museums of this system. He designed the Halls of Arkadelphia, and also the Chancellor's villa on Eden. Then he went back to his *real* job."** When both AC and Kima moved closer to see the name of the artist, they were shocked; Logan Cain. That was one of Nicky's aliases! Neither of these women, him being so dear to them, had any clue that this was inside of the Alpha Paladin's soul.

It was no wonder he used so few words, AC thought. *Why use words when your soul is capable of this?* Kima knew from the tone in her voice that this woman was more than just Nick's teacher. Someone that can read minds is rare but not uncommon among Paladins; Nick has tricks for how to deal with that. Antonius' little sister is different because of her connection with the Alpha Paladin on an emotional level. Kima is also an empathic; she can read both the cognitive and emotional content of any subject that she chooses. One touch can reveal a great deal of information.

She stumbled upon a memory of the curator spending an intimate moment with her big brother. Kima immediately reached out and hugged Arielle; it isn't everyday that you get to meet the love of the Alpha Paladin. The young paladin didn't mention it to her mother; she knew that AC had no knowledge of who this woman *really* was to Cain. She didn't dare mention this discovery to Kira either; she knows about her crush on Nick. *Kira would be beyond pissed if she finds out about this woman*, mused Kima. Red heads were relatively rare on Earth and they are even rarer in the Alliance and the IGF. *At least Nick has really good taste*, she thought to herself.

As they walked throughout the rest of the museum, they noticed several other pieces of Cain's labor and it was as Ms. Star-Fire had intimated, magnificent. That is when they noticed that the majority of the pieces of artwork in this section of the museum were actually completed by Nick. There was an incredibly accurate picture of AC, down to the minutest of exquisite detail. Arielle kindly explained what inspired the artist to complete these works. Finally they came upon the Eastern ocean of Mu painting that Nick completed; it occurred to both AC and Kima that this painting was why he was on Mu that fateful day already.

Nick has a tendency that when he goes to work on his art to travel to the most remote areas of a planet or moon to draw his landscapes. Nick refers to them as his artistic disengagements. He usually is in a location so remote that many of his comrades have no idea where he actually goes. It was not a coincidence that he was in the Mu system. He was working on his art; he had been waiting for the Chancellor to call him to kill the renegade Paladins but he was never summoned. Tears were rolling down all three of these heart stopping women's faces. **"Nick was too humble to show you; but you needed to see just how much he loves you both."**

Cain's loved ones were so shocked and moved, they did not notice the page from Sayied indicating that the preparations were complete. At that time, Nicolas snapped them out of their awe, **"time to go to work. We have a briefing with the Chancellor in one hour."** Before Antonius went on his way, he caught up with his Scarlet Carson. **"Thanks for showing them,"** he said. Before Arielle could respond, he kissed her. It was so unexpected, so typical of Nick. His kiss was gentle, yet passionate; the artist at work. Ms. Star-Fire's cheeks were the same color as her red hair.

This is the typical pattern of the Alpha Paladin. Just when things start getting good between him and someone, duty calls. That is one of the major drawbacks of being the Alpha Paladin. His deep space missions take him far away from loved ones. His immortality leads him to duties that keep him away for the equivalent of centuries. Even though he is a tough act to follow, his lovers must go on with their lives. Time doesn't matter to an immortal; but the pain of leaving a loved one always hurts.

It was ironic that he met Arielle; it was actually Kush's doing. Kush and Cain were having a quiet discussion when Kush suggested that Nick have some other pursuits that didn't have anything to do with violence. Kush was concerned that Nick needed to do something that brought him peace where he didn't have to do anything with bloodshed in any way. He had told him to either meet up with his newest Humanities Chair, a stunning woman named Taylor Driax or he could meet up with Arielle Star-Fire, the best art instructor in the quadrant. Kush felt that either proposition would make him happy. Cain said that he would agree only if Kush pulled rank. He liked the thought of being ordered to enjoy life. Kush gladly obliged. Cain then went to Arcadia because it got him away from planet Eden.

When Cain arrived, he met Arielle for a special instructional session arranged by Kush himself. Cain, a man who doesn't impress easily was infatuated by the instructor. She had the most delicate sense of touch that he had ever felt. Her fingers were perfect as far as Nick is concerned; she touched his arm and he actually had goose bumps. He has no idea why he felt this way or how she touched him on an emotional level; he just knew that he liked it. He was intoxicated and had no idea why. For the first time, he was completely out of control, but in a good way. She smelled like Jasmine and he was completely smitten by the sound of her voice. There was something about the sound of her feet when she walked. It was the most incredible sound that he had ever heard.

She was equally love-struck with the handsome Terran officer. He didn't tell her what he did initially because he didn't think that it was important. It was supposed to be one lesson to get Kush off his back. Then it became something else. What was supposed to be a onetime meeting turned into an extended encounter. He spent a few weeks with her and began to create some of the best art that a human being had ever produced. They talked and walked for hours and Nick even cooked for her; something that he rarely does. Nick began to smile and even laugh. He was happy in a way that his wife had never made him or destroying his target never did. The rest is history.

Arielle and Cain spent the night together, but in the back of her mind, she knew that their time was coming to an end. She tries to keep it together. Flustered, she said **"Its time already huh? Back to work?"** The artist replied, **"Yeah. Back to work, back to death, and back to the madness. See you next lifetime."** Realizing that this might be the last time that she sees her dearest Cain, she hugs him tightly; squeezing him and hoping she doesn't have to let go. Whipping the tears away, she gathers herself to speak to her lover, knowing this may be the last words that she may get to say face to face to him. **"It's too soon baby. This is not fair."** Nick put his index finger up to her soft lips and kissed her forehead and replied, **"It *never* is."**

One hour later at the Arcadian Regis' antechamber, several very important people were having a confab with several dozen other individuals via telecom. An important issue has been brought to all of their attention and the decisions made at this time will resonate throughout the Terran Alliance as well as also have an impact the entire Inter-Galactic Federation and indirectly the Dark-Siders as well. It comes down to this simple equation: the Earth's 600 million people versus the 11 trillion humans in the Terran Alliance and also the 80 Octodecillion sentient beings in the 800 systems of IGF, spread across a vastness of space incomprehensible to people who still measure distance in miles and think that 6 billion people on a planet is too crowded.

Yes there were once almost nine billion humans on Earth, but isolationism, paranoia, intolerance, and greed lead to the demise of most of the planet's ecosystem, which in turn lead to starvation, which eventually lead to a war that consumed nearly every remaining resource on the planet. A blue-green world that had an arctic and desert ecology has been mostly destroyed. The remaining people are divided still and mostly leaderless, trying desperately to survive; not learning much if anything from the mistakes they have made. Would it be easier to accept that this planet was a total loss and let whatever beings who want it to have the Earth? The nickname that the Terran Alliance members have for the native Earthlings is the *Savage Landers*; based upon their actions, the name seems appropriate. That is the issue that stands before these Politicians, Clerics, Economists, and Warriors. For one Paladin in particular, the decision will be an easy one.

For the Regent from Eden, the current capital system of the Terran Alliance, the issue is simple: the Terrans no longer have any need to claim the Earth. Cornelius Katsina, Eden's charismatic leader spoke words of both wisdom and clarity. **"Earth is the most back-water planet in this part of the damn universe!!! I know that some of you want to keep it and maybe it will ascend to its rightful place, but I respectfully disagree. The timetable that the IGF has given us does not make it feasible to reach even level 1 of the galactic stages of growth. They've had the means to make clean energy feasible and they fought like spoiled children over who has the right to receive it. These people let their fellow man, woman, and child starve to death!! They had the teachings of every version of the Father that existed and still decided against doing what is right. Their time has been spent. We must move on for the sake of all humanity. The cost just doesn't support this benefit."**

The Nubian Regent, Alexander Halima, a man of great compassion and vision chimed in to second Kastina's position. **"I also agree that** this must be considered. **According to Nari's preliminary report, Earth has lost over 90 percent of its population and several areas of the planet have been bombarded by radiation. And who bombarded it?** *They did it to each other.* **Can you imagine if the Rioans hadn't intervened? None of us would be here today. While I am deeply disturbed that it has come to this, we have no time. One Earth year to create clean energy, faster than light travel and also usage of the other planets within this system; all three levels in one year? I seriously doubt it. Didn't the Savage Landers demote a planet because the scientist changed their minds? How arrogant is that?** *They are afraid of anything different and the Landers always hate what they fear.* **There almost all of us would have been limited in the hope of our endeavors, why should we save a planet like that?"** Several other prominent individuals stated their positions were clearly with Halima and Kastina.

It was not that these were sinister humans with their own agenda; it's just that from a logical point of view that Earth clearly at this point was not worth the risk. Furthermore, the Genesis Accord, an contractual agreement stating that the Terran Alliance would never interfere with the home world, Earth's natural development, whatever that was, and the leadership had no intentions of breaking that pact. The rebuttal side of the argument however had yet to be made. Chancellor Alron Driax would be a deciding vote if it there was a tie and it looked as if that was going to happen. It may all come down to whether she would be convinced to leave or stay.

One of the most powerful orders of Clerics, The Order of St. Thomas, had a representative of their position on the subject of Earth's future in the Terran Alliance. Namon Ka, one of the most prominent of this sect made this argument. **"Greetings and Blessings to you all. Our position is that not only should Earth be saved, but if necessary, the Genesis Accord should be abandoned. It is not a divine document; it can be broken. While I am grateful personally to be living in these times, I am fully aware that the only reason that we are here is because God wills it. The Rioans would not have intervened if not for God's will; much like the Iconians intervened in the Rioans' development. Can't you see? This is our opportunity to serve our brothers and sisters as others have served us. It is a circle, a bond that must not be broken. Our entire foundation of who we are comes from this planet. Need**

I remind you that *every* foundation of our race can be traced back to Earth; only when it became too dangerous was the prohibition on pilgrimage to the home land. I am no politician or economist or warrior; but saving Earth is the right thing today, tomorrow, and forever."

Admiral David Kun, commander of the Terran 9th Naval Squadron brought up another crucial element that had not been addressed. **"Blessings and Grace to all those assembled. I think that saving Earth is the right thing to do. However I do have some concerns that have not been addressed at this point. First off in Nari's report, there was an additional notation completed by Major Armanuel Arazar. He states that Earth is within the star system that would most likely be the sight of the main Dark-Sider invasion. It would take a full contingent of Paladins and a minimal five totally stocked legion of Terran Alliance and IGF military to deter the siders from using that region as a base of operations for their incursion. Militarily, it makes more sense to let them have Earth and gather strength in the adjacent system. However, I am of the belief that if there was ever a reason to go to Earth, now would be the time. I am a soldier and mathematician; I know what the odds are. At the same time, I would like to believe that if God is on our side, it's time to find out. I'd like to think that He is. Because without Earth, none of this, none of us matter."**

At this point, the Regis of Mu, Maia Quintus, asked the Admiral about the time table of the siders and he responded 15 to 18 Earth months. At this point, the Paladins, the most powerful and resourceful warriors in the Terran Alliance, gave their position. It was from a voice that normally doesn't speak much, but this was a crucial time. A hush entered the room. Most of the leaders of humanity had never seen him in person, much less heard him speak. He had always been more legend than real; a spook story. Many who had seen him had never lived to tell the tale, he usually only shows up to eliminate enemies. Today on Arcadia, at the most crucial period perhaps in Terran History, that was about to change. There he was, the Executioner, the monster, the weapon, the tool; in the flesh. The Alpha Paladin had something to say.

"Greetings and Blessings to you all. Normally whatever the will of the leadership of our race is, I will obey without question. This is not one of those times. Everything that Regent Angelis and Halima

said is true. However, things are in motion that cannot be stopped; things are in motion that must be seen through to the end. I agree that Earth is a difficult issue. But this is not just some economic or diplomatic issue. This is not an issue of whether it is a strategic issue either," he spoke with his voice cracking with anger. He touched the bracelet that Kima gave him as he spoke. **"This is Earth!!! *Our* home world. We are not losing it. It is our home; we all know who was born there. Anyone who thinks they want to take it will get the business; that includes the Erixes, Gondronians or anyone else. The Dark-Siders can't have it either. We are not only going to bring Earth to where it needs to be, the people of that planet will earn it. Earth has to earn the right to be the Hub of the Spoke; Eden will remain the Primary planet. Period. The Blood Knights will take this responsibility. We will help Earth rebuild and will defend it to the bitter end."**

Erik, AC, and Petamauck were astonished at what they were hearing from their dearest Cain. He is not known for very long conversations in public. He is also not known for rhetoric so this verbiage from Nick has disturbed all of them. What was the angle of the Alpha? To Nick, never saying more than he had to didn't mean not speaking at all; it was about *when* to speak. He addressed the more obvious issues that needed to be answered. **"I know that one of the bigger concerns about this is the fact that the Gondronians control that part of the star cluster. I am also aware that Admiral Kun's other concerns are more than legitimate. Whoever goes to Earth with also have to deal with the most disjointed part of the Virgo Super Cluster. Furthermore, they would almost be completely alone. Reinforcements would take a long time to get there if things get heavy. I am aware of that. That is why The Janitors will be in charge of handling this situation. In many ways, this task isn't dissimilar to many of the charges that we have undertaken throughout our service to the Alliance and the Federation. What I will not do is supersede the chain of command. If it is the will of the Chancellor Driax, we will depart for Earth immediately; there is no sense in creating anxieties for the Alliance. Especially since there is no true consensus among all of you. You don't have to ask us; we willingly volunteer."**

This is the first impression that many of the leaders of humanity had ever had and Cain had created a tremendous first impression. He had smooth, bronze skin and a beautifully shaped bald head. His musculature was barely contained in his formal uniform. His eyes said that he is a predator, but not just any predator, but the *apex predator*. He is a soldier; he was not comfortable in the bourgeois circles of the Alliance, but he was able to acclimatize well. The leaders saw his character; his courage, his love, and devotion to his people. He was in his formal uniform; they saw the regality of his silhouette. He was a noble man of both Nubian and Roman heritage. His mother's ancestors were descendants from of legendary General Taharqa; they could feel his strength. This is a man of action, not words. However, he is also adaptive.

These people could also hear the wisdom and charity of his words. He continued on, **"For the first time, the Alpha Centauri will utilize the entire arsenal on those who would present an adversarial position. Petamauck, my brother, has trained all of these Paladins for this conflict and this opportunity to be a builder of worlds. This is exactly why the senate had the training regimen changed. God has willed it from the beginning; from the V'idozans to the Iconians to the Rioans to AC to us. I am excited about bringing Earth back from the brink. So excited that anyone who gets in our way will get completely shredded. God has given us what is needed; the rest of the IGF will be shown the way. Tell the IGF that we will be ready in one Earth year that is my vow. If not, Earth will leave the Terran Alliance and go it alone. The Alliance and IGF need each other to survive; and both groups need Earth."** Then the Centauri's second in command, AC, sent Major Faris a texted communication. *Set the course for Earth, leaving in 45 minutes.*

Chancellor Driax, realizing the quality and succinctness of Cain's words, saw no need to call for a vote. The die was cast; either Earth is able to be fixed or the Blood Knights are alone; it is either madness or a true leap of faith. All the leadership wished the Knights well. Erik the Red, Cain's comrade in arms, and his best friend, Petamauck the Prudent, both gave him encouragement and their prayers. Regent Kastina was pleased that Eden would remain for the immediate future as the capital planet of the Terran Alliance or the Knights would fail and Eden would still remain the primary planet. *This is a win-win*, he thought.

For a man not known for his compromising disposition, Nicholas Cain has gained several knew allies among the Regents, Clerics, and Economists who thought him merely a necessary evil. None of the

Regents save Quintus had ever spoken to Cain or even had seen him in person. In all the eons that Cain had been in service to the Terran Alliance, very few had actually seen him; his name only spoken in hushed tones. Until that evening, Cain had always been an *it*, never a *he*. Intelligence, Nobility, and Faithful were among the descriptive words attributed to this noble warrior; for those who had been lucky enough to stand by his side in battle, this was no surprise. In both AC and Erik's minds, they were both surprised that he hadn't spoken sooner. But both of them were stunned at how polite he was. It was a sign of growth from Cain that he didn't just threaten death to the Regents who were against the chancellor's position.

As Cain finished speaking to the Clerics and the political leadership, a sense of calm reached him in his soul. *Time to go to work,* he thought. He knew he didn't have time to talk to Arielle. There is a strong possibility that he would never see her again; that is the life of an immortal. *Don't worry Nicky,* she was listening. *I made sure that everyone was listening;* the voice in his head spoke to him. Nicholas was happy that Kima was a telepath. For where they are going and who they are going to be dealing with, those skills will certainly come in handy. The Centauri was ready and so was the crew; next stop, planet Terra or Earth, for one Earth year or the rest of their lives. A total contingent of 600 Terrans, including 300 Paladins, are returning home. It will not be a hero's welcome; one of their first hostile encounters will be with their kinsmen. Getting those wild, back water humans on the same page will be among the first orders of business. Before the humans can get their respective acts together, unity of purpose must not only be found but accepted. For now, chasing down the siders that attacked Arcadia would have to wait.

When the Paladins were leaving the conference room, Petamauck, AC, and Erik were walking with Nick. They were all looking at him in a shared silence. It was more awe than anything else. Nick hates talking to the Terran leadership, in part because he has disgust for the self-important. Nick felt it was imperative that the right decision be reached about this acute set of circumstances. He didn't want to leave anything to chance. Furthermore, he knew that the Janitors were going to Earth anyway; however, he wouldn't undercut his Chancellor's authority. Luckily on this issue they were on the same page, even though they still haven't officially met.

Erik couldn't take the silence anymore and tried to tease Nick about him showing up in full dress attire, something that he has never done. **"My God Commander, I didn't know you could be so persuasive. Maybe it's the uniform; you look so handsome and well spoken. What do you think AC?"** AC, his second in command couldn't resist either. She put his arm around her shoulder and kissed him sweetly on the cheek. He hated that; he loved that. **"Indeed. Women love a man in uniform; where are all your medals cutie? I am going to get the security feed and replay for everyone on the ship."** Finally his mentor, Petamauck, got his shots in. **"I didn't realize that you had a future in politics brother."** At his point, Nick smirks and responds coolly to all of his friends. **"It's nice to have friends. I love the fact that all of you have jokes. For your information smart asses I disabled the video but left the audio system operational so don't even try it. You are all lucky that I need you for the mission."**

As Arielle was getting ready to close up the museum for the evening, an unexpected visitor has shown up. Dr. Kima Darius, one of the deadly Paladins that serve with her dearest Nick has shown up to have a quiet chat. She knows her brother; she did something that has never done before, she found something in Nick's mind without his permission. The situation is even more difficult because she accidentally found it in Arielle's mind first. Considering the circumstances of the situation, she is sure that he wouldn't mind. She is not sure if Nick doesn't know that Kima is an empath or not; it is one of the byproducts of the Paladin process. Kima discovered that Nick doesn't really know how to truly express himself so that his dearest Arielle will understand what she means to him. Kima knows exactly what to do. His dearest little sister has to help her brother in a way that she has never aided him before. She in essence is actually serving him through helping clear up things for Arielle, which in turn helps Nick in a tremendous manner.

Kima is Nick's little sister, in part because when he met her, she reminded Nick of his foster sister, Maya. At the beginning of his journey, his foster sister died from the abuses that his first set of foster parents had given them. He eventually killed his foster mother and got his foster father put in prison but he always felt a sense of loss because he didn't kill them *quick enough*. She died because of the trauma from the abuse. When Kima was being threatened by Petamauck, Nick was successful in killing his target in time to save Kima.

To Nick, Kima grew into what Maya wasn't given the opportunity to become. When he was at his most frightening, she was completely at peace. Most of the adults who have been around Nick during combat are paralyzed with fear, but she wasn't. She kissed his wounds from trying to save her; in that instant, they were bonded. She will always have a special place in his heart; Kima being AC's baby girl doesn't hurt her standing either. If any person would ever have standing to speak on his behalf from his personal perspective, it would be her. Knowing that she has this special relationship with Nick has given Kima the confidence to have this difficult conversation with nearly a total stranger. But she felt comfortable for one reason: it was for *her* brother.

Kima walks up to her and speaks sweetly. **"I knew that you would be beautiful. I just knew it. I knew that you were real."** Arielle sits down. **"What are you talking about Dr. Darius? I know that Nick has never mentioned me."** Kima sits down next to her. **"Please, call me Kima. No you don't understand, he mentions you all the time. But not by what he says, but by what he does. You are the reason that he is better. You are the catalyst Arielle. I am so delighted that I got to meet you. You are everything that I hoped you would be; in fact, you are more. Lovelier than I could have possibly dreamed and you are more beautiful both inside and out, than I could have ever anticipated. You have fixed him."** At this point, the radiant red head was confused. **"Okay, could you start from the beginning? I know that Nick loves me, but in the end that wasn't enough."**

Kima was almost out of breath as she spoke excitedly to her new friend. She didn't know where to begin. **"No dear lady, you are wrong. You are the reward Arielle; you were the gift that fixed my big brother. How long have you been together? I know, since the Tronic Reconciliation right?"** Arielle looked shocked. **"How did you know?"** Kima smiled and touched her hand. **"Because that's when Nick became more human. You were the reason. You are the blessing that I prayed to God for. You have no idea how honored I am to meet you!"** Kima continued. **"You have given Nick a reason to love; you have no idea do you? He has only been in love one other time. She died and their unborn child. You didn't know that did you? It changed him. His mother died at his birth; his big sister died because of child abuse."** Arielle was both shocked and shaken by that sentiment. **"I had no idea that those things happened. He never talks about the past."**

Kima continues her thesis to her brother's beloved. *She doesn't know a thing about him,* she thought. **"No he doesn't talk about the past. Why would he? If your past was filled with the kind of sorrow and pain that his past is filled with? I don't think so. He was sent to a facility which was the equivalent of a prison as a child. My brother was taught how to kill before he was taught how to love. He was taught how to be the best warrior, the best *assassin* for one reason: the protection of all the innocent and helpless. This is his life."**

Kima was crying. Just the thought of this life for her brother brings her such sadness and anger. It's not fair at all. She wipes her eyes and continues. **"But you know what? For a little while, that wasn't true. For a short period of time, *you became his life.* Your love had too high a cost. Entire star systems quake in fear of his name being spoken. The fiercest warriors whimper in fright at the thought of him. You've never have to worry about that at all. When he is with you he is the sweetest man isn't he? You haven't seen anything like that have you? He can just be an artist when he is with you. He can just love you and be loved by you. You have given us so much; he is better because of you. You are *all* his reasons."** Arielle was completely stunned.

Kima looking at her watch, smiled. She was almost out of time. **"He expresses his love through what he does. He is so much sweeter to all of us because of your presence. Look at his art; you gave him an outlet to express himself in a positive way. He didn't tell you who he is did you? He is not just a Paladin; he is the *Alpha* Paladin. But when you are with him, he doesn't have to think about the awful things that he has to do. I am so sorry but also I am so happy for you. Only two women know what it is like to have Nick love them like you have. The first one was taken away and the results were shall we say destructive. But you? You will have a positive impact on the rest of the universe. You have no real idea about the depth of your impact. His job is to be the immortal protector of the universe and he was ready to leave *all his responsibilities* for you."**

At this point, Kima was crying again. She leaned her head on Arielle and a woman whom she had never met shared the most intimate of moments. It became clear to Arielle that their love, no matter how short a time it may have been was an exquisite gift. She saw in Kima's eyes, the love that Nick had for his people, that it hurt him on such a desperate level to leave the love of his life. To once again go charging into the endless night. How these brave souls were willing to follow her beautiful Nick to whatever end that it would be.

It was difficult for Kima told it together. She loves Nick so much and it had occurred to her just how unfair Nick's life is. He is an immortal solely for the good of others; to meet the Father's agenda. Now she understands why he can appreciate the rain. In that instant, she connected to her brother in the deepest way. Arielle must be made to understand. **"He never told you that did he? Of course he wouldn't. All of his burdens, just for you. For a man of his intelligence, a moment can last a *lifetime*. That's how hard he fell for you. He has the right to love and be loved *that* hard. From the bottom of my heart, thank you. You were so kind to my mother and I; the picture that you showed us was a memory from an important day. It was the day that we met; he saved my life. I have loved him ever since. I wish I could tell you more, but I just thought that you should know that. Oh and one more thing."** Kima then pulled out a portfolio and handed it to Arielle. Kima knew the code to Nick's quarters; the number 0124. It was Kima's birthday. It was a portfolio of all these pictures of Arielle and him together. He drew an entire portfolio of her and him. She held it close to her chest and smiled as Kima left the building.

After the confab with all the leadership of the Terran Alliance, Nick was happy to take off his "monkey suit." He put his battle gear back on, including his katana. *This is more like it*, he mused. Cain is a warrior; he had little use for formal attire. Whenever it was time for any official political or military affairs, Nick had a tendency of making himself scarce. He always had sent AC, Sayied, or Petamauck to such functions. One reason was that he hated wearing that outfit and the second reason was that he liked the thought of the Alliance and Federation leadership not getting to know him on a personal level in any way. When he had to do what was needed, he didn't want any biases about the job that had to be done. As long as it needed to be done, it was better to know that his duty was going to be unencumbered by special interest groups. If they got to know him, the leaders would feel that his opinion about other things that mattered; that these leaders would try and use his reputation as leverage in matters that were of domestic origin. His policy has always been to protect democracy, not to practice it.

Before Cain left on the Centauri with the rest of the Blood Knights, he received an encrypted message from his boss. She wanted to see him before he headed for Earth. Nick sent them ahead; Wing Alpha can catch up to the Centauri. Usually before Cain heads out on a potentially way of life altering mission, he has a consult with the chancellor to discuss final preparations before racing off into the abyss. This is the first time that the Alpha Paladin has had the opportunity to meet with his newest chancellor. In the short time that she has been in charge of the Terran Alliance, several incredibly difficult situations have occurred and Cain has done his very best to handle these situations as efficiently as possible. It is now time for a much more personal conversation between the monster and his mistress to occur.

Cain entered the conference suite where the Arkadelphia Eleven made their final stand against the Dark-Siders. The chancellor said that he could dress in the way that made him most comfortable. He showed up in his combat attire, complete with guns, knives and swords. *This was far more comfortable*, he mused. The room was cleared out already. All of her senior staff had been instructed to leave the room and her security detail had also been told that they would not be necessary while these two people were going to have their first official consult.

Nicolas Cain has an affinity for red headed women. Petamauck always said that Nick was a sucker for a red head. Nick is fully aware of how much of a head turner that AC, Kima, and Kira are, but a red head will always be at the top of his list. Maya was a red head, which is probably were his affinity began. His current love is a red head; his first love, Quenas, was also a beautiful, sociopathic, red head.(*His favorite kind*) Perhaps the only reason he did not torment the Attorney General of California, Jean Wilcox, was because she was a radiant red head. That being said, Nick is fully aware of how attractive his female chancellors have been also. Of the sixteen incredibly alluring women he has served, Chancellor Driax is the most stunning. Of all the attractive female leaders in both the Federation and Alliance he had served, she is the most exquisite. He didn't think that he would have another Alron as remarkably dazzling as Chancellor Nyota. That was until he met his new Alron.

Nick noticed that she was tall and had beautiful ebony skin and sparkling, kind eyes. She had a sharp outfit; she cut a striking silhouette in her navy blue business attire. He tried not to stare, not just out of respect for her position, but also because he did not want to give anything away; he was still sizing her up as a leader. Still, it is difficult to focus on the task at hand. It was hard for him not to stare though, she was beyond stunning; she was startlingly gorgeous. She began to undue hair; it had been tied in a bun and she also removed her glasses. Driax didn't need them, it was part of her subterfuge. He liked that. She asked him to come and sit down next to her. Nick was weary of being in close proximity to his boss; he never lets his guard down. However, that is exactly what the chancellor wished for him to do.

Cain had never really spoken to Driax face to face before. The first time he had words with her was on Mu, but that was when Petamauck had decided to play madman dictator. Everything they did was by audio-link. For the next 20 rotations, he returned to deep space to eliminate another rogue anti-IGF faction; no one in the Terran Alliance was privy to what it was. The second time he heard her speak was at the event of Arcadia; again by audio-link. The first time that he had actually seen her was during confab about the Earth issue. The thing about that was that he was consumed with the issue of returning to Earth, nothing else mattered. That took priority then, but not now. He was well versed in her tendencies; he had several allies who had dealt with her and found her to be a shrewd leader and decision maker.

The Alron's reputation was also that when she had to, Driax could be a real hand full; a spitfire. The other things that he had heard were from AC; that she was inquisitive and always incredibly prepared. AC likes her, but that meant little because AC likes everyone she has ever met but *one* person; and Nick knows why. Aya never said a word; she figured that it wasn't relevant. He would see what she looked like when he met her. Danyzer and the Commandant were both impressed as well. That might be the most important endorsement of all because those two rarely agree on *anything*. However, no one had told him just how beautiful she is. When he first saw her in person, he was startled by it. Now she wants to talk. No one ever *wants* to talk to Cain; they usually *have* to talk to Cain. The Alpha is curious about her angle. She smiles at him and speaks as if they are long time friends.

"That was quite a speech you gave today Commander. You let everyone know exactly what's what didn't you? I guess we politicians can sometimes talk too much for a man like you. Now tell me how you *really* feel about going to Earth. If this is going to work my dear Alpha, I need you to trust me as much as I have already come to trust you. I must admit that you are everything that Kush said that you

were. **In fact you may be more. What did he tell you about me?**" This took the mighty warrior somewhat for a surprise. The only person who had been that comfortable around him so quickly was Kush. However, under the circumstances, it was probably imperative that these two become on friendly terms as quickly as possible considering the troubles that lie ahead for both of them.

He finally spoke to his new chancellor in a calm, yet measured tone. **"Well the leadership didn't give me much of a choice. They don't understand because they are stupid. We were going to have to go Earth regardless of the decision that was made here. But you already knew that didn't you? The course that the Dark-Sider Armada is taking will bring them through the Earth Solar System. We have a chance to stop them there. My former Alron left you on purpose, of that I have no doubts my chancellor. It is apparent to me that God and Kush both think highly of you and therefore I will also think highly of you. I loved Chancellor Kush and if you let me, I shall also love and protect you at all cost. Your leadership will see us through this conflict. Of that, I am certain."**

The chancellor smiled pleasantly at Cain's words. She then decided that it was time to talk to him about why she asked him to come and meet with her. She touched his hand. **"My dear Alpha, compared to you, most of the universe would be considered stupid. Commander Cain; do you mind if I call you Nick?"** He nodded in agreement. **"Nick I must admit, this is a daunting job. I am chancellor during the most unsettled period in the history of the Alliance. All of our enemies are at our doorstep, but our charge is the same. We must safeguard the people at all times and if I am in real trouble I hope that you will come protect me. Kush told me that you are an acquired taste. He also said that it would take time for me to get used to how you operate. That because of the brilliance of your mind, your candor, and the swiftness by which you act can be a disturbing thing. He said don't read anything into it because deep down, you're a *pussycat*."** That description brought a smile to the monster's face.

The chancellor yawned and stretched. She decided to take her shoes off and she rubbed her feet. Driax hates wearing her monkey suit as much as Cain hates wearing his. She continued. **"I appreciate the fact that you were kind to the leadership today. From what your Admiral friend tells me, you have been known to severely damage people who mock** or try to insult your Master; or Mistress. You may be my *monster*, but I am not *your* mistress. I hate that title, because I know you are only following me because *you* want to; I know I have no true dominion over your actions. By the way, please never refer to me as anything but Lady, Chancellor or Driax. When you are ready, you can call me Taylor, but only in private times though. This only works if we work together." The Alpha nodded in agreement and simply smiled at her.

Lady Driax was comfortable with her shoes off. In that manner, she reminded him of his dearest Arielle. She paced around the room with her arms folded, occasionally tapping her chin. Nick was watching her move; it was as if she mustering up the gumption to say what was really on her mind. She looked out the main window and sighed slowly. She put her hands together against her face, shut her eyes, and continued on. **"Nick when I am terrified or anxious about what I must ask you to do, I pray. I constantly ask God to guide my decisions and I constantly ask him to guide yours. You are so far away from us; you have no help. Everything that you are asked to do is of the most terrible intentions. I fear that it will be my fault that you or someone dear to you will lose their life because of my orders. I ask you in advance to forgive me for what I will ask you to do."**

Alron Driax invaded her Apex Predator's personal space and looked at him directly. In that instance, she was a contrast, both strong and vulnerable at the same time. The chancellor then asked a personal question, one that will evoke trust or will crush their relationship in its infancy stages. **"Do you get lonely Nick? From what I have read in your file, you have been doing this since before my great great great great grandparents were even alive. I know that you are much older than you look. Aya told me about her, I won't ask you about it now. Does it ever get to you that so many people need you? To tell you the truth, the strain does get to me from time to time my friend. If you ever feel like venting about the madness of your life, please don't hesitate to do so. My colleagues always marvel at your resolve, but everyone needs to talk to someone sometime."** The Alpha nodded his head in agreement.

The chancellor at this point had her hand sitting on top of Nick's. Usually Nick wears gloves and doesn't like being touched. He has never had much physical contact with others unless violence is involved. However, this interaction seemed natural. The Alron was happy that she had reached her monster. She pressed on. **"I need you to know that my life is also incredibly lonely. I was getting married to one of the cabinet members who were assassinated by the Kurgax; dating is pretty difficult when you are leader of humanity. How do you deal with it? Do you tell your dearest about the horrible things that you have to do in order for us to have a better life? Or do you leave it at the door?"** For the first time in almost 20 rotations, he was perplexed. *Damn she is good.* Nick finally replied, **"Why do you ask Lady?"**

Driax then made her point. **"People in our position are often under incredible stress. It will let me sleep better at night knowing that you deal with those stressors in a productive way. If you go rogue, there is almost nothing that I can do really. I just have to trust that your relationship with God is better than your relationship with me; and I expect us to have a wonderful, sweet, special affiliation. I cannot be something that I am not when I am around you. You will see right through that and I don't have time to find another Alpha Paladin. I have to trust in that. I know that you understand; I have read your file and I know how smart you *really* are. I will always be like this with you when we are alone. I hope that you don't mind. I need you to be honest and free to speak your mind and also speak from your heart. Because I need a friend Nick; in the time that I have been chancellor, our Alliance has nearly been brought to its knees from within and our enemies are everywhere."** At this point, her voice began to trail off. He gave her a truly sympathetic look, letting her know she was in the presence of a true friend. Just talking about the madness of it can be overwhelming. She sighed and spoke slowly. **"And now, we have to deal with Earth."**

Driax then did the unexpected. She then leaned her head on his left shoulder. That was significant because Cain is left handed. *Damn, I don't have a chance; this is worse than AC and Kima put together,* thought the Paladin. It was as he suspected: his boss is exhausted. Cain doesn't do warm and fuzzy by nature, he had to be taught those actions. Nick now had to speak to her in the way that AC and Kima had taught him. **"The old man said that you are fearless. No one ever does *that*. Or *this*. You are one of those people that trust in their heart to do what is needed. I understand and deeply respect that point of view. I also am appreciative of the fact that you are direct and ask questions instead making assumptions. That shows an intelligence that I will always** respond to. Well I meditate my Chancellor and I also am an artist; every significant other I have had has always known that our time together will always be short, but I will do my best to give them a lifetime in whatever time that we have. Many of them are somewhat aware of what I do but for the most part, I keep them in the dark. It isn't worth it. There were only two women that I truly loved; you know about one of them and the other I keep a secret. Only Kima knows who she is and she works for me. Don't worry about me and God; *He is the only one that I will serve better than you.* If being your friend is what you require, then I shall be the best friend that you've ever had." He thought to himself, *thanks Arielle.*

The mighty Khan Antonius is a man of view words. He is comfortable in the madness that is his life. Dear comrades have died in his arms, in service of people who can hardly comprehend his duty. He knows that this new chancellor is once again about to ask of him and his mighty warriors. To do the improbable, but not the impossible. To bring Earth back from the brink and protect it from all foes at all costs. He quietly inquired to his dear chancellor. **"What is that you ask of me, my dear Chancellor? You have my love and my blade. What do you ask?"** She sighed comfortably, kissed him on the cheek and then gave him his marching orders quietly. **"I want you to kill them *all* Nick. Anyone who endangers the Earth, slaughter them. I want everyone to know that to try and occupy our world will be the end of them. Annihilate everyone and everything that would be in your way. My beautiful monster, close their eyes. I am asking that you destroy the Dark-Siders. I am asking you to obliterate the Gondronian Empire also; don't leave any of them alive. Cut Atlas' fucking head off my monster. He has lived far too long, don't you think?"**

This response is different from the requests made by the other chancellors. She made no bones about what she actually wanted from her deadly servant. Cain will never go against the wishes of his chancellor. If they want the best out of him, they actually have to ask him. That is usually all the incentive he needs to do his thing. But this Alron seemed happy to send him to do it. *That's so cool; I don't have to hold her hand* thought the mighty Paladin. She continued. **"The council is a bunch of bitchy little girls aren't they? Don't worry about them, no one will get in your way. I am in agreement with the IGF; their orders are my orders. Kill them. I am not as angry with Atlas as I was with the**

god-king, but he needs to die just the same. I don't care about any of the decisions and resources that you deem necessary to carry this out; you have my total and complete support. Demolish them my monster. Make sure that anyone who ever thinks about harming one human in the universe will be an endangered species. Now go."

With that mandate from his chancellor, he smiled and replied, **"good bye my sweet chancellor. By your request, it shall be done. Please pray for those foes that would cross me; they shall need it."** He then took off in a dead sprint towards Wing Alpha, comforted in the fact that he had his leader's full support. *Wow, she is the only person that makes the word monster sound like a term of endearment*, thought the Alpha. As Nick was about to head off to catch up with his team he brought the ship to the suite where Driax was standing. He looked at her and she looked back at him. He smiles and salutes her. He doesn't say anything; he doesn't have to. *Thank you God, she's a keeper*, the mighty Alpha mused. *Kush was right about him; he will be a wonderful friend*, thought the Alron. Chancellor Alron Driax smiled, knowing full well that the Milky Way Galaxy is about to become the most interesting place in the universe.

CHAPTER 4

The Spook Story

As Cain and the rest of the Blood Knights had just left to head towards Earth, the confab of Regents, Clerics, and the Economic Guild were still in session. Many of the Regents, especially Lucian Angelis, had many more questions about this noble operator, Nicolas Cain; questions that needed answers. Many of these men and women had been glad to have Nicolas and the rest of the Terran Military handle these complicated situations, but it never occurred to any of them until now to learn about their mightiest protectors. The Commander said that the Blood Knights would resolve the issues on Earth in one year or they would go it alone. There was no political capital or forethought; he made the decision for them and asked nothing in return. Leaders like that are easy to admire. And a man like Gaius Nicolas Cain is deserving of that admiration.

The confab was continuing after the Knights had left the Arcadian Star System and were headed towards Earth, but many of these leaders, from the politicians, clerics, and the guild were buzzing. All of these men and women were left desperately wanting to know more about Antonius. As Nari the Wise began to resume his report on Paladin issues in the Terran Alliance, Oceania's Regent, Lucian Angelis, decided that Cain needed to be discussed right then and right now. **"I think I speak for all of us, Madam Chancellor, in saying that we would like to know more about the Commander. No, I miss spoke; we *need* to know about Cain. I was always left under the impression that he was somehow more of a monster than a man. He is a person, complete with thoughts and eloquence; not the boogie man. The previous OceanianRegent left me with the impression that he may be a monster, *but he's our monster*. Please tell us more. Where did he come from? What of his family?"**

Chancellor Driax was hesitant to discuss the subject. **"Let me be clear about something: Commander Cain doesn't answer to us; he answers to *me*. The only information in his Alliance file is documentation on his mission successes. We are political actors, not military ones. The majority of his file is classified. Being honest with all of you, no one in this room, including myself, has enough clearance to read it. What I will say is this: I trust him and that I need all of you to do the same."** What she told them was *partially* true.

Commander Nicolas Cain has one file and Khan Antonius has another file within the IGF. The IGF report has a far more accurate recording of his exploits, psychological, and personality profiles. No one within the IGF civilian governance could read it either. However, she has seen the most accurate record of her monster and that is because she was privy to the Ocularian dossier on Commander Cain/Khan Antonius; no doubt the most accurate information in the Universe. It is said that only God knows more than the Oculari and there are some who believe even *He* doesn't have enough clearance.

Yes, the Alron didn't have enough clearance to read it, but she read Cain's file because the Ocularian Commandant had let her read his *personal* summary. The clerics and the guild were of the same opinion; there was more that needed to be known. Essentially since he convinced all the Terran leadership that his Knights could answer the charge of the IGF; furthermore, why did the IGF trust him as well? What did the IGF know about Cain that the Alliance didn't know? The Alliance officials were irritated that the Federation knew more about their super warrior than they did. So Driax decided to tell them the story of her first encounter with Cain.

The reason that the Cain/Janitor topic became a point of discussion was in part because Regent Aegir sent her personal aid to retrieve the file on Commander Cain and the aid didn't find anything within the file. Further digging kept leading to more dead ends. Only one actual report existed that the Regency had access to and nothing was in the document. It simply had his name and then the word classified. Furthermore, there was concern because when there was an audit of the Blood Knight's primary summary; there was nothing in it either. Not only was there not any information on the Alpha Paladin that the Regency has access to, there was nothing on the Blood Knights/Janitors either. There was simply one statement: Classified-*Clandestine Services*. It was time for answers; a lot of answers.

The regents were so impressed with Cain's conversation they almost forgot about how deadly he really is, but the Sichuan Regent was not satisfied. Both Qin and Aegir shared the same concerns about one warrior having that type of ability who essentially answered to no one. Just how far is he above the other Paladins? Just how far is he beyond any of the warriors in the IGF or the Alliance? Qin is the newest Regent of the Alliance. He is the closest in age to the Chancellor. He was unaware that Cain had been a high value asset to the Alliance and the Federation for eons. It was hard for him to comprehend that a warrior could be that much further ahead of all the other Paladins; he was of the understanding that the Paladins had no true equal in combat and then he finds out about a Paladin who is not only the superior to all the others, but that the comparison is not even close. His questions while brief, was filled with both wonder and concern. **"Chancellor honestly, just how dangerous is Cain? Is he really that much better than all the other Paladins?"**

Driax realized that he was going to press the issue until she addressed it. The Alron revels in having strategic advantages, even over her own subordinates. She took a sip of her Ynarian Fire tea, smiled and spoke with a cool yet flirtatious tone. **"So you really want to know how good Cain is? I don't think you understand the ramifications of that question. I will try and answer it in a manner that will not insult you but my answer probably won't be very clear either. You see there are two classes of Paladin: *Cain and everyone else*. It isn't close. His IQ is often considered beyond any quantifiable measurement. In his spare time, Cain designed some of the greatest pieces of architecture ever by a humanoid."**

Driax loved telling her subordinates about her dearest Cain. Many were arrogant enough to think that he was just some brute who served their bidding. She loved letting them know they were gravely mistaken. **"He is considered to be the best battle strategist that has ever served in either military. Commander Cain has drafted treaties for several warring factions who decreed that they would not fight each other simply because it would have *annoyed* him. Alron Nyota asked him to help our xenomorphologist once and the result was the creation of a language algorithm that is still in usage within the IGF. Chancellor Kalila once discussed her students having a problem finding** something within the archives because it was so vast. She said that the data was both so vast and old, no one never figured out how to modernize the research process. For her, he customized the entire Genesis archives in *one* day; that was significant considering that the archives are more than 9 million Earth years old. To display his genius to Chancellor Apollo, he drew a perfect circle, *free handed.*"

When she placed emphasis on the word phrase free handed, it garnered a deafening silence; exactly what she wanted. She knew that her casual tone was the element in evoking such concern. As if what she was saying to them wasn't the most incredible story that they had ever been told. The Chancellor continued her assault on their comprehension. **"Wing Alpha is the deadliest star fighter that has ever been created by either the IGF or Alliance. The great Rioan engineer Dr. Okx once admitted than he should have *never* built it. Everyone who has used that fighter for more than three missions had either died from the physical stress or become psychotic. It was in storage for more than 150 rotations until the commander began using it. Cain has used it for more than six hundred rotations. There are about 1800 known forms of bi-pedal combat that we know of; Cain is a master of at least *seventeen hundred and ninety* of them. Whose brain could store that much information just about *combat*? There is *nothing* that his brilliant mind cannot do."**

The statement that the young chancellor made about her dear, sweet monster didn't put anyone else at ease. That was exactly what she wanted to do. She wanted them to understand that *he* is the primary reason that other systems will continue to have a positive working relationship with the Terran Alliance. The delusions that her Regency had been under was being shattered in the most intimate way possible. Other Alrons left their regents with the impression that Cain was just another soldier; another tool for the Alliance. She was not of the same opinion.

The reputation of the Alliance military is a strong one indeed. However, Cain's reputation throughout the Federation territories is even greater than in the human territories because of his status as the Federation's *Janitor*. The word Janitor has a common translation in the Terran language but in the Ocularian native tongue, the word Janitor literally translates to "Terrifying Servant." The Oculari are considered the deadliest, clandestine unit of the IGF; Cain is considered the deadliest agent that the Clan of The Oculari has ever produced. The regents inquired about his training as an Oculari; one of the regents' staffers once told her that no human could ever complete the Ocularian Killing Academy only to later find out that Cain was the *Master Oculari.*

At this point in the conversation, Driax was smiling intently and listening to the regents discuss the ramifications of having an Oculari as the leader of the Blood Knights. She almost laughed out loud when one of them suggested that Cain's training as a Paladin was more important, meaning he was a Paladin first and an Ocularian assassin second. Driax informed the leaders that he was neither one nor the other; he is both. She further explained the benefits of having a human warrior with ties to both disciplines. **"His training as an Oculari has molded him into an efficient and deadly killer. They believed in the purification of pain and cruelty, leaving him damaged both emotionally and mentally.** *Or at least, it should have left him damaged,* **he isn't. Our warrior is so powerful that not even the Oculari could break him. Here is an example of the kind of life that he has led: his** *lover* **allowed herself to be captured and murdered in order to bring out to most destructive tendencies of his nature. His** *wife* **did that."**

Chancellor Driax had everyone's full attention at the absurdity of that notion. It was inconceivable for any of them to do something to that extent for a greater good. They got a glimpse of Cain's world and it scared them *shitless.* She continued. **"Through prayer and meditation, he has kept his anger from getting the best of him. When truly angry, he can go beyond berserker rage; coupled with his intelligence and other vast abilities, he may literally be the most perfect killing machine that God has ever created. That being said, he is without question the most deadly Paladin to have ever lived; even deadlier than his mother, and that is saying something. Once he decides that death/destruction is the logical conclusion, no one in the known universe is better. If there is a warrior that could make Cain tremble, I fear for the universe. His training, both in the Paladins and the Oculari, has made him** *very good at very bad things.*"

Her Alliance colleagues and subordinates were starting to get a picture of who Cain was and the quite frankly, the picture is beyond nerve racking to say the least. Cain is beyond their scope of understanding; he might be beyond anyone's understanding. But what about his troops? Sensing the next question would be about his origins with the clandestine strike unit, *The Janitors* or The Blood Knights, would be the next subject brought up, she addressed that issue also. **"Because of Cain's truly unique skill-set and nature, the Paladin leadership decided that he was better off in a much more uncompromising unit. It would be a smaller, much more mobile detachmentof warriors and battle equipment. Going into deep space and performing high risk, high speed attack runs is a lot easier with one ship rather than an armada. Danyzer essentially wanted to duplicate the *Iconian Black Project* within the Order of Paladins; which made sense considering Cain's success as an Ocularian Operative. The Janitors are considered *superior* to the Iconian Black Project, the Rioan Warrior-Core, and every other attack force within the known universe. It is believed that his troops consist of the most creative, adaptive, and easily the most hyper-violent Paladins within the order. These warriors serve under Commander Cain only; regardless of the charge, it is their duty to answer the call. These warriors would specialize in the preposterous. The project would be known as the Blood Knights."**

The Chancellor was in the mood for shock and awe. She was sick of their shit; it was time to throw her weight around. All of her constituency had heard of the Iconian Black Project. The Iconians were the precursors to everything that the Rioans are; the first to ever defeat the Dark-Siders. These were the first heroes of the Virgo Super Cluster; and the Janitors were thought to be even deadlier. Driax smiled at her nervous staffers and continued on. **"The warriors chosen were the most deadly, the bravest, and also the most versatile of all the Alliance Military Operations. Janitors don't negotiate and they will *never* surrender. Killing their enemies was usually the first, second, and last option. The running joke through the IGF Senate is that no enemy of the Federation has ever seen Antonius and lived. Most of the beings within the Federation are literally scared to death of the Janitors. The Blood Knights don't have any enemies; they've killed all of them. We are a little more judicious when sending them out to fight, while the slightest aggressive provocation will send them into Federation space."**

Chancellor Driax had the luxury that many of her predecessors never had: an audience willing to listen to the truth about Cain. The Blood Knights and their master had never been explained to the leadership in the manner which she was speaking. **"The Janitors believe in wiping our enemies away. They leave nothing; no man, woman, or child.**

They burn everything, sometimes they destroy entire star systems. When we send them, star charts usually have to be re-made. Cain has more than one hundred trillion troops at his disposal for any discourse that he considers them necessary, but he hardly uses anyone but the Janitors. In many instances, if the Federation has given him orders and if those issues concern the Alliance, he will only carry them out with confirmation from the Alliance; the IGF will just have to wait. He is not only a Terran, but a loyal Terran. You really don't want the leader of the Federation Military, who is also a master assassin, pissed at you would you? He is the deterrent. *For everything.*"

Realizing that her new Cabinet didn't understand why Cain and Antonius were described as two different people, she informed them of the reason for that supposed discrepancy. His official title amongst their Federation comrades is what he is known for throughout a majority of the quadrant. In the Alliance, he is Commander Nicolas Cain. However, within the IGF, his title has a much more grand orientation. "He is the Inter Galactic Federation's newest military leader; Khan Antonius. The Khan is an immortal protector who serves the interests of all free peoples of the Federation. Of all the deadly operatives within the known universe, he is considered the apex; the best of the worst. He has this interesting dichotomy: the most vicious and the most disciplined. He is the youngest to ever have that IGF designation; he is also the deadliest. His interests are greater than just Alliance needs; he is only serving us because he chooses to. Humanity is not his primary concern, protecting all the beings of this region of space are. Think about the advantage of being immortal. He will outlive the stupidity of his political leadership. When someone is an immortal, they really have little use for the biases of others. He doesn't have a political position; it is his desire to do what is best for all people."

What the chancellor said was a mouthful. She also made it clear that he serves Driax not out of some ancient obligation, but out of love for his people. Cain is Terran to the core, but he also knows that a secure Federation is also good for the Alliance and vice versa. As Cain stated to them earlier, these mighty factions need each other and both groups would need Earth. She concluded the conversation. "Can you think of a better way to keep political leadership accountable than having an immortal as the commander of the total military? Knowing that he will outlive all of you? That is the price paid for our security ladies and gentlemen. You have never seen his combat record people. All of the previous Alrons who ever encountered him understood what I do now; he is the gifted, the deadly, and the necessary. His obligations are the Blood Knights' obligations. The Alpha Centauri is the flag ship for both fleets. Admiral AC was chosen to be under his command, in no small part to aid in keeping his humanity relevant to Janitor/Blood Knight bottom lines. It has become, without question a full time job."

What Cain and his dearest Alron were both aware of was that the Dark-Siders were a threat to all the free peoples of the universe. Earth is a planetary system of strategic significance and it had to be addressed. It was a tricky proposition because of the immense distance that this system is from both the Federation and also the Alliance. What both of them are aware of is that the Earth may have to be the hub of its own inter galactic network eventually. When that eventuality occurs, the Terrans and Federated peoples will have an opportunity to return to the Milky Way and Andromeda Galaxies at some point. This could dramatically change the geographical and political landscape of the thirty-eight million light years and more than 860 quadrillion sentient beings are potentially affected. He knows that the territory leading up to IGF occupied space isn't as numerous but that is still a large population of sentient beings. These beings are now under his protection as well; a concave of friendship has to be made. Cain's charge is to make that prospective opportunity an actual reality.

However, where the planetary system is located has been long considered the most capricious locality of the Virgo Super Cluster. Many of the more evolved species that call the Virgo home never go anywhere near this area. There are scores of contemptible and merciless races who are thriving at the expense of the exploitingof weaker races in this expanse of space. Some of the most feared species within the Virgo Super Cluster call this territory home. They will not be happy to see two military and political powers, that both believe in equality and free will, return to this region. Lines will be drawn and issues will abound. Cain knows that many of the potential threats will need to be neutralized before the task of reclaiming their home system could be accomplished. In addition, the Alliance and Federation scope of influence could literally double; another enticing incentive. Driax and the Federation leadership are leaving that monumental task to the Khan and his valiant troops to address thisconundrum. The *Janitors* will do what they do best; clean up the evil in that area.

From time to time in her first few rotations as Chancellor, Driax has had to accommodate the Alliance Leadership. She is younger than almost all of her cabinet, the clerics, and also most of the military leaders as well. She has this beautiful, youthful aura; sometimes it makes for difficult conversations with her elders. If not for the death of Kush, she would be following their lead instead of the other way around. The only person who saw her potential abilities as a leader was Kush. Nick trusted his favorite Chancellor's thought process. He knew that Kush would not have done what he did unless he was certain about her potential. Kush was a shrewd leader and excellent judge of character. Driax is an intelligent, stunning woman from the Nubian Star System; beautiful ebony eyes and mahogany skin; she reminded Antonius of Nefertiti but she was different. Driax was warm and inviting from the start, while Nefertiti took some warming up to. From his experiences with Alron Driax as his boss, he thinks that they will have a solid working relationship.

Alron Driax realized that she had not been as fair with her new subordinates as she could have been. The Alliance is a lot more stable than what it was when she first became the Terran Chancellor. Many of the current leadership were not there during the chaos of the Kurgan Assassination. When she ascended to her current position, she was even younger than what she is right now. Over 25 rotations ago, the Terran Alliance was on the brink of coming apart from the seams. Every civilian leader of note besides her and a few others had been thrust into leadership situations they hadn't been briefed on. Now things are better. The new leaders are now properly acquainted with their responsibilities. Many of them had heard of the terrible tragedy that had occurred, but no one but Taylor Amani Driax had actually lived through it. She had a grand story to tell and her rise to power coincided with the actions of the Alpha Paladin.

Chancellor Taylor Driax realized that she had another advantage over everyone either in the room or via comlink and decided to press her advantage. She was tired of her subordinates looking over her shoulder, especially when those matters pertained to the Alpha. She was the only person within the Terran leadership that had any real knowledge about their most dangerous operative; the rest is just the opinions of the uninformed. What information she had given them about Nick was surface knowledge at best, but she wanted it known that he is loyal to her and any slight of her could evoke a hostile response from Cain. It is not because she uses him to bully others, but because Cain believes in the value of protocol; disrespect of his Alron doesn't compute. Cain has already proven that he will remain loyal to her and is willing to kill on her behalf if necessary.

The fact that she has stated that the file on this agent of the Alliance requires a security clearance that no regent apparently has the security rating high enough to actually read it further strengthens her position. One cannot be betrayed if someone has no leverage to use against them. One of the primary reasons for the Paladin coup was because many felt that she was ill equipped to lead such a vast and diverse group of planets and people. Nicolas disagreed with that sentiment; he believed that nothing happens without a reason; that God doesn't do anything random. Cain's actions on planet Mu indicated that she has the Alpha Paladin's full support. Considering the way that he dispatched his former comrades, that is a significant point. She then gave the leadership her understanding of the facts that led to her becoming an Alron.

Alron Driax is the youngest high Chancellor in the history of the Terran Alliance. She was barely in her thirties when this opportunity had been pressed upon her. She was chosen to be the new Vice Chancellor of the Humanities when tragedy struck. Kush only left her because in case of a terrible tragedy, he must have been certain that she would be up to the task. Otherwise why would a vice chancellor have not gone to negotiate the peace accord in the first place? Many of her fellow vice Chancellors and Alron Kush had been murdered in an attack initiated by the Kurgax Federation. In what was supposed to be a peaceful territorial negotiation, the Terran Alliance leadership officers were murdered by the Kurgax elite guard.

The Kurgax Federation had always been a problem for all the free peoples within this quadrant. Their leadership has always believed that they were the most important creatures in the universe. If these people wanted something, it was their right to have it. That didn't work well with the Federation or the Alliance and it was inevitable that these powerful groups would eventually be in some sort of conflict. As far as Cain was concerned, their number had come up a long time ago and he wanted nothing more than to burn the Kurgax Federation completely out of the consciousness of the quadrant. There was one thing keeping them alive; the attitude of the leadership that the Alpha Paladin served. The Alliance never thought of the Kurgax as a true threat. This thought process angered the Kurgax and also irritated Antonius. This encounter was only a matter of time.

In many ways, the Kurgax are similar to Terrans, especially in their past. The Kurgax believed in a monarchial society and practiced governance similar to slavery and/or indentured servitude. The aristocracy believed that the non aristocracy of this empire was born to cater to their needs only; never to serve the people, but for the people to serve them. The way that the Kurgax had crossed the Alliance was seemingly innocent enough. One of the most remote planetary systems of the Kurgax had suffered a cataclysmic event. One of their planets had been tilted off its axis, affecting its weather pattern. They suffered a tremendous drought and famine. The Terran system closest to them, Aquilonia, decided to intervene. The Kurgax leadership did nothing to help its own. However, they were offended at Terran interference. What theseAlliance missionaries discovered was beyond cruelty.

They saw how the Kurgax had treated some of their underclass. This planet was home to the Oucuz, but the Kurgax controlled them. The Kurgan leadership didn't leave these people the proper resources for survival and how they were forced to work day and night for the Kurgax Federation's benefit. The Kurgax high class cared little for the people that were under their dominion. In fact, the Kurgax were alerted only by the presence of the Terran missionaries from Aquilonia. Terran interference was based on the fact in Terran society that no one had the right to enslave and disenfranchise others. Since the Kurgans had left several of the races to fend for themselves, the Terrans decided to aid them; to try and make their lives better. The Kurgax Federation sent a force to repel the "invaders" only to find out that the Terran angels of mercy were being protected by an Alliance Naval battle groupthat was a more than formidable foe; millions of Kurgan elite died that day.

Their government had reservations about having a society that believed in liberty and equality that was in proximity to their territorial borders was too close for comfort. Several Alliance sponsored missions into Kurgan star systems had created several small conflicts. A Terran medical vessel and a Kurgax science vessel were two ships destroyed in this particular conflict. At this point, Cain sent fourteen Anubis Class Star Destroyers into Kurgan territory. Two divisions of the Kurgax Navy, more than 90 ships were obliterated. Many Terran political leaders complained that Cain's methods were too severe and that they were not bullies. The political leadership's argument was that the Terran Alliance Military was a peace keeping armada and not a bunch of vigilantes.

As far as Commander Cain was concerned, the Kurgax Federation's number had come up and it was time to slaughter them. The high counsel was not of the same opinion and wanted to find another way to resolve this issue. Kush and the Chancellor's Cabinet decided to negotiate a peace accord and the Kurgax agreed to terms. Unfortunately, the Cabinet was deceived and then murdered. The Alpha Centauri was away on IGF business when this occurred. They had been in IGF territory for 8 rotations handling an IGF-related conflict when AC received word that the cabinet had been murdered. Cain, who was especially close to Kush, was deeply wounded emotionally by the incident.

The Kurgax were a people noted for being of immense self-importance and possessing a will to dominate. What they did not know was that Kush was trying to save *them* from a potentially species altering event; Nicolas was ready to destroy them. As far as he was concerned, it was either *them or us*. And every one of his officers and Alron Kush knew he didn't mean *us*. Kush always said that Cain was always the one right tool; if he has been sent, there is never a need to send a second.

The Janitors and Kush were in conference about the Kurgax before the Knights were supposed to leave for IGF territory. Nicolas told the Chancellor that the Kurgax would be a problem and that he planned on sending them a message to let them know that the Terrans were not to be trifled with. Kush then received a report on the tactical deterrent that was being proposed. AC gave the overview of the plan; she told him that Cain planned on putting an electric-magnetic pulse device on Kurgan Prime, the Kurgax capital planet. He planned on stopping their planet's core from spinning just to show that he could. That was just the start of his destructive actions. He would threaten to destroy their planet's core to show them how far the Terrans would go to prove their point. If the Kurgans didn't respond to that dis-incentive, he planned something more deliberate.

Cain had dealt with the Kurgax before, they were bullies and they had to be reminded of who the *real bullies* of the quadrant were.

Antonius' experiences with them was that the Kurgax only negotiate in good faith when they know the opposition is willing to go one step further than them to prove their point. The Kurgax are known for aggressively trying to enter another species' territory and create chaos until that group backs down and acquiesces to their demands. This strategy has extended their territorial boundaries for eons. That was until they attempted to try to punk the wrong group of people.

When the Kurgax attempted to pull a similar aggressive action against the IGF, the Janitors destroyed one of the Kurgax Federation's primary weapons facilities. Using an electro-magnetic smart bomb, Cain rendered most of the weapon depot's primary defense systems useless. Once the defenses were down, nine Wing fighters, including Wing Alpha proceeded to destroy the facility in 6 minutes. More than twenty-eight million Kurgax died in the attack.

The attack was only 3800 kilometers from the Kurgan capital. The message was clear to the Kurgax: don't *cross* the IGF. Not only was the facility destroyed, but it happened so fast that the Wing fighters were already out of the territory when the Kurgan Military attempted to respond. That action was to prove that whenever the Alpha decides to, he could destroy the Kurgax Federation. This was an irritant for Cain because he considered the Kurgax a loose end and he *hates* loose ends. The message was received; the Kurgax could never prove it was Antonius, but they also knew he was capable of this kind of damage also. The Ocularian's reputation was a serious disincentive. The Kurgax never bothered the IGF again.

This circumstance was an example of the multiple and sometimes conflicting bottom lines of the Alpha Paladin. The Federation had grown tired of the Kurgax Federation, Senator Aya had given Antonius specific marching orders; kill all the Kurgax as soon as he was prepared to. These people were no longer infuriating the IGF, it was time for their disposal. However Cain wouldn't exterminate the Kurgax until he received permission from Alron Kush. This annoyed the IGF but they also knew how Cain felt about Kush. Kush was the former head of a religious order within the Terran Alliance; his ethics required him to not use Cain to slaughter a race unless he had to. Cain deeply respected this point of view. The IGF would have to wait.

This set of circumstances also had a certain tragic synergy to it. The Kurgax Intelligence Division had no idea that the Alpha Paladin and the

Master Oculari were one in the same. Antonius and Cain are usually discussed as if they are two different people instead of the same person. The Kurgax were so busy creating discord within the quadrant, none of their clandestine operatives learned that Khan Antonius *is* Commander Nicolas Cain. Had they known that little tidbit, it might have saved their race. Nick likes to say that losers *always* find a way to get beat. Or in this case, losers find a way to become *extinct*.

Before leaving to attend to Federation business, Cain planned on doing something similar to the Kurgax in terms of scope, but not necessarily scale. Cain wanted to do something even more bent and twisted. Kush asked how many people would potentially die from this action and Faris told him at minimum 250 million and the chancellor stuttered and stammered, **"Two-Hundred Fifty...."** He almost passed out. He said to Commander Cain urgently. **"Wow, I, I wasn't expecting such a high number. 250 *million* Nick? Is this really needed? Don't you think that is a *little* high?"** To which Cain retorted, **"nah; two hundred fifty would have proven our point. My other plan was a *little* bit worse."** Kush asked how many did he originally propose? Cain smiled and replied sweetly. **"All of them. We are Janitors, Alron. *This is how we get down.*"** Once Chancellor Kush found out, he was against that course of action. **"No Nicolas, we will try a different path,"** said Nicolas' boss. **"I know that the IGF has approved that action, but I cannot. Wouldn't be very Christian would it?"** Cain smiled when Kush said that.

Chancellor appreciated the duality of the Cain's existence. He always referred to him as Nicolas as a sign of specificity. He knew what Khan Antonius was considered in the IGF; he was the dirtiest of the dirtiest secrets of the Federation. He is the most accomplished of the Oculari. The man that Kush had come to trust and admire deeply was Cain. He knew that because of the terrible things that had happened to him and the deadly training that he received, Cain was considered the most expendable of assets. Nick's Christian beliefs sometimes are not held in great emphasis with the other leadership within the Alliance and the IGF.

Kush once asked Nick why he felt so little remorse for his actions. He responded that he was simply doing the Lord's work and that someone had to. He felt humbled that God would choose him for such a task; Kush was taken aback at his sincerity. Kush was quick to remind everyone who would listen that Cain was more than just a deadly, violent asset of the Alliance. He was also a dear friend of the chancellor. Kush once remarked that he loved Nick and he was proud of the man that he had become; *that Antonius was needed and Cain was wanted.* It was a gift that Antonius would never forget. The Kurgans would pay dearly for taking Kush away from Nick.

Of all the Chancellors he had served over the years, the Alpha Paladin respected and loved Kush the most. Cain admired the fact that the chancellor always wanted to resolve conflicts with compassion and grace. That wasn't Cain's world, but he admired that none the less. Before Kush became Chancellor he was both a cleric and professor at the University of Eden; Nick and Kush had many deep discussions on faith, redemption, and service. These men were a great team in many ways. Kush was a visionary, while Cain was the instrument that made the chancellor's visions plausible. In many ways, these two driven men were a lot alike, AC always said. That statement always was considered comedy among the Federation officials, in particularly the Ocularian Commandant; they knew what Nick was truly capable of.

Chancellor Kush had always made Nick feel comfortable to the point that when he was in consult, he never carried a weapon. Kush often had Cain come to family gatherings. He was considered an extended member of the family. Kush's wife never knew what he did for the Alliance government; she merely thought that he was one of the new bureaucrats that had joined his staff. Kush's wife had immediately taken a shine to him. Lady Kush always remarked that her husband should be glad that Cain hadn't met his wife first or he wouldn't have had a chance. She was always doting on Cain, much to Kush's amusement.

Kush's oldest daughter decided to collaborate with AC and Lady Kush to plan a surprise party for Cain. It was an especially difficult task to pull off because there was no record of Nick's date of birth. Nick didn't attend the funeral for Kush and his favorite chancellor's family was deeply hurt by him not showing up. Lady Aya then informed them of who Cain *really* was and what he was about to do. Kush's children and grandchildren were completely surprised; the chancellor never gave any indication that there was anything unusual about their relationship. These people had no idea that this sweet, dear friend of the family was in fact the fiercest operative in the history of humanity. Nick and Riley, the youngest of the Kush clan had an annual fishing trip that would need to be canceled, because Nick was going to be **"busy"**. They caught the best fish and now, all that was taken away. The Kurgax Federation had *really* fucked up.

On planet Acre, the Ocularian Commandant, Danyzer, and his wife, Senator Aya, had just received word that Alron Kush and his party have just been assassinated by the Kurgax Elite Guard. The Commandant was excited because he knew what the response would be: the total extinction of the Kurgax race. **"This is going to be the most beautiful destruction that we will be witness to. My son did not allow us to watch the decimation of the Unori; we will get to watch him this time. I am so excited, aren't you Aya? I know Danyzer will complain that Nick will go too far, ramifications, blah, blah, etc."** Aya smiled. **"Yes it is going to be incredible. Kush shouldn't have stopped Nick the first time. The Chancellors keep acting like Cain is not doing what God made him for. He is an exquisite assassin. The Kurgax knew better than this. Their god-king is an ass; he deserves to die. Don't you agree husband?"** The great leader closed his eyes and sighed.

There has always been a doubt, a sense of dread that has always been in the back of Danyzer's mind about Cain. He is not just a Paladin. Nick is the externality of a bargain made long ago. Paladins are peace keepers as far as the Rioan General is concerned. That was his vision for them when he had the Paladin Corps created. Cain is something more than that. There is always the fear that he would go too far. The problem is that Danyzer's wife and comrade never think that the Apex Predator has never gone far enough.

Danyzer was Nick's first commander in the Paladin Command Unit. He was never a Paladin, because he is a Rioan. He is the mighty general who was deemed a Khan, a high protector within the Inter Galactic Federation. As Khan, the warrior's obligations are to protect those who cannot protect themselves. To wage a never ending war against those who would oppress the weak. General Danyzer was the primary trainer of Nick's mother, one of the most deadly Paladins to have ever lived. Danyzer believed that there was greatness in Nick's mother. It had always been Danyzer's hope and wish that she would eventually become the next Khan after Danyzer; she was *that* good. This warrior was so good that Danyzer considered having her enter the Ocularian Killing Academy, she was *that* deadly.

Danyzer was the commanding officer of both Cain and his mother; as deadly as his mother was, Nick is considered far more dangerous. She was emotional, much like most of the Paladins. Nick's pathology is far more unnerving. While many warriors use their heart and passion to fight for the Cause, the apex predator is so different. His training has made him become a confident but subtle operative. He moves silently and with purpose. Circumstances such as this one make Danyzer nervous because Cain believes in elimination of a complete threat. No negotiation. If he has been invited to the party, there is only one conclusion. Danyzer doesn't adhere to this absolute belief, but Cain doesn't care. Many, including his superiors, are never completely sure what his objective is unless he decides to tell them of his intentions. Even then, he may not reveal the complete truth. A warrior with his combination of experience, power, and intellect, makes many within the leadership of both the IGF and also the Alliance incredibly uncomfortable. *Just like the Alpha Paladin likes it.*

None the less, this current situation has made Danyzer pensive. **'It's going to be a nightmare my wife. Why did the Kurgax have to kill the entire contingent? Nick never needs much incentive and now these people have killed his favorite Alron? All they had to do was steer clear of us and they could have continued to exist. We could have used them against the Dark-siders. That species will pay an expensive price. The Terran Alliance is in desperate straits my wife. They are not prepared for the long night to come. Who is the new chancellor? Is she up to the task?"** The Ocularian Commandant laughed at his old friend. *He is so dramatic,* he mused. As far as the Commandant was concerned, this couldn't have happened any better.

Whereas Danyzer saw despair, his wife and friend saw a tremendous opportunity. Aya sat in Danyzer's lap and hugged him. **"Driax is her name. She is young, but I will prepare her. Husband, I need you to go see her and deliver Cain's file before I arrive. Let her think that it came from you; she doesn't need to know its OC's file. She's already nervous enough as it is; let her know when she is ready. Tell her that it is some light reading material and tell her I will come and see her soon. She will be prepared. My dear friend, I need the assistance of some of your excellent assassins. Eliminate all of her boisterous opposition; especially that cheeky bastard from Carthage. He talks too much anyway. Make their deaths all look like the Kurgax did it; we will not have a better opportunity. I already discussed this course of actions with Antonius; he agrees that their deaths are a**

necessity. Cain will take care of the rest of her immediate problems when he finishes off the Kurgax. Kush did a good job grooming her; everything is going according to plan." The head of the espionage network smiled and concurred with the senator. The Alliance just got a lot more interesting.

Cain sent Petamauck to assist in making Chancellor Driax's transition smoother. Cain knew that she was youngest chancellor ever; challenges would come from everywhere. Cain believed that Petamauck could help her in this difficult period on one end, while the Blood Knights would be able to help the new chancellor on the other. Eliminating the Kurgax Federation would be their inauguration gift. The rationale was that if a Paladin of Petamauck's stature was her counsel, the rest of the leadership, both military and political would be less likely to make waves.

AC, Faris, and many of the senior staff were in consensus about this view of the situation. Petamauck was not so sure. He felt that she was too young and naïve for such a tremendous task. But Cain pointed out that Kush had a reason for leaving her out of the delegation purposefully; it was always the policy of Kush to leave one leader out of potentially dangerous situations, just in case the worst case scenario occurs. It just did. Petamauck didn't see it that way totally; he felt that if the Centauri had not been charged with aiding the IGF whenever they needed it, Cain could attend to Alliance business. Both AC and Nick were irritated by their dear comrade's lack of vision. AC then quipped, **"Well I am glad my father didn't think that way. The Terran Alliance is merely *one tree in the forest*! Nick has already given us our assignments. Go do yours!!"**

Cain ordered then Lt. Cmdr. Sayied Faris to set course for the Kurgax Federation. Cain addressed the crew stating that they were about to do something that the last Chancellor did not want, but he felt it was a crooked that needed to be straightened. The crew knew how Nick felt about Kush and they knew he was really salty about this set of circumstances. The only reason that the Janitors hadn't already wiped out the Kurgax was because Kush wouldn't let them. It is ironic. Faris knew this was going to be bad because Nick had come up with a battle plan in 11 minutes for how to wipe out their whole race. Imagine that; he figured out how to eradicate an entire species in *eleven* minutes. The angrier Cain is, the faster his mind tends to work. It is not that he rushes into things;

it is because he can process more information when he is focused. The Kurgax have just moved to the top of Cain's shit list. It's never a long list.

When Petamauck met the new chancellor, Alron Driax, he told her that Commander Cain would speak to her when he returned from dealing with the Kurgax Federation. When Driax asked what he meant by deal with, stating that this was not the time for revenge. Petamauck was to the point. **"Revenge is not what he is after. This is a *reckoning*. This is not an emotional response, but rather a tactical one. The rest of the universe needs to understand that this *will not be tolerated*. The entire Kurgax Federation will have to pay a heavy price. Madam Chancellor, there will be *no more* Kurgax Federation. He will not return until there are no Kurgans left anywhere in the universe. As far as my commander is concerned, the Kurgans need to meet God. *Personally*."**

Cain doesn't always like this part of the job, but this is the most efficient way to handle these kinds of circumstances. The total elimination of an entire species is a messy proposition and it shouldn't be done without proper planning and preparation. Once it goes bad, kill them all. It can be an emotionally taxing thing to slaughter an entire race because there are so many that might not of had anything directly to do with their current state. To kill everyone literally means *everyone*; the old, the young, the children. Every strand of DNA of that species must be completely destroyed. And no one is better at this horrible task than the Blood Knights aka the Janitors; no commanding officer is better suited to such a task than Nicholas Cain aka Khan Antonius.

Cain believes that it is brutal but necessary duty because if these people weren't angry before, they will be angry when their kin are being obliterated. Cain's belief is that it is more logical that once the Janitors begin, they must complete this disgusting task. The commander is aware of how powerful the need for vengeance can be. He always says that he doesn't want an enemy out there holding a grudge. Better to sweep every remnant of an enemy species completely away. As far as Antonius is concerned, it is better to get messy right then than wait and try to deal with the mess later. Once the decision is made, leave no one alive; *ever*. It was a chilling, brutal, and frighteningly efficient cost benefit analysis. This is what makes Cain, Nicolas Cain.

As Cain and the Blood Knights began to cleanse the quadrant of the Kurgan problem, Petamauck became the trusted counsel of Chancellor

Driax. She was a patron of the arts and had a love of music and also possessed a deep compassion for other races and her own. The nuances of politics were relatively new to her. She was however an incredibly quick study who couldn't be manipulated. Much like Kush, she is a Christian and often let her faith guide her decisions. This often put her at odds with her advisor, who despite his faith, often made decisions based upon his logic and reason.

Captain Pax Voss, a valued and trusted member of the Paladin order, was a close friend of Petamauck. She finished the academy in the same class as Petamauck and served in the Intelligence Division. Voss knew the dangers that would soon be at the Terran Alliance doorstep. This was the worst time to have a novice chancellor. She didn't like the direction that Driax was taking the Alliance and she insisted that Petamauck use his influence and do something about it. Kush had begun negotiations with the IGF for entrance before he died; a move that even Cain was not highly enthused about. Since he died, it was naturally assumed that the negotiations would cease. Voss and many other Paladins felt that the Federation needed the Alliance far more than the Alliance needed the Federation.

Driax, much like Kush, saw it as an opportunity to spread charity to other races that had been generous to the Terrans. *To share our knowledge of God*, she informed the Regents. As long as the Paladins were supportive of her actions, so would the rest of the military. As long as she was alive, the Alliance would head in that direction. As long as Nick felt it was prudent, the rest of the Paladins were more likely to follow the Alron. The chancellor would also confess her secret concerns to Petamauck; believing his counsel was also in the name of friendship. She had no idea that Petamauck saw her as weak, but he could afford to be patient. Once AC and Nick saw what he and Voss saw, they would also be of this opinion. At least that is what he and several other prominent Paladins thought. The actions on Mu would confirm they were gravely mistaken.

Meanwhile, the Alpha Centauri had begun its deadly game. One by one the planets of the Kurgax Federation had fallen. The various races subjugated to Kurgan cruelty were being liberated, only their oppressors were being killed left and right. This tactical genocide was unnerving to say the least to the Kurgan leadership. On one planet, Cain detonated an anti-matter ordinance near the core of a planet, destroying all life there in less than thirty seconds. On another system, he used a moon to crash into another planet, killing 25 billion Kurgans. Those two actions were in the first *hour* of his campaign. On another planet, the master assassin used a tactical weapon that super heated the atmosphere of this planet, burning all the people on the surface; microwaves literally cooked the planet. Planets throughout the Kurgax Federation were being destroyed in ways that couldn't be easily understood. It was as if the plagues of death the Kurgan religion described had been unleashed upon them. These people considered Cain to be the visceral image of death itself.

That is exactly the type of panic that Cain wanted to invoke. This was not rage; this was cold blooded, brutally efficient intellect. Throughout Kurgan space, word had spread that the Janitors were coming. The Terrans had sent their most deadly warriors to kill all the Kurgans and there was nothing that anyone could do to stop them. These warriors are known for destroying everything and killing everyone who they deem expendable.

When the Blood Knights went to one of the central planets to kill all the Kurgans, the aristocracy had taken desperate measures to keep their lives. The governor of that planet had decided to use a Goethean infant to protect himself from harm. The attack unit, lead by Lance Blood-Joy didn't pursue the governor any further. The governor then tried to escape, only to feel his hands begin to burn. The organs of his hands, from bone to muscle tissue began to rapidly decay until there was nothing remaining. He literally wasted away on the spot. At this point, Lance reached through the government official to recover the child and return her to her mother. Apparently, weeks before they even reached this particular planet, Cain used some neurotoxin that destabilized Kurgan DNA had put been introduced into the planet's food and water chain. Once the Kurgans began to stress, the physiological processes became a catalytic agent that caused the meltdown. It happened all over the planet, all at once. Cain knows that dramatic deaths are effective tools in psychological warfare.

Many of the outer territories had been taken over by liberated races that had once been under Kurgax Federation dominion. The Janitors had been dismantling the Kurgans, one system at a time. The Kurgax Federation had decided that it was time to accept the terms originally proposed by the IGF on the territorial borders; that was *before* the Kurgans had murdered Kush. The time for third party negotiations ended as soon as Cain received word that Kush had been assassinated.

He was also made aware of the taunts that the Kurgans made about how weak the Terrans were and how their god-king mocked Kush before he had his warriors kill the Chancellor's soldiers and then his cabinet members. Once the Kurgans had done this deed, many of the races that had correspondence with them had ceased to do so. The Federation knew better than to get involved in this situation. Collateral damage meant little to the Janitors at this point. The best thing for every other group in the quadrant was to stay out of this situation before they also go in the shit list.

The IGF citizens, from their civilian leaders to its military commanders to its everyday citizens, all knew that there was nothing to say because Cain was going to kill *every* Kurgan in the quadrant. The Janitors were going to kill any group or species that would grant the Kurgans *asylum*. There would be nothing that anyone or any group could say that would be a deterrent for the Blood Knights; these fuckers were about to get the business. The Janitors were going to burn and destroy any existence of the Kurgax Federation. There would be no DNA of that race of people anywhere in the universe. This type of extermination is disturbing for anyone who would witness it; which is why the Janitors' exploits are often spoken about but rarely ever seen in action. There are no curses or angry swears. These vicious operators do their jobs with smiles; and their victims wouldn't hear a thing.

This is their job, to kill and destroy. The Blood Knights were experts in killing a species in an efficient manner. They literally sweep the universe clean of that group's existence, hence the nickname. Nick and his crew were aware of what they are; monsters. They are the gifted, the deadly, and the necessary. The newest Alron had remembered reading notations in her comprehensive leadership reports that were marked *Clandestine Operations* in the past, but no one within the senior staff had ever discussed the codename Janitors. Every time that a notation had the word *Janitors* on it, it was quickly dismissed. It was an open secret; no one ever talked about what Cain had done unless they had to.

At this point, all of the people who had prior knowledge about the Blood Knights had been murdered and now these operatives have decided to respond to those actions with *extreme* prejudice. Those members of the hastily promoted leadership within the Alliance were now cognizant of the existence of the Blood Knights. However, they didn't know what that *meant*. The military leaders, in particularly the Naval Command

Operations didn't make any retaliatory plans against the Kurgax Federation. When the interim Corinthian Regent Aurelius inquired as to why there was no battle plan being proposed, Admiral Noelle Christopher replied unperturbedly to the question. **"No Lady Aurelius, you don't understand. They killed Kush; they killed Cain's *friend*. He is already aware of it. The Janitors have a way of solving problems that those problems remained solved. The Kurgax Federation has become Cain's problem. *He will handle it*."**

The rest of the regents were stunned. The military representatives all nodded in agreement. There was a chill in the room, a level of tension that many of these newcomers were not accustomed to. Interim Aquilonian Regent Daniel then inquired. **"Um okay so what does that mean? What are you preparing as a contingency if they fail at their mission? Actually a better question might be *what* is their mission?"** Christopher then responded coolly. **"I understand now; you don't realize that Commander Cain is our commanding officer. He doesn't answer to us, we answer to him. Sir, there is no contingency plan. The mission is simple: the extermination of Kurgax Federation. It is better for the rest of the Navy to stay out of Commander Cain's way. All of you are about to be witness to the true power in the quadrant, and *they're pissed*. They are the Janitors sir; Janitors don't negotiate. The Janitors' mandate is to kill; everything. The members of that unit will show no remorse and they will have no pity. They will not stop until all the Kurgans are dead. Anyone who gets in their way could end up dying on accident; and the Janitors won't give a shit. The Blood Knights have absolutely no intentions of leaving anyone with Kurgan blood alive. This is what the Janitors do. I can't make it any clearer than that."**

The Janitors were the secret behind the reputation of the Terran military. No part of the Terran war machine was as imposing. The Terran Navy is impressive and the star fighter core is also highly regarded. The Alliance Special forces and the light infantry were also well, thought of. The Paladins were known also as the fiercest warriors in the quadrant, but the Janitors were different. No group made the balance of the region quake like they did. The rest of the quadrant was already painfully aware that the Kurgans were an endangered species. The Kurgan people were on Cain's shit list; and it is *never* a long list. These people were marked for death; *all of them.*

There would be also be no sign of Kurgan innovation or commerce throughout the rest of the Virgo Super Cluster. When the Janitors decide that a species must be destroyed, they make sure that literally nothing is left. The mocking of Kush was the part that really put Cain in such a salty mood. Compassion is a representation of true strength as far as Nick is concerned; Kush had an abundance of it. The god-king took that as a sign of weakness. Driax was made aware by her mentors that this had to be done and there would be no reason to negotiate with the Kurgans. The Federation and Alliance ignored any vid-communications because what these condemned people had to say was of little consequence; in a very short period of time, the Kurgax wouldn't *exist.*

Donalwden, the most heavily fortified system within the Kurgax Federation was the last to fall. These beings of will preyed upon the fear of others were about to know what fear truly was. The commander of the planet declared they were prepared to die for their god-king and that they would be remembered for their bravery. Nicolas replied gleefully, **"your god-king gave you pride. My God gave me this. It seems to me that you picked the wrong one. Besides we aren't leaving any Kurgans to remember your bravery."** At that point, the Alpha Centauri's most powerful weapon, the (*fuck you cannon as it is affectionately known*) nova cannon, was activated. A powerful blast with the equivalency of a supernova destroyed the entire system. Eighty-four billion Kurgans had been eradicated.

Once the Kurgax Federation leadership received word that their most powerful system had been totally decimated, panic struck their entire race. Negotiations for peace were sounded off by the military. Up to this point, the arrogance of their aristocracy had been in abundance. They were made aware that only one Terran warship had been used to this point and they had no intention of showing any mercy what so ever. It was no longer a game. Changing their entire way of life was being discussed by a panicky group of people. The problem with those actions was simple: *the Blood Knights don't negotiate.*

Arrogant to the end, the god-king of the Kurgans said that they would not negotiate with the Terrans. His warriors were just as powerful. His most trusted operational commander declared that this position was madness because of the destructive actions of the Alpha Centauri. His reward was being hung by his entrails at the capitol building on Kurgan Prime. The god-king then promoted another soldier to his supreme commander and then demanded that the bulk of his forces attack the Centauri and destroy it. He also refused. This process of killing his military leaders continued until the king found someone willing to fulfill his mandates; 134 soldiers died at the hands of the king, who fancied himself a god.

48 hours after destroying Donalwden, the Blood Knights attacked what was left of the Federation's armada. The Delta-Wing Raptors, all 200 of them went out to face fifteen thousand star ships; and it was NOT a fair fight. Before attacking the fleet, Lance Blood-Joy, a man considered an artist with his raptor declared, **"I am making my mother's recipe tonight boss. And I am getting top kill also. Low person has to clean up the kitchen. Deal?"** Nathan, Lance's best friend and wing man was not happy with that proposition, because the kitchen will be mess when Lance is through cooking. Cain laughed and simply said, **"then don't be last. Top kill eats first. Deal?"** The destruction was incomprehensible. In a matter of 283 minutes, another 258 million Kurgans were killed. All fifteen thousand warships, star destroyers, and star fighters had been completely wiped out by the Raptors. Again, the god-king's arrogance would not allow him to accept the fact that the Terrans were not to be trifled with.

The god-king was angered at the results of the destruction of his mighty armada. He sat on his throne and one of his wives came to comfort him. The woman began to dance seductively and declared that Antonius was nothing compared to the great king and kissed him sweetly. She smiled at him and he snapped her neck and then he laughed; *useless*. He declared that the Alpha Paladin would die at his hand. He had reached the end of his rope. He demanded that his people prepare for a victory celebration that evening. His royal court and all of his key military staff were demanded to be at this celebration. He raised his glass and declared victory at this event, but didn't drink. Instead, he walked out of the room and it filled with poisonous gas and the rest of the people who were considered vital to the continuance of his species had been murdered at the hands of their king.

The god-king knew that the end was at hand. The Kurgax Federation had reached the height of its opulence. His people were weak and self important; not worthy of the greatness of their past. He looked around and realized that his kingdom should have never been brought to its knees by one man. He knew that his ancestry would be most disappointed with him in the after-life. His war strategists had miscalculated the strength of his people; he decided that they were too weak a race to survive. If the Terrans could send one ship to decimate his people, then his people's reign as a dominant race was now over. He could accept that, but his subordinates would not. He smiled as he walked amongst his dead subjects; his useless aristocracy. They were perfectly preserved and he sat on his throne and drank to victory in front of all his subjects.

26 hours after destroying what was left of the Kurgax Federation armada, the Terrans reached Kurgan Prime. The Alpha Centauri and the Blood Knights had reached their quarry. For the first time in this bloody campaign, Nicolas gave thought to the carnage that had been wrought on these people. *They have to be out of their minds*, he thought. The god-king was in need of a final lesson brought to his door-step. Cain told the Knights that it was time to take a look at their targets face to face. Lance and Nathan would accompany both AC and Antonius to the palace. It almost seemed pointless to kill so many and never meet the idiocracy responsible for them being massacred. He calls himself a god-king, even still after all that had been done to his people. *Time to show the Kurgans that a god-king can bleed*, AC thought.

She had known Antonius for most of his life; sure as anything if the king does anything to piss him off, Cain will kill him with his bare hands in front of what's left of the planet's nobility. Over the eons, he has gained a reputation for snatching vital organs, such as a person's eyes, out of the bodies of his enemies when agitated. As the knights entered the hall, they saw nothing but corpses, but the knights hadn't killed them; the god-king had. Only one Kurgan maid-servant, a blue-skinned woman with silver hair, remained. She begged Cain to not kill her, to show mercy. *I'll deal with you later*, the monster thought to himself. Mercy however was not on his mind. He now only had one target, the god-king.

The god-king was dressed in a garb of purple and green, in a material similar to silk. He had handsome features, save the red-skin; he and Cain could have been related. But the similarities stopped there. He was Cain's mirror, as conceited as Nicolas was humble. The god-king smiled warmly as if he had met a dear friend. **"Welcome Cain or is it Antonius, I forget,"** he sneered. **"You have so many names don't you?"** Nicolas, realizing that he was going to have to kill at least one more Kurgan sighed, **"I only have one title: executioner. You should not have killed**

Kush. He *wanted peace*." The king sneered again as he spoke, **"if he was the man that you are, he would have done to me what you have. The strong survive in the universe; not the weak or compassionate. The god he served must be weak; yours must be strong, like me, in order for you to do this to us. In your time, we have been here 4 billion years. Our time is at an end. I accept that fact. End it mighty Antonius. Yours has just begun. How does your musician say it 'always look a man in the eyes before you kill them'."** The Alpha Paladin replied to the arrogant god-king's request. **"No you are wrong. We both served the *same* God. I think that it is time for you to *meet* Him. And you are no king. But Kush was."**

The king was quiet and calm; it was a disturbing conversation to witness in person for AC and the others because the god-king was ready for Nick to end him. He had this almost joyous demeanor about the circumstances, as if he was honored for this to happen. He understood what many had come to know over the eons, crossing humans can be a species ending event. Once a race crosses the Terrans, the potential for that race's extinction goes up dramatically.

In truth, this is why the god-king of the Kurgax Federation was so excited about this set of circumstances; the finality of this encounter. The Terran Alliance and the Inter Galactic Federation were already allies whose view on society was opposed to the Kurgan way of life. His military advisors told the king what he wanted to hear; that even though these groups were powerful, neither could contain the power of the Kurgax Federation. The Kurgans had been long considered one of the true powers in this part of the Virgo Super Cluster. The king knew that it was only a matter of time before his mighty faction would have to deal with both the Terran Alliance and also the IGF; he believed that those groups would make excellent additions to his Federation and also cement his name in the lore of his people.

The dilemma was that the god-king knew that there were two warriors that he would have to deal with in both mighty factions. He figured Khan Antonius was far too dangerous to try and get into a conflict with because he had already experienced how precarious and unpredictable that he was. The IGF's champion had already proven how far he would go to prove a point; that he was the most deadly of all Oculari. That he was creature who danced between sanity and madness. He heard that Cain was controlled by a weak leadership; he could have killed Atlas but they stopped him. From that, he postulated that the humans had to be weak. The Kurgan monarch secretly hoped that he could defeat one of them and had the warrior who was subjugated would be his champion against the other. The god-king was of the hope that they would wage a glorious battle to the death. He didn't know they were the same person. Such a pity.

Now the monarch stands before the mighty Oculari who happens to also be the Alpha Paladin. By the time that his military was aware of the fact that Cain and Antonius were one in the same person it was too late. The God-King had already attacked Alron Kush's contingent because he had been given assurances that the Terrans would be so overwhelmed that their defeat would be a certainty. Furthermore, that the IGF would have so many issues with negotiation of a peace accord that his forces could decimate both groups potentially. The Kurgan best case scenario was that they could break the unity of the Alliance and IGF; either proposition was considered a win for the god-king and his people. He was surprised that the Terran response was to begin the total devastation of the entire Kurgan population did this terrifying reality become apparent.

When the god-king tried in secret to use the IGF as a mediator, his request was received by the Terran Senator, Aya, who laughed and replied, **"You idiot. Did you not learn from the last time you did this? What, you didn't know that Cain and Antonius were the same? The Janitors are about to give you the *business*. You didn't know that we had already given the kill order but *Kush* said no. You killed the only person who could have saved your species!!! I don't mediate for the soon to be dead."** Now there will be no more Kurgan people, there will be no Kurgax Federation. The great race of the Kurgan people will be nothing but another target that has been crossed off the Janitors' shit list. There is nothing left for the god-king to lord over because he now knew that the Oculari and Terran Paladin were one in the same. And now, he is standing right in front of him.

The monarch smiled and spoke sweetly to his executioner. **"How will I be remembered Cain?"** Nick was annoyed at the sheer arrogance of his foe, they all died for nothing. He began to take off his gloves, something he rarely does. Nathan began to turn away, but Lance steadied him. Nick began slowly walking towards the king, cracking his knuckles. Nick was ready to prove that this king was no god. *Time to bleed*, thought the brave Alpha. **"You talk too much; you have no kingdom. Your people** died because of your need to be remembered. So disappointing. Well back to the matter at hand; it's time to see if you have one." The king, the last of his race inquired. "Do I have what?" To which the Master Oculari replied, "A heart." With tears in his eyes, he spoke softly to the king. "You should really be thanking Kush. If it were for anyone else, you would die slowly." He then reached into the chest of the Kurgan. Kurgan skin is incredibly dense, much like stone. Cain was moving his hand around in the God-King's chest, searching for his prize.

There we are, thought the deadly servant of humanity. As he was reaching for the monarch's heart, he put his right index finger up to his lips and said, "Shhh." He then slowly ripped the monarch's heart out with his bare hands. The god-king died looking at his still beating heart, the last thing he would ever see. After the blood of the god-king had been spilled, Cain looked at the remains of the leader of a dead race. He then noticed the female servant cowering in the corner. She had no idea if he was going to end her life because she had been servant to the monarch. An even more disturbing prospect was that none of his troops were certain what he was planning to do next either.

At this point, Cain began to walk over to the woman and his second in command called his name. He continued walking towards the female and AC grabbed his hand. Commander Cain smiled at his subordinate and said, "it's okay AC, just one more loose end." The problem for AC and the rest was that the woman seemed to be speaking jiberish. None of the party had ever heard the language that the woman was using. All that is but Cain. He responded to the woman in her native tongue.

She was bare-foot and shivering with fright. She was surprised that he reacted as if he knew what she was saying. When they first walked in, she spoke a language that their translators had been able to decipher, but the more fearful she became, she began to speak in her native tongue. The servant bowed to her new master and cried softly, "Please don't kill me. I am the last of my kind." Nick looked at the woman and spoke, "close your eyes." She closed her eyes and began to cry. Lance began to object and Nick looked at him harshly. Lance then remained still. AC and Lance held hands, not knowing what why their master was leaning.

Antonius pulled out his katana and swung it violently; she screamed. The chains that were binding her had been cut. He sweetly spoke to the citizen, "dear lady. I know who you are. I know what you are; I have no quarrel with you or your people." The woman cried and tried to grab Nick's feet. She had never known freedom before. It was really hard for her to accept. She jumped into his arms and was shaking with fright. He gently embraced her and sang to her in her native language. It was a lullaby that he picked up in his travels. She was overwhelmed with both relief and fear.

The noble Paladin carried her to the god-king's throne and placed her there. Nick bowed to her and kissed her hands gently. She finally calmed down and spoke in a measured tone. **"I know of you; you are Lord Antonius, The Executioner."** Cain smiled. She then touched his handsome face, **"you know who I am don't you?"** The predator nodded and smiled. He spoke quietly, **"what's your name?"** She responded, **"The god-king never gave me one."** Antonius looked at her and said, **"what a dick: may I name you then?"** She cried. **"Yes my Lord."** He snapped at her, **"no, I'm not, you have no Lord; you are free. You are a queen, you always were. How does the name Trinity sound?"**

Cain recognized what his colleagues didn't: Trinity was the last of the Royal House of Lycoria. It had always been thought that her race had been extinct; apparently, that was not entirely accurate. The god-king thought it was humorous to make a noble woman of a race become his personal maid. Nick fixed that. Nick kindly explained that people of Lycorian blood when frightened revert back to their native tongue in a panic. It sounds much like baby gibberish. They also have a paralyzing fear of the sight of blood; in their culture, blood is sacred and they cannot be touched by someone who has shed it. The actions by the Janitors evoked a mania that she couldn't control. The only way to alleviate such fright was with a song of lamentation; which is what Nick sang to her. The kissing of the hands was also a custom of grace and good will to the Lycorian people. Antonius was just being polite.

Lady Trinity would become a devoted member of Janitors; she swore that as long as Cain was alive, she would follow him, no matter how much he told her that she didn't have to. She said that she would serve the Janitors because Nick had given her a home. He even gave her permission to end the Kurgan home world. She made the command to fire the nova cannon and removed the Kurgax Federation from existence.

By the end of the report on how the Kurgax Federation had been removed from the universe, every one of the new cabinet members, from Regent to vice Alron had been left speechless. There was a silence that was almost deafening. The Janitors could do this to anyone who they considered an obstacle to their objectives. These warriors led by the Alpha Paladin should always be given a wide birth. They answer to no one but Cain; he only answers to Driax. Everyone realized that being crass with the young chancellor could lead to a violent death. Chancellor Taylor Amani Driax should be given the best of their endeavors, save they face the wrath of the Master Oculari. It is safer to be polite.

Once Chancellor Driax told the Terran Leadership about the story of how Cain and the Knights destroyed the Kurgax Federation a great many things were learned about Nicolas' character. He was not to be trifled with and was prepared to do what was necessary. Petamauck seconded her stance by stating that when he went rouge, Cain was sent to deal with him and his band of usurpers; mercy was not given in that case either. If anyone can meet the expectations of the IGF and the Alliance and be willing to do whatever had to be done, regardless of the mandate, it would be Cain and his Knights. It would be wise to never doubt anything that Cain had to say; under estimating his resolve could yield deadly results. Nari the Wise then entered the room. Driax asked him to give a report on what could be known about Cain. He then reported the following:

Khan Antonius

Real Name: *Gaius Nicolas Cain*
Eye Color: Brown
Hair Color: Black
Height: 6'3"
Weight: 215
Earth Age: 33

Abilities
1. Immortality
2. Total Night Vision
3. Perfect Reflexes
4. Super Human Strength (Ability to lift up to 40 tons in Earth Gravity)
5. Super Human Speed

6. Knowledge of all forms of Terran Martial Arts and Several Iconian/Rioan/Oculari Combat Techniques
7. Super Human Agility

After hearing the "report" from Lt. General Nari the Wise, the regents were convinced that Cain was up to the task and also was comforted in the fact that if things were to ever badly, that he was on their side. Additionally, Driax position would be safe as well. She had gained the Alpha Paladin's trust and that was important. Now the leadership had a better understanding of why his word was so important. His nobility and faith were reasons to revere him just as much as his power was the reason to fear him.

Chancellor's Log: Alron Nefertiti

Personal Log: I have recently been rescued from the Gondronian warrior-king, Atlas on Colleria Beta, a mining colony. This has been as disturbing an experience as any that I have had in my career of service as Chancellor to the Terran Alliance. Today I was a witness to something; well to be honest, I really don't know exactly what I was witness to. A monster came to rescue me, *my* monster. However, I was mistaken on just who the monster actually was. I was always under the impression that the monster that we had at our disposal in case of terrible circumstances was always *the big guy*. He turned out to be Erik the Red. I was under the impression that he was the strongest and most resolute of all the Paladin order. On the day of my liberation, I found out that I was greatly mistaken about a great many things. I met the monster that day and I must admit that I am beyond terrified. It frightened me on a level that I cannot easily comprehend.

Let me start off by being honest about something; I was beyond petrified at this state of affairs. I had never been in operational circumstances before. How these people can keep their sanity in situations like the one I experienced is beyond me. I have a much better understanding of what I am asking of my troops now than ever before. Atlas was a sadist of the highest degree. When he touched me, I just wanted to jump out of my skin. If he decided to rape me, I knew he wouldn't just do it once. Even for a Gondronian, he was huge and he had told me that he was going to keep me as a prize. I could barely breathe inside; I knew what kind of existence that was going to be. Shit, where are my people; why haven't they come? Do they even know where I am? When I told him that my warriors were coming for me, I was bluffing. I was so afraid I forgot that my homing beacon had been activated. I was so glad when they came in. Then I only saw two men; I figured that one of them must have been Cain.

I actually heard them before I saw them; the sounds were so disturbing to my soul. You could hear this awful whistling sound while flesh was being carved up and there were these blood curdling screams and squeals. At one point, I took notice of an almost joyous cackle and then the words, **"Stop squirming and hold still; I am only going to ask you once. Where is she?"** The bigger of the two men had walked in first and he had already cocked his very large hand cannon. A smile crossed his handsome face; finally my liberation was at hand from these vile creatures. I had seen him before; he must be my monster. He spoke with a robust authority. **"She is in here Commander."**

At this point, I was shocked. He wasn't Cain; I had no idea of who it could be. The smaller man walked in and smiled. He was someone that I had never seen before. His eyes had a twinkle, he was handsome; his entire face lit up as he smiled. I felt a certain sense of ease when I looked upon him. He momentarily made eye contact with me and then he winked. I mean he actually winked. He spoke with a gleeful tone; as if he was going to enjoy the next few minutes. **"Hi. I am Commander Cain and I will be your executioner for the evening. Erik, please secure the hostage."** Then it happened.

It transpired so fast. I blinked and three of the Gondronians holding me hostage were dead. Blood was gushing from so many different places. Then he grabbed one of the warriors by the eye sockets and poked them out. As the blind Gondronian screamed, Cain then threw him against the wall, crushing his skull. Another had his throat ripped it out. One man actually shot his weapon and Cain dodged it. He jumped in the air and kicked the Gondronian in the sternum; it snapped liked a twig, Cain then pulled his sword and cut four more into pieces. I was petrified with fright. My God, what have you done? You made him like *this*.

At this point, he came upon Atlas. There they stood; two creatures of monstrous renown. The most terrifying thought to me was that the most dangerous monster was my own soldier. Atlas didn't even have a chance. Before Atlas could draw his weapon, Cain pull his own weapon and shot him in his knees. After that, he quickly head butt the Gondronian and then kneed him in the abdomen. With the blow to his abdomen, blood gushed from his mouth. Cain laughed and said, **"Look at him Erik! That's so gross!"**

At his point, my monster had a sad look on his striking face. Atlas was writhing in pain and moaning. Cain seemed mildly annoyed at the fact that he wasn't more of a challenge. My monster then grabbed him by his throat and lifted him off the ground. He spoke with a whimsical tone, **"*This* is the mighty Atlas; what a letdown. Time to meet God**

chump." Then he began to squeeze and Atlas began to struggle for every breath. I was so frightened; I almost pitied my kidnapper.

He was slowly, methodically squeezing the life from Atlas' body and I finally snapped out of it. I grabbed the monster and begged him to stop. Erik and Cain looked at each other and mouthed the words 'is she serious?' and Cain seemed amused at my reaction. He continued squeezing Atlas' throat; you could hear his neck being stretched. I said stop again. Cain looked like a child who had been told the word "no" for the first time. He frowned at Erik and he finally let him go.

The Commander threw Atlas to the ground and grunted with a disapproving tone. Then he smirked at Atlas, pointing his index finger and spoke **"You're lucky. Next time you die screaming."** Erik took me by the arm and began to escort me out of the room. This was the first encounter that I had ever had with Commander Cain. My God, what have we released upon the universe? He looked at Atlas and said the next time that the Gondronian would die screaming. I mean, who says that?

Whereas Erik was so attentive to my needs, Cain treated me as if I were a nuisance. He never spoke to me while we were traveling to the Alpha Centauri. Not only did he not speak, he never even looked in my direction. I was so shaken by what had happened; I was shivering cold. He never checked in on me once. While Erik could tell that I was still shaken by this ordeal, I don't believe my emotional state made Cain the least bit of difference. I thought he was still pissed about letting Atlas live. I could literally feel his anger. Being honest, I was more disturbed by the rescue than I was the actual kidnapping. I was still trying to get my mind around what I had just seen. At this point, I truly believed that Cain was evil. In fact, I believed that he was a different kind of evil; perhaps a worse kind.

Cain's display left me unsettled to say the least. I had never been around someone as gifted as he was in the art of death. What am I saying? He makes death seem elegant. I had been briefed on the gifts that the Alpha Paladin possessed, but those descriptions never did him justice. I kept thinking about the Angel of Death and wondering if Cain encountered him, would it be a fair fight? I had never known true fear until I was in his presence; Atlas made my skin crawl but Cain emotionally compromised me. His wit, his proficiency, and his ferocity in combat were frightening. That sword that he used was such a weapon of mass destruction in the hands of its master. I now understand the value of sending the *one right tool*. This is why the Alliance only sent two people; one to kill everything in his path and another to ensure that I wasn't collateral damage.

This experience was as if I had been witness to something that I was never supposed to see. Because of what the Gondronian had done, I got a chance to witness in person what so few had been witness to. To show just how out of sorts I was, I originally thought that Cain was angry with me, like I had intruded on his affairs. Erik assured me that wasn't the case at all. He informed me that Cain was angered at the fact that the protocols for my protection hadn't been followed to his specifications. Furthermore, he considered Atlas a loose end and Cain hates loose ends. He knew that he is going to have to kill Atlas sooner or later; he'd rather have done it then.

At this point, I had this terrible feeling about the course of actions that have taken place since I have been named Chancellor as well as all the terrible things that as leaders that we have all sanctioned. I have always delegated from the Golden Tower on Eden; I have never contemplated the damage, death and destruction that we sanction for the protection of our interests. I felt like a hypocrite because I was okay with authorizing such deadly and destructive actions, but as soon as I had to witness it in person, I was afraid of what I had seen.

The Paladins were always described as peacekeepers; but their outcome reports were wrought with violent and often bloody encounters. These warriors had always seemed so useless to me; I had never seen anything that had been remotely a dangerous situation. I always thought that having the Paladins around was not necessary. I didn't want to seem like I was using the resources of my station needlessly. I always wanted to use the Elite Guard because they seemed so much more impressive to me. In my mind, they dealt with issues in such delicate and beautiful ways. That my guardians had to be represent the ordered and advanced society that the Terran Alliance had become, at least that is what I told myself. Looking back on it, I actually had no reason to believe why that thought process was accurate.

I remembered once that the Ocularian Commandant suggested that I get to know Cain on more than an authoritative level. Senator Aya also requested the same thing and I was dismissive of her point of view as well. Both of these people said that Cain is actually a person that I need to make a friend. I rebuffed that position, stating that Cain worked for me.

That was wishful thinking on my part. After witnessing him in person, I am not really sure any more; the truth might actually be that *I work for him.*

Cain is nothing like I imagined. My monster really takes joy in what he does; he has this pleasant demeanor about his actions. He is efficient, sadistic, andpicturesque. When he was killing the guards, I wanted to turn away from the violence but I couldn't; he is actually quite stunning to watch. I really don't know how I feel about what he does. I am smart enough to know that what he does is necessary; but to witness it in real time is as disturbing an experience as I have ever had in my life. A part of me actually enjoyed watching him. What does that say about me?

I always wondered why we never saw the video reports of their missions; now I know why. *My God, he does this every time we send him.* I will never question the notation of *Janitor* ever again in our reports; from this day forth no one will. He cleans up evil. As a political actor, I don't have the point of reference to understand the tasks that have been performed by Cain and his warriors. From now on, only a recorded report of the mission summaries are necessary. We would merely be getting in the way of what they do best. Besides, I don't think that any Alron would ever truly understand what has to be done anyway.

I have an entirely different point of view on what the Paladins are now, that is solely because of Cain. My rescue gave me nightmares. I just wanted to get as far away from him as I could. I had been around dozens of Paladins, including Nari, AC, Petamauck, and had a friendly relationship with General Danyzer, but this young man was the first Paladin that actually *frightened* me. I have even met the Ocularian Commandant and he didn't even frighten me like this man did. I realize now that Cain could literally kill any of us or he could kill all of us if he felt it necessary. He could kill all of us just for fun.

When I was kidnapped, Atlas told me that an interested party wanted to create discourse in the quadrant. He told me that this was the least of my problems. Atlas' minions killed some of the best soldiers in the Alliance; my entire legion of Elites had beenexecuted. The Alliance response was to send only *two* men. I now understand why. In spite of what has occurred, I know that I am incredibly well protected, but if Cain had ever decided to go rogue there was nothing that we could do about it. The protocols designed to keep me safe literally mean nothing. There are groups of ignoble people out there; they have no honor nor play by the rules. I discussed it with the head of the IGF and he just laughed at my response. He told me that he was never nervous because he knew that Cain was the *very best of the very worst*.

It is difficult to admit, but both the Commandantand Senator Aya were right. She told me that Cain would be the most valuable asset that I would ever have as Chancellor. He told me that I should try to get to know him on some level. That he is actually nothing like the rest of the leadership has intimated. I didn't want to. I always thought that my job was to oversee the more important aspects of our people. Defense, in particularly the clandestine units of the Alliance, I always believed were far too messy. I hoped that I never had any direct dealings with Commander Cain. I even created layers of bureaucracy to ensure that I would have little to no contact with the Paladins unless I decided to. I felt as if he was just another member of my staff and I couldn't have been more wrong. That was my fault.

In my arrogance, I felt that my actions were enough. I see now that Cain will require a more personal touch. I cannot leave our dealings with him to people that don't understand him. Before the encounter with Atlas, he had never even heard my voice, much less seen me face to face. I must be more available to him. Major AC said that he had no family and that his parents died when he was just a child. What kind of upbringing could create such a being? Cain has nothing, but he ensures that the Alliance and the Federation have everything.

He deserves far better than I have given him. He deserves far better than we have all given him. It was my mistake that I took my most valuable asset for granted. I never even gave Cain the courtesy of a personal, face to face communication. How could I have been so arrogant? To his credit, he adjusted to the circumstances. He was completely comfortable with never speaking to me; I am ashamed. No matter how ridiculous the task I demanded, he always delivered on those mandates without question. I've never honored him. Not even a proclamation of a job well-done.

I must do a better job of dealing with him. I must make the first move in that direction. He never said one word to me when I was on the starship or even when he was rescuing me. Erik asked Nick why he never spoke to me; Nick said that there was no reason to speak because we had never spoken before. If that statement had been uttered by anyone else, I would have been haughty about it, but since it came from him, I knew that I deserved it. Erik told me that he was his partner, but that partnership wasabout to be severed because a tactical unit to carry out Cain's missions had been created.

When I returned to Eden, I realized that no one said anything about what had happened to me and honestly, I don't blame them. What was there to say? We never once mentioned the incident. It seemed so odd to me that no one in the leadership ever addressed my kidnapping or the security breakdowns that lead to Atlas creating so much havoc. I was told later by Regent Arcie that Commander Cain spoke to the regency when I was kidnapped, **"It doesn't make me any difference whose fault it was; I am going to get her back now. If this happens again, I am going to blame all of you. And then I am going to kill all of you, *because you are bad at your jobs*. This is the replacement business. Everybody gets *one*."**

The first people that I met with when I was returned were Senator Aya and the Ocularian Commandant. Neither of them was happy; I had never had an unpleasant conversation with either before this incident. When I spoke to Aya after I was returned, she was irritated with me. The Ocularian Commandant was furious at the fact that I hadn't spoken to Cain, except to tell him to *not* kill Atlas. He was so disgusted by my decision that he couldn't even look in my direction. Aya inquired why I didn't let Commander Cain kill Atlas. I told her that there was no need and that I was safe. She scolded me. **"I can't believe that you were so selfish. This was the perfect opportunity and you chose to think about yourself. That was so *human* of you."**

I realized at this point that Cain wasn't just a Terran operative and that he had obligations that were far more complex than I had believed. The IGF looked at my predicament as an opportunity to dispatch a problem and that my actions took that opportunity away. Atlas needed to be taken down, but because of his loyalty, Cain didn't get a chance to fulfill the second part of the mission. Aya told me that Cain had been given two mandates. The first was to make sure that I was safe and the second, more important priority was to make sure that Atlas was dead. Atlas had already left our territory and it would have taken Cain and Erik too long to hunt him down. He couldn't go back and finish the job because he had another pressing duty to take care of instead. Like Erik told me, it was a loose end.

Within 48 hours of me being returned and debriefed about the incident on Colleria Beta, Cain was gone again. I inquired to Major AC as to where he went and she said that it was classified; she had no idea where hehad gone. If I wanted to talk to the Commander, I was going to have to wait. I was taken aback at the fact that I was not privy to where *Khan Antonius* was going. I always *hated* that name; Nicolas sounded so much better.

The Major told me that he had IGF business and if I wanted to know, I should consult the Ocularian Commandant. At first the Commandant was hostile; **"so now you're interested in Cain eh? Well, he is *busy*."** I apologized for my previous stance and asked in a more polite tone. That seemed to please Nick's mentor. He informed me that the Dec'Lense had become a problem and the Oculari were being dispatched to eliminate them. Cain was tasked with carrying out the orders of the IGF High Command. I asked the Ocularian Commandant how many of them were they assigned with eliminating. He replied coolly. *"All of them."* It never occurred to me that Cain must navigate conflicting bottom lines at all times.

When he returned from slaughtering the Dec'Lense, I still never had the chance to speak to him because he was off again within 24 hours of his previous success. This time, it was another clandestine tasker that was beyond my clearance. I didn't even see Erik or Cain again for the immediate future; they were off to deal with another situation in deep space. I think that he left the entire Virgo Super Cluster; once again, it was *classified*. When he finishes his duties as an Oculari, he has obligations with the Paladins. My God, he never has a chance to rest!

After seeing what Atlas did after I allowed him to live, I now understand that Aya was right and that Cain had a right to be annoyed with me. Cain and Erik had two objectives and because of my actions, they only got to accomplish one of them. I will never make that mistake again. I now understand the term, the gifted, the deadly, and the necessary. I decided that he would never be referred to as a Paladin again. He is a stealthy predator who doubles as protector. The predator was seeking out new prey; the rest of us are just the bait.

A funny thing happened the second time that I had an encounter with the Alpha Paladin. It was a function in the Zerbian system. I had to make a speech on the value of stewardship and good will. It was nothing really, a speech that anyone is my position would have made many different times. When I retired to my chambers for the evening, I had a gift waiting for me on the mantle. I had received a single red-crystal rose. I was so touched because the rose was a *Red Fire Maiden*. It is one of the rarest plants in the entire quadrant. Not many know where these plants are grown, and the planet where they are found is nearly impossible to reach. With the flower was a hand written note that simply said, **"Your speech is just like my image of you; beautiful and rare."** I knew who it was. He never comes to events like that; he is always at events like that. At that point, I felt like the most well protected person in the universe. *Because I am.*

Chapter 5

Be Ware the False Prophet

As the Alpha Centauri races towards an uncertain future on Earth, a sense of both calm and anticipation grips the crew. AC, the brilliant second in command, is especially upbeat about the opportunity. She knows that Commander Cain, also known as Khan Antonius, has unfinished business in the Milky Way Galaxy. An old enemy has resurfaced there and it gives the Alpha Paladin an opportunity to address an obstacle to the main objective. And history has shown Gaius Nicolas Cain's favorite tactics for dealing with obstacles.

The Alpha Centauri is not only the most powerful star ship in the Virgo Super Cluster, and possibly, the known universe, it is also the fastest. In a time when light speed is common, warp speed necessary and hyper space folds are a luxury, its propulsion system is at the top of the food chain. Dr. Okx, the great Rioan engineer, and his then project assistant, AC, devised an engine that could only come from imagination. The system, Tachyon Pulse, is unlike anything that has ever been actually utilized in this section of the known universe. It is so unbelievably fast that many beings in the IGF and also the Terran Alliance don't believe that it exists.

The very essence of this propulsion not only violates every known belief about how the universe works, but it also violates every principle *which every other propulsion rule bends*. The rules that make FTL (Faster than Light) speed aren't just bent; they are completely obliterated. There are five levels of TP speed; its cruising speed already stretches the limits of comprehension. Not only is the Centauri equipped with it, but the Delta Wing Raptors as well. The fighters all have level one, but Wing Alpha has all five. Only two people understand the theoretic behind such power besides the genius engineer; one is the second in command of the Centauri, while the other has no known predators in the universe.

Furthermore the only other people that are even close to having the knowledge necessary to understand this propulsion system are actually members of the crew. That advantage alone makes this dreadnaught the most dangerous weapon in this stretch of space.

Major Sayied Faris was asked by Admiral Kun to describe the speed that Centauri can travel when necessary. **"I think the best way to describe the Centauri's maximum propulsion is this simple: think of something Admiral Kun; think of anything. In the time that it took for you to compose that thought, the Centauri can not only reach its objective, it will destroy it and already be on its way back home. It is literally beyond the speed of thought."** Between the Alpha Paladin, AC, and the Alpha Centauri as well as the Wings, it's no wonder that all relevant parties, the IGF, Terran Alliance, and the Dark Siders give Cain such a wide birth. The Milky Way Galaxy is 40 million light years from the nearest outpost of either the IGF or the Terran Alliance. In the last 32 hours, the Centauri has already traveled 39.9 million light years. They've already returned to their home galaxy and the ship barely used level one of its Pulse Drive.

Now that the Centauri has traversed the incredible distance of space between Planet Arcadia and the Milky Way, it is time for the senior staff of the mighty battle ship to begin preparations for the offensive on Earth. Cain also has another assignment that must take his attention temporarily away from his objective on Earth. There are more than seven thousand sentient species in this galaxy, a remarkable number for the size of this spiral galaxy. Usually only elliptical or merged galaxies are this numerous, where two galaxies have collided; this makes the Milky Way incredibly unique. Eventually the Dark-Sider Armada will attempt to take over this quadrant of the universe and because of its proximity within the Virgo Super Cluster; the Milky Way is strategically significant. Two billion Earth years ago was the last time that the siders attempted to invade this part of space was when they attacked the Andromeda Galaxy, the Milky Way's neighbor. The armies of the Andromeda, lead by the Rioans, rebuffed those attempts but at a great cost. More than 90 percent of the Andromeda Galaxy was deemed uninhabitable after the more than 300,000 Earth year struggle. Over fivethousand sentient species perished in this conflict, but the objective was met, the Dark-Sider Armada was defeated.

These victories indirectly lead to the development of the Terran Alliance and the framework of the IGF. More than four thousand bi-pedal sentient species that survived began to leave the Andromeda Galaxy and began seeding the rest of the universe. Several hundred species formed the IGF almost 60 million light years from Earth while the species like the Ne'Celadons and the A'mmonze remained in the Milky Way, just in case another Dark-Sider Armada attack was possible. Now after all this time, the siders are preparing to return. However, this time a group of Paladins will stand in their way, prepared to give their last breath to defend Earth and everyone else in this part of the universe. The IGF had given the Alpha Paladin and his acolytes' specific instructions to destroy the Dark-Sider Armada, no matter the cost. The Chancellor of the Alliance was even more specific; cut Atlas head off. The Gondronians were now on the Alpha Paladin's shit list. As stated previously, it is *never* a long list. Earth would be the base of operations for this galactic star cluster's defense. The people of Earth would have to fight; and the Blood Knights had only 12 to 18 Earth months to prepare them for this conflict. But first things first.

As the senior staff of the Centauri enters the main conference room the initial feelings of calm have been replaced with feelings of reflection and pensiveness. Finally the three senior members of the Blood Knights, Major Sayied Faris, AC, and then Nicolas Cain came in. Following these three was a fourth person. One of the youngest and newest members of the Paladin order, Kira the Strategist. As they sat down, another holographic image also was present. Chancellor Driax, the youthful, visionary leader of the Terran Alliance was present for the briefing. It was important for her to know just what the Janitors are going to be facing and also the big picture ramifications of what is about to happen over the course of the next year.

The strategist, Kira, the stunningly beautiful ivory manned daughter of AC the weapon maker began to brief all twelve people in the room. **"Greetings and Blessings to all. Madam Chancellor, Commander Cain, Lt. Admiral, Major Faris; here are the findings from Nari and Arazar's report. Earth has roughly 600 million people left out of a population of over 9 billion. From what our archivist have been able to gather, this is the course of events that lead to the demise of the population. Eighty-Six Earth years ago, the population was 9 billion and there were shortages of essentials to life; food and water, as well as fossil fuels. An American business found the means to cheaply remove salt from water. With the massive population of the planet,** the rest of the Earth felt a sense of relief. However, the Americans used this technology as leverage against the rest of the planet. It sold the technology to its allies, NATO, Japan, Israel, and Australia. They essentially bankrupted the rest of the planet.

There was desperation on a level that had never been seen. Muslim countries converged on Israel, which responded with nuclear force. Africa and the Middle East burned. 900 million humans died within the first eighteen months. Russia, desperate for the technology, joined forces with China to attack both NATO countries and Israel while India and Pakistan would attack Australia and Japan. As the war began to consume the planet, the United States didn't get involved until the Chinese and Koreans attacked Canada and Alaska. Then it got really bad."

As her comrades looked in horror at what their kinsman had done to each other, the Paladin continued her report. "During the conflict the Russians were double-crossed by the Chinese, who were using the Russians to keep the NATO countries occupied. No other country knew that the Chinese had developed a microwave-based weapon that could evaporate an entire country's water supply. Its weaponry could literally cook all the moisture out of any living thing. The Chinese used this leverage to force the countries from South America to attack the United States. Since the South American economies were being bled dry by the American's water based technology anyway, the Chinese threat didn't seem like such a bad proposition."

For many of the Paladins, this was the first time that they had heard a description of the depravity that their kin were capable of. The term Savage Landers seem to take a stronger hold for all of them as Kira continued. "Britain and France then upped the ante by destroying the Amazon rain forest. India and Pakistan and part of the Unified Korean Navy attacked both Japan and Australia simultaneously. America and Russia joined forces to attack China. The NATO countries, angered at America's actions to join with Russia then destroyed a water cleaning station in the Atlantic ocean forcing the Americans to respond. Israel then destroyed what was left of both Britain and France. India flattened Israel, based upon its treaty with Pakistan. Australia then bombed Shanghai and Japan destroyed Moscow. Japan also destroyed the entire western coast of South America, which in turn destroyed seven water cleaning stations along the Pacific Rim. The war never stopped. Eventually almost all the fresh water was destroyed. There are about 600 million scattered on five continents; Australia is unlivable. Most of the technology is destroyed. More than 90 percent of Europe's 3.4 billion people are deceased, both of the Americas are desert wasteland now; 88 percent of Africa is deceased and 92 percent of Asia is gone as well. The troops still fighting aren't fighting for anything in particular at this point; it's mostly out of habit. They don't know anything else. There was no one left to pull the plug."

Major Faris, being a fan of Earth history, as well as being an eternal optimist asked a question that would spark Cain's brilliant mind. **"What about Switzerland? Is it completely destroyed? Because if it isn't gone we might have a chance to turn this around."** At this point, Commander Cain had a perplexed look and then almost immediately after, a look of hope. As he looked at Sayied, they then looked at Kira; all three shared the same thought. All three of them made the same utterance **"CERN!!!!"** Even if Kima hadn't given them the same thought, she might as well have. Kira then let the rest of the staff in on the simultaneous discovery. **"CERN might be the key to everything. If Switzerland hasn't been completely destroyed, there is a particle laboratory there. Over 80 countries have ties to that place. The scientists there had been working with anti-matter. The facitlity was deep enough in the Alps that it might have survived. It was a better example than the United Nations; they actually worked together."** *Not bad*, thought Cain. However he knew that the other shoe would eventually have to drop.

Chancellor Driax sat through the meeting at this point with both hope and caution. She knew what was in the rest of the report that had not been addressed yet. **"What about the damping field? Please tell me that it is still intact. Since all that radiation has shown up on the planet, how long can the Solar System hidden from the Gondronians?"** Driax learned from Nick's adopted father the value being well informed; her inquiry brought a smile from the Alpha. Kira reported that Atlas already knew and was planning to invade. That's where the problem was; should the Knights attack Atlas and his minions or head straight to Earth? What to do, what to do? Then the commander, Nicolas Cain, spoke of his plan. **"That will be resolved now Chancellor. We shall split up into two groups. Kira will lead a contingent to Earth;**

their primary mission will be to protect the planet. Anyone who isn't a friend will die. I know that Atlas already has an occupation force on Earth; the knights will eliminate those who have no business there. Secondly, the engineers will use the CERN concept on the planet. Lance and Nathan are the best engineers we have and Thomas is our best agricultural specialist; the rebuilding of planet Earth will begin once the elimination of the Erixian vermin is complete. Ensign Uchida is our best strategic planner and is the best at resource development; they will start making the people ready for a better life. Honestly, this couldn't have turned out better."

Perplexed as to her apex predator's enthusiasm, the chancellor pressed him for more clarification. The Alpha Paladin answered. "The reason that this couldn't have turned out better is that if the Erixes hadn't interfered, there would have been only one way for the Earthlings to realize the strength of their kinsman. That would have been combat. They are that stupid. We would have had to kill a lot of them to prove our point. Effective? Yes. Efficient? Not in the least. There wouldn't be any reason for them to trust us. It would have been one occupying force taking over for another. Oh yeah, by the way, there are *only 30 million left,* not six hundred million. Your intelligence is old; Ocularian information is *always* more current. The Erixes have been busy."

Not only would the Earthlings not have stood a chance, it would have painted the Blood Knights in an unpopular light. Not that Cain had an issue with that, but it would have been inefficient; resources that would be expended unnecessarily. Yes, the planet was his number one priority, but killing his fellow man for no other reason than to show them who was stronger would have gone against the doctrine of his favorite chancellor, Alron Kush, and his new chancellor, Alron Driax. *Not very Christian,* he thought. The Erixes provided them an opportunity to be helpful without being hurtful. These people don't know the Paladins, the siders, the Terran Alliance, or about the IGF; first impressions were going to be placed at a premium at this point in time.

The second aspect of the plan would be a simple one. The Milky Way Galaxy has been under the siege of an old acquaintance of the Federation and the Alliance, in particularly Cain. Atlas is not from the Milky Way, he is actually from the Andromeda Galaxy. He is a famous warrior from the original Dark-Sider conflict. He is a Gondronian, a race of conquerors. He is known for his incredible hubris. They are everything that the Rioans are not; hostile, vicious, and cruel. The only reason that the people of the Andromeda Galaxy worked with them against the siders is because the siders were actually worse than the Gondronians. This race had crushed many free peoples of the galaxy and they were on their way to attack the Rioans, the last hope for freedom in the Andromeda Galaxy, before the siders invaded. Only out of a sense of self preservation did the Rioans and Gondronians have to put their mutual disdain for the other aside to fight against a common foe. Once their common foe was vanquished, the Gondronians resumed their quest for domination.

These beings are similar to both Terrans and Rioans; they are bigger in size than either race and have grey skin with red eyes or they have pale blue skin with pale yellow eyes. The males and females are equally deadly; they give no quarter and show no fear in combat. Even for a Gondronian, Atlas is huge. They live by one code in particular though and that is that the strongest shall rule. This is the rule that Cain hopes to exploit. If the Alpha Paladin can best Atlas in single combat, he would rule the Gondronians and all that the empire controls. It is believed that the empire controls almost 40 thousand light years, with nearly 19 quadrillion beings on over ninety two hundred star systems. Those numbers will come in handy for the conflict to come. The game is on.

It is Nick's favorite time now; right before the beginning of an operation. This is when he gathers his thoughts and goes over the action plan inside of his head. The process by which Cain prepares mentally for the operation is actually quite fascinating for the rest of his fellow comrades to watch. He thinks about the infinite possibilities and worse case scenarios and then he thinks of how he would counter all of those things. His preparation takes him to the deepest corners of his mind and also the depths of his very soul. No one in his senior staff has ever disturbed him during these moments, in part out of respect and more importantly out of fear at disturbing him needlessly. However, Ensign Emily Uchida, one of the newest Paladins was either incredibly brave or foolish. Now that he is aware of her presence, she will find out which one.

For a Paladin, this warrior was relatively unremarkable. Emily Uchida wasn't the best graduate in her class. She wasn't a deadly fighter pilot on the level that Kira was, nor was she an empathic like Kima, nor did she have any distinctive skill or noteworthy accomplishment that made her such an important member of the graduating class under Petamauck.

As a cadet, she was never tapped for special missions or anything else. Her secondary disciplines were architecture, project management and infrastructure. The most remarkable thing about her career at this point was that she was known for asking very interesting questions; she tended to see what others didn't.

Everyone was surprised when she was tapped for the Janitors. When Nick picked her, she didn't move because she thought that he was referring to her classmate standing next to her, Hayden Don Arthur. Don Arthur was a big, strong warrior who was considered in the same class with Kira in terms of combat ability. It seemed like a natural mistake. He began to follow Nick and the rest. Without looking, Cain replied coolly, **"I wasn't talking to you. I was talking to *you;* come along little one."** He even smiled; Cain's reputation was that he *never* smiles. It was time for her to try and get answers as to why she was there.

At this particular time of preparation, the mighty Khan has chosen to be in the Centauri's greenhouse. The Alpha Centauri is capable of producing both oxygen and carbon dioxide naturally and with the solar collectors; it also has the ability to create photo synthesis artificially. The agro/eco engineers have done a remarkable job. An entire Terran ecosystem exists on the ship; the central eco/agri hub is a place of Zen for the Alpha Paladin who constantly takes advantage of it. Emily notices that Cain is sitting in a gazebo watching the waterfall be a waterfall. He speaks to her without looking. **"Come and sit down Ensign."**

A moment of panic washes over the young Paladin. **"I didn't mean to disturb you; I didn't know you were here."** Nick smiles and speaks in a nonchalant tone. **"It is okay, lying is so unbecoming little one. You can stay."** Emboldened she began to ask him a question. Nick cuts her off. **"That doesn't mean that you can *talk*."** Emily was watching him as he was surveying the environment. There was so much going on; she had no idea what had captured his attention. She couldn't help herself. **"What are we looking at?"** Nick puts his right index finger up to his lips. **"Shhhh, you're going to miss it."** She tries to follow his eye movement but can't keep up. **"Miss what sir?"** He smiles and says pleasantly. **"Everything; just watch."** He then looks towards his left and speaks again. **"Right there; you see that little one? That is so perfect. Just look at them; so efficient, so beautiful and so deadly."**

Uchida has no idea what he is talking about. She doesn't know if she is stupid because she can't follow his thought process or whether she should be angry because her commander has decided to play a joke on her for disturbing him. Before she can say anything he speaks again with more urgency. **"I love coming here because it clears my head. I love watching how the ants operate. They go up into the tree and get only the resources they consider necessary, go back to their home and then the rest of them either organize theprovision or prepare to defend their home. I have been coming here for a long time and no other creatures have ever conquered them. They are out manned; they are small force, but look at how incredible they are. They stand their ground and safeguard who must be protected. No other force in this ecosystem has ever beaten them; I admire that."** Emily finally begins to see what her commander is witnessing with glee. She began looking at the ants, the tiny ants; the mighty ants. A colony of bulldog ants was about to attack the smaller ant's mound. The smaller ants began to defend their encampment and then they proceeded to slaughter them. It was efficient, brutal, and uncompromising. The display of complexity and brutality seemed familiar to her. These vicious, noble predators shared commonality with her family; the Janitors.

Since Cain had been in command of the Alpha Centauri quiet moments told him many things about his crew. He knows that all of them are incredibly capable of following his orders and every once in awhile, one of them even understands why he has chosen some specific course of action. In this case, this was a special time because this young Paladin actually gained insight into Nick himself. He knew that she was the right fit for this very important job. Cain always trusts his instincts the first time. Second guessing is never a good thing for an Oculari; lives could be lost in his hesitation. Eons of combat experience and faith in the fact that God doesn't do anything random tends to align the commander's frame of reference.

She understood everything that she needed to know about her commander. Emily began to leave and Nick smiled. **"Understand Commander?"** Just like that, Cain had made a decision that would change the course of the young Paladin's life. While he did put Kira in charge of the defense of the planet and the solar system, he didn't specify who would be in charge of the entire operation. Someone would have to be in charge of this daunting task; someone who knew what questions to ask and would be smart enough to marshal the resources to fix their problems. In that instant, he sharing that moment with her was all the time that he needed. The youngest officer in the Blood Knights just received the fastest command promotion in history. She wasn't asked if she was ready; she proved it by her actions. By his actions, Cain told her that she had his trust. No more words needed to be spoken. Emily smiled and replied excitedly to her commander. **"Understood sir."**

In two different directions did the Blood Knights split; a squadron of Delta Wing Raptors, led by Kira was racing towards Earth, while the mighty Alpha Centauri was headed towards a meeting with a hated rival who Cain has decided has lived far too long. Both groups have their orders and will execute both of their charges with brutal efficiency. This is the first combat command assignment for Kira, she is lucky to have both Nathan and Lance by her side. Nathan is usually the second in command of the Wings in combat, but he doesn't have a problem with taking orders from Kira. In part because he trusts his commander to make the right choice and furthermore he knows that AC's children are probably the most prepared of all the new Paladins. Lance is Nathan's best friend and right hand; if Nate is fine with it, then so will he. Emily is known as a brilliant orator, her skills will be put to use.

As the raptors, thirty-five in total, reach the edge to the Terran Solar System, all the pilots stop their chatter to begin their moments of silence before the deep breath. There are nearly 4,000 star ships between them and their objective. It should not be a difficult task for a group as accomplished as the Blood Knights, but this is different. This is for their *home*. Never has a task seemed surreal as the one that they are about to partake. There is no doubt amongst any of them; the vermin will be slaughtered with Paladin competency.

Even though this is not another day, the routine is kept. Lance finally makes the announcement, **"Kira, I know that you are squad leader, but it's still your turn to cook!!! You know the rules, top kill eats first and,"** Nathan, Lance's best friend chimes in, **"low kill has to clean up. It won't be me!!"** A smile flashes across Kira's beautiful face, her cheeks flushed red and her emerald eyes sparkle. She appreciates the fact that neither Lance nor Nathan has complained about her appointment as strike team leader. Nathan and Lance have both been with Nick since before she was born and they accept her as commanding officer. She says only two words. **"Let's go!!!!"** The slaughter was glorious. In one hundred eighteen minutes, more than 3,950 Erixian ships were destroyed. The rest were in full retreat mode. Never had their enemies seen such incredible defeat. They never saw it coming.

The Paladins, not known for their generosity reached Earth but hadn't penetrated the atmosphere. All of the beautiful instruments of death had surrounded their home world. *Amazing*, Lance reflected. Even with all the war and destruction that had taken place on this planet, it still glowed. With all that the inhabitants had done to it, the Earth was still beautiful and green. You could see the damage that had been prevalent, but you could also see the resiliency of this world. A world so beautiful that only God could have conceived it. How could the Alliance ever consider giving this up? Lance had grown up on Aquilonia; he thought that his home was the most beautiful Terran world, until he came home.

Still with a job to finish, Kira gave instructions to Emily, an orator that rivaled Petamauck himself. *Okay Commander, do your thing.* Emily opened up a channel to the Erixes that were left on Earth and also to the Earthlings who could hear her communication. Her words were of strength, compassion, and wisdom. **"To the vermin who have unfairly occupied a star system that does not belong to you, I have a message. The Blood Knights of Terra have come home. Almost all of your fleet has been destroyed and the few ships that survived are in full retreat. We did this in a matter of moments; imagine what horrors we have for you on the planet that remain. Today is your lucky day. Because we have not been home in so long, we are going to do something that is against Paladin nature, you have an hour to vacate our home. In the 61st minute we will kill everyone who isn't a Terran and because you insulted us, we will go to your planet and kill everyone there. This is the extinct of our mercy. We do not want to, but if you think that we are mocking you, try and communicate with your fellow Erixian ships. There will be no answer. To our liberated kinsman, we expect your hospitality. The clock is ticking."** Within nineteen minutes, remnants of the vermin that invaded the Terran home world have left the planet. The exiting force was relieved to tell the tale of the horrors given by the Blood Knights of Terra.

As the wave of Blood Knights led by the youthful Paladins met their objective, their accomplishments were being matched and exceeded by their master. As the mighty Alpha Centauri reached Gondronian territory, the mission became clear: the complete extermination of the Gondronian species. The Blood Knights showed no mercy to the Gondronians, a beautiful display of annihilation that these warriors had not known since the time of the Dark-Sider offensive. The difference was that the siders were an endless hoard of warriors and battle mecha. The siders were known for sacrificing millions to achieve one objective. This destruction was different; only one Colonial Class Ship with a contingent of 165 star fighters was doing this.

This destruction was as brutal as it was effective. In three hundred twenty-seven hours, more than 259 billion native Gondronians had been laid to rest by the Paladins of Terra. The Paladins didn't try to reason with them nor did they try to negotiate with them. One slaughter was particularly chilling. A transport ship carrying only 10 Paladins, led by Cain had crashed their ship into the flag ship of one battle group. Those Paladins then proceeded to kill a crew of nine hundred without using a blaster, just hand weapons. All while the Centauri broadcast this show of glorious mayhem to the rest of ships within this battle group. Bones were broken, screams were heard and blood was being spilled, this was the Paladins, in particularly Cain at their brutally destructive best. The Gondronians, warriors who were known for their strength of will were having it broken in ways that they could have not possibly imagined.

As Nick and his strike team had decimated the crew of the mighty flag ship, the brave commanding officer demanded that Cain face him in hand to hand combat. Since they were ahead of schedule, Cain decided to grant the captain's demand; *he had a few moments to kill.* The soldier took of his battle uniform and attacked Cain in a full sprint. He tried gashing Cain with a shard of glass, but Nick sidestepped him and the used a roundhouse kick to the captain's ribs, cracking them in the process. The Gondronian then attempted to punch Nick and he dodged that also, then the master assassin broke the soldier's right ankle with another accurate kick. As he was on his knees, Nick then snatched out both of his opposition's eyes.

The officer was screaming in both terror and pain; the noise was irritating Nick. Cain then incapacitated his vocal cords which made him squirm even further. The squirming bothered the Master Oculari even more than the screaming so Antonius then snapped the officer's spine. *That's better,* thought the Oculari. Whistling the tune Whistle While You Work, Nick then dropped a plasma module into his ocular cavity; he melted his brain and his head exploded. What a glorious picture! *God*

I love my job, thought the mighty Alpha. After killing the commander of the flag ship in hand to hand combat, Cain, with the blood of his victims all over his handsome face looked into the view screen and made only one statement. Smiling, he said quietly, **"Atlas, your time has come. I am a man of my word."** This was a chilling reminder to all, including the Paladins, Terran Alliance, the IGF, and even the Dark-Sider Royal House, that Khan Antonius was indeed a *monster*.

Atlas saw the images, graphic and horrible as they were, and was happy. The final veil removed. *I knew that the boy had this inside of him*, the king mused. He summoned his most trusted aide; finally, someone worth killing. *He is so strong; I will have to be at my best*, the mighty warrior king pondered. *His queen must have died. There is no way that she would have let him kill so many of my warriors. That means he will show no restraint. Not like the last time I saw him. The monster is so revolting, so striking; I cannot wait until Cain gets here.* As his adjutant returned, the mighty Gondronian sends a word. **"Tell Antonius that he does not have to kill anyone else. Give the Centauri free escort, not that they need it, here. I will have no more of my warriors die without cause. He is just warming up, it is all about me."** At the same time, in two different parts of space, the two vicious predators smile. This has been a long time coming.

Over 470 rotations ago, these two warriors met in combat. Atlas was given a contract to kidnap the Terran Chancellor. Normally a warrior of his reputation would not involve himself in such matters because there was nothing to be gained by doing it. This however, was an exception because of who this Chancellor was. Nefertiti was the first female high Chancellor of the Terran Alliance. By kidnapping her and holding her hostage, this could destabilize the entire quadrant. The IGF would immediately be blamed for such an incident and war would be inevitable between the Alliance and the Federation. This is exactly what the Kurgax wanted. The leader of their people is a friend to the Gondronians; it's also an opportunity to get a look at those Paladins up close that Atlas had begun to hear about.

The Gondronian monarch knew that the Rioans had been involved in their creation and wanted to see what these super warriors actually looked like. Terrans are not naturally strong like Atlas' people; they had to be made that way. He wanted to see what happened and store that information in case he ever had to see the Terrans in combat later. After all, Atlas knew he controlled the Milky Way and Andromeda galaxies; eventually it would come down to the Terrans or the Gondronians and the time would be sooner than later.

Atlas and his warriors attacked an IGF function and kidnapped the chancellor. They took her to the Collerian system to wait for their reward. Even for a human this chancellor was beautiful. She was tall for a Terran; she had caramel skin and brown eyes. Atlas was smitten, he thought about making her his instead of following through with his contract. She will make an excellent prize. *The Kurgax would just have to be angry*, he mused. At this point, the Chancellor asked him what he was going to do with her and Atlas told her that he was going to take her to his system to become his property. Nefertiti then told the great warrior king of his dilemma. **"I am not a prize; I am Chancellor of the Terran Alliance!! Going with you is out of the question!! I suggest that you use me for leverage instead. In a few moments, my monster will come for me. It may not be in the mood to negotiate. If you let me go before it gets here, hopefully I can stop it from killing everyone in your race. My monster delights in dispensing pain."**

At this point, the warrior king realized that the chancellor was trying to protect *him*. Then before he could respond, he heard something unknown to him before. A sound. A song was being whistled while bones were being broken. (Time is On My Side) He had never heard a Gondronian scream in terror before. Not till then. There were nine of his finest warriors, all killed in the most gruesome of circumstances. Then the monster walked into the room with an inappropriately gleeful tone in its voice. **"Hi my name is Nick and I will be your executioner for the evening!!"**

When Nick and Erik came for the Chancellor, Nefertiti was shocked. She had seen Erik the Red; he was powerful and handsome, from the moon of Carthage. That being said, she never actually knew his name. She was miss-informed; he was not the Alpha Paladin, but she made the mistake of thinking that he was. He carried two huge broad swords and huge hand cannon. Aya had tried to get her to meet the leader of the Paladin's but Nefertiti had declined. Aya told her that she had made a mistake. Then she saw the man. He was so young. He had a shaven head with bronze-like skin.

To the Alron, she had no idea just how misinformed she had been. Nick isn't as big as Erik, but in many ways, he is far more frightening.

He had his katana already pulled out and had already killed four of the Gondronians within a manner of moments; he was so efficient in his actions. The chancellor couldn't get over how young he looked. *This is the monster*, she pondered. *Why he is just a baby*, was the thought that continued going through her mind. Then the youthful operative showed her why he was known as a monster. He punched a warrior through his chest, destroying his heart. Then Nick reached into the rib cage of another warrior, pulled out three ribs and threw them like darts, killing the other three remaining foes. It happened so quickly, so violently; the chancellor could barely comprehend what she had been witness to.

Before Nefertiti could get her bearings on what had just occurred, the Alpha Paladin, the age of a young adult had already snatched up the warrior king by his neck and was about to deliver a final death blow, she ordered him to stop. The point had been proven; the chancellor's monster was the *Ocularian Master Assassin*. When she told him to stand down the chancellor was so disturbed that she grabbed the young Paladin and softly said, **"that is enough, you have done enough."** In all the time that she had called the Paladins to duty, she had never thought to meet Nick. She had tears in her eyes when she made the command; how could she be sending such a child to die? She commanded, he responded; that had always been the ebb and flow of their relationship. The thing was that the chancellor had never *seen* Nick before. She had no idea that he was *so young*. How could this boy be so deadly? Cain then smiled and as Erik escorted her to safety, walking out the door, quietly the monster made a statement of fact. **"Next time, you die screaming."** Atlas knew that would not be last of that monster. *He is only going to get worse*, thought the kidnapper.

Never before or since had had Atlas dealt with such a menacing presence. From what the mighty Gondronian champion could gather, Cain was more. He was stronger, faster and far more vicious than he remembered. The agent that was dispatched by Cain was one of Atlas' best warriors. He was in the ballpark of Atlas in terms of combat ability and Cain quickly dismembered him. Atlas knows that his best may not be merely enough to handle Cain. This time, Cain had come for him and no chancellor or anyone else was going to stop him. Atlas was unsure of why Cain had come or what the endgame was because it really didn't matter. One of these warriors was not leaving this planet alive.

The mighty Centauri had reached Gond Prime, home planet of the Gondronians; the powerful weapons were pointed at the capital. To prove the level of peril of their situation, only Wing Alpha headed towards the surface. No escort for the Alpha Paladin; no wing man for the Master Oculari. As Cain walked into the great stone castle on Atlas' capital planet, the only thing that was heard was the psychotic whistle. There were whispers amongst the Gondronian Aristocracy of the fact that no one had ever dealt with the Terran and lived to speak of it. *This* was the monster that was in the stories that scared children.

Unlike the Kurgax Federation, the Gondronian hierarchy had been made aware of the fact that Khan Antonius, the Master Oculari and the Alpha Paladin, was actually the Terran known as Cain. These two apex warriors of the Oculari and the Paladin clans were one in the same. There was even a rumor that as a boy he once had Atlas by the throat and only his queen had stopped him. Or how he had killed the god-king of the Kurgans and destroyed their entire race. It was revealed that he was the one who had obliterated the Unori, smashing their system to dust. That there had been several factions throughout the Virgo Super Cluster that had crossed this warrior and none of them lived to tell the story. The entire great meeting room was buzzing with dread.

As the mighty Antonius continued walking towards his meeting with death, a young Gondronian officer crossed his path. He was huge, standing nearly 3 meters and he was seemingly at least twice the size of the warrior that he had dispatched on the flag ship. The young warrior bellowed at Cain, **"Where are you going little man? No human has ever passed through the halls of my ancestors. And no one ever will."** Nick smiled at the proud warrior. The great hall heard a shriek, then nothing but footsteps and a whistle. The giant Gondronian walked in first, smiled and then his head fell off of his neck. He fell dead and several of the high society of the Empire stood in shocked silence. His head rolled and stopped in front of the adjutant. The mighty Alpha Paladin walked in and stepped on the warrior with blood gushing from the wound that he created.

The Gondronian war drums beat slowly and had an ominous tone. A smile crossed Nick's face and then he spoke, **"you owe me something Atlas."** The king confidently responded, **"And what is that?"** The Alpha Paladin repliedpleasantly, **"your life. I have been letting you borrow it; time to collect on your debt. *Oh yeah, how's the knee*?"** Nick then put his trusted blasters down and took off his coat. He carried only his Katana. Cain's favorite weapon was a Japanese sword but created with a material unknown to many in the universe. Atlas, the greatest warrior of his people pulled out his own bladed weapon; a staff made of the finest metal in the empire. The two warriors smiled, knowing that the end would be swift for one of them.

These two predators begin to circle each other, like two vicious lions fighting for the right to be king of the jungle. Atlas spoke softly, but confidently. **"The things they say about you; that you are the best and strongest of all humans. Is it true that you snatched the Kurgan's heart out of his chest? And how is that pretty thing, Danyzer's child? I'll bet she tastes so sweet!! I can't wait to see her after I am done with you."** Nick was irritated but not at what Atlas said; it was just the fact that he was talking period. Nick finally smiled and spoke to the Gondronian champion. **"I am happy that you have an audience; they will get to see you as I do. You are nothing but a coward and a bully. You only attack groups of people when you have advantages; you are a front runner, not a warlord. You remember the last time we saw each other? I haven't. My old mistress had to keep me from ending you then and there. My new mistress doesn't mind the blood. She likes to** *watch.***"**

The crew of the Centauri watched on the view screen. Many were taking wagers on whether the Gondronian would even *touch* Cain. The apex predator was ready to send the Gondronian into the after-life, just like everyone else who was unfortunate to cross the deadly Paladin's path. He pulled out his Katana from its sheath. Cain, serene and secure smiled and said softly, **"are you ready to begin?"** Then it happened.

Their weapons clanged and sparks flew from the weapons with great speed. Cain rarely makes noise when he fights, he is normally whisper quiet. The mighty Atlas did what very few warriors ever do to Cain; he knocked him off balance and Cain lost his sword. Then again, Atlas is almost a meter taller than Nick. For eight minutes it seemed as if the warrior king would be able to stay in the fight. Until he made the mistake of mocking Cain, the Paladin had intended on letting him die in front of his people with dignity. Atlas said assertively, **"Little man, maybe your whore queen was protecting you from me. If this is best you can do, I should have taken her from you!!"**

With a look of annoyance, Cain decided that his life had been long enough. Antonius decided to get up, but he didn't even bother to pick up his blade. He dusted himself off and then smirked; AC shut her eyes. She knew what that look meant. Atlas' end was near and it was going to be ugly, very ugly. He ran straight at Atlas and at the last instant, avoided Atlas' blade in the process by dodging his spear thrust. As Cain made the Gondronian miss, he took advantage of Atlas being off balance. Cain bent down on one knee and punched Atlas in the same knee that he shot him in when he rescued Nefertiti. Atlas winced in pain. Nick smiled and said, **"Sound familiar?"**

Atlas again tried to attack Cain, but the Alpha was again too swift. Nick rolled off the emperor's back and in the same motion of gathering his balance, he kicked Atlas right in the face, shattering his right jaw bone. Atlas slashed at Cain with weapon, cutting him across his forehead. Cain sneered and said sweetly, **"I'm bleeding. This is good. I am glad that you finally decided to participate."** Atlas then tried to cut Nick down in a chopping motion, only for Cain to grab both of his hands in a test of strength. Neither had a weapon, but the Gondronian was still outgunned.

As Cain began to force the mighty monarch to the ground, he changed tactics. Cain broke the hold, speared him with his bodyknocking Atlas into wall, and in the same motion rammed his head into Atlas' chest, splitting his sternum. As Atlas slumped over in pain, Nick then used the crown of his head to lift the victim quickly. Blood spilled violently from Atlas' mouth. Cain then giggled, **"I told you that she didn't mind the blood."** At this point, Cain was ready for this exhibition to end; he drop-kicked his opponent in the face. The kick was so hard and accurate that Atlas went blind in his left eye, with the ocular bone crushed from the force and his eye burst from the pressure. Atlas had been dismantled in front of his Gondronian leadership. As the fight had ensued, there were low murmurs of joy at every blow that Cain landed. The monster that was Atlas was near his death, but some of the leaders, in particularly Congo became concerned. What if the Terran was worse than Atlas? Cain was a different kind of evil; perhaps a worse kind.

This was cruel and unusual punishment in the truest sense of the word. As Atlas was trying to crawl away, Nick walked up behind him and crushed his right ankle and lower tibia. As the warrior was screaming in agony, Cain picked up the steel bladed weapon and skipped back to

Atlas. Using speed that the warrior had never seen, Cain severed all of his limbs off Atlas' body; with his personal weapon no less. *My, this is sharp*, thought the Alpha. Sayied and Kima were on the ship giggling. Nick let her into his mind so that she could feel his satisfaction. Kira was wondering when Nick decided to start integrating White Lotus into his primary attack. *He must be trying something new*, she mused. As Atlas was lying on the floor writhing in pain, Nick laid down on the floor next to him mimicking his murmurs of pain. Atlas' weapon had been the symbol of his cruelty over his reign; he would be the last person killed with it.

On planet Eden, the youthful chancellor, the Ocularian Commandant, and the Terran Senator from the Federation were having a conversation. The senator spoke gleefully. **"What did I tell you Driax? I told you that he would kill Atlas in less than 15 minutes! And you need to pay up on our wager friend."** The Alron looked puzzled. **"Senator did you expect him not to kill Atlas quickly? So Cain is now the King of the Gondronians? Doesn't that go against his code?"** The Commandant laughed. **"I told you she was smart. The reason that we had that wager was because if Nick really doesn't like the person, he is known for taking his time. He's only efficient when he has other things on his agenda. Yes dear Driax, Nick's plan is right on schedule. We are going to have to wait awhile for the *next* part."** The chancellor understands that she is in the presence of two of the most cunning, intellectual, and sadistic citizens of the IGF. She was afraid to know what plans that those two and her monster could have contemplated, but felt she had to ask it anyway. **"What plan are you speaking of?"** Aya patted the chancellor's hand and while Aya shrugged her shoulders, sighed joyously. **"It is better that you don't know dear. *Plausible Deniability* is the term that you need to become familiar with when it comes to the actions of our son. God, you are so lucky that Nick loves you or he might be doing these things *to you instead of for you.*"**

What the Chancellor was finally becoming aware of is the agenda of the Alpha Paladin. Nick understands that many of his activities are monitored. It is not enough to kill his targets; he must also put on a show for all those that are able to see him at work. He wants his potential opposition to know just how painful their deaths will be and also to his allies for them to never forget just how brutal and sadistic he can be if the mood suits him. Everyone in the Milky Way knew how deadly and powerful that Atlas was and saw that Cain dispatched him rather easily. It was apparent that Atlas would no longer be on the shit list; these actions were examples of why Antonius' list is never very long.

Atlas had caused so much suffering to so many peoples of both the Milky Way as well as the Andromeda Galaxy. He is the epitome of the vile, the crass, and the condescending leaders in the universe. As he lay on the floor bleeding and panting in extreme pain, Cain lamented on the position that his kaepa, Danyzer had been placed in. He was forced to negotiate with this beast. To his credit, Danyzer kept his word and left this section of the Virgo Super Cluster after he had to destroy most of the Andromeda in order to defeat the Dark-Siders assault. The general had always hoped to return to this region of space and remove Atlas, but circumstances didn't allow for such actions. Now Nick has the opportunity to send the piece of filth into the after-life. There would be no pity shown to Atlas, mercy was not in the Oculari's protocol.

Danyzer and many of the Rioan High Command were also watching these events unfold from their headquarters. Many of the leadership of the Rioan Corps were watching at how their supreme warrior, Antonius, had rather easily dispatched their greatest enemy. It was Atlas' actions that created the situation for the Rioans and many of the free peoples of the Andromeda to leave this part of the star cluster and form the IGF. Danyzer's youngest son had faced Atlas in combat before the truce had been approved. Atlas killed him in a very sadistic way and Danyzer swore vengeance. However, a stronger sense of duty made him table his personal feelings for the good of the galaxy. A feeling of peace had not just washed over him, but many of his comrades in arms. Still, there was a sense of fear over what had happened. Many were angry because Cain was far superior to his mother and every other Paladin. He was a different kind of evil; *a worse kind.*

The Cain issue is something that is of great concern for the leadership of the Rioan Corps. These men and women of this proud race have always been uncomfortable with Danyzer's involvement with Cain. There was always a fear that he couldn't be objective. Colonel Elisma was so talented, but she was also emotionally fragile. Danyzer showed little concern about her emotional state and now he has an operator that is so dangerous that he would wipe the floor with the Colonel. She had always been considered the best Paladin ever and now the Federation has someone so much better, and worse, than she could ever have been.

Antonius is so much stronger and better prepared. No one had ever been schooled by both the Oculari and the Rioans before; until now. The unintended consequence of those actions was having a warrior with no apparent weakness that no one had any control over. General Ponz, one of Danyzer's closest comrades has often commented that having Cain train with and eventually become an Oculari was possibly one compromise too many.

Smiling, Cain then whispered to the fallen warrior, who was screaming and panting in pain, **"the wolf has laid with the sheep long enough dear Emperor. Before this day, your people were convinced that you were a wolf; but you knew better didn't you? It's frustrating isn't it? You knew I was coming to kill you and there wasn't anything that you could do about it. False bravado is so unbecoming Atlas. I told you that you would die screaming. It isn't personal; it's just that you and your people came up on the shit list. Your death is merely an obstacle to the main objective. This is how I deal with obstacles."** Then he removed the giant's head, blood rushing from the wound like a fountain; the monster was pleased. Glorious is the word that his mistress used to describe his actions.

The Empire now had a new master. While he was killing the last and mightiest warrior, the Janitors had dispatched every other being of Gondronian blood in the Empire. The Alpha sighed and looked down at his artwork. With blood all over his face, he slowly turned towards his new subjects, smiled and softly said, **"The Gondronian Empire is under new management."**

Commandant's Log: Unknown

Commandant's Log: I knew as well as everyone who was involved with this situation that this could very well be the last night of my life. If that is the case, then it has been a good life. Nick has just returned to us, probably for the last time. His time with us is up now; he is returning to the Paladins. They won't know what to do with him, but what's fair is fair. He has learned everything he needed from us anyway; far more than Danyzer intended. That is okay; Nick learning about love and loss was an inevitable conclusion to his training here. Of all the members of the Ocularian Assassination Unit and graduates of the Killing Academy, he is by far my favorite. He is so humble and honorable; he is brave, vicious, dangerous, intelligent, and dedicated to the Cause.

He is so strong, but not just physically strong. He is spiritually and emotionally strong as well. My favorite pupil is a strategist that is without peer. I never play chess or moguri with him because of how his brain works; Nick can tell you how many moves it will take for him to beat you in either game after the first move. His mind solves problems in such unique ways. He never fights or kills the same way twice. His brain is this incredible decision engine that is full of files on combat experiences and scenarios.

Cain has more knowledge about the physical strengths and weaknesses of all the races than anyone else within the quadrant. He not only knows about their respective anatomies; Cain is also well versed in their fears, limitations, and strengths. Cain understands his target's motivations, their shortcomings, and the most base of desires about his opponent and his allies. He is always studying tendencies, looking at what someone does and more importantly what they don't do.

One of the greatest misconceptions about him is the fact that he is *insane*. The truth of the matter is that he incredibly *sane*. To call my son insane shows a tremendous amount of shortsightedness; it's typical of the leadership that we follow though. Cain has a tendency to make the most complicated issues sound so simplistic. He completely unnerves his comrades and subordinates because of these actions. It always seems like he is doing something randomly but one thing I have learned about Nicolas is this: he doesn't do anything random. Everything he does has an objective. There is always a reason. He considers most circumstances as obstacles to the main objective. His combat record has shown all of us what his favorite tactics are for dealing with obstacles.

He knows that there is so much riding on his ability to navigate both the Federation and Alliance's multiple and sometimes conflicting bottom lines. For that purpose, he made a curious decision; he decided to bond with both Aya and me. Based upon our reputations, making us a part of any family unit would be considered absurd to anyone besides him. It makes sense from a tactical perspective because he needs to be privy to everything that we know and we need to be privy to everything that he will have to do.

He has been an orphan; he trusted us enough to call us father and mother. It's ironic that he calls me father, because I am absolutely nothing like his father and calling Aya mother is even more hilarious because she is definitely nothing like his mother. No one has trusted me enough to bond with me as family, but that is typical of him. My biological children have long since died in the service of the Federation; he is an excellent replacement. Aya is considered the most dangerous Terran perhaps behind Nick because of her mind; even Danyzer is afraid of her. She is so powerful, so seductive; so driven. For some twisted reason, he finds comfort with us both. That being said, he could kill us if he needed to; especially if we got in the way of him completing his objectives. I have always admired that.

Of all the warriors that I have trained, I know that he is the best. He merges the best of what we are and the best of what the Paladins are. I must admit, he was well trained before he got here. We were just able to take away the hesitance to do what is truly needed to be done. He has just finished off one of the deadliest enemies that the IGF has ever encountered; scary, it only took him two rotations to do what we couldn't do in nearly 90. I mean we had to deal with the Unori far too much. None of the warriors that were at the IGF's disposal had the ability to do what Nick is able to do. The IGF could no longer afford to wage extended conflicts. We needed something, someone different. The Unori's destruction couldn't come about with brute force. The Oculari needed something unexpected. The IGF's Assassination Unit needed strategic, efficient intellect. That is my son's specialty.

Even though Nick endured more cruelty and pain than any other Oculari under my command, he actually bonded with me. I was so humbled, but I am also frightened. Nick could just be doing this for some operation that even I don't know about. He does that; it's always dangerous because he is so much smarter than all of us. At least with the familial bonding I will always have access to his thinking; Nick will never lie to us. The key is asking him the right question; he always knows what to ask us, but being honest, it is usually a guess with him. On the contrary, we can no longer lie to him either. That's pretty difficult for a person well versed in espionage to do, to tell the truth.

It was a daring, brilliant plan really. Quenas had heard about Nick after seducing a Paladin, can't remember which one though. All she said was that he was big and strong, but not very bright. In reality, that could be any number of those guys. We made Danyzer think that we were on the way to get him, knowing that they could reach him before we could. It was far easier to get them to do the work for us; idiots. Nick was stuck on Earth; he had already created the sort of damage that was similar to the type of tactical actions that I would have authorized. He was only twelve years old then; remarkable.

Yes, I knew that they would get to him first, but they would figure out what I already knew: they couldn't control him. Now after being trained by Petamauck and the others, Cain has even more potential. The problem was that they were holding him back! Paladins have so many unnecessary rules. Then again, their screening process is not as comprehensive as ours. That's why my results are always better than my friend's. I know it pisses Danyzer off deeply that I was able to get the best out of Cain and he knew that I could go where his morality wouldn't allow. This is *exactly* why we are better than them.

Quenas arranged for his ship to be damaged and that was a great risk. This action could have started a war between our groups, but it was necessary. The Paladins were not capable of bringing out the best in him; that was a job for an assassin. He is not a peacemaker, Nick is a problem solver. His abilities are an incredible deterrent for anyone looking for a fight. The Oculari protect democracy and freedom by being ruthless andcaustic. It is an interesting dichotomy; Nick is the epitome of that action.

I must admit, when Quenas took him under her wing, I thought that this could be either the best thing for the Oculari or the very worst thing. He was so powerful, so deadly, and so intelligent. In our hands, he did reach his potential. Truthfully, he surpassed every expectation, both good and bad. Cain dispatched his fellow students faster than anyone else on record. He really began to enjoy the hunt; he really became a panic inducing predator. He could have finished them off so much sooner, but he took to our teaching. My son, learned the greatest strength of an assassin; the power of patience. Patience in a warrior of Cain's renown makes him harder to defeat because he thinks about not just the job that is in front of him, but also the job that will soon be in front of him. Patience and preparation are close cousins; arrogance is not a member of that family tree. Nick's physical ability could have made the objective easier for him to complete, but he said that would have cheapened the process.

He believed that if his powers had been taken away, he would still be deadly because of his training. That was so beautiful to me. He is so methodical and disciplined. He is also adaptive; he has no consistent pattern of combat or assassination. Cain is totally unpredictable; I love that about him!! My Paladin counterparts were always trying to stop his creativity; we always felt that it was his greatest strength. There has never been an Oculari that combined that kind of strength and that kind of intellect. He even figured out that Quenas was not a kaepa, if she wasn't as sharp as she is, he would have killed her too.

Quenas told me of her plan; I told her that even for an Oculari, this was beyond madness. She said that it had to be done; the Unori had to be stopped. No matter the cost. Then she reminded me of the fact that even Danyzer, Nick's kaepa, approved of this course of action. Nick could deliver fear and destruction on a level that none of us could ever do. The IGF approves this action; my son will connect the IGF and the Terran Alliance. The only people sacrificed were his wife and their child. Quenas said that she was positive that if the roles were reversed that Cain would do the same thing. He would have sacrificed everything for a greater good. I truly hope so; if not, I can continue this conversation in the afterlife with Quenas and everyone else that Cain decides is responsible.

I have always wondered how he dispatched the Unori. When he left on his campaign, all he said was that they now had his *attention*. He never said a word about what he was going to do. Did he use the direct approach or did he do something more subtle? Sometimes he just destroys a planet and everyone on it; other times, he kills all the people and leaves the technology intact. He decides that the resources are valuable on a planetary system, but not the people. There is no telling with him. I know how much he loved Quenas, but I have always wondered if my son was destroying the Unori because it was tactically necessary or was it because of anger over them killing his wife and child. Being honest, neither his mother nor I truly want to know. Before this opportunity presented itself, he had never taken out an entire species before. I guess there is a first time for everything. God, Quenas was brilliant!!

I know that when he is really excited, Cain will hunt someone down and kill them with a sharp weapon like a blade. I remember when the Moxx king and the royal court had to be taken out. He killed every member of the royal house in one night; he killed every member every 18.75 minutes until he killed them all. He actually let them make preparations to defend themselves and killed them anyway. It was so delicious. I heard that he finished off the Unori by destroying all of their planets, but I know that he savored killing the leadership right up close. Killing a warrior in hand to hand combat is one thing, but killing a queen in a crowded room in front of her elite guard and no one set eyes on you in plain sight? Well that is right up my son Nicolas' alley. That's why the Federation fears him so much; he could do that to anyone of us. He is so magnificent.

It has been a long time coming. Danyzer has been ready to name his replacement ever since he met Erika. As much as I love my friend, he was in over his head. He spent all his time being seen. Too much pomp and circumstance; it cost him Nick's mother. I know this: *she would have never left me.* It is ironic that even though she was reluctant to even be a Paladin, her bloodline has produced the most impressive killing machine in the history of either the IGF or Terran Alliance. I am so excited. I have given instructions that if Cain kills me before he allows me to speak, that my wishes will be placed on this video disk. He will watch it after he calms down, but I am certain that it will not come to that point. His insanity is so logical; the people that he should have been pissed at were the Unori and he has already made them a memory. I haven't been able to contact Danyzer, he probably already killed him. Then again, this might be one of those kinds of jokes that old friends play on each other. The odds that Cain has already killed Danyzer and I hadn't heard about it are pretty low; one of my people in his office would have let me know by now.

I have already picked out his new name. He will be the first human Khan. He will be *Khan Antonius.* Antonius means the 'Loving King.' His new name is consistent with the oath of the Khan; I know that Quenas would have liked that name for him. He will protect the totality of both groups and he will protect the innocent and helpless. He will fight and kill those who would harm the weak. *Antonius doesn't play that shit.* He will be here any moment now. I knew that by letting him enter the Oculari there was a possibility that this scenario would occur. He might decide that our clan was too dangerous to survive and just kill the rest of us, but my son understands that we may be evil, but we are a necessary evil. Besides, he knows that Quenas wouldn't approve. Then again for the types of things that I have done, I deserve to die. Almost every Oculari has done something so vile that death is an acceptable conclusion. All of us but my son.

Ah, I can feel him in the compound. This is so exciting, because I truly have no clue as to what is going to happen in the next few moments. There are 200 of the best of the Oculari and they don't have a chance against him. They would be foolish to interfere because Cain would kill them. No one has made a sound in the facility for more than 10 minutes. Either he has knocked out the guards or he has killed everyone in this facility. The door is opening slowly. My favorite Oculari, Nicolas Cain, has something to ask me. **"I guess you have heard Quenas' message and have questions. Or I guess you only have one?"**

CHAPTER 6

One Empire under a Groove

The citizens of the Gondronian Empire had been led to believe by Atlas that he was the most destructive and powerful warrior in the galaxy and perhaps the entire universe. His power and level of depravity had kept the people who weren't of Gondronian blood in fear for eons. However that statement had to be tempered some. Until the Alpha had come home, Atlas *was* the most powerful being in the galaxy. Once he knew that Cain had come to the Milky Way, Atlas knew that it was a matter of time before Cain would come for both him and his kingdom.

Once Antonius and his warriors had killed the entire Gondronian race, many of the remaining citizens had a temporary sense of relief, but that relief was tempered with the fact that they now had a new master who was more powerful than the previous one. None of the remaining citizens were sure what having the Alpha Paladin meant for their lives. Whatever the Alpha Paladin wants, he can have. Even if that means that their way of life come to an end. The empire must wait to see what their new king wishes and obey. For all they know, Cain could be a different kind of evil; a far worse kind.

This has been a very productive 448 hours in the Milky Way for the Blood Knights. Not only have they liberated their kinsmen, they have expanded their sphere of influence in short order, with the Gondronian Empire now to be counted amongst its allies. This also presents another challenge. How does one go about educating an empire on the nuances of democracy without allowing it to plunge into civil war? Hopefully the Blood Knights have not bitten off more than they can chew; looks like Antonius doesn't have empire to rebuild, but rather two.

The Alpha Paladin has a new title for now: King of the Gondronian Empire. There is a serious dilemma that has to be addressed amongst many issues of the new monarch. His tribulations on Earth notwithstanding, he has inherited a whole new set of problems. The enemies of the Gondronians, the Altarian Federation has declared war and has every intention of seeing that through to the end. The Altarians are a humanoid race on the other end of the Milky Way, with a territory that spans nearly eight thousand light years. These beings' physiology is similar to Terrans except for the fact that they have hair that looks like bird feathers. Their males primarily resemble eagles and cardinals for the females. Since their bodies are less dense than almost any other race, they essentially can fly. In hand to hand combat, this can be an advantage. They are a noble race that at one time were allies to the Rioans during the Dark-Sider conflict, but that was a long time ago. The Empress of the Altarians, Alvanari, has a personal blood debt that the King of the Gondronians has to pay.

Almost 25 rotations ago, the Altarians were a small system of people that was being swallowed by the Gondronian war machine. They were not a war faring people in any of the sort, but they were explorers who wanted nothing more than to make new relationships both culturally and technically. In galactic terms, the population of thirty-five billion is not a significant number; some races of people have more than that number on just one planet. They controlled a planetary system that had more than 40 worlds in the inhabitable zone of a binary star system. Because of the kindness of this group of people, they were willing to share resources, such as their planets with other systems that were not as blessed as they were. In the Altarian Star System, more than twenty different species and 3 trillion sentient beings called the Altarian system home. With an abundance of resources and technology available, this system was the kind that Atlas and his warriors considered to enticing to resist. The Gondronians did what they always do; conquer and destroy.

In a desperate attempt to keep the free peoples of this system from falling into darkness, the Altarian Federation decided to try and reason with the mighty Atlas. They knew that did not have the resources to fight such a powerful and savage enemy; Atlas' reputation had preceded him. The Federation had hoped that some type of agreement could be reached with the despot. The leader of the Federation, Avis IV, led the contingent, which also included his daughter, Avari. King Atlas allowed the contingent from the Altarian system to reach his flagship undeterred. Upon beginning the negotiation, everything seemed to be proceeding well and then Atlas saw Avis' oldest child. She looked radiant, with red features, graceful and beautiful. He asked for her to come closer so that he could look upon her beauty.

Atlas, however was not just a savage despot, he was also known as a collector. Upon that instant, he *had* to have this creature. She will make an excellent addition to my collection. She was not a person, but property for him to do with what he decided. Since he was Atlas, he decided that she would be his. Avis, of course was totally against this proposition, his daughter would be part of no negotiation or would she considered as something to be claimed. Atlas then sneered at the father, **"there is nothing that you can do. I own everything that I gaze my eyes on. You need to decide if your daughter worth an entire system of people. Either you give her to me and I leave your system alone or I take her and then take everything else that I look upon. It makes no difference to me."**

In reality, he did not want Avari as bad as he wanted the system. The Gondronians wanted more land, more planets subservient to them and the Altarians would make a good addition to the empire. But being the tyrant that he was, Atlas wanted to break the spirit of the leader; he reveled in the fact that Avis could do nothing to stop him. The head of the Altarian Federation was given an impossible set of circumstances; either he places the safety of his beautiful child above all of his people or cost billions of lives and loose the system that had always been their home. His daughter agreed to be the property of the mighty king. The Altarian leader wept, but he knew that was what was best for his people. Why did I even bring her, he thought to himself. Little did he know where this road was about to take them.

The great Atlas, the slime, ordered for the annihilation of the Altarian Federation even though they had acted in good faith. Avari's sacrifice had been totally in vain. Many of her people, friends and loved ones that she had known all her life, were slaughtered without mercy. Atlas laughed as the father watched as his people were destroyed. He lunged at the warrior king, attempting to right this terrible wrong, only to fail in vain. Atlas' warriors then began to beat on the Altarian and then his daughter intervened. She shielded her father from the punches and kicks, pleading for his life and the life of her people. Amused, Atlas then gave the noble woman an ultimatum; become a whore for his soldiers and she would let either her people or her father live. Desperate, knowing that he had only one play, he begged for his daughter to let him die so that what was left of his people could live. Reluctantly she agreed to her father's, the great leader, request. In a chilling insult, Atlas then violated the noble woman of Altaria; right in front of her father's dying eyes.

The carnage of the Altarian Federation was catastrophic. Of the almost 3 trillion beings of the Federation, barely fourteen billion remained. Atlas, having had his fill of rape, murder, and carnage decided it was time to retire for the evening. He allowed what was left of the federation the opportunity to leave the system, based upon the promise that they would never return. Alvanari, the only surviving child of Avis IV, and youngest sister to Avari, vowed revenge. Even if it took a million lifetimes and the blood of every member of her race, she would have retribution. And she would return to the home land of her people with Atlas' head on tip of her star ship, a chilling reminder to anyone who would be foolish enough to cross the Altarians ever again.

Over time, the Altarian Federation reached the other side of the galaxy, offering protection to any race of people that had been damaged by the tyranny of others. By becoming a safe haven for others, the Federation grew. Much like the phoenix of Earth mythology, the Altarians rose from the ashes to become stronger than ever before. They grew from 14 billion to an *army of four trillion*. Alvanari developed a reputation as a leader and warrior. Much like her sister, she was stunningly beautiful. But there was one distinctive difference; unlike her sister who radiated warmth, she was cold. She is far more predator than prey; much like Antonius, she reveled in the destruction of her enemies and the use of lethal force was often her first thought and when it comes to the death of tyranny, her only thought. And she was on her way to meet the new king of the Gondronians, the Alpha Paladin. *This couldn't have worked out better,* thought Nicolas. *I don't have to look for her; she will come looking for me.*

In the present time, the Paladins had finally made first contact with their kinsman on Earth. Since there was no formal government to speak of, it was really hard to communicate with all the remaining groups of people. Almost none of them spoke the same language and there was a great deal of hostility on all sides. Instead of trying to organize the people into one cohesive group, such as one nation for the planet; the Knights decided on a different course of action.

Emily and Kira had been in counsel with Major Faris, who had been a scholar on ancient human customs. He had a radical proposal that seemed both ancient but at the same time modern in its approach. **"Remember to read up on the CERN concept. It was collaboration between groups of people that had decided that working together for a common cause was beyond any personal, religious, economic, or political differences for the betterment of mankind. If it worked before, it can work again. Let that be your guide for helping the people,"** said the wise commanding officer. **"These people haven't had your training, either socially, or emotionally. This can be a tedious process. Take this to heart though, if God hadn't done what HE did, you couldn't be there for them now. I will be heading your direction as soon as I make a delivery on planet Arcadia. Probably one Earth week; Cain has a special assignment."** *What it could be,* wondered Emily. *Nick is always up to something and no one really ever knows what that is except for Kima, and she will never tell me,* thought Kira.

Using the CERN concept, the Blood Knights began to start getting their tasks completed. Nathan and Lance's job was to get the power system on track. Shiro and Thomas' job was to get the eco/agri system back to working optimally. Once those systems were ready, the metallurgist, Nicolai would work with natives to develop the material needed for use in inner stellar travel. Furthermore, the best educators amongst the Paladins, Deana, Jasmine, Alex, Simon, and Isis, will start getting the natives up to speed on the goings on of the universe. None of the beings on Earth have ever actually been *off the planet.* There is so much for them to learn and understand coupled with the fact that in less than 12 months, Earth has to be ready because within fifteen months, the siders will be here. Earth may very well be the battleground for the rest of the universe.

Nathan and Lance are not just best friends; they are brothers in every way. These guys finish each other's sentences and have the same taste in women and clothes as well as are incredibly competitive when it comes to combat. They always have each other's backs and short of Kima and Kira; work better than any duo in the Paladin order. These two brilliant engineers are the possibly the only people who understand theoretical propulsion anywhere near AC or Antonius; another advantage that the Blood Knights have over every other military unit in this part of the universe.

The two close friends have found on Earth seven scientists who have the knowledge of fusion that they require to keep in step with the Genesis

Accord mandate. Dr. Adam Samuel Hockins and his colleague, Dr. Michelle Blaska have made the most progress so far. However, Matias Martinez, Henry Musoma, and Parker Igeleke, science students from what was left of the United States have refused to work with them, in no small part because of Hockins' participation in the creation of a particle weapon founded on stolen technology. Technology that was proprietary to Igeleke's mentor, Dr. Christiana Nikitin and her colleague, Dr. Carmen Acosta, which has caused a great deal of unrest because theladies haven't arrived yet. Igeleke says that once that is cleared up, they will work, and not one second before. Once the doctors did arrive, personal prejudices, and petty squabbles ensued for almost 45 minutes. Nathan was not amused.

Nathan the Magnificent and Lance Blood-Joy, two of the deadliest Paladins of the Order, have decided to end this useless debate. Just before Nathan was about to snap the neck of young Mr. Martinez, an ivory manned woman entered the room. Smiling, she asked Nathan to put the youth down. Strike Team Leader Kira Darius, a woman not known for her patience, asked the incredibly intelligent Earthlings what was their issues with one another. They spoke of the mistrust between each group and how there were still hurt feelings that needed to be mended. Kira then smiled and asked all of them, including Nathan and Lance to follow her. They all then flew on a transport to the North American continent. The entire time, she never said one word; she was humming a tune. Nathan and Lance were disturbed, because the only other person that seems happy during these kinds of situations is their *boss*. *Weird*, Lance thought.

It turns out that these incidents of the Earthlings arguing with each other were happening with *every* one of the Paladins all over the planet. These incidents had happened to all of them; from the eco/agri group, the educators, the metallurgist, and finally the energy experts. Over three hundred eighty thousand men and women all Earthlings were bickering amongst each other as if they hadn't both been liberated from their oppressors, the Erixes, and had been made aware of the impending difficulties of the time table that all of them were under. These men and women were under the impression that their opinions counted and that their jealousies, paranoia, and anger would be tolerated. These Paladins however, were unsure of how to deal with this issue. It had been more than one month and none of the baseline needs to reach the mandate by the Terran Alliance and IGF were even close to beginning production, much less any legitimate progress report. The Alpha Centauri, the mighty warship was in the middle of an unexpected encounter; Emily and Kira would have to resolve this issue. Antonius was certain that he had made the right choice.

Commander Emily Uchida, a beautiful Paladin of Roman and Japanese descent, was the first to speak. She was not only a brilliant and capable warrior, she was well versed in both political policy and theory, and she was also well trained as an orator. She rivals her teacher, Petamauck himself, the greatest teacher of logic and reason of the Terran Alliance, in her ability to move a group of people to act in the manner that she deems reasonable for the cause that she has been chosen to serve. And no back water, close minded, lunatic humans were going to stop these proud and brave warriors, so far from home from meeting their objective, set forth by the greatest warrior that humanity had ever known.

These men and women killed countless peoples who would stand in their way and now it has come to this, whether or not to kill off what was left of Earth's humans and concede that they must start over. Once the crowd saw her face, they realized what kind of true danger they were in. It was possible that these humans from another place had decided, that they were too stupid, arrogant, and close-minded to work with one another and therefore they were too stupid, arrogant, and close-minded to live. **"Greetings, Grace, and Blessings too all those assembled here today, as well as all those assembled around the planet and watching from our mighty home, the Alpha Centauri. We have called this assembly because all of you are the best and brightest of what this planet has to offer the rest of the universe. However, I am saddened by the actions of this group of incredibly accomplished, incredibly foolish people. It is time for you to see what we truly are and what you are truly not. Obviously, you are misinformed; our goal is not the protection and deliverance of the people of Earth. *Our goal is the protection of the planet Earth*. The people are a *bonus*."**

There was a sense of fear moving throughout the crowd. They could see several of the Paladins begin to move into position. Weapons were being locked and loaded for use. **"You see, there are only about 30 million Earthlings left on this planet. You killed nearly nine billion of your kinsmen; something that we find completely deplorable. That alone makes some of us want to kill the rest of all of you and be done** with it and begin again. Lucky for you all, we find this illogical, or you would have been crushed. We could have easily let the vermin kill off the rest of you and then came back to claim what is ours. Instead, we chose to attempt to save the remnant of our ancestry," said the brilliant orator. She was not even close to being done.

"Instead, we want to show you what the rest of the universe looks like. Very soon a terrible army will attempt to re-enter this part of the universe and because of our proximity in the Virgo Super Cluster, this will be one of the first places where they will strike. Humans have a prominent place in the universe; you have earned none of that equity. Our Master is feared and respected throughout the universe, as are we. You have done nothing to earn that fear or respect. Because you are NOTHING. We are trying to change that and you are not letting us help you." As she was speaking several of the Paladins who had been standing amongst their Earth counterparts had begun moving out of the line of sight of the snipers who had begun aiming at their targets. This was the bad time.

As she paused for both dramatic effect and also to catch her breath, the young commanding officer continued her soliloquy. "He said that the Earth was worth saving, he did not say that the people were. You are *expendable*. Of all the humans, and yes there are almost 11 trillion of us spread across an incomprehensible distance to you, you are the weakest and the most intellectually inept, no matter what your arrogant minds may believe. You have never even left the planet. You live the shortest life span; physically, you are by far the weakest. Our *children* could best your strongest man in combat in a matter of moments. Any of my fellow Paladins could kill anyone of you in a matter of seconds; if my master were here, his Oculari would probably have killed several thousand of you to make sure that he has your attention, you are lucky. In the bible, countless stories have been written to describe the value of stewardship. We believe in that, however we also believe in never letting the stupid from getting in the way of God's agenda. You have tested all of our patience; we don't have the right to judge you. However," the budding leader then paused to collect her thoughts. Then Commander Uchida finally made her ultimatum to the crowd.

"We have no time for your bullshit any longer, we are behind. You all are getting in the way; that makes everyone of you back water, arrogant, and paranoid people expendable. This communication is being beamed to the rest of the planet. It's time for you to set a positive example for the rest of Earth. You are being given exactly *one hour* to get your act together. Not a week; not one day. One hour. Otherwise, we will have to eliminate the obstacle. It will be bloody and it will be permanent. The rest of the people of Earth will learn from you, either how to get beyond their petty differences and do something greater for God or they will learn that all are expendable when we *fucking kill every last one of you*. It can be the easy way or the hard way, the choice is yours. *You either get down or you will lay down*. We don't have time for you to act like this, the clock is ticking. You now have 59 minutes, 45 seconds. 44, 43, 42." The Alpha Paladin was incredibly pleased. They will get the message. One way or the other.

Even still an example had to be made; some people just have to be shown. One man from America said with confidence, **"well what if we."** He never finished the statement. Kira, standing nearly 1800 meters away, shot him in the mouth with a tracer bullet, killing him. She killed him and also killed the man standing next to him. Two people with one bullet; the crowd was both impressed and alsoconcerned. The best snipers on the planet would have had difficulty if not any real chance to have accomplished such a feat. At this point, the Earthlings realized that as much they may look like their kinsmen from the stars, the similarities end there.

For the first time, the Earthlings looked at their fellow Terrans. They noticed Kira. She was so powerful. She was as tall as any supermodel that they had ever seen, but there was something different. She was strong but seemed limber. One of the scientists who was standing relatively close to her when she shot her pistol remembers trying to pick up her weapon. He remarked how heavy it was and that she didn't even move from the recoil of the blast. There was no way that any human from Earth could have done what she just did. To think that a being had so much physical strength and dexterity was difficult for them to comprehend, but the message was clear. Any of these soldiers could kill anyone of the humans whenever they choose to. They could kill all of them just for *fun*. Accept this was no laughing matter.

The thought that Kira hit her target from such a distance just with her eyes was what truly agitated her kinsman. Antonius once displayed his genius by drawing a perfect circle free handed; Kira just brandished her genius in a beautiful yet brutal fashion. Typical of the stunning, brutal officer. The man had only said four words, but he had already gabbed too much. Then the ivory manned warrior said, **"Don't push us and we won't push you. You're talking too much. Look at what we did to the Erixes; what do you think we'll do to you? If you get over yourselves, you may be able to save your, I'm sorry, *our home.*"** *Faster than I expected*, Nicolas thought. *I figured they would have done this in another two weeks. Excellent, ahead of schedule.*

The Alpha Paladin was being briefed on the vastness of his new kingdom by his adjutant, Congo. Cain was being given the schematics of the resources that were now at his disposal and was surprisingly delighted at what he found out. Cain discovered something that was important for his plan; that his adjutant was incredibly capable. Congo would become an unexpected gift, an asset, an ally. His adjutant's incredible brain would come to be just as important as the vast resources of the Gondronian Empire, if not more.

The truth was that the Gondronian Empire was incredibly diverse and that the Gondronian race was actually the smallest race of the entire empire. Coupled with the fact that the Paladins had actually killed almost 75 percent of the ruling class. The remaining twenty-five percent were not of Gondronian blood. Many were like Congo, people who were forced to serve Atlas. Most of the people were glad that Antonius had liberated them of such a cruel tyrant. Several members of the empire's leadership were hoping that this day would come ever since they heard that Antonius existed. They knew that the mighty Terran Alliance were originally from the Milky Way and several of them, including Congo felt that it would be a matter of time before they came to retake what belonged to these people.

The hope was that the blood thirsty Khan Antonius would demand the territory and they hoped after a struggle that Atlas would be bested. Secretly, they hoped that Cain would be provoked into killing Atlas. The problem for all of them was the fact that Antonius had killed Atlas so easily and his warriors killed every Gondronian in the empire in a relatively short period of time. There was nothing heroic about their victory but rather it was an extermination of an entire race. It was atrocious, efficient, and at the same time, beautiful. Many were frightened that so few Terrans were required for such a brutal campaign. There was a fear that these warriors may not be liberators, but rather that they were conquerors, these creatures could be even worse than their Gondronian overseers. Sometimes prayers are answered in the exact fashion that they are asked and sometimes they are answered in greater renown than originally proposed. This is one of those times.

The adjutant of the empire was the only being within the remaining leadership that had actually spoken to Cain. His wife feared that every time that she saw her husband that it would be for the last time. If he could kill Atlas so easily, what was his plans for the remaining citizens? Fortunately for Congo and the rest of the remaining citizenry, they were off base in terms of Cain's intentions. The new Emperor had no intentions of harming Congo because he was not Gondronian. The mighty Terran did have big plans for the empire, but these tactics were not of a selfish nature at all. In fact, upon their first encounter, Nick told Congo that he was completely free as were all of the people. He was politely asked if the adjutant stayed on through what he considered a potentially difficult transition.

Taken aback by the Khan's charity, Congo quickly accepted his request. He was a genius fromthe Archimedean system that had been made the property of Atlas who marveled at the brilliance of Congo's mind. He had been forced to serve Atlas to ensure that his people would not be slaughtered; this is the kind of leverage that the previous ruler used to get his agenda done. It was because of Congo's organizational skills could such a vast empire be maintained. Atlas actually just wanted to conquer a race; he had little use for what to do with those people after. In reality, Congo usually allowed the system to elect their own leadership and many rivalries between races had been subsided because all of the species had been under mutually cruel tutelage. The Gondronians didn't have the means or technology to maintain the empire; it was far too vast.

Because Atlas was their champion and since Nicolas killed him, it was his entire kingdom, much as it was. The infrastructure of the empire had been crumbling because Atlas cared so little for it; he was more interested in acquiring more than he was in maintaining. Cain knew that there was a window of opportunity that existed in Atlas' death. If he could keep the various peoples united under one banner instead of fighting at each other's throats, the empire would not have to undertake a destructive transformation. Cain planned to have the Gondronian Empire converted into a Federation. He had Congo assemble all the regional governors on the home world, Gond Prime, where these articles of confederation could be drafted. There, Congo's brilliance was on display.

The combination of Congo's intellectual brilliance and knowledge of the Gondronian Empire coupled with Cain's ability became an incredible asset for this new day. Congo would become Steward of the Federation until the second phase of Cain's plan could be completed; finding a suitable heir. Congo became fast friends with Cain; even though he refers to Antonius as his master. Nick admired the fact that even under these most precarious of circumstances that he put his personal feelings aside for the good of others. Antonius has deep admiration for his newest ally. Cain promised that he would not rule the Federation long because that was against his code. He said that he would defend it against all usurpers, both foreign and domestic.

For many of the systems that had been under Atlas' cruelty, it seemed that this was their opportunity to try and carve up the federation with the belief that they were strong enough to deal with the Terrans. These beings were not trying to do what was in the best interest of all, but rather what was in the best interest of a few. This point of view clashed with the Alpha and it became apparent that enough people hadn't been slaughtered yet, fortunately for many, Cain and his warriors had already eliminated the Gondronian species, but Cain was aware now that he still had work to do to eliminate the Gondronian *mentality*. That is where his Oculari come in and do what they do best. These silent, almost invisible assassins are now going to address Cain's loose ends; he *hates loose ends.*

One system lord attempted to kidnap Congo's wife and children to leverage a political advantage. At this point, it was time for Cain's Oculari to re-establish their reputation in this part of the quadrant. Not only did the Oculari rescue the adjutant's family, for good measure, Cain had the governors of nine of the more prominent systems killed in their sleep just to prove his point. All of these loose ends were dealt with in less than 100 minutes. Over the vastness of Gondronian space, these powerful leaders were eradicated with ruthless proficiency; and no one heard or saw a thing. Nick knew they conspired against him; he settled that issue quickly. When addressing the governance, Cain snapped his fingers and the heads of all ten leaders were dropped from the roof. He needed the potential dissenters to know that Cain could be *anywhere*; that he could be *everywhere*.

Then Cain's hypothesis about the behavioral patterns of Atlas was proven correct. When he saw the harem that Atlas possessed, his heart ached for the cruelty of the former emperor. AC was traveling with him as Congo had taken him on tour of his new kingdom, she could see that he was actually disturbed. She was glad that he saw this after he had already killed the king; if he had known the extent of his cruelty, he may have killed him slowly. Of all the evil he faces constantly, nothing truly angers Nick like an abuser of women and children. *The thought of anyone doing that to one of us would yield a fury from Cain that would have been beyond comprehension,* thought the Centauri's Executive Officer.

AC remembered when the Hunian Prince once tried to make her his by force; a cold shiver went up her spine, remembering how Cain killed him, deboning him like a fish but not allowing him to die. Cain kept him alive for 37 hours with his brain stem intact, looking at his dismembered body; God help anyone who ever hurt Kima's *feelings*. If someone had ever hurt Kira enough to make her cry there would be no where in the universe that they could hide. Nefertiti once commented that the course of the quadrant could very well be changed if she felt truly insulted by someone; all it would take was one vid-link and they would be gone. All of the women in Nick's life are careful not to overreact to anything. He may execute half the universe.

As Congo, Cain, and AC kept walking, he came upon a child. He looked like an Altarian, but he had ox-blood looking skin with bluish eyes. Turned out that Atlas had fathered a child with Avari and he didn't know it or he didn't care. That's who I have been looking for, thought the wise and noble king. This is exactly what I need. He looked like a hawk, piercing gaze, regal and strong. His father didn't claim him and his mother died while giving birth to the hybrid; much like with Nick, the child's birth literally ripped his mother's internal organs in half because her physiology wasn't designed for such a large fetus. The harem had been taking care of him. AC, with her eyes watering, picked up the small child.

It was no doubt; he was an Altarian/Gondronian hybrid. Finally Atlas was helpful, thought Antonius. Then the commander contacted his trusted friend, Major Faris. **"Sy, I need you to take this package to Arcadia with the greatest possible speed. AC will fill you on the way. I want it in Alliance space as quickly as possible. Take my lady to Level Two."** Faris with a puzzled look replied, **"Am I hearing you right?**

You, you want me to do this? Level 2? For a package delivery sir? Are you serious? That'll take like 5 hours." Antonius then said, **"Deadly serious. I am trying to actually *avoid* a war."**

AC and Congo both knew his plan, since Atlas didn't have any children besides this child, he can make a legitimate claim to this kingdom. Nick adopted this young child as his own; he would now have a claim to the new Gondronian Federation. The only way to dispute his claim was to best Nick in combat, as if that is going to happen. Congo made sure that the articles were iron clad and the Alpha was the other deterrent. While Nick was dealing with those issues, it would be AC's duty to raise the child and make sure that he will be properly educated.

It would also be better for all parties to remove him from this region of space. The child would be in danger if he was raised under these conditions. AC informed Congo that if anything were to happen to the child, it was likely that Cain would wipe the entire species that was responsible. Furthermore, if something happened to his adopted child, he may decide that his plan needs tweaking and slaughtering the majority of the species in the federation would be his most prudent course of action. *Yeah, Cain's mind works just like that,* is what she said to the adjutant.

If the heir was trained properly, he can take over this region of space and keep it from plunging into war. Plus the fact that the child's biological aunt is on the way to start a fight also creates a sense of relative urgency in Antonius' mind. It is the new king's hope that she may see things differently if her nephew is actually as noble as her father and her sister, who happens to be his mother. *God, this has to work. If she forces me to, I may have to kill her,* pondered the mighty king. Cain is aware that the Altarian Queen's rage and need for revenge may cloud her judgment. This could fix all these issues. The Altarian fleet is traveling fast, warp speed, but even at the fleet's maximum velocity, he felt theat he had plenty of time. *If AC and Petamauck can fix me, they can fix the child,* the mighty monarch pondered.

"What are we going to call him?" asked the heir's new foster mother. Nick never looked at the child. **"Michael. That is his name."** AC looked down at the child, **"Michael?"** The boy smiled and giggled. Perfect. AC said that he likes it. *Of course he likes it; he's my son,* thought the Alpha Paladin. *What the Hell are you up to my brother,* thought Kima. Smiling, Nick thought back, *it's a surprise baby.* AC tried to get Nick to at least pick up the child and Nick rebuffed both Michael and AC's attempts to bond. **"It isn't time yet. Don't worry AC. When it is time, I will be there for him."**

Faris arrived with Cain's lady, the Alpha Centauri. He wanted Michael and AC out of the galaxy quickly. The Centauri's propulsion system is capable of level 5 TPulse drive, but it is hardly ever used. The main reason is that Level 1 already stretches the limits of human comprehension. That Cain wanted them to use *Level 2* displayed his level of urgency for this situation. To travel more than 40 million light years in less than 5 hours sounds ludicrous. That is until someone realizes that at level 4, the Centauri could reach Alliance space in less than *10 minutes.*

AC and the rest of the Centauri crew then raced towards Arcadia so that the greatest teacher of logic and reason could begin to teach this youngsovereign. Namon Ka, one of the clerics from the Order of Saint Thomas, has also volunteered to become an influence on the infant heir, the adopted son of Antonius. Eventually father and son will be brothers in arms; they'd better, because the Dark-Siders are still on the way.

Another three weeks have passed on planet Earth, it is almost spring now. After the ultimatum given by the Paladins, the Earthlings have begun to get the message. Several thousand humans still believed that these mighty warriors were still to be trifled with; all of them were dispatched with typical Ocularian efficiency. The strike team had no idea that there were Oculari on the planet, but that is the point. The Oculari, much like their master, can be *anywhere*; they can be *everywhere*. Nothing or no one would get in the way of the strike team's mission. The Paladins, understood it was about them teaching their kinsman how to get things done, remarkably the Earthlings, once they started looking at the big picture, could see that their limited knowledge, while impressive for ignorant people, wasn't anything compared to the vastness of knowledge that their brethren were trying to prepare them for.

Commander Emily Uchida, in particularly empathized with their plight, but the job had to be done. She knew how many of them felt because a tremendous responsibility had been thrust upon her shoulders as well. Like her Earth kin, the Commander was not given the option to ponder whether or not she was ready for this responsibility, she was just told to address this task anyway. She also began to understand the brilliance of her commander, Nicolas Cain. It didn't matter whether these people actually met the goals set about by the IGF or the Alliance; the Dark-Siders were coming regardless of whether they were ready or not.

Nick liked to say that both pride and fear can make a person overlook the obvious. The only way to make the people of Earth allies to the Terran Alliance was to convince them to become allies to each other. It is hard to be able to stand against potential enemies, if you cannot stand with one another. It was brilliance that she was certain that no one had ever pondered, especially the regents.

When she had finished her academic training, her favorite cousin, Shiro, told her that his father, Admiral Sho Uchida, was not going to add Emily to the Intelligence Division. Instead she had been ordered to enroll into Paladin Academy for advanced combat training. She had hopes of being an analyst; overt combat wasn't her particular cup of tea, but she was never given the choice. Shiro came to her graduation and immediately had her shipped off to the secret Paladin Command center. Her parents were distraught when Shiro came to what should have been a festive occasion and left with his uncle's youngest child. Her parents didn't want her in Deep Space Operations because her brother had died during the Mu Occupation; the family couldn't take losing their baby. When Emily had told them that she was entering service, she had promised them that she wouldn't go for combat operations. She believed that she was going to be in the Intelligence Division like her uncle. On the day of her graduation she found out that not only was he not in the Intelligence division of the Terran military, that youngest Uchida child would not serve there either. She hasn't seen them since.

Apparently Commander Cain had eyes for the youngest Uchida all along. He never told Admiral Uchida why his niece was now to join the Paladins, in particularly the Janitors, in part because Cain didn't have to. Nick is the Supreme Commander of all Terran military forces, Cain doesn't normally tell his subordinates why he has made any of his choices, and their job was to obey. This situation was no different. She had no idea that Cain wanted her and he always has first choice in the Naval Operation Corps.

Those who were in the know believed that Cain is the shrewdest judge of both talent and character in the history of the Alliance; he doesn't make those mistakes often, if ever. That is why her cousin trusts him so much. *This is why I couldn't be under Uncle's command; Cain wanted me here* she thought. This is where she was meant to be and now she *outranks* her uncle. *God is so much smarter than me; all this time I thought that I was being punished*, thought the emerging leader. She smiled at the thought of learning more at Cain's side.

It makes sense now. Emily, then decided to talk to Lance about this new contemplation, he smiled and said, **"Whatever you do, please don't start trying to understand Nick. He freaks me out. I mean don't get me wrong, I love and trust him deeply. Understanding him? I would say that he is crazy, but no form of insanity is this *logical*. To show a chancellor how smart he is, he drew a perfect circle; free handed. *Free handed*, Commander, which is just crazy to even think about it. Wing Alpha's operating system had to be upgraded *twice* to keep up with his reflexes; that's just stupid."** Lance stood there shaking his head at his commanding officer.

In that instant, Lance realized that even though Emily was his commanding officer, she was still the youngest Paladin there. In many ways, for all her brilliance, she was still a novice. This is exactly why he thinks that Nick is such a crazy person. Only Nick would have done this to someone. She is so young. He smiled and continued the conversation. **"Think about that for a second. A machine had to be upgraded to keep up with an organic brain. Just be glad you have some breakthrough. Only person who really gets him is Kima. Ask her; then again she's crazy too. By the way, the fusion system had its second successful test. We should be able to complete a propulsion test within the next 10 to 14 days."** The results were excellent, but the commander knew that Cain wouldn't care until all three levels have been reached.

As the Earthlings are nearing completion of stage one of the levels of interstellar development, Antonius is checking on the progress of his adopted son Michael. He has left the Gondronian Federation in the capable hands of Congo; he will alert him to any significant issues that arise that need his attention. Even though only a week has passed to Cain, Michael has been on Arcadia with AC, Petamauck, and Namon for the Altarian equivalent of 17 years. Michael is still considered a boy by his mother's cultural customs; the Gondronian's customs meant little since Cain and his troops made them all extinct. The prince is strong, even though he has not undergone the Paladin process; he is almost as strong as any of them. He also has another advantage that his hybrid heritage has afforded him in combat; the power of flight. But Nick is there to check on the progress of his son's mind.

The Altarian/Gondronian hybrid is not being trained to just become a warrior; he is there to learn how to become a king. As far as Cain is concerned, warriors don't have a large enough frame of reference; Michael Cain needed more. At this point, Nick has decided that it is time for his son to face his deadliest potential adversary; Michael himself. Nick has him placed in the Revelation Chamber, a sensory deprivation tank where only the strongest of Paladins dare to venture. Many of these potential warriors never return. Some become psychotic or even worse. No one has stayed in the chamber longer than Michael's adopted father; it is time for the son to become more than just a warrior.

The Revelation Chamber is a place that only the most resolute of Paladin will go. It is device that reveals all; your inner most thoughts, the most vulnerable of emotional content. It shows images from a person's past, their potential future and how their shortcomings can create horrible outcomes for those that they hold dearest. The chamber displays that person's innermost pain. Many of the Paladins could never stand to be in there very long, it is too painful. Cain has spent more time in the chamber than anyone else in its history. He personally spent more than the equivalent of 450 Earth years in it over the course of his life. That length of time is significant considering that the average Paladin spends an average of 180 *minutes* in their entire careers.

He finds it a delightful treat; the pain keeps him accountable to whom he serves. Spending time in the chambers aids Nick in his quest to find balance between his emotions and his logic. Cain believes that this is a tool to keep him respectful and faithful to the Cause. It is difficult to become arrogant when you are painfully aware of how much greater God is than you. Even though Cain is the strongest and most capable Paladin, he is humbled by the fact that his favorite prophet is so much more than he could ever be. When that is your level of understanding, it is incredibly difficult to become too full of yourself.

Here in the chamber, the young warrior saw the truth about who he was and who Nicolas Cain was to him. He saw that his biological father was a cruel despot and how he was the product of his father raping his mother and how his father, Atlas, has cruelly destroyed a large population of his mother's people. How she and his grandfather sacrificed themselves in honor of a greater good. That despite all that had happened and how he was conceived didn't matter to her and how she died knowing that he would one day become a great Altarian, perhaps even the greatest.

She did not die in vain. He also learned of how his adopted father, the mightiest Terran warrior ever, had come to kill his biological father. How he efficiently did it and took glee in the death of such a cruel foe. It was also revealed to him that Nick had the opportunity to kill Atlas many eons earlier and didn't. When he left the chamber, the young warrior was shaking. AC, his surrogate mother was there waiting on him, to provide comfort for him, but he wanted none. Michael saw Cain and knew exactly what he needed to do. He grabbed a sword and was ready to fight his adopted father, mighty Antonius. Cain smiled at his foe. *This is why I am here,* thought the mighty Paladin. It was time for Nick to see what his son has learned.

Michael and his father began to circle each other. Michael stood almost one half meter taller than his father. He noticed that Nick was not as tall as some of his instructors, in particularly Red. He noticed that his father looked strong and was confident. Even though he hadn't seen him in almost 17 Altarian years, the prince had been studying him most of his life. He noticed that Nick's katana was in a unique position along his left hip. He also knew that Nick preferred using his left hand and was cautious about what to do next. Michael is ready to strike, but he knows that Nick wouldn't hesitate to attack if provoked. He was incredibly angry with Cain, but he wasn't stupid either. This is the best human warrior, the one who killed Atlas. *Why does everyone love such a monstrous creature,* he pondered. *What twisted ends do I serve by adopting me?* This sinister warrior is far too dangerous to leave alive any longer. **"Defend yourself Oculari,"** the young warrior bellowed. Cain yawned and slowly unfastened his blade from the hilt.

With blood in his beautiful eyes, he screamed, **"you knew what he was!!! You should have killed him sooner!!! They would still be alive!!!"** Antonius was somewhat amused. He smiled at his son, a boy that he hasn't spoken to in his entire life. As disgusted as Michael was with Atlas, he was even more disgusted at Cain. He knows what the Oculari are and that of all who were members of that clandestine order, Cain was the most accomplished; which is to say that Cain is the very best of the very worst. During the prince's academic studies, he discovered that the Oculari were not heroic, but rather they were the "problem solvers" of the Federation. These are the type of people who could destroy everything and let other people die in order for their agendas to be met; much to his chagrin, his adopted father is Master of the clan. Nick is the very essence of what the Oculari represent.

As far as Michael was concerned, there was nothing noble about Cain. Just cruelty, malice, indifference, and a twisted logic were the character traits of his adopted father. As he was being educated and trained, Michael constantly heard of how much his father was truly feared; the traits that were not heroic at all. In his mind, Nick was more evil and mad than the foes that he vanquished. A different kind of evil, a far worse kind of evil. Michael concluded that someone of Cain's infinite wisdom and patience was secretly plotting to control the quadrant and he needed to be stopped. The rage that Michael had was so strong that it was oozing out of the pores of his skin. Cain replied that if blood is what he wanted then blood is what he would receive. AC begged him not to fight the boy; she knows that once Cain decided to fight, he decided to kill. **"Out of the way woman, this is what he wants,"** the mighty Alpha replied. **"Time to teach my son a lesson that he won't forget."**

Michael was angry at Nick for a lot of reasons. One of those primary reasons was the fact that he was abandoned. For all of his life, he had been told that he was heir to a mighty kingdom that he was being prepared to protect the innocent, the helpless, and to destroy the wicked in all its forms. It wasn't fair. He had no say in the matter. That he is the son of the mightiest warrior to ever live; that he was the most capable and noble of all warriors and that when it was time, he would willingly cede Michael a kingdom that Cain had valiantly defended. That information conflicted with the character traits that the prince had studied. Michael had never even met his father; he felt unloved and manipulated. He believes that he is strong enough to kill Nick and it is time to teach his cruel and loveless parent a lesson. How could AC, Petamauck, and Namon care so much for him and Cain care so little? Time to get answers.

He spoke withall the brewing disgust in his soul. **"Cain, I hate you. I have always hated you. *I will always hate you.* I know what your plan is; you wanted Atlas to kill them because you knew that they could stop you. You allowed her to die and my noble grandfather to die just so that your agenda could be served. What a coincidence monster? You are just as cruel and vicious as any of the Oculari are you not? You are the master of espionage and manipulation aren't you? You could have killed Atlas a long time ago and didn't and why?**

You could have commanded your Oculari to kill and they would at moment's notice and you didn't. Because it didn't suit your needs. My mother's people suffered because of your choices didn't they? You don't care about me at all, just what purpose I can serve for your twisted ends. Why did you have them raise me? Where were you?" Cain was no longer amused at the banter. "**Shut up and fight.**"

Then they fought, katana to katana, Michael giving everything that he had, Nick barely trying. *He has been taught well, very well*, thought the monster. Michael was screaming at him and cursing him, finally Nick spoke to his son. "**You fight well warrior. Let me ask you something, have you not learned anything? It's never about you, it's always about God. Silly boy. If your biological father hadn't done what he did, you would not be. Your anger does not change the fact that all these terrible things happened to you. You were created for a reason; you could have died and you didn't. I killed Atlas because it was time for him to die; it is never about us fool. You have a chance to stop a genocidal war because your aunt is pissed about what happened. This is why I am here, because you think too small son. Look at what she and her people, your people, accomplished. Protecting the lives of innocents,**" the father spoke to the young heir softly, but sternly.

At this point, Nick dropped his sword. Michael was still in a rage. He attacked his father, who was unarmed. Cain sighed and shook his head at the young warrior. Nick dodged Michael's attack; he then performed a beautiful leg sweep. After Michael was on the ground, Cain pushed him almost 5 meters, hoping that he would realize that he was over matched. Michael was still determined to fight. He then got up and ran at Nick and jumped in the air to kick him from above his head. Nick then grabbed his son's left foot and dragged him to the ground. He laughed and said to the noble, furious monarch, "**excellent technique Michael. My have you grown. So gifted; so foolish. You are showing a tremendous amount of talent and a spectacular lack of vision. But you lack focus because of your anger. Your fury has clouded your judgment son.**"

Michael again screamed and Nick easily dodged his attacks and making him fall in the process. Every time Michael fell, Nick would let him get up. Every move that Michael made was nearly perfect in execution, but Nick had a counter move that was even more impressive. Michael attacked using the deadly Iconian fire star technique. Nick countered with a lethal combination of Japanese Aikido, Kindarian Jujitsu mixing in some Neo Thessalonian hand to hand combat. These techniques were never heard of being used together.

For Cain, the eclectic styles made sense. He was consistently using Michael's vast power against him, leaving his opponent furious in the process. Michael was panting heavily, while his father was laughing. **"So which is it? Am I out to subjugate the quadrant or are you upset that I allowed them to die? It can't be both. You are not thinking straight. You are just tired aren't you? You've been carrying all that rage in your soul for a long time haven't you? I love you son. It's okay. I get it."** At this point, Cain was dodging every aggressive punch and kick that Michael attempted. He wasn't swinging back; Michael split a concrete slab in half with one of his kicks intended for his father. If anyone besides Cain was fighting with the young warrior, they would've been dead a long time ago.

Cain smiled at his son. ***"Your* anger doesn't change the fact that Atlas raped her and killed your grandfather. Your *anger* doesn't change the fact that I am your *father* and you are my *son*. It's not *always* about you. *My mother and grandfather died and it's all your fault; blah, blah, blah.*"** Cain then changed to his Carthaginian combat stance. **"Now attack."** At this point, AC wanted to intervene, but Petamauck held her back, whispering to her that he understood what Nick was doing.

Michael again tried to punch Nick several times and missed; the last time Nick put him on the ground with an arm bar. It is apparent that regardless of what amazing physical powers he has acquired over his career, Nick's skill in hand to hand combat is far above reproach; there are 8,000 versions of hand to hand combat that a bi-pedal is capable of performing and Cain knows them *all*. Most humans think there are around eighteen hundred, but Nick is privy to more information. No one but the Ocularian Commandant knows this about Nick, but he remembers every attack ever attempted against him. His mental library of physical encounters is almost as large as the Genesis archives on hand to hand combat itself; remarkable.

It was at this point that Michael finally spoke to his father without all the rage, he was tired. **"Dammit, you are cheating. You know more styles of combat than I do. You are a snake, a deceiver. When you had Atlas by the throat all those years ago, were you beating him like** you are beating me? Taunting me as you fight. I hate you. You had better not let me live after today Cain. If you do, I will train even harder and learn more than you. Then I will know what I need to kill you!" Michael grabbed a bow staff to attack Nick. Nick watched him manipulate the heavy staff like it was a hollow stick; Nick waited for him to attack and then he punched through the staff, hitting Michael in the chest. The young monarch then flew backwards three meters.

Nick smiled and spoke to his son, "what will you do then? Will you protect the innocent and destroy the wicked? Or would your entire life be wasted on trying to kill me? Many have tried son, I can tell you that you are blessed because you are my son by love, if not this would have been over with a *long* time ago. I would gladly cede my life if that means that you would take my place. But you won't; you are too selfish. I will always be better than you because you fight for revenge; I fight for your *mother* and for your *grandfather*. Who do you fight for? Oh yeah, you fight for no one but yourself. Selfish. Obvious. I made a mistake; I should have come sooner. You are not a warrior; you're a selfish little boy. Like you're the only person whose life is fucked up. It's not about you. You fight for nothing; I already killed Atlas dummy. You have learned NOTHING; what a shame. You will be better after today's lesson. Attack."

Michael ran at his father in a dead sprint. He leaped into the air and prepared to kick Nick. Cain leaped in the air he deflected Michael's kick with his left foot, spun around in the air, and kicked him in the face with his right foot. Michael was bleeding. AC and Petamauck cringed. Nick is no longer taking it easy. Michael angrily spit out the blood from his mouth, courtesy of his adopted father's accuracy. He was in pain, but not ready to concede anything to Cain, much less that he was learning something from the combat. "Lesson? You think that you are teaching me? How dare you Cain! You don't get to talk about my mother or grandfather. You don't fight for anything but glory. Now you die."

Michael screamed again and picked up his blade. He attacked. He ran at Nick in a dead sprint and tried to cut his father down, Nick moved out of the way, disarming his son as he ran by. He then kicked Michael behind his left knee, knocking him down in the process. Cain paralyzed his son temporarily with a tap to one of Michael's nerve clusters in his lower back. He had his blade against Michael's throat, with his son in a head lock. Michael closed his eyes; he fully expected to die at the hands of a superior opponent. He knew of Cain's reputation, he had already lived longer than he should have. Fortunately, Nick is a lot smarter than his son. He kissed him on the top of his head and pushed him down. Cain smiled. **"My God you are deadly! You fight like Kira. She always fell for that move also. When she was a *kid*."**

Michael was crying in frustration at the proposition that no matter what he did, Cain was *better*. *How could the king of assassins not kill me*, he thought. It was in this moment that he realized that Nick could have killed him but his restraint was keeping him from doing so. *Maybe it is love*, he thought. Nick spoke softly. **"Have you not learned from Ka, many great things come from perceived tragedy, if those things are of God? Have you NOT read the bible son? Have you not paid attention to Christ? Have you not paid attention to what Paul wrote? My beginning was just as cruel and in some ways worse than your own. I've been where you are. You've been building your resentment day by day, haven't you? I did the same thing. Like you, I felt vengeful every day. That's no way to live. I know your pain. God has already taken your measure and finds you approved. I have been and will always be proud of you."**

The mighty Cain dropped the katana and smiled at his powerful, noble son. He beamed with pride at what kind of man he had become and the type of leader that he would soon be. He knew that as much as Michael loved AC, Petamauck, and Namon, his growing resentment for Antonius had to be addressed. Nick is not one to wait to deal with such matters; it was time to deal with it now. Nick has been there.

He was beyond angry with Quenas, Danyzer, and the Commandant about what happened. He also understood that it was for the greater good. God does things that are necessary that he would never understand. Nick has learned that to be a tool of the Father means to cooperate with Him; understanding is not a necessity of cooperation. **"This is a good start son."** Nick then did something that his dearest friends have never seen him do. He walked up to his pupil and kissed him on the forehead. **"Remember son what God wants of us is here and here."** He touched his son's head and his heart. **"I love you son. Always have. Always will. Class dismissed."**

The son fell to his knees. All he ever wanted was to be loved by this man, his father. The father embraced the son as the son cried. Seventeen years is a long time to wait for a present. Nick was hugging Michael and stroking the top of his head. Nick was quietly saying to the son, "**its okay Mikey; its okay. Shhhhh. I know. I know. Rest now.**" The son sobbing in the father's arms saw the nobility, the love in his father's soul. "**All I have wanted to do since I have been here was become strong enough to kill you. I am sorry; I am so sorry. For, Forgive me father, I didn't see the big picture. I can't believe that I have been so stupid. Her love, her life is the greatest gift that my mother could have given me.**" The mightiest warrior of Terra, Nicolas Cain, was not this warrior's father by blood, but by love. "**It is time for you to see where I come from.**" AC, Petamauck, and Namon were all overwhelmed at what they had seen.

For the first time ever, Nick revealed to them everything that helped make him Khan Antonius; all his pain and suffering. All of his joy. Michael cried as he learned that his father had no family, how he was taken from one awful circumstance to another. How he had to fight for his life daily with the Oculari; how Quenas took his love and made it into a weapon for the greater good. In spite of all that has happened that Cain was able to smile; to enjoy the light. How serving a greater cause than himself gave him comfort. All of them learned how watching Michael grow up gave him an incredible amount of joy. They all saw how it hurt him to treat his beautiful son like this but that this was the only way to get the results that would benefit so many. To Nick, some lessons simply have to be *lived*. Michael is his father's son.

Commander Gaius Nicolas Cain has always been an enigma to his colleagues and also to his loved ones. He has always had an advantage over most of his friends because he always seemed to know so much more about them then any of his dearest friends and loved ones ever knew about him. They knew almost nothing about his family and it was always a great debate amongst all of them, why Nick was so giving and caring, even though most of his upbringing had consisted of him essentially being moved from one cruel set of circumstances to another.

AC knew a lot about his mother's combat record, but she never knew why she left the Order and almost no one knew anything about his father. Nick's understanding of concepts such as free-will and equality were almost at the level of a cleric even before he began his training and his understanding of the Cause was to the point that he could be able to perform such feats of destruction but never feel overwhelmed by the situation. Nick then decided to sit down and explain the story to Michael while his loved ones intently listened.

Nick asked Michael to sit down at the dining table. Cain knew that his son was hungry and also exhausted. He asked him if he was ready to eat. Michael asked him why and the father replied sweetly, **"In the Altarian culture whenever the child is going to be told the story of his family, it is usually done over a meal. Since we are about to talk about your de facto grandparents, I figured it is appropriate. AC, you and the rest need to sit down also. You have questions and it's time to answer those as well."**

Petamauck was in tears because he knows that Cain almost never talks about the past, nor does he hardly ever cook unless it is for the dearest of loved ones. Michael smiled and said, **"Father, I didn't know that you know how to cook. It smells delicious. What is it?"** Nick was in the kitchen with is back to all of them. He replied in a cool manner consistent with his reputation. **"It's Avari's best dish."** Everyone stopped chattering. Michael said to AC, **"How does he know that? Did he know her?"** AC and Namon looked at each other. Nick could hear them. **"Son, I am an Oculari; I *always* know things that I shouldn't know."**

Petamauck knows that Cain had been from one end of the quadrant to the other. It was totally possible that he had met Avari, but he never mentioned it. This is the exact thing that his friends and loved ones always talk about. The only person who might truly know the truth is the Ocularian Commandant and he will never say. They will all have to wait until Nick decides to tell them anything. Today, the father decided to tell the son about his birth parents. It was the only log that he ever had; until he was much older, he had never seen a picture of his parents. This compu-log that OC had was part of the file that he shared with Driax. Driax then shared it with her deadliest friend.

It was revealed that Cain's father was both an artist and scholar was from a nation in central Africa, it is uncertain which one, because so little is known about him. Rumor has it that he was a professor of the arts at a university in southern California. It is said that he was also dedicated to the betterment of all people regardless of their race, religious beliefs, and anything else that usually kept the ethnic groups of planet Earth separate. One thing that was known was the fact that he was also a humanitarian who worked in several relief campaigns to fight poverty and terror all over the globe.

Colonel Erika Elisma was one of the greatest warriors in the history of the Terran Alliance. She had been revered and feared throughout the entire quadrant for most of her life. She was one of the most effective combat warriors to have ever been trained by the Order of Paladins. The mighty Federation General, Danyzer himself had taken a special interest in her talents and was her primary instructor; he told her that it was her destiny to bring all the enemies of humanity and the Federation to their knees.

There was one problem though: she didn't *want* to be a killer. She was from a proud family whose roots could be traced back to the beginning of the Alliance. Once she had been tapped for military service, it was expected that Erika would serve in the Paladin corps, much like her other relatives. She was an artist as a child; but her masterpieces had always been of death and destruction as an adult. Danyzer and the rest of Alliance command were telling her of her obligations to the Cause and how she should feel honored that God had chosen Elisma for such a difficult calling.

Erika had been pushed so much harder than other Paladins, in part because her natural abilities were so much greater. Her entire life was one constant battle after another. It seemed to be an existence of woe and sacrifice. She would never know love or joy, but it was her job to ensure that others had those opportunities that she had nobly sacrificed. Her dearest friends would die at her side in battle after battle; there was always a new campaign. No rest for the weary indeed.

After one particularly brutal conflict, she lost her taste for bloodshed. The fact of the matter was that she never had a taste for bloodshed to begin with. In the Faxcillan Galaxy, she was tasked with leading a unit of Paladins to destroy a Dark-Sider research facility. The purpose of the facility was unknown; the speculation was the facility housed their drone creation center. In the attack, the Paladins were overrun; they failed to destroy the facility and also all but two of the warriors were killed. After barely making it out of the galaxy with their lives, Danyzer ordered her to return and finish what she started. Her closest friends had died right before her eyes and she was told to ignore the pain and do what was necessary. Danyzer said that the Cause mattered more than anything else, even her pain and sorrow. It was not that he truly believed that point, but Erika was the only person within the Paladin ranks capable of completing such a dangerous assignment. Instead of completing it, she did something else.

Erika decided that she was through with this life of bloodshed, through with this life without joy, and most importantly, she was through with Danyzer and the Alliance. She enlisted the help of an old friend who she knew had left the Alliance and was hiding on Earth, living as a normal human in America. She asked the Rioan scientist, Ryxadrona, to help her. She wanted to live on Earth as a regular human; to be normal. The process was called the *agroge*, the ancient Iconian word for purge. The problem was that it had never been successfully completed before. It was even trickier for Erika because her powers were even greater than the average Paladin. Every so often, a one in seven hundred trillion chance in the Paladin process occurs were the person's powers are beyond that of a normal Paladin; it is unknown why this anomaly occurs but it has happened three times in the history of the Order. The other two warriors became unhinged; unable to handle all the power, they became psychotic. She was the third.

After completing the process, it seemed as if it was successful. The scientist then used an experimental gateway module to allow her to reach Earth without a starship and then she destroyed it after Erika was on Earth. Rxyadrona always felt sorry for Erika; too much had been asked of her. They arranged for her ship to be destroyed, to make it seem as if she died in an accident. The Alliance and Federation would be none the wiser. On Earth, Erika assumed the name of a deceased child and lived with that same friend who was sympathetic to her situation. She would pose as her adopted mother. For the first time in her life, she was free. Free to become anything that she wanted to be.

While on Earth, she met a handsome graduate student named Antoine via a mutual friend in college. They connected instantly and eventually fell in love and got married. She was attracted to his character and also his charity; how he was passionate about making the lives of others better. Dr. Cain became a well known advocate for human rights. He was a poet, a martial artist, an artist, a musician, and a professor. A true renaissance man. She was enjoying an awakening of her own; she was also a professor of Woman's studies and Education; she loved having students come by their home and discuss free will, equality, social justice and faith. For the first time, she was truly happy. Then Erika discovered that she was pregnant.

Erika had also made a startling discovery; her powers were beginning to return. This was different though. She was not able to control her emotions, she had no equilibrium; she was dangerously unstable. Her husband had no clue; he was on a humanitarian mission and he hadn't even known that his wife was pregnant yet. She was traveling through the California desert when she finally reached her beloved husband on the phone; the reception was terrible. All he heard her say was **"you're going to be a daddy."** The next thing she heard was a gunshot.

It is unknown which country that he was in when it happened, but Professor Cain was killed somewhere in western Africa when he was delivering supplies, such as water and grain. The commandos of that nation accused him of being a spy and revolutionary and had him executed via sniper. Dr. Antoine Cain, a man of incredible compassion, was gunned down by some of the very people that he came to aid. She heard the shot as she was driving. She drove right into a telephone pole. In that instant, everything that she had ever wanted was taken away; she couldn't take it. Erika began to go into labor on the spot; she barely reached the hospital. Her child was literally tearing her internal organs in half. Nick was being developed in minutes; he grew the equivalent of 8 months in 15 minutes. The rest they say is history.

At this point, Cain had just finished cooking the meal for his son and his friends. They were barely able to speak when they heard the story. Michael felt awful because he saw the environment he has been raised in and compared that to what his father had been raised in. Petamauck had never heard that story before; he had other questions but never had the courage to ask them. Namon was shaken by his past also. Michael then asked another burning question. **"Tell me about my brother. What happened to him and his mother? Quenas died before giving birth. I have heard many stories, but I want to hear it from you."** Nick smiled. **'Okay son, you deserve to know."**

The others heard about how much Quenas meant to Cain but no one ever felt bold enough to get Nick to talk about it. Only the Commandant and Senator Aya knew that Cain had actually married Quenas; one of his many secrets. He truly loved this woman; he never wanted to give anyone else a child but Quenas because she would understand. Standing up and being a protector of the innocent meant that all your loved ones would be in constant danger. Quenas had an eternal hatred for the Unori, but through her love for Nick, it was possible that these two warriors could find comfort. Quenas once told the Commandant that she saw that it was possible for her to be happy and that it frightened her. That Cain could look into the darkness and always see the light; she felt that she was not strong enough for his love.

When Cain stopped talking, everyone could hardly think through what he had told them. Petamauck once remarked to Erik the Red that learning about the mechanisms of Nick's soul was the most frightening experience that he had ever had in his entire life. That learning about how Cain felt about his birth parents and even learning a little bit about his relationship with the Ocularian Commandant was hair-raising. Looking at life from Cain's perspective is like staring into the abyss. Except the difference between Cain, his mother and his wife was simply this: when Erika and Quenas stared into the darkness, they *blinked*. When Nick stared into the darkness, *the darkness blinked.*

Whereas Michael began to hate his father, Nick loved and adored his father. When Cain first entered the Genesis Chamber, his pain was far greater than Michael's. Unfortunately for him, there was no compassionate person waiting for Nick to help him to deal with this pain. The Commandant of the Oculari wanted him to embrace his pain and use it as fuel for all the terrible things that Nick has had to do over the course of his life. How someone can still smile and not let his anger consume him is still beyond the understanding of his dearest friends.

Nick is aware that the ones closest to him are always afraid to truly invest in him because he is an Oculari. The Oculari don't care, the Oculari don't invest. The Oculari will kill their own if they find it necessary. His mother was just as proficient in killing people as he was; but she had bottomed out. She had lost her taste for it completely. Truth be known, she *never* had a taste for it ever. Nick will never have that issue; he lives to serve. This just happens to be the way that God has chosen for him to serve. To terminate evil in all its forms and to protect the innocent and the powerless. He is the out cost of that faith; he knows that he is not a hero. He is a Janitor. He cleans up evil; *he is the very best at the very worst.*

Many things have been discovered over the first quarter of this Earth year. The humans were capable of growth just like their brethren and Nicolas Cain, always more monster than man, could also grow. It is only by the will of the God that they all serve that set of terrible circumstances have the potential to become so much more. AC is especially pleased that the mighty Alpha Paladin has taken time out of his busy schedule helping to protect the universe, to become a Daddy. This action takes place of the child that had to be sacrificed so that Nicolas could become the Alpha Paladin. Fate has rewarded him with a son. The Lord works in mysterious ways doesn't He?

Personal Log: AC

Personal Log: It has been almost 18 Altarian years since Nick and I were walking through the harem with Congo. I have known Nick since he was fifteen and even after all that time together, he still never ceases to amaze me. He has suffered through so much, from the death of his parents right after his birth, him being a ward of the state, the psychiatrists trying to "help" him, to the Ocularians; don't get me started on Quenas. In spite of all those experiences, he has this incredible capacity for compassion. I know that he hates when I am affectionate towards him, but I know that he loves the fact that I am affectionate towards him. He has this interesting dichotomy; he isthe greatest assassin in the history of the Oculari, which is saying something, but he is probably among the kindest men that I have ever known. His relationship with his adopted son is no different.

Here my dearest Nicky has taken the son of an enemy that he has slain and made him a part of the family. He named him Michael; when I asked him why, Gaius told me that that was his favorite angel. I mean who says that? Michael is the key to a better future as far as Nick is concerned. Nick wanted him strong and resolute, he had us educate him. However, when Nick felt it appropriate, he stepped in and became the parent that Michael truly needed. Nick has never had a stable life; much of it has been filled with pain and anger. Yet when it truly mattered the most, he has become the father that he never had. It is incredible to watch. He is compassionate, yet stern. He is strong, yet tender. Michael will have an opportunity to become what Quenas could not allow; Nick's child.

The actions when Nick and Michael were fighting really disturbed all of us. What were we going to do, stop him? Nick is the Alpha Paladin; wewouldn't stand a chance. Besides, he had already killed Petamauck once. That's *a fact*. I underestimated Nick's compassion and focus; we all did. It was Nick who knew that Michael needed to address his pain, suffering, and circumstances. Probably because at some point in Nick's life, he had to make a similar decision. I make it a point not to talk about the past with Nick; it is far too painful for me to think about it. I was afraid that he would kill Michael, Nick is not known for his ability to be patient or negotiate. I mean Michael is just a kidbut Nick understood exactly what his son needed. He got it out of Michael's system and now he can concentrate on the task at hand. So much is riding on both of their shoulders. But both are up to the charge; I see that now. I am glad that these two powerful, brave souls found one another.

It is as if each filled the hole in the other's heart. They finish each other's sentences and Michael is beginning to sound a lot like Nick. They both have this frighteningly efficient, brutally complex logic. When he is with Michael, Nick even laughs; he actually laughs. It's such a wonderful sound; I wish I heard it more often. In all the time that I have known Nick, he has never had so much joy as to when he is training Michael in hand to hand combat. He talks to him as they train. We are talking complete paragraphs worth!! Not the eight words or fewer sentences he is known for either. He talks about respect, honor, sacrifice, and freedom. After every lesson, he always kisses his son on his forehead, telling him that he must always use his head and his heart for the greater good of other people.

The other thing that Nick is constantly talking to Michael about is the value of being blessed. That God knew that with all the terrible things that happened to both the father and the son that in spite of all that, look at what they both have become. He says **"God knew you before you knew Him. He is smarter than us. There is no such thing as random. Remember that."** That God took their measure believed they were up to the task and would be ready to answer the call of duty. That Michael's mother and grandfather were beings of such renown; that he had so much to be proud of. Sometimes Petamauck, Erik, and I stand in the room as they talk, listening in awe. It is so amazing.

Nick and Michael also gave both Petamauck and myself a special gift. You see I love my girls, but I am a Rioan first; service will always take priority. I have an incredible relationship with both of my children but I didn't raise them. By the time, I entered their lives; they were ready to fight by our side. I never got the opportunity to bond with and raise them like my mother had the opportunity with me. With Michael, I was essentially able to raise him from being an infant. I know that Nick thought that entire scenario through long before I did; I am so thankful that he is so much smarter than I am.

I wanted to talk to Nick about my emotional state but that will never happen. In no small part because my dear Nick doesn't look at things that way. He is so solution oriented. He considered me raising Michael as a means to an end. He would say that my relationship with Michael is important for the Cause and everything else is merely a bonus. I will forever be grateful to him. Michael is my son by love. Petamauck has had the opportunity to become a mentor and good friend to Michael also. He really regretted the things that he put Nick through and more regrettably what he allowed Nick to be put through. Michael was a way to remove the stains from our failures with his father.

It finally dawned on me that no one has ever talked to Nick about how he felt about the actions that Quenas chose. She took his son from him, she took herself from him; how could he live with those actions? Nick smiled and kissed me. It was such a sweet way to tell me to shut the fuck up. He then told me that he would always love her with the whole of who is and would ever be. Of all the people that he had crossed in his life, that she understood him best of all. It hurt me a great deal when he first said that to me; but I was the one who asked him. I know that he is right.

No one ever taught him more than she did. My father, my Uncle, and my mother don't come close to touching her level of teaching. He has never had a better instructor. He was angry about what happened, but not angry with her. He once said to me, **"If there was no evil in the universe, I would have never met her, Petamauck or you. It had to happen just like it did. Basically this is my way of turning a frown upside down."** Who says that? It sometimes frightens me how his brain processes data.

Nick considers what she did was for the greater good; that her sacrifice was from the depths of her very soul. The Cause matters more than anything, even love. I truly believe that she felt that Nick's love for both her and his child would have gotten in the way of the main objective, which is the Cause. That is how much he loved them and that would have been a problem; Nick's ability to focus beyond self interest is his greatest strength. A noble sacrifice; that is how he chooses to remember her actions. Nicky considers it hypocritical for him to look at this situation any different. He would have done the same thing; that's what she believed about him. He would honor her sacrifice. God blessed him with a son to raise and protect after all. Nick believes that God is smarter and he never questions that fact. His simplicity is so beautiful.

Michael is so much his father's son. He is so capable physically; he has mastered many of the killing arts and is incredibly strong; he is certainly formidable. He adapts to situations and combat circumstances quickly. While he is very intelligent and well trained, he does not have his father's brilliant, tactical mind. That is not a knock against him at all; no one has a mind that works like Nick's. However, he does have Nick's heart. His commitment to us and his commitment to the Cause are beyond reproach. Michael loves Kima and Kira as if they were his sisters and loves me like his mother. He loves and deeply respects both Erik and Petamauck. Nick created this entire environment for this child; for all of us. I understand Nick so much better from watching him with his son. Damn you Quenas; bless you Quenas. Forgive me, I could not see. Look at them. So much power, so much love, so much commitment. They are truly two peas in a very unique pod.

CHAPTER 7

Homecoming

The Earthlings and Paladins have made remarkable progress over the past seven Earth weeks. The natives have an energy system, atmospheric fusion that would rival some of the more efficient energy systems within the IGF. By using this system, they have been able to replenish a large portion of the food and water chain on planet Earth. Coupled with the fact that the emissions from this procedure are clean, the planet is being healed daily. Thanks to the agri/eco practices taught by Thomas and Amanda, the Earthlings also have rebuilt a large portion of their globes' atmosphere by restocking the forestry destroyed in the global war as well as the Erixian's occupation. Meanwhile, the present Steward of The Gondronians, Nicolas Cain, has been busy getting resources together for the upcoming conflict with the Dark-Sider Armada.

Throughout the galaxy, Cain has used his reputation as leverage to get groups of people who would more than likely be in deep conflict to see that there is a greater foe on the horizon. He has actual control of more than forty percent of the Milky Way; control that he will eventually cede to his adopted son Michael, heir to the Gondronian and Altarian thrones by blood. The last true hurdle to be met is with Michael's aunt, Alvarnari, who has sworn vengeance against a foe that her nephew's adopted father has already sent into the abyss. Only by convincing her that she has bigger concerns, can the galaxy be more than a stopgap for the siders. In this region of space, everything hinges upon the relatives being able to get along.

Commander Emily Uchida, project manager of the Earth's development and Kira, strike team leader of the Earth's defense forces are in conference with their various department heads. Each of these leaders, proponents of life, are the exact types of Paladins that the new training specifications that Chancellor Alron Driax and Petamauck had in mind. When it is time to go into battle mode, these conscientious people will revert back to their original duties of vicious, deadly warriors, prepared to die to protect the innocent at all cost. The project manager is being accompanied via holographic conference by nine Paladin Unit Commanders, including Erik the Red, Vice Admiral Sho Uchida, Petamauck, Terran Naval Commandant David Kun, as well as four members of the Chancellor's cabinet. It is time to update everyone both in this conference room and also back in Terran Alliance territory on where they are and what work is left to become. Commander Emily Uchida, with a greater understanding of her master's intentions accept for perhaps Kima, is prepared to brief everyone, whether they are ready for the truth or not.

The sharp young leader begins her presentation of the facts at hand. **"Greetings and Blessings to all assembled, both in the flesh and via telecom. This is where we are at the moment. As of one Earth week ago, the engineering group, led by Lance and Nathan, have completed a successful test of the fusion propulsion engines on a make shift star fighter. It is primarily of Earth origin, mixed in with some of our updated technology. The test pilots were Jamie and Jaylun Harris, these two brothers are the best pilots that Earth has to offer so far. Thanks to the materials developed by Nicolai's group, we may have a working Earth-centric fighter group by the end of the month. Dr. Kima Darius has been working with the medical staff, led by Dr. Marni Chandler to develop a body suit that can withstand the gravity pressure on the Earthling's bodies. It should be prepared for field testing by the end of the week. Lance, Dr. Igeleke and chief engineer, Brad Beadle, should be having completed designs for an Earth-centric, battle fortress by the end of next week as well. And,"** the project manager was interrupted by a midst of angry, frightened chatter.

Many of these seasoned leaders had no idea of how and when Emily and Kira were given the authority to speak on operational concerns. Nari the Wise bellowed out a bunch of concerns at once. **"What the Hell is going on? How the? What the Hell? Fucking Cain! He's *always* doing this? These are *children*. Where is Faris?"** Admiral Uchida was also pissed, **"By the way, where is Nathan and Lance? When did Ensign Uchida and Chief Darius get placed in charge of this venture?"**

Astonished by what they had heard, Admiral Noor Gibran barely knew where to start. **"First off, why are you developing weapons for the Earthlings? At what stages is the team on the galactic development mandates? Have you even begun the fusion procedures? Has AC, Sayied or Cain approved of such measures? Better yet, when did you believe that you had the authority to begin preparing them for war? That's supposed to be *your* job."**

Perplexed as to the tone and depth of this inquiry, Kira, strike team leader of the defense forces spoke in her trusted colleague's defense. Nothing truly aggravates Kira like a lack of respect for protocol. She gave a steely gaze, sighed loudly, and finally she spoke harshly. **"Are all of you people out of your minds?! First off Nari, you obviously didn't talk to Commander Cain did you? None of you could have!! Why? Because he is *busy*. Oh, I get it now; he must not have thought that any of your opinions mattered. Since this new data is upsetting your apple-carts, I will brief you all to make sure that the project director is no longer interrupted for such tedious matters. Cain split the team long before we even reached the solar system; I am in charge of leading the fighter squadron and *Commander* Uchida is our leader until Antonius returns. You all need to settle down; she *outranks* all of you. If you or anyone ever interrupt her again or take a disrespectful tone, I promise you that the next sound we hear will be the blood rushing from your cut throats. I know something that you don't know."**

No one said a word, not even Erik; he trained Kira, she has already said more than normal. She looks at the chain of command much like Nick does. Furthermore, there is a strange air in the room, like they weren't alone. Master Chief Kira Darius is not known for making threats as much as she is known for guarantees. The contingent all knew that there was a strong possibility that there were Oculari nearby; perhaps even in the room. Everyone knows that they could be *anywhere* and that they are known to be *everywhere*. Violence will ensue if she has to keep talking about this point.

The deadly Paladin continued, **"Commander Cain is somewhere in the Gondronian system, assembling reinforcements for the pending conflict. Before we parted company, he split most of the leadership duties. I am in charge of the defense; I will lead the fighter group for the immediate future. Lance and Nathan are the best engineers, so** they will lead most agri/eco projects as well as the development of the military armaments with the natives; as has been reported, it's going well. Finally because of Emily's *outstanding* organizational skills, policy making abilities, and her charisma, she is project manager of all the endeavors related to the Earth. Everyone answers to *Commander* Uchida. She was promoted her to Commander before parted company; not a field commission, either. This is a *full* commission ladies and gentlemen."

At this point, Kira, a woman who is not known for long conversation, stops to take a sip of her tea. She knows that she has given the leadership a lot to digest. She then reaches a deductive conclusion about this set of circumstances. **"Ah yes, once again, my master didn't give a damn enough to inform you did he? If you need confirmation, consult Major Faris. Chancellor Driax is fully aware of what the commanding officer decided to do; if you have any queries related as such, you should take them up with him. Otherwise, be quiet. We don't have time for this. Commander, my apologies for speaking out of turn, please continue."** This was as polite as Kira usually is, no one but Nick uses less words to make a stronger point. It seems as if Kira's reputation for not taking bullshit from anyone was grossly underreported.

Because of the tone of her friend's words, the youngest Commander in the history of the Terran Alliance was taken aback by their intensity. She had to gather herself because her brain was moving a million miles a minute at that point. Who would have thought that she would be leading a briefing to the Chancellor, the Commandant of the Terran Navy, veteran Paladins such as Erik and her uncle, Sho? Emily took a deep breath, calming down and realizing that this is exactly why Cain made the decisions that he did. He truly sees the big picture and she was humbled by the fact that she was able to see some of it.

Commander Emily Uchida sighed deeply, smiled slowly, and then continued her briefing. **"There is more than one way to show the appropriate levels of galactic growth required by the Federation and the Alliance. What better way to show that then this course of action? Besides we are going to need a battle ready Earth force anyway, so why not now? The reason that I am placing so much emphasis on the military buildup is that the Dark-Sider Armada is on the move. They will be here in this galaxy faster than we could anticipate. Our only advantage is the fact that our propulsion**

technology is more advanced than any opposition that the Alliance or IGF could have. These people have been fighting for years, it won't take them long to adjust to their new foes."

Emily does sympathize with the emotional state that her comrades are in. Many of these decisions happened without their knowledge and furthermore, an entire set of new realities has been placed at their feet. Not only do these veteran leaders have to deal with the youngest Alron ever, they now have to deal with the youngest operational commander in the history of the Terran Alliance, and the campaign that will take place is nearly 50 million light years from their present location. Coupling that with the fact that the savage-landers are going being relied upon as integral parts of the battle plan created by their Commander who isn't even in their home system. To the untrained eye, this could be considered a Molotov cocktail of epic proportions.

That is an awful lot to digest in one setting; in addition to the fact that Kira has already threatened them with death in the first 15 minutes of the report. She smiles to herself, *my master has them right where he wants them.* Emily sips on her mint tea and continues. **"For the first time in the history of this planet, the natives are all on the same page. It does not matter that the IGF or Alliance approves of these people's existence as a member of humanity officially or unofficially;** *the siders are still coming here!!!* **They will have to be ready to fight for their, or should I be saying our *home.* That is what Commander Cain has always understood. We were going to need to come here either way; he was just being efficient. And just what did you expect the natives to be doing while we are fighting? Hoping and praying for our success while they watch? No my dear counsel, they have just as much right to fight and die for the Cause as we do, in some ways even more so."**

Uchida went on further to say that the engineers, led by Beadle, may have developed an alloy that will make their warships at least as capable as the Terran Naval fleet all on their own. By creating the alloy in absolute zero temperature and then heating it to more than forty thousand degrees Celsius and then cooling it back to absolute zero, this alloy may present a key advantage for the natives. That being said, the Earthlings, the back water close-minded Earthlings, have come a long ways in a short period of time. Emily and Kira have become a formidable duo in a short period as well, with Emily being a visionary and Kira being the instrument to carry out those visions. Erik smiled. *This is starting to look and sound very familiar,* he mused.

Vice Chancellor Halima, after hearing the mission briefing was more than pleased with the progress of the project leader and the defense commander. Terran Naval Commandant David Kun stated that the 9th Naval Squadron and also the IGF's Omicron Assault Group were going to be deployed into that area of space within the next week and should arrive to the Milky Way within the next quarter of the Earth's year. He indicated that these troops would number somewhere north of ten million warships, star fighters and support ships. Until otherwise specified, the Earth battle group should continue progress as planned.

Chancellor Driax had been in consult with her deadliest servant. Nick met with his boss on planet Eden to discuss the realities of the situation that would soon play out in the Milky Way Galaxy. **"Greetings Lord Antonius."** Cain looked at her with a frown. Driax shrugged her shoulders and kissed him on the cheek. **"Kidding."** He quipped. **"Very funny."** Driax then addressed her most pressing concern. **"Nick, just how bad is it really? How many troops do you think that we will need to send to help you? Or do you not think that you will need our help? Just let me know what you need my servant,"** the chancellor inquired. She always seems so cool around Cain, but inside she cringes every time she has to ask something because he might answer her. His answers are always direct and honest; always efficient. As few words as possible.

The Alron's manner was steady but still concerned. She could always be honest and comfortable with her warrior, in part because he already understands the ramifications of his actions. **"My Chancellor, it will be okay. We can't have a prolonged conflict with these guys. I am putting all of our chips on the table. My son is being trained right now. His aunt is on the way. Once they are ready, we will destroy the Dark-Sider fleet. You know that I have a plan; it is in progress as we speak. Everything is going according to my design, even Kira and Emily shitting on the other Paladins. I heard about that; I would have figured Kira would have shot *at least* two of them, she used words instead. That's pretty cool. I need you to trust your monster my dear Chancellor."**

The two most important humans in the universe continued walking. Driax put her arm in his. In this moment, Driax understood why Kush loved Antonius so much. No matter the task set forth by circumstance, Cain is always ready and willing for the good of others. Nick thinks that it is never about us and it is always about God; it is such a true but difficult way to view life. The discipline it takes to actually believe that is incredible. Driax has also come to the realization that he doesn't take any of the gifts that God has given him for granted; there is something beautiful and noble about that sentiment. Coupled that with the fact that more than likely, *he has thought of everything.*

This understanding is what makes their bond so special. Nick almost never takes his gloves off in public, but when he is with Driax, he never wears gloves. Cain doesn't just let anyone touch him; he almost killed AC when she first tried. Cain understands that even though Driax is a steely leader, she from time to time needs to be comforted. It is a difficult life to know that countless peoples depend on you to always be at your best. Driax knows that Nick understands that. She can be herself, much like Kush could with Cain. Cain and Kush often played chess while discussing problems; she has Cain walk with her or sometimes they sail in a boat in the sea. Just them; like she needs a better bodyguard. She has Cain!

The night was especially beautiful on Eden that evening. As the two of them sat in the gazebo, the southern breeze began to pick up. Driax noticed that Nick was just smiling with his eyes closed, almost as if he was humming a tune that only he heard. He is completely aware of the disheartening tasks that lie ahead for all of them, but he still has the ability to appreciate the little things, such as an evening breeze. Driax, trying to get a sense as to where her noble warrior's mind was and she inquired about his joyous demeanor. **"Why are you so upbeat all of the sudden, did I say something funny?"** Nick opened his eyes and smiled, **"not at all. It's just that I love the breezes. That's why I designed the villa like this. On a good night, the breezeways make a melodious tone, like a song. When I was inside the juvenile and foster systems while I was on Earth, I could never feel the breeze. It was like prison; no warmth, no comfort, not even a breeze. When Petamauck saved me, the first thing that I noticed was that there was a strong southern breeze. It was as if God was giving me a warm embrace, letting me know that everything was going to be alright. I didn't know what was going to happen to me; certainly not this. But that breeze was** the first time that I felt that God loved me." Driax realized that Nick was another of his amazing qualities; the ability to see God in *everything*.

Driax also decided it was time to bring up another of her concerns. **"Erik brought up a good point, why did you put the youngest officer in your command in charge? Of all the people that you could have chosen, you picked one of the least accomplished Paladins that you have at your disposal. I know that you always have a reason and I know that I am going to regret this, but why her?"** Nick smiled at his chancellor. She cringed; she knows that Nick's reasons usually make other people feel stupid. This is not because he tries to, but when you have 50 percent of your brain functioning, everyone else does seem stupid. **"Driax, she is the best thinker that we have. She understands the value of using the resources that are available, she is highly creative, and she always focuses on the main objective. Commander Emily Uchida has this subtle, brilliant intellect. I love that. Her greatest skill is problem solving. That's why. I will have to spend most of my time outside of the Solar system. I may not be with my troops, but because of her, I don't have to be. If there is an adjustment that needs to be made, she will know what to do. Furthermore, she reminds me of you. I trust that most of all. Does that answer your question?"**

The chancellor smiled and said that the matter was closed then. **"Lighten up Nick, I was just asking."** She leaned her head on his shoulder. **"For shits and giggles, when did you make that decision?"** He kissed her on her forehead. **"I made it when you had me punking the politicians, economists, and the clerics. I can multi-task you know. It doesn't take much brain power to outsmart that group. I know you know what I am talking about; you do it all the time."** *Damn, this is why I need to be myself; the smartass already knows,* the chancellor mused. If they knew how smart he really was, the leadership would be even more fearful than they already are. Nick is a monster, but not because of his brutality; because of his intellect.

The Alron decided to inquire about his relationship with the Commandant and the Senator. They intimated that their relationship was of some significant importance to Cain. That they knew him better than Danyzer and AC does. **"Yes Mistress. Mother and Father do know me better than Danyzer and AC; much better. Who do you suppose taught me how to *think*?"** Aya is head of the Federation Intelligence arm of the Senate and The Ocularian Commandant is the head of the counter intelligence network of the Federation. Danyzer is the statesman; those two are far more likely to get their hands dirty. They look at things much in the way that Cain does. He should; they adopted him while he was in the Ocularian Killing Academy.

Driax was confused; wasn't Nick an orphan? **"I don't understand. The Ocularian Commandant and the Senator are your parents? How in the Hell does that work? There is nothing about this relationship in your file. In fact, it's not in any file in the Alliance. Are you being cryptic?"** Nick laughed at his chancellor. **"No. You have done your homework haven't you? No Alron, it's an Oculari thing; you wouldn't understand."** The chancellor decided to leave this alone. The more she knew about Nick, the less she understood. **"Is this another one of those 'Plausible Deniability' circumstances that Aya and the Commandant told me about?"** Nick kissed her on the cheek sweetly as they looked at the stars. He leaned his head on her shoulder and closed his eyes. This was a sign of comfort that Cain hardly shows anyone but Aya. **"You catch on fast. So you aren't just pretty huh?"**

When Cain completed the Ocularian Killing Academy, one crucial element of the completion of the Academy is the choosing of the "family." The operative will know everything about them and they know everything about the operative. For most Oculari, this is a secret pact, but for Cain, he decided that he didn't care. Nick chose Aya because of her position as head of Federation Intelligence and the Ocularian Commandant was chosen because of all the information that he possessed as well. Because his parents have both died, he decided to make them his adopted parents. This is an Ocularian custom, but it seemed appropriate to Cain; both OC and Aya were beyond honored that he would refer to them as Mother and Father. The ceremony took place right before he left the Oculari; he told them that they could reveal the truth when they felt it appropriate. It felt right to Nick, to have two sociopaths for parents. It is consistent with the madness that is his life. The Alpha Paladin wouldn't have it any other way.

The chancellor inquired as to why he told them about the course of actions that he planned. Nick simply replied, **"They asked."** The chancellor was confused. **"Would you have told me if I asked?"** Nick kissed her on the cheek. **"Yeah, but you wouldn't have understood. I am *a lot* smarter than you. I plan things eons in advance. My brain works in ways that would truly scare people. Besides, you said you** need a *friend*. **If you knew what I was thinking you might not be my friend anymore. Aya has taught you well; but she didn't teach you *everything*."**

Driax kissed Nick and understood that if Nick kept things from her, it was for her protection, not his. She was satisfied with that sentiment and changed the subject. She further inquired about Nick's new familial obligation. **"So your adopted son has accepted what you did to his biological father?"** Nick smiled and replied, **"Yes he did. His name is Michael. He wanted to kill me because I hadn't acted *sooner*. Then he tried to kill me with a damn sword. I love him so much; it's going to suck for him being my kid though. He is up to it. He showed no fear at all, he is right on schedule. We both laughed about it after it was over."** Everything was happening according to the Oculari's original schedule. It was all part of his strategic plan. He specializes in beating an opponent *before* the fight begins.

Antonius felt that the warriors would have a different level of motivation because the galaxy was their home. The mighty Khan was certain that he was correct, but he would do the right thing at the right time. She then inquired as to what would happen if they fail. He responded sweetly to her. **"You're missing the point; if we fail, then it won't matter anyway. The only thing that stands between the Dark-Siders and their complete and total domination of this quadrant of the universe is *us*; the madcap warriors ofthe Virgo. There isn't any force left to oppose them in this part of space. They have already conquered the Phoenix, the Proteus, the Alborian, the Columbian, and also Cressian Super Clusters; those are the just the few that we know of."**

At this point, the Khan reminded his Chancellor that the Dark-Siders are one of several groups vying for universal supremacy. Just because his comrades and superiors hadn't seen them did not mean these predatory groups weren't out their watching and waiting for the chance to strike. The fact that they keep standing up to the siders has done nothing more than make their potential opposition aware of their existence. The Dark-Sider War is just the tip of the iceberg. He continued speaking coolly about these future events. **"They have been gaining capacity and technology for a showdown with the Virgo Super Cluster; that's *us*. You haven't seen what I have seen Mistress. There are few species that are as capable as the Dark-Siders. Everyone that is in their league will** eventually come for us as well; our problems will never cease. **The more brutal and destructive our campaign is against the siders, the greater our reputation, and the greater concern we create for other despotic races. Besides, we won't fail my dear Driax.**" He then kissed her on the cheek and left the planet to continue preparations. *Dammit, I knew I shouldn't have asked*, thought the Terran Chancellor. Driax had been thinking about the fact that her troops had been barely holding their own against these Dark-Siders without Cain and now intelligence has something even more grim to report. *It can wait; he has enough to think about*, she thought.

Aya and OC were on Acre drinking Ynarian Fire Tea. It is an acquired taste; the smell of it always makes Danyzer and AC sick. Whenever the senator and the commandant wanted to discuss something that her husband shouldn't be privy to, that's how they get rid of him. Danyzer is an incredibly capable leader and visionary, but his wife, the beautiful, talented, and brilliant Aya is probably smarter than he is. She is the most powerful and influential senator in the IGF. His comrade, OC, his best friend, is also incredibly bright. He doesn't have a name anymore; it is part of his cover. The Oculari are now the most powerful clandestine organization within the IGF. He has spent the majority of his life authorizing assassinations and gathering intelligence; the great irony is that he doesn't really like doing it. It is the fact that this job must be done and no one is more capable than he is. Their connection? Their adopted son Nicolas Cain. They are discussing the progress of their brilliant son's plan.

The Paladins are trained primarily to be peace keepers; Nick doesn't always adhere to that point of view. To the present day, Nick still believes that killing an entire group of people is far more logical than trying to negotiate a peaceful coexistence. Dead people can't start trouble. To Cain, the only peaceful existence was one where one's enemies were disposed of. This particular juxtaposition is disturbing to most of the leadership of both the Federation and the Alliance. Their normative discomfort is the price paid for their security.

The senator spoke sweetly while sipping her tea. **"He is something isn't he? He is actually going to pull this off. His plan is beyond insane; it is beyond brilliant. The Federation and Alliance are going to be pissed."** The commandant concurred with that sentiment. **"Of course they are. They only think in linear patterns. They won't** complain long because he doesn't care about their viewpoints. Our son is an artist. He is about to create his masterpiece. Your husband is going to complain. A lot." She laughed, almost spitting up her tea. "I know. God my husband is not that bright is he? I am glad that he is so pretty. He still believes that Nick cares about what he thinks doesn't he? Driax is smarter than all of them. She is ruthless isn't she? You think that she has figured out the plan?"

OC looked puzzled at his dear comrade. "Driax? No, not yet. But I think that she has a clue. But since Earth is not her responsibility there isn't much that she can do about this set of circumstances anyway. Her subordinates are all fucking idiots. They gave Earth away to Nick without any thought about what he could do." The senator was laughing so hard that she couldn't breathe. "I know. 'We want Eden to remain the Hub of the Spoke.' They fucking fell for that? When Nick ran that by me I said that there was no way that they could be that fucking stupid. He said yes they were. *God, I am glad that Nick works with us instead of against us.* By the way, is Driax ready to be trusted? It will be her job to groom Uchida. Furthermore, do you believe that Nick has changed his mind about Kira yet?"

The nameless officer smiled and sighed warmly. "No, Nick hasn't changed his mind about Kira. He says that she is too limited; I agree with that assessment. She still burns far too hot. I think that he is angling for Michael instead. That makes a lot more sense. We need gender balance anyway. He has a plan for how to address that issue. I met with Congo right after Nick took control of the Gondronian Empire; I mean Gondronian *Federation*. He is changing the quadrant right in front of them. Congo is prepared to follow Nick's orders. When he gives the word, it will happen. It's so perfect; it's so cruel. It's so Nick. After Nick finishes remaking the Milky Way, Driax will be ready. Like our beautiful son said, you taught her well; but you didn't teach her *everything*."

Cain had spent several weeks observing and testing the progress of his adopted son on Arcadia. He knew that his preparation was vital to the war machine that was going to be necessary to fight the monster that is the Dark-Sider Armada. Intelligence reports indicated that a massive build-up within the Phoenix Super Cluster meant that the Dark-Siders are preparing to head towards their direction. Considering the distance between the Phoenix and Virgo Super Clusters, the fact that their instruments can even detect it means they are in for a huge fight. The Alpha Centauri is really an exquisite piece of engineering and its crew has handled the siders as well as every other foe countless times, but this will be different. Looks like the siders are sending in everyone. A billion years is a long time to hold a grudge and it looks like they are going to bring everything possible to win this time.

If they can stop the armada in the Milky Way, the rest of this part of the universe will be safe; *we can go back to killing each other*, thought the Alpha. The thing that helps the United Fleet's cause is how the siders tend to attack. They always attack in linear patterns, always parallel; they never cross them. But their numbers are usually so overwhelming even if you destroy a lot of them; they usually still have large enough reserves to keep up their offensives. The siege attack is their primary strategy, much like Saladin's Muslim armies attacked Jerusalem in Earth's past. But the Paladins cannot force the siders to terms; there is nowhere else for the IGF, Terran Alliance, the Gondronians, or anyone else to go. *The line must be drawn here*, pondered the noble warrior.

If it takes the might of every sentient species in this part of the universe, the armada cannot be allowed to pass them. *God, give us the strength to make this stand here and be with us; we cannot win without You*, the mighty warrior prayed. *Let us drink from this bitter cup and not be afraid; if it be Your will, we shall not be moved. Please God, give us the strength to endure; we have to outlast them. I am weak, I am flesh; but in You, I am victorious. I will bow to no one but You, Father. Amen.* The lines of the Dark-Sider Armada must be broken; it's the only way. They fight as a single unit, Cain knew that there has to be a way to split them and disorient them. That's it!! *That's how we do it; the siders would never see that coming*, Nicolas thought to himself. Antonius knew that Michael's aunt was vital to the battle plan that was formulated. That being said, if she proves difficult, the plan could still be successful without her. Altarian technology was an important asset but not necessarily the Altarian people. Hopefully it doesn't come down to that decision.

No one foe has ever had as much consistent success against the Dark-Siders, the Gondronians, the Kurgax, and the Unori as the Alpha Paladin. The crew of the Alpha Centauri has always been able to excel against greater numerical foes in part because of the way Cain's mind works. He has devised a methodology of combat that allows the crew of the Centauri to take advantage of superior numbers. He is a master of misdirection; he has this incredible ability to convince his opponent to pay attention to one action, while being completely blind to another more crippling behavior. The Khan understands that the siders are prepared to utilize their vast resources at all costs because if they are successful against the Janitors and their allies this time, there would literally be no other significant force left within the Virgo Super Cluster to stop them. Unfortunately for the armada, Cain is aware of that dilemma also.

Cain was so deep in thought that he didn't hear AC, Petamauck, Erik or Sho. Finally, his son snapped him out of it; with a roundhouse kick from an angle that only someone capable of flight could have done. **"What the? Why did you kick me? That hurts son, sneaking up on your father like that; excellent. Never hesitate Michael when you have an advantage because,"** thenthe father showed the son a move from the Ocularian killing arts. Kicking him in his shoulder, he then pulled out a blade and put it near his throat. Michael, unfazed, had a knife near his father's ear, only to see Cain point to him another blade near the young prince's crotch. *How did dad move his hands so fast,* thought the young warrior. The father wins again. **"Excellent. But always remember that your most powerful weapons are,"**the son finished his father's sentence. **"The head and the heart. A person with a brain and the will to use it can do anything."** The proud father kissed his son on the forehead, a sign of his approval.

The son asked the father what was on his mind; everyone had been trying to get his attention for at least twenty seconds, that's a long time for Cain to be in deep thought. **"I was thinking about how to kill our enemy, stop them cold in their tracks."** The son looked at him and sternly said, **"Break their lines. They have to be broken; they fight as a unit, just like a phalanx. I have been studying them; it is the best and most logical option based on the resources you plan on using. Take that away and they will break. It will be easier said than done. You haven't considered using the Andromeda tactics have you? What did Atlas and the Rioans do to beat them?"** Nicolas smiled at his brilliant apprentice, easier said than done though indeed. What Danyzer did was so destructive, most of his galaxy ended up making the IGF; Cain was certain that his troops not do the same thing unless there were no other choices. *Not unless we utterly have to do so,* thought the Alpha. The price is too high. But the son and the father are both right though, those lines must be split. Maybe the material they are developing on Earth is just what we need. Either a fleet or one moon-sized monster ship. *Yeah, that will do*, thought the genius.

As the months went by, the Earthlings had continued to make remarkable progress. The natives were able to complete their fusion system, as well as complete a propulsion system for light speed travel. Dr. Genero and his new protégé, Dr. Matias Martinez had completed a propulsion system for star fighters that could at least reach warp speed. Dr. Chandler, a beautiful blonde with kind and soft eyes, was in constant consult with Kima on how to inoculate the Earthlings from diseases that the Terran Alliance had dealt with eons ago. Kima, in her personal journal remarked at how these people, just a few decades earlier would have never been able to work together have become more than just brothers in arms; they had become family.

One of the test pilots, Jaylun Harris, had become quite friendly with Kima and she began to have feelings for him. He was a tall and strong African American; he reminded her of Nicolas in a lot of ways. First off, he is absolutely brilliant; an incredible problem solving intellect. The way that he didn't say anymore than he had to and was really quick witted. She didn't dare tell him though, she was far too shy. Besides there were a great many other details that had to be addressed before she could even think about telling him how she felt. At this point, her number one priority was developing the kinds of medical procedures that could be implemented in the field. Isis needed to be taught them by Kima and Dr. Chandler so that the pilots and other support staff could be ready in a moment's notice to become medical officers in the field. Isis has a remarkable ability in that anything that she has been taught, she can teach others with equal if not superior aplomb.

Nathan and Jaylun had made preparations to implement an early warning net that was specifically designed to detect energy signatures that were not human, via Earthling or Terran Alliance in origin. By implementing the design that Alex taught about energy signatures, Jaylun figured out how to create a detection system using their opponent's own technology against them. He then took his theoretic to Dr. Igeleke who then took it to scale with the help of Nathan. Because of the time crunch, they worked on it for 43 hours straight; that is nothing to a Paladin, but to a normal human, that can be dangerous. It was operational and the good doctor then fell asleep in the lab. Jaylun and Nathan then took off in a Delta Raider, one of the fighter ships that the Earthlings had created. It was heavier than a raptor but the design is similar; because it can't travel at the same velocities that the raptors can, the Raider needs to be sturdier. Coupled with the fact that it is a multi-use vehicle, it is in some ways a more functional design for the newest members of the Faster Than Light propulsion club.

While Nathan and Jaylun were developing the detection grids, Lance and several other natives were building several support stations throughout the solar system. Because of the rediscovery of the CERN labs in what were the remains of Switzerland, the Earthlings were again using anti-matter. There in the particle lab was the foundations for anti-matter equipment. *Remarkable*, thought the Paladin. *They were so close to making the breakthrough.* Since Lance had a background in quantum mechanics and anti-matter applications, he taught several engineers how to use anti-matter in a much more weapons based form.

By using electromagnetism as the base, they were able to create several million antimatter projectiles. Coupled with what the humans already knew about nuclear radiation and astrophysics, in a short period of time the Earthlings had produced quite an impressive armory. Most of this equipment was too dangerous to be used on Earth, so they created several dozen weapons depots all around the system. Most of it was for deep orbit such as the Kuiper Belt and the asteroid belt between Mars and Jupiter. Another base was secretly designed on Mars, which could act as a safe harbor in case the war began to take a turn for the worse and they needed a place to regroup. With their newly discovered warp speed propulsion technology, reaching Mars would be a matter of minutes. Once the battle begins, everyone who is unable to fight, children and the injured and the elderly will be sent to Mars for safe keeping. Everyone else when the war begins who is on Earth will be expected to fight to the death, devoted to something that is greater than themselves.

It was early August and the Earthlings, along with the help of some devoted Paladins, had reached the levels of development required by both the Terran Alliance and also the Inter Galactic Federation. Antonius was pleased with the progress as was Emily, but he was more pleased with the defensive developments that had been implemented to make the star system more secure. Both the project manager and also the head of Earth Defense were in agreement that formal entrance into the greater collective would have to wait. There were much bigger issues at stake. AC, Faris, and Nicolas were all in agreement with that fact. What was important now was getting the Earth warriors up to speed, prepared to fight to the death. Their star fighters were ready and it was a matter of time before the Mega Star Carriers would be ready for long term space flight. Mega Carriers would be between twenty-four and twenty-nine hundred meters. The super destroyers would be between thirty-four and thirty-eight hundred meters in length, all of which would have warp speed propulsion, enhanced up to Terran Alliance standards.

The flagship of the Earth armada was bigger than all of the other ships, coming in at a massive forty-eight hundred meters. With the humans understanding of antimatter, the primary weaponry are three energy turrets; each was more than 400 meters, bigger than the guns on the Centauri. That plus sixteen 75 meter rail guns and missile battery of five thousand modified antimatter and thermonuclear warheads means that firepower won't be an issue. The Earthlings had shown themselves approved; it was time to make sure that they were battle ready. The Dark-Sider Armada war machine would not be merciful. It is imperative that the Earthlings are not in a giving mood either. Kira smiled, knowing that her kinsmen were prepared to give no quarter to the siders or anyone else. It was just a matter of time before it was time to be battle tested.

In October, the opportunity for testing the Earth defense network was given its best opportunity. The Erixes, still smarting from the devastating defeat handed to them by the Paladins had returned. This time, they brought a much larger invasion force, almost seventeen thousand star ships. That many ships would have been a nice warm up for about a dozen raptors but this was different. It was time for the Earthlings to let the rest of the universe know what happens when you come to Earth's territory looking for trouble. The early warning nets had alerted Earth to the group of vermin heading towards their system. One million antimatter and nuclear warheads began hitting the Erixian fleet; several thousand ships were severely damaged before reaching the Kuiper belt. On the moon of Triton, another weapon of mass destruction had been activated.

A binary fusion weapon of terrible ability had been activated, destroying several thousand starships and damaging several thousand more. Before entering the inner part of the solar system, the Erixian Fleet had been cut in half. At this point, the *Wig Splitter* star fighter squadron, led by the two Harris brothers, led the contingent of seven hundred into battle. Their fighter ships were the Sigmas, the modified F-22 raptors, or the Omnicrons, modified SR-71 Blackbirds. The Harris brothers had distinctive ships from everyone else, with their ships being upgraded versions of the American Aurora spy plane. Each of the fighters with a full armament of antimatter, nuclear and binary fusion warheads. Coupled with fusion based energy beam cannons, these ships were not going down without a fight.

The Earth-based techno weapons had been more than effective. The fighters destroyed most of the Erixian Fleet star fighters without much of a fuss. The only ship that made it past the lines was the mother ship, only for it to have a devastating reward. An antimatter blast came from the surface of Mars, obliterating the remainder of the rest of the fleet. The Earthlings had their first victory. A ship was watching from a minimally safe distance taking notes of what they had seen. A sider ship had been their just to observe the action, no doubt to scout out the competition. The Earthlings were not going to just lie down.

As the squadron returned to Earth fresh off their first successful test of its defenses, a pensive Kira and Emily stood above hanger bay. The two leaders talked to each other dispassionately about the events that unfolded. **"Commander, you are going to have to talk to them about what happened. We can't let too many see what our people can do yet; but it was a good start, do you want us to prepare to sweep the rest of the Erixes away or,"** the warrior was interrupted by her commanding officer. **"No, we are going to need them; the Erixes won't bother us again. Still, we are the *least* of each other's problems. There will be a time very soon when we are going to have to put aside our differences to address a much larger common threat. We could use their bodies and mecha, besides the siders were watching. I just wanted your guys to give a good show. Jaylun and Jamie are *really* good. The fighters held up well and that wasn't even the good stuff. The siders will come soon. At least you know what you have to work with."** The Chief nodded in agreement with the commanding officer's assessment.

Kira, cautiously proud of her new troops, pondered another issue that eventually has to be addressed. **"Commander, when we send the mega cruisers into battle who are we going to have command the flag ship? Because I was thinking about,"** Commander Uchida smiling, cut her off, **"that's easy. *You are.* I discussed it with Nick a long time ago;**

I was just waiting for the appropriate time to let you know; sorry about that. Very soon, we will have the first unified armada in the history of our home planet. I have no doubt that you're not just the right choice, you're the *only* choice. We still have a lot of work to do, but when the lights come on, we go where you lead. Admiral." At this point, Commander Uchida proceeded to pin a Admiral's medallion on Kira and the entire room filled with cheers of approval.

The father and son are on the capital planet of the original Altarian Federation. Michael is feeling apprehensive about the situation for multiple reasons. One of the biggest issues for him is the fact that his biological father was responsible for the destruction of the original planet and its people. A part of the noble young warrior was deeply troubled and ashamed at what Atlas had done. That being said, there was another part of him that felt incredibly proud of his mother's people. That even after all that tragedy, they could find the strength to go on and become more than they had ever been. The son speaks to his father about the immediate future and how it could be changed. "Father, I am afraid that they will not accept me as one of theirs; that they may only see the Gondronian in me. I want to love them and be loved by them. I know that you have given me much but a part of me has always longed to connect to my Altarian roots. I hope that you do not take offense."

Nick was looking out at the courtyard, he could feel his beloved son's concern at what his answer would be. "Son, you have nothing to fear. Your family will always stand by you; nothing has changed. There is nothing for you to feel apprehensive about. Your kin will see the good that is in your soul. It doesn't matter how you came to be; God knows what He is doing. Only He can take something that was of darkness, beat the *Hell* out of it, and use it for the light. If the circumstances hadn't have happened none of these great things that we are on the cusp of would even be possible." Michael smiled when he heard his father speak with such clarity and confidence. The young monarch continued. "So what do you think? I have been studying the *Language of Tears*; I believe that everything is in order. What if my aunt doesn't see it that way? I heard she is a hot head like Kira." Nick turned and smiled at his son, he began to sharpen his blade. "Nah, she isn't. She is just suffering. Once she takes one look at you, all of that

shit will stop. She will see you as what you are, her nephew and heir to the Altarian Federation."

Even though he could hear his father's confidence in the situation, he knows that Cain hasn't completely answered his original query. Michael knows that the next response will have nothing to do with the fact that his father loves him dearly. If anything, he has learned that when left with a choice of sparing his son's feelings or being honest with him, Michael's father will always choose honesty. The young prince also knows that Cain has contemplated whether he would consider her anger and grief an obstacle to the main objective. He already knows the answer but asks him anyway. The son looks at the twin stars as they begin to set. He doesn't want his father to see his tears. Michael then repeats the second half of his original question. **"Commander, you didn't answer my question: *what if she doesn't see it that way*?"** Cain put his katana back in its sheath. **"Then your face will be the last thing that she will see."**

The time had come. Antonius was in the king's study, meditating when Congo entered the room. He informed the mighty Paladin that his guest had arrived. **"It's time my Master."** A smile has surfaced over Cain's handsome face, the thing that he was wanted the most, a face to face with the cold-hearted beautiful leader of Altarian Federation was about to happen. She would no doubt be frustrated because both her and her fleet of almost fourteen billion had come looking for blood and there was none to be had. Nicolas had ordered Congo to tell inform his army of more than 29 billion warriors to not even come close to bearing arms. Let them come through. He knew his foe well; the Altarians will not strike down an enemy who has not picked up a weapon to arm themselves.

As the mighty Altarian fleet moved closer inside Gondronian territory, Nicolas had the flagship of the Gondronian fleet meet the war birds. Congo, Nicolas' valued and trusted aid would carry his orders and make his request to his guests. Alvarnari is a wise and cunning leader, who no doubt is confused by the actions of her sworn enemies. Her last memory of Atlas was the cruel and twisted mind games he played with her father and sister before he killed them; she was not going to fall for his devious tricks. She was however inquisitive about the fact that every ship and system that was supposedly of the Gondronian race didn't have any of the Gondronian people on them.

From the time that she had entered their territory, she had yet to encounter one Gondronian officer, much less even a Gondronian child.

Everywhere the Altarian Queen and her mighty fleet had gone, there were many other races of people, from the Asgaries to the D'ashren to the Sprogranix peoples, but no damn Gondronians. Even the adjutant of the king was not even Gondronian. *What arrogance do they have to believe that asking us to meet the king in our home system would yield some type of mercy? Or maybe this is the where he has his palace, over the blood of my people? I will enjoy killing him,* the warrior queen thought. *I will kill him slowly; Atlas deserves a perfect death. I hope that there are Gondronians all over this planet, so that my warriors are able to gain some satisfaction in their bloodshed. They took our home, we shall take their lives.* Her bridge officer informed her that Congo had something to say.

The fleet was essentially surrounded, there were Atlas' star ships all around them, but they had given a wide birth. Cloaked maybe, if they were there, the ships were in hiding. *What a coward, you shall die slow,* the predator thought. **"Alvarnari, my great king is on that planet waiting for you. You can bring down as many of your warriors as you wish; he says that if you want him, he will face you in single combat. No sense in so many of your warriors needing to die. A fair fight if that is what you desire. The opportunity for retribution on the soil of your people, of your father and sister. Only he and his ward are on the planet. As long as your warriors don't interfere, my ships will not attack yours. They may be in deep orbit, but they are here. Do you accept his terms?"** Her lips could barely make audible sounds; she was shaking with anticipation of a one on one encounter. **"We are on the way. Your king has but a few moments to live and then we will kill you for serving him."**

The delegation of the Altarian Federation, men and women representing the races of all the people that were slaughtered by Atlas long ago had accompanied the warrior queen. They had all dedicated their lives to fighting tyranny in all its forms; hoping to one day is strong enough to seek their revenge upon those that had wrongly taken from them which not theirs to begin with. This place looks as it did when she was a child. Every building and every other structure was just as if it had not been razed by this cruel and manipulative monarch. What sort of madness was this? Her people were conflicted; this was just as it was, accept for the horrible bloodshed.

There was one distinctive difference in the before and after on the planet's surface. There was a memorial statue in the courtyard with an inscription on it. The inscription was in the *Language of Tears*, the Altarian language of the dead. This angered the party even further. Coupled with the fact that the king dared to face her in combat. Only his ward was on the planet with him. *Does Atlas think so little of us that he created a memorial to torment us as he waits? No matter*, she thought. *My mind is stronger than this; he will die a perfect, slow death. Then will his ward, and then the rest of his people, wherever they hide.*

As the party entered the great conference chamber, two figures are in the shadows. In the Hall of Kings, all of the fallen kings of the Altarian Federation were there, including one new edition; Avis. This was too much. Then the party saw the two figures. One was the king, the slime, the filthy king, and his ward. No doubt an assassin trained to protect him, as if he needs it. There the two figures remain in the shadows, with their faces hidden by cloaks. These clothes were those of Altarian monarchy. The king was in the colors of red with black trim while his ward was wearing the opposite color pattern, black with red trim.

The king sits in the chair of the head of the Federation; much like her father once did, while the assassin stands beside the chair, waiting at a moment's notice to protect him, to die for him. The beautiful would-be executioner spoke, **"get up and face me. Don't stand in the shadows. Face me as you said you would!!!! Rise you coward, look at me; I want to see my father and sister's killer!!!! You took everything from me and my people; it's time we took it back."** At this point, she lunged for the king and his ward intervened, stopping her with a blade, a katana, just like his father.

Nicolas Cain, the mighty Paladin, with no known predator didn't move. In the shadows, he sat patiently and finally he spoke to noble warrior queen. **"I am the new king of the Gondronians. I am Antonius of Terra. You are the warrior queen of the Altarians. You have no quarrel with me or anyone else in this part of space. This land is yours; I had every planet within your star system rebuilt, just the way that it was, save a few changes that are consistent with your death customs. You have no quarrel with me or my subjects, Alvarnari of Altaria, noble warrior, and enemy of tyranny. Everyone of the foes that you speak of has been vanquished. My warriors and I have removed all Gondronians from existence. It is only the Gondronian Federation in name only; I just haven't decided to change it yet."**

The queen and her party had come too far to be denied. She knew of Khan Antonius, he was a human whose reputation for his hatred of evil was greater than her own. But they had come too far not to fight. **"I know who you are; Lord of The Oculari. Antonius, I don't care that what you have said could be true; the Gondronians are going to pay and since you represent them, it is you who must pay for our pain. It is you who must pay for our sorrow. I am sorry, we could have been allies, but this cannot be undone."**

The Master Oculari realized that this conversation wasn't going as planned, but it wasn't inconsistent with Altarian Queen's reputation. Much like his own son, her anger had clouded her judgment. *It's too bad, we could have used her for the campaign,* thought the Alpha Paladin. If this had been for anyone else but his son, he wouldn't have done what he isn't known for: reasoning with the opposition. Antonius, realizing this was Alvarnari's last chance before he would have to end her life spoke again. **"We have bigger issues my friend. The Dark-Sider Armada is on the move into the Virgo Super Cluster, that's concerns *all* of us. We need you to fight alongside us; the rest of the galaxy is concluding preparations. We need your warriors, we need your guidance. However, if you are so selfish and close-minded that your immediate pain supersedes the greater need in this part of the universe then you are not the person I hoped that you were. I shall take your life and then the lives of all of the Altarians who believe their pain is greater than our plight. How many of your people will die needlessly until I find someone who will listen and fight for something greater than themselves? Let me know when you are ready."** To which Alvanari quipped, **"ready for what?"** Nick sighed and unfastened his gun belt, **"to die."**

As Michael's father, tired of the immaturity shown by his aunt, reaches for his sword andthe son decides to intervene. This is the only blood that he has left and she must be made to listen. Even if that means to fight his adopted father, the human who showed him so much compassion and taught him how to be more than just what he was, it must be. Alvarnari, a warrior of great skill with two swords, prepared for combat. Cain, seemingly both amused and irritated by her actions, got in his combat stance. She ran at the mighty king with full speed, leaping in the air, prepared to swoop down on him as he remained perfectly still.

At the last instant, her blades struck something, but not Antonius. The ward moved so quickly; he blocked her attempted strike with his forearm. His body amor was stronger than the queen's blade. Michael, with the ability to fly, caught his aunt in midflight and threw her to ground, saving her from certain death. **"You fool!! He would have killed you! And for what? They are gone!! My mother is gone and my grandfather is gone; I will not lose my aunt as well."** At this point, Michael removed his hood, looking like the image of his grandfather, accept for the oxblood feathers; the hawk is revealed. **"I am Michael, my queen. Son of Avari and Grandson of Avis IV and also the son of Atlas. I am the *only* heir to the throne of Gondronia and also to the Altarian Federation. The Lord of The Oculari is also my adopted father, the Gondronian Steward, but I am the kingdom's heir. Not him, me; your nephew".**

The Altarians looked at Michael for the first time. He is the spitting image of Avis III. The only difference was his hue. Avis was white, while the young monarch looked like a hawk. Alvanari's grandfather also looked like a hawk. It was unmistakeable. He continued. **"If there is blood to be spilled it will be my blood. I am the *last* of the Gondronian race. But on one condition; you stand with my father, Antonius and the rest of the galaxy and fight against this terrible foe. This system, the one taken from you so long ago, is your payment. He had it rebuilt brick for brick save a few things. My father had nothing to do with the memorials because he is not of *our* blood. *It was I who had it commissioned, not my father.* If this is the blood you must have then take it. We don't have time for Cain to kill everyone of you until he finds someone who is sensible. Do it now!!"**

The young king laid down in front of all of the federation, his people. The queen grabbed her blade and prepared to kill her nephew, knowing that it might kill the rest of her soul. How could he not be of Avis? Michael looks like her father, but sounds like her sister. He was willing to lay down his life for a greater cause than revenge. Even in this situation, Antonius is quite pleased. His child has become a man; his wonderful, beautiful son. *How he has learned*, thought Nick. Even still, Michael knows his father; Cain has that look in his eye. He is taping on his katana, waiting to strike if the queen does anything but embrace this new reality.

Michael was hoping to avoid the very scenario he was facing, but it is too late and cannot be avoided. He knows that his aunt's life is in serious peril. *God, allow her to think this through.* Nick has already made his assessment of the situation and has but one conclusion. *If she lunges at him, I will kill her and all the rest; we need him, she is expendable.* The noble queen takes one look at her nephew; so noble, just like her father. So giving, just like her sister. Her heart is conflicted, as are her warriors. This is their king.

Oh God, please don't let her be that stupid thought the mighty Paladin. *How much more greatness do these people have to see from my son,* he mused. Cain had reached the end of his patience. He had already made his assessment of how he was going to kill not only Alvanari, but all the rest of the contingent. *Might as well kill all of them,* he thought. *They are probably just as stupid.* This is an inefficient use of resources as far as Cain was concerned because he was about to eliminate a lot of experience and talent, but he felt that killing them was the lesser of two evils. He was disappointed that she couldn't see the big picture. He figured he needed 9 seconds. It is absolutely terrifying how quickly his brain works.

Oh God, Alvanari, don't be this stupid, thought the adopted mother. *Oh shit, Nick is going to kill everyone in this room in less than 10 seconds.* AC has been with Nick longer than anyone and she knows that Michael has stalled him as long as he could; the Altarian Queen has to make the right choice. Namon told Michael that Cain is an awful person to play games with because he has normally worked out the hows and whys long before you sit down to actually play. AC knew that Michael's aunt and everyone that was with her was dead the moment that they walked into the hall. They had at the most three seconds to do the right thing or Cain would decide that killing all of them was the most efficient use of time and resources. *Don't screw this up,* thought the mother. AC closed her eyes; *damn, they didn't have to die.* The father looks at the son and smiles. The smile reminded her of when Nick went after Kima and Petamauck; she remembers the outcome of that day. Michael will not have one hair misplaced.

It couldn't be a coincidence, thought the queen. In Altarian prophecy, a king would come forth who was not of Altarian blood to make the people whole once again. He would be raised by a mighty warrior and they would make the universe a safer place for righteous. There was no way that the boy in front of the queen and her warriors was not the king of legend. Then she dropped her blade. She uttered to the mighty hawk, **"forgive me my King. I did not see. I am at your service. We all are at your service."** The blue–hued queen became red and she sobbed at her nephew's feet. All of the Altarians fell and wept. The king of the Altarians had been returned.

Personal Log: Lady Alvanari

Personal Log: This message is to my father and my sister. Father, you were the greatest leader in the history of our people and Avari, you were gracious, kind, beautiful, and joyous. Both of you sacrificed so much for our people to become what we have become. Our Federation is vast and strong; we have more than 700 different races of people represented, we control more than nine thousand light years, with well over three hundred thousand planets, moons and stars. Your sacrifice has not been in vain. Father, I remember the last words that you said to me, **"protect the people, allow them to grow, and remember that I love you."** I swore that we would have revenge for what Atlas and his people had done. I used your death and Avari's death as motivation for everything that I had done. In that regard, I deeply apologize. Because I failed you both.

You see, I didn't learn anything from your great sacrifice. I couldn't see why Avari went instead of me to meet Atlas. I understand now. I would have tried to kill him and would have failed. Our people would have been completely obliterated. In my short sightedness, revenge would have been too great an incentive to do what was right. You and Avari's sacrifice represented everything that was great about you both instead of the cowardice that I displayed. I thought that I was using strength, but instead I was not doing what was in the best interest of the people. Our people have thrived in spite of me, not because of me. As many people as we have protected and gave a home to, I was so busy being consumed by revenge and hatred. I hated both of you most of all, because you left me. I was so unprepared for such a responsibility and both of you knew that I would eventually be up to the task. I thank you both for your faith in me. Even as we grew in size and strength, I was consumed with vengeance; I became blue instead of red. I almost plunged us back into war for no other reason than I felt that retribution was my only purpose in the universe. Forgive me for being so selfish and close minded.

You will both be happy to know that I have met someone that would make both of you very proud. He is strong and handsome, he looks just like grandfather. A beautiful hawk. He is regal and strong; he is wise beyond his years. He is your son Avari, he is named Michael. Father, I believe that he is the *one*. The one that the ancients talked about. His beginnings are not as important as his present and certainly not as important as his future. He is so strong and brave. His father is such an honorable and decent being.

Before you say anything dear sister, no I am not talking about that monster Atlas; I will get to him momentarily. I am talking about his *real* father. Father, you might have heard of him. The Khan, the mighty general of the human tribe. He is so powerful and deadly but that is not why he has earned my devotion. He is also wise and noble; much like you father, he has a servant's heart. He truly dances between the realm of wisdom and psychosis. I have never met a creature such as he. He is known for his ability to dole out death, he is the enemy of tyranny in all its forms. He killed Atlas and liberated the people of the Gondronian Empire. Truth be told, he eliminated all Gondronians from the universe, except for one.

Michael is the hybrid of the Gondronian and Altarian bloodlines. I was so angry went I met Michael, I could have killed him, but I knew that probably would have been the end of the Altarian Federation because Antonius would have surely killed *all* of us. He loves Michael so much and his people are Michael's family. His Rioan mother loves him like I believe that you would have my sweet sister and the most amazing thing is that they have embraced all of us as their kin. Antonius' influence on Michael is so apparent, but his father wants him to know his heritage. I am preparing the annals so that he can learn about the nobility of our family bloodline. I am so excited.

Michael and Lord Antonius have done something that is still beyond my comprehension father; they have returned our home to us. Every planet within the system is ours once again. They rebuilt everything; it is as if nothing has been destroyed before. Michael said that whenever we wish to claim it again, it will be there. Several of the elders are preparing a pilgrimage to our home. It is ironic that many of our people have never set foot on the home world; I look forward to them having that opportunity.

I must tell you both that we are once again on the brink of war. The monsters that the ancient ones spoke of, the Dark-Siders are coming back to the Virgo Super Cluster. The Federation will be involved in the fight. I want to help protect our new family father and protect Avari's son; he is our last one. I believe that he is the child of prophecy; the king groomed by a warrior of a different tribe. Even though he is a capable warrior and leader, he is still only a boy. If in this conflict, things become eventful, I have instructed our generals to protect him at all costs. He must live in order for our people to survive; which is what I have to tell you about.

You see father, I am dying. The physicians say it is because of too many reckless encounters, far too many life and death struggles. My body is slowly being broken; I cannot have children. The bloodline was going to die with me. I selfishly was willing to kill Michael to satisfy my bloodlust. Antonius had told me that he had killed Atlas and that we had no reason to fight, but I didn't care. He said that the Dark-Siders were coming and I still didn't care. Michael even told me that he was your son dear sister and again, I didn't care. I felt that if I was going to die that the Altarian Federation shall die with me. I am so glad that I turned out to be wrong. I have a human to thank for that gift. I will not live long enough for Michael to become a great king; that will be someone else's charge. I am proud of him. In the short time that I have been around him, I have come to love him with all of my soul. Forgive me for my actions father and forgive me sister for my selfishness. When you see me in the after-life, please be kind.

As for now, I have much to teach my nephew. He has a tremendous task ahead of him. But with the help of his noble father, powerful mother, and his dedicated tribe, I believe that he will fulfill the prophecy and make the wicked of the universe tremble. *Just like his father.*

CHAPTER 8

A Khan is Born

The time has finally come for Commander Nicolas Cain. He has been waiting to finally take on the Dark-Siders since he can first remember becoming a Paladin. No more isolated skirmishes; not another unfulfilled encounter. Something will be settled. The war with his enemies will finally tip one way or the other. His comrades, the Blood Knights, the Gondronian Federation, the IGF, the Terran Alliance, the Altarians, and the United Earth Defense have all made their way to this unremarkable solar system that houses the planet Earth and her seven sister planets. None of his allies have any idea why he believes this is place that the war with the siders will turn nor have any clue as to how this battle will change the Alpha Paladin. There are many questions, but only one answer.

Seven months have passed since the Earth warriors had their successful offensive against the Erixes and more than six months have elapsed since Nicolas' adopted son Michael has connected with his beloved aunt. At this moment, the IGF and Terran contingents of their military have entered the Earth system's territory. A gathering has been called for on the planet Mars. The solar system's fourth planet houses a secret stronghold for the Earthlings that has been deemed either too young or too old to fight against this terrible foe, the Dark-Sider Armada. This mighty, heavily armored enemy has plans on a full scale invasion into the Virgo Super Cluster; thus having subjugated the Phoenix Super Cluster recently.

Alliance and Federation intelligence reports reveal the scope and scale of the invasion force. On this tiny red planet, the gathered warriors are ready to hear from their commanding officer, Cain, on how they will wage war against this seemingly endless hoard of machines and resources bent on making the Milky Way, the new base of operations for their assault on the Virgo Super Cluster. There is little surprise that Nick has been chosen to lead this offensive against the Dark-Siders. If these warriors can hold the Dark-Sider assaultthere in this solar system, there is a chance that the war can truly turn in their favor. The Dark-Sider Virgo offensive may be halted before it truly has begun. Even with as large a force of contention as these groups may seem their combined quantity is but a fraction of the beast that they now are facing within the next few Earth weeks. As far as Cain is concerned, they have the Dark-Sider Armada right where they want them.

Here on Mars, Admiral Kira Darius, the leader of United Earth Defense and the reportedly best warrior that the Order of Paladins has produced since Khan Antonius delivers her preliminary report on what the unified forces will now be soon facing. **"Greetings and blessings to all assembled as well as all those present via Holcomb. Here is what we know so far. The siders have crossed into the Virgo Super Cluster as of 10 Earth weeks ago. They crossed into the Milky Way as of 10 Earth days ago. All the groups that said they would decline joining this defense directorate, from the Angorians to the Thezon Alliance have been completely wiped out. More than eighty trillion beings have been decimated by the armada so far. It seems as if their fleet has been gaining in strength and capacity as they move forward. The total length of the vessel that is the mother ship of the armada is estimated at around 15,000 miles in length and also more than three thousand miles wide. Its best described as a runaway train in space."**

As Kira looked over the faces of the leaders in this room and via holocom, she saw several looks of despair; fortunately, none of those looks were from her mother, Cain, Michael, or Emily. This gave her even more hope that this great battle will be a successful venture for them, when she saw her loved ones so unfazed by the daunting task of their charge. Queen Alvarnari, Michael's aunt and newest ally, spoke at this point, hushing the crowd. **"Admirmal, I don't care how big that ship is they have to be stopped. I know some people have been disturbed by what you have said, but I am not moved. None of what you said does not mean that this cannot be done; please continue your report."** This pleased Nicolas; because for his plan to work, he will need all of his newest comrade's courage for his preparations to be feasible. Kira continued her report. **"Thank you Lady Alvarnari. Intelligence also reports something of significant importance; the siders are being lead** by one of the members of the royal house during this offensive. The Dark-Sider Assassin, Nex, will be in command. He is considered the deadliest warrior (that we know of) from the siders. But..."

At this point, Erik the Red, one of the oldest and most accomplished members of the Order of Paladins interjected. "**Excuse me Admiral, did you say Nex? Son of a bitch! Nick, you are one tricky Ocularian Bastard! You knew he would be leading their forces already didn't you? Damn Ocularian tricksters; they** *always* **know too much! When we kill him, the war will definitely turn in our favor. Isn't that what you were thinking? Kira, I think that the commander has the rest of this report covered.**" Confused yet convinced, Kira nods her head in agreement and cedes the floor to the Alpha Paladin. The telepath was also confused. *When did you met this guy before, you never told me,* she thought to her big brother. *A long time ago before you were born; ask me about it later,* he thought back. Kima realized that she could only read as much of her brother's mind as he allowed her to. There were things that he would never share, no matter how far she dug. For the first time in a long time, Erik knew something that his young Paladin comrades did not.

Nicolas Cain, a man of few words, but vast actions, knows that the time has come. This is the crucial element of the war that has Erik the Red, a warrior who helped train him in combat and a dear friend over his life, excited because this pending conflict provides an opportunity to close the chapter on whose form of combat is truly superior; the assassins of the Dark-Siders or the Order of Paladins. This is a unique opportunity presented by Nex being present. Once he is gone, there will be no replacement for the Assassin in Dark-Sider society.

The truth about the Dark-Siders is that their resources are almost infinite, but their key citizens are finite. There will be no replacements for the lord of the assassins. Once he has been vanquished, there will be no more assassins. In order to beat the siders, one must kill every member of the royal house of their kingdom. The problem is that during an offensive that their key warriors are well protected. If that person is considered to be in danger, the sider armada will change tactics from offensive to defensive to insure that the warrior will be protected at all costs.

Many of their prolonged offensives over the years have cost the Dark-Sider Royal House many. The last campaign into the Virgo was in the Andromeda Galaxy more than two billion Earth years ago; that offensive cost the royal house five hundred-eighty members. Each of those members was irreplaceable; it took eons for the siders to recover from those huge personnel losses; it was considered the greatest victory ever achieved by the great Rioan general Danyzer. It was then decided that the siders would never send more than one member for any major incursion.

But this is personal for the siders because the Virgo Super Cluster has been most troublesome to their ambitions. This will be the *third time* that the Dark Sider Armada has attempted to enter this galactic star cluster; the other two times have ended in failure. There have been seven Empires or Houses of the Universe. The Dark-Siders have been desperate to make it number 8. The people of Iconia were the first group to truly stand up against them. To stop them, the Iconians sacrificed their entire species to defeat the Dark-Siders. The previous Dark King's father was killed at the hands of the leader of the *Iconian Black Project.* This action nearly drove the new king mad with rage because he could never have vengeance on the Iconians. Instead, he intends on taking his anger out on the rest of the Universe, especially the Virgo Super Cluster.

The second attempt, more than 950 million Earth years later had been thwarted by the people of the Andromeda Galaxy, led by Danyzer and Atlas. The reward for the defeat of the mighty Dark-Sider Fleet was making the Andromeda nearly lifeless. This indirectly led to the creation of the IGF and also the Terran Alliance. Now the great Dark King and Queen are prepared to take the Virgo Super Cluster again. They have no intentions of under estimating the resolve and skill of their opposition.

The Dark King and Queen of their empire have activated their most deadly asset to ensure that victory would be reached this time. The monarch has decreed that within his lifetime that this section of space would fall and no species, especially a human, is going to stop them. The Assassin will be sacrificed if necessary to finally kill the human Khan, because the King knows that Cain's death literally stands in his way of conquest of this part of space.

The commanding officer of the Milky Way's united defense against the Dark-Sider offensive has decided that it is time to reveal the strategy on why the Earth system is the perfect place to mount their most spirited defense and just how the great assassin of the Dark-Sider Armada will finally fall. **"Greetings and blessings to all assembled both here and afar. This is an exciting time. For the first time, the combined strength of the mighty Gondronians, the Altarians, and the warriors of Terra will stand together as comrades in arms, we shall stand** together in blood. We shall stand together in victory. From my colleagues to my son to my son's beloved aunt, war is upon us. Here we shall stand, fight, and die, to protect this part of the universe."

Cain was looking over the faces of his comrades in arms. He knows that this is the most incredible undertaking that he has ever asked of them. He is cognizant of the magnitude of the task; the sheer absurdity of it. Cool confidence is what he radiates for his friends. **"The basis that this system is the best place to engage the armada is simple: this system negates the sider's primary advantages. We know that the siders use dark energy to power its war machine. Since dark matter makes up the majority of the residual energy in the universe, they have an almost endless supply of it. The Milky Way and Andromeda galaxies are perfect areas for the armada to travel because they are both overflowing with it. However this system where the Terrans call their home is not. This system has an inordinately low amount of dark matter, plus the fact that the star is yellow creates another disadvantage. Our star is just the right combination of brightness and also relative coolness that renders many of their defensive and propulsion systems tremendously diluted."**

The officers who would be carrying out this action plan were speechless. Even for Cain, this operational plan seemed crazy. He wanted to wage an extended conflict with the Dark-Sider Armada. He wanted to stare down the most deadly foe of all the proponents of liberty in the universe. Even though the Paladins had achieved success, it had never been in an exhaustive encounter with the siders. He smiled at the thought of this glorious battle. **"The key to our strategy is to keep them in this system for an extended period of time in combat with our fleet, depleting their reserves in a comprehensive conflict. It would also give us time to locate the primary ship where the Assassin is and close his eyes. Permanently. The primary objective of this encounter is to kill him; we fail if we don't complete that task. We have to force the siders to break up into smaller vessels, with all the chaos occurring, he will be easier to find. The United Fleet will be responsible for destroying their armada while Erik and I deal with Nex. We will hunt him down and,"**

At this point AC, one of the United Fleet's fiercest operators, interjected. **"You and Erik aren't going to fight the Assassin without us so just stop right there. Personally, I am tired of you two having** all the fun. Petamauck and I are going too and there is nothing that you will say to change that fact Commander. As a point of question, how are we going to break them up and how in the Hell are we going to find him?" Nick smiled at his troops and then spoke with a cool vibe, "excellent question Admiral. And the answer is coming in three, two, one." At this juncture, Dr. Igeleke and Nathan the Magnificent entered the room, Nathan exclaimed about their discovery. "We have found it Commander!! We can track them. We can locate the damn assassin!! Our design for energy signature detection has been modified for dark matter. It is experimental, but it should work. The key is the distance though, if we can get within forty thousand kilometers, Dr. Martinez can track him."

That's when it became clear that this action plan had more than a fewcrucial issues. To be that close to the armada meant being literally in the middle of the fire fight and the equipment wasn't designed for a star fighter. A bigger, slower ship would have to be used. Or a ship that could hide in the corona of the sun without melting. There was only ship that would be able to do that; Alvarnari's flag ship. There was also another problem as well. Alvarnari's ship could only be suspended within the corona for a finite period of time. Once the ship had exhausted its time there, the ship would be extremely vulnerable; if it can't find the primary vessel from a minimum safe distance, it will have to go into the fight with the Altarian flagship being severely weakened, it wouldn't last long.

Another crucial issue was how to force the siders to break apart and fight individually. The strength of the armada is the phalanx; to fight as one unit. The Dark Siders resemble a school of predatory piranha fish in motion. The ships will be so tightly compacted that the armada actually moves and functions as one entity. Their primary target is somewhere within that monster; where the assassin will be hiding. The Paladins have always succeeded in making the siders fight individually, but those were drones. These would be complete star destroyers with a contingent of drones. Furthermore, how to keep them fighting without being overwhelmed by the sheer numbers of the Dark-Siders. This battle has to just be long enough to wear them down, but not too long as to wear the Milky Way fleet down. Because of the fact that the planets are uninhabited in this solar system, the entire arsenals of the Earth Alliance, which includes anti-matter and the Alpha Centauri which includes gamma and nova level firepower, coupled with the Gondronian/Altarian solar battery weaponry, the collateral damage should also be kept at a minimum.

The final problem is breaking up the siders; some ship has to stand in front of the monster, stare it down, and not flinch. The question was not which ship had the firepower, but rather what commanding officer would be crazy enough to make that deal with fate? The phalanx must be broken. Admiral Kira Darius then volunteered the Earth Flagship, the Kronos, for that mighty honor. It had the type of antimatter firepower needed to make the sider armada not only stop, but dissipate. The board was now set. In about 44 hours, the battle for the Virgo Super Cluster, the most coveted space in the universe, may very well be decided.

As the meeting was adjourned, Cain had one more announcement. **"The IGF and Terran Alliance will not be involved in this fight. Commandant Xian, you shall move your forces to the adjacent sector, just as you originally proposed. If they get past us, bring in the Omicron, Gamma, and Sigma squadrons of the IGF and Admiral Agyekum, mobilize the 9th, 42nd, and 3rd Terran Naval Squadrons. Admiral Uchida, have the Scarlet and Crystal Paladin units prepared to join the Terran Alliance and the IGF. If they get past us, you will have to hope that we have weakened them enough for you to take them down. Besides, we have booby trapped the entire solar system. Eighteen million antimatter and nuclear warheads will zero in on the dark matter radiation signatures if we fail."** All three commanders nodded in agreement. That was not the response that he wanted, but it was the one he expected. His instincts were correct.

The Terran Regents were not pleased with decision made by the Alpha. That wasn't even the main thing that was their difficulty. The problem was that they all knew that Cain didn't care. Their opinions and anger meant little to him. Regent Halima in particularly was angered that the majority of the primary assault force from the Alliance and the Federation were told essentially to stand down. How did Cain expect to defeat them with such a small battle group? Driax has had enough history with Cain to know that he always has a reason. His track record says that he has earned the right to be trusted completely. The IGF High Command believed that the Dark-Sider Armada issue was too grave a concern to be handled by such a small force. Driax smiled and simply replied, **"He doesn't work for you."**

Nick had made the decision on how many troops that would be in this conflict based upon his faith and remembering the story of Gideon. He knew that the Terran Alliance and the IGF were interested in the fight against the siders, just not interested enough to fight for the Milky Way. The troops that were coming had no vested interest in the planet Earth, the Milky Way or the Andromeda. These were people who had never even seen their native star systems; it was just another assignment. For the people who were from that section of the star cluster, it meant so much more. The Paladin, IGF, and Alliance warriors were so far from home; these troops had no emotional investment. Nick believed that fighting for a reason that a person holds dear to them is always vital. The universe is too big, that's not a worthy basis to fight and possibly die. The reasons must always be smaller. Cain knew that the Altarians, the Earth Knights, the Janitors, and the Gondronian Federation would be ready to do the unthinkable, to do what was necessary. To be bloody but unbowed. He knew that the IGF and the Terran Alliance troops did not feel that same sense of urgency or sentiment.

The commander knows that time is not on his side when fighting this foe. This battle must lead to the proper conclusion; a prolonged offensive does not favor the warriors of the Virgo. He knew that he normative battle tactics that his colleagues had been taught were not going to be effective in this offensive. This would not be a contest but rather it will be a street fight; it will be a question of who wants it more. Even though he was leaving a lot of firepower and experience on the table by asking them to remain in the adjacent region and wait to see if they would be needed, it told Nick everything that he needed to know. His decision was a wise one; he knew that everyone there wanted to be there and was prepared to follow his orders. There would be no retreating, there would be no regrouping, and there would damn sure be no negotiating. Either the siders were going down or they were. There was no way he could have asked his son, Alvarnari, Congo, United Earth, or the Blood Knights to stand down. He needed everyone who was going to fight to *actually* fight. The game is on.

On Acre, Danyzer is fuming about the decision that Cain has made. He has been in consultation with Driax and she appears unwilling to order him to take more troops into the conflict with the Dark-Sider Armada. And he knows that there is nothing that he can do about it. Aya and OC have just entered the council chambers laughing at Danyzer's rant. "**Dammit Aya, what the Hell is wrong with your son! That defense contingent is far too small! I can't even reach Antonius via com-link or any other way either. I want to know what is going on and he shut me out; I hate when Cain does that. I know you have talked to him, both of you have. I need to give the High Council answers and I don't have any to give them. What is he doing?**"

The Commandant chuckled at Danyzer's anger. "**Stop bitching. You're acting like one of them; you're not. You trained Antonius, why are you acting like this is some new action from him? He is just as much your son as he is ours; you're embarrassing yourself. He *always* goes quiet before a major battle; this is no different. Furthermore, you know that he doesn't give a shit about what the Council, the Alliance or what anyone else thinks. You know that Nick has a plan and it has been working so far; why would he deviate from that?**" Aya concurred. "**Husband, my son has never failed and he has no intentions of failing now. Not when he is so close to completing his objective.**" The Commandant spoke with glee. "**Our son knows exactly what he is doing. Driax is making you look bad. She trusts him more than his kaepa; you are acting like a human. Nick has planned for everything; including your fucking hissy fit.**" Aya kissed him and spoke softly. "**Husband, Nick is doing his job. Please, go do yours. He is counting on you. And so are we.**"

It is not that Danyzer isn't a powerful and wise leader; it is simply that the way he looks at things is not always in the best interests of the quadrant based upon the current realities. He tends to look at the issues that Cain deals with through the lens of a soldier. That particular scope of reference is far too small. For the majority of his tenure as Khan, it was considered a golden age of peace and prosperity for the Federation. The Unori Massacre was the beginning on the end of his tenure. His replacement, Antonius, is Khan during the most uncertain period of the Inter Galactic Federation's modern history. Nick deals with more conflict in a rotation than some Khans have dealt with during their entire tenure as Operational Commanders. Sometimes OC and Aya's combined condescension is the only way to get the right action from Danyzer and therefore the right action from the Federation or the Alliance.

Cain's problems are far more complex than Danyzer's career as Khan. The bottom lines of those issues are often in conflict with one another. Cain has to make decisions that none of the previous military commanders *ever* had to make. Between his previous vocations as an Ocularian Assassin to his tenure as leader of the Federation's Zero Squadron, Cain's life has been filled with life and death decisions that affect millions of light years and quadrillions of people. When it was time to decide who would replace Danyzer as Khan, there was no list of candidates. In fact, Nicolas Cain was the *entire* list.

Many of those choices are far too disconcerting for the IGF leadership. Many of the races that make up the Federation are pacifists. These are statesmen, entrepreneurs, and scholars. Many of these races are not warriors. Many of the leaders have no idea what it's like to have a weapon pointed at them, much less have a friend die in their arms. General Danyzer and the rest of the Rioans are constantly attempting to describe the varied difficulties that Antonius has faced. This reality makes many of his conversations even with the Military leadership problematic. The mighty Khan cares little for the opinions of the under-informed. He will do what is both ugly and necessary for the good of others, even if they cannot fathom the price that must be paid. Cain's belief that the Cause matters above all might be the most extreme of any Paladin, Oculari, or any other leader that has ever lived.

To many within the IGF as well as Terran political and economic leadership, Cain is far too brutal in his methods. The problem is that they know that he doesn't care. Those in leadership look at Antonius with a hint of fear and rightfully so. Of all the Oculari, he is considered the most dangerous, he has no true peer among the Paladins and every other military officer is at his disposal. The Oculari are used as his personal hit squad in most of the Virgo Super Cluster. Everyone who has ever faced him has been executed with extreme prejudice.

In many ways, Cain is both pitied and envied. For all of the potential problems these peaceful people face, he is the perfect solution. He has no biological family, and those that he holds dear are also soldiers so they can't be used against him. His mentors are considered the most devious and feared within the quadrant. Cain is not considered a good person by any stretch, but he is considered far more deadly than the foes that he destroys. This is why so many follow him, because the ramifications are too perilous to imagine. Many look at Danyzer with both scorn and confusion as to why Cain was ever made Khan; many have wondered what was the Rioan General thinking?

To protect his people and the innocent, Antonius is prepared to go to extremes that no one else would ever dare to go. He doesn't care if the Terran Alliance or the IGF leadership understands him or is afraid of what he is. His reasoning is that he is doing horrible things for purely righteous reasons; that is his comfort. Nick has far too many problems to have to continue negotiating peace accords only to have to renegotiate later. It is far more efficient for him to just eliminate the threat. All the enemies of liberty have decided that the IGF and Terran Alliance must be eliminated; the Dark-Siders are just another of Cain's rouges gallery. It is better that Danyzer never know what Cain is really planning; he would have a coronary attack everyday for the rest of his life.

As customary, Cain met with Driax for his final consult before the goes off to execute his operation. While she will never question his decisions in public, she is more than a little concerned with the battle plans that her noble Alpha Paladin has chosen. At this moment in time, Nick is fully aware that his decisions may alter the course of the Milky Way, the Virgo Super Cluster, and perhaps the rest of the universe as well. So far, the only beings that have ever had any real success against the Dark-Siders on a large scale were the mighty Iconians, who are extinct, and the warriors of the Andromeda Galaxy, led by Danyzer and Atlas. The price of that victory could be considered far too high; this victory was considered Danyzer's greatest triumph. His reward was making their home galaxy nearly lifeless. That was a proposition that neither of the two most important Terrans in the universe deemed acceptable.

"Nick, you sure don't believe in making things easy do you? Why did you ask the aid from the Federation and the Alliance to stand down? People from both the Alliance and the Federation have been complaining ever since you made that decision. I know that you told me before, but you said it so casually that I actually thought you were joking. Make your reasoning make sense to me please my servant." Driax needless to say was more than disturbed. Nick smiled and replied. **"Mistress, I cannot wait until you get here. I am going to take you the beach. You will love walking on the sand."** Driax pressed the issue, something that she rarely does with the Alpha. **"Nicky?"** Nick sighed, realizing that she really needs an answer.

For the first time in their relationship, his boss is truly concerned and confused by his actions. **"Lady, because my comrades don't understand the ramifactions of this action; they think too small. We are about** to do the improbable, not the impossible. Impossible is a word that humans say far too often. The Janitors are experts in the absurd. Don't think that for one minute that what we are about to do doesn't border on the side of madness, because it does. It really does. The Dark-Siders are mad enough to believe that one group could actually conquer the whole universe. It's not like they don't have precedent; it has happened seven other times. The problem is that they are good enough to pull it off and make it *eight*. I am aware of that. The only way to fight that kind of madness is with *more* madness. Everyone who is going to war is completely prepared to do the ridiculous; to do the absurd. You know what I learned from Danyzer? To stop the siders is to be willing to go one step further to prove our point. In other words, we have to risk *everything*. I never understood that until now. How big a sacrifice is considered too big? We may have to destroy the solar system, maybe even the entire galaxy to stop them. Everyone here with me now is unruffled by that proposition. That is the choice that my kaepa had, that is the choice that I am faced with now."

Cain could see from the look upon his Alron's face that even though she is highly intelligent and trusts him, she needed more clarification. She needed to know why, if for no other reason than the fact that her comrades in the Federation will need to understand his actions. When a decision of this level affects so many, she needs a better answer than "I trust my monster." This why he loves and respects Driax so much. The mighty Khan has reached a point of devotion for her that rivals Kush and it is more remarkable because he is at that point in such a short period of time.

Even though most of the Federation leaders have known Cain longer, that doesn't mean that they know him *better*. **"Dearest Alron, I could have ordered my IGF troops into this galaxy a long time ago and probably not had to even concern myself with Earth or anything else but that is not the point. For the greater good, I could have just wiped out anyone who I thought was going to be a problem; it would be one master taking the place of another. That was not my intention. What I want is for the people of this galactic region to be accountable to each other. To develop a friendship that will define all of us in ways that none of us even realize yet. Look at us my sweet Alron. There are more than 450 different species represented in this** coalition. People who used to be mortal enemies are now willing to fight and die beside each other under the banner of freedom. This is all part of the plan. Some people have more courage than others. If everyone knew just what was on my mind, they would be too freaked out. Danyzer is probably having a fit right now and my father is somewhere laughing. You have your hands full with those two don't you? Danyzer thinks that I am *beyond* crazy; the Commandant thinks that I am *beyond* sane. They are two aspects of the same face; both comedy and tragedy. God, your friends have a lot of problems."

She was beginning to see just how his mind was working on this issue. It was dizzying to say the least. "**My Chancellor, once this is over, the other free peoples of this part of space will see that the humans aren't to be trifled with, that the Altarians and Gondronians are unified, and that a new day of freedom and peace is within their grasp. All we have to do is kick the Dark-Sider's ass. That is the *easy* part. To me, having the people of this galaxy do the job is an imperative; that's the only way that what we are doing will matter. I know that the Federation and the Alliance are thinking that this is madness, but that is what I want them to think. They need to know that the universe doesn't revolve around their wishes.**"

The chancellor was astonished by this level on clarity and honesty from Cain. It is not that she didn't expect the truth, but rather that he revealed so much of himself in this conversation, including his reasoning behind one of his most well kept secrets. Why did he follow Driax instead of his brother when the commander had no reason to believe in her? He decided that his mistress had earned the right to know the truth. "**Which brings up another query you have been afraid to ask. Why did I kill my brother; why did I kill Petamauck? I know you want to know. I didn't kill Petamauck because he was wrong; I killed him because he was *stupid*. I ordered him to support you and what did the supposed greatest teacher of logic and reason do? Petamauck, of all the fucking people, tried to usurp your authority! I was *not* cool with that. He acted selfishly, he acted in arrogance. I didn't kill him because of the space station slaughter or even the Mu System occupation; it was because God doesn't do anything random. God made the choice to elevate you; I have no doubt. Even if we don't understand, it doesn't matter Mistress. God has *never* made a mistake; their actions indicated that they thought that God did make a mistake. That's** unacceptable and inefficient. **To challenge that put my brother and his comrades on the shit list. And you know, it's *never* a long list."**

Cain was talking faster than normal. He actually was opening up about his thoughts and feelings. It was hard for her to keep up with the rate and tactical proficiency of his mind. When you are as smart as Cain, it is hard to not seem crazy. The Ocularian Commandant always said that Cain danced between sanity and madness; Driax finally understood the breath of that assessment. *This is why Nick talks so slowly; not for him, but for all of us*, she mused. He never talked about his aggravation at the Paladin Liberation Party's stupidity; until today.

"As brilliant as Petamauck is, he is still stupid. This was about selfishness my dear Chancellor; the Paladins who tried to take over were only thinking about themselves. They tried to take advantage of this tragedy to press some fucking political leverage; to reshape the Alliance as they saw fit. If they had gotten their wish, none of these things that are about to happen would have been possible. To prove their narrow minded point, they would have destroyed the damn quadrant." As she looked at her brilliant servant, Taylor Driax could see the frustration and anger that this situation caused Commander Cain. In this moment, she felt the loneliness and at the same time, the steely resolve that one must have in order to be the Alpha Paladin/Master Oculari. *Oh Nick, I am so sorry*, she thought.

At this point, Alron Driax saw her Master Oculari from an entirely different perspective. The leadership actually had the nerve to ask Cain to kill his dearest friend. The maddening part was that he obliged them without hesitation. They expected him to eliminate the obstacle; that obstacle happened to be his loved one. Cain must've been terribly conflicted but yet he completed the task that was laid before him. She then thought of the fact that in order to make the entire quadrant more secure he had to make sacrifices on a level that very few understood. His actions are a reminder of the fact that he was retrieved from Earth for a singular purpose; to make the universe safer for other people.

He doesn't care about glory or adoration; just service. Love, peace and personal happiness are luxuries that the monster has chosen willingly to give up for the good of others. *I don't know if I am strong enough to be the type of Alron that Cain needs, but I owe it to him to try*, she thought. Cain was so certain that God was right about her that he thought killing his brother was logical; Driax was overwhelmed, but tried to keep from hyperventilating. Taylor Driax realized that his actions were a ringing endorsement if there ever was one.

No person who had been involved with the Mu situation had ever discussed the state of affairs from Nick's point of view. Driax was saddened by the fact that in this situation, it was Nick who was in need of comfort and it wasn't provided. They asked him to kill his mentor, his best friend, his brother. In spite of all the awful things that had happened to him over the course of his career in service to the Terran Alliance and the Inter Galactic Federation, the Paladins and the Oculari, this had to be one of the worst things that had ever happened. Only Quenas' actions could be considered comparable; and Driax knew how that turned out for the Unori.

These mighty factions ordered Nicolas Cain to kill Petamauck. How could they? *How dare we*, she thought. To his credit, Cain was merely waiting on her orders to act; the Federation had already made their position clear. He could have carried them out without actually speaking to his new Alron, but he wanted to let everyone who was a potential usurper know that she had his full support. Driax has always been disturbed at the proposition that everything Cain does has an objective that others don't see. He is always seeking an advantage through misdirection. To that end, he killed the man who meant more to him than anyone else. This action was not just about doing what was necessary, but rather a political statement. Chancellor Driax had reached an entire different level of understanding of what the term, *Apex Predator* meant. It frightened her deeply; it comforted her profoundly.

At this point, Nick's voice began to trail off; just the thought of these circumstances brought up a tremendous amount of anger. **"And for what? Because they felt you were too young? Really? That is why I am always calling them *stupid*. No person truly knows how to govern a federation, kingdom, or an empire. It is absurd to think that *any*one could do that. There was no guarantee that they would have been a better choice than you anyway. That is pretentious at best and idiotic at worst. Besides, where was their outrage at the Kurgax? Those assholes were the ones who took Kush and your future husband away; yeah I knew about that before you told me. Did the PLP decide on their own that the Kurgax Federation should be eliminated? No. Did take out their hostility on the people who put us in this situation? No they didn't. They were being simple-minded,** backwater, arrogant jackasses; and my friend was the dumbest genius of them all." His eyes were watering; he is just as incensed now as he was back then. An inconceivable scenario that had been created by his closest friend. These actions made his brother Petamauck expendable. "**I am lucky I got him back.**"

At this point, he felt better, laughing at the madness of his people. It was cathartic. Terran stupidity is a punch line to the Alpha. "**He allowed himself to be manipulated into thinking he was destined for something greater than what he already was; being the greatest teacher of logic and reason wasn't enough? It isn't possible to be *happier than happy* Driax. I thank God that you are so strong, dear mistress. My dearest brother would have plunged the entire quadrant into the most *uncivil of civil wars*; and the Dark-Siders would have wiped all the free peoples of this Super Cluster out. That's how the Phoenix Super Cluster fell to them; infighting. God's timing is perfect. No one who tries to speed up God's timetable has ever been successful. Earth is important to God, therefore it is important to me. Killing him was expensive, but necessary. Pride only hurts, it never helps my lovely Alron. Tell the leadership whatever you wish, it makes no difference. This is going down and there is nothing that anyone can do to stop it.**"

At this point, the chancellor understood what Nick was primed to do, what all his Milky Way comrades were all set to do. It is a horrible scenario to ponder. How could he ask his brethren from the Alliance and Federation to participate in such a zero sum scenario if they were not completely ready to do that? Nick continued. "**My dear, sweet chancellor, you really don't want to know what I am prepared to do. I am so sorry, I have worried you beyond any reasonable measure. The price of liberty and freedom is *never* too high. Remember Driax, I am not just a Paladin; I am also an Oculari. And you know that the Oculari specialize in the preposterous. The place that everyone else including the Paladins will consider as insane is where I am at my best. I learned from dealing with Alron Casamayor, its better you don't know; my mother explained to you the concept of 'plausible deniablity' already. This is as good an example as ever. As I told you before, you will always have problems, but the Dark-Siders will not be one of them.**"

She could see his unyielding resolve; the fearless demeanor. The Terran with an unconquerable soul. Once again, Cain showed why there were two classes of Paladin; Cain and everyone else. For a man who is usually neutral in politics, he has displayed an incredible amount of savvy. **"This should make sense to many of them but it won't. I should be able to share my reasons with them, but I can't. The reason why is that all of you care about power. You see I don't care about power. *I use it.*"**

Driax looked at her noble, deadly servant. She saw it in his eyes, the unyielding resolve. At this very moment, she understood why Cain is able to do such incredible and often times horrible things. This type of perspective is what makes him such an enigma; a warrior with a commitment to the Cause is nearly absolute. In his brilliant mind, this scenario has only one possible outcome. Whether or not this is a pyrrhic victory or not makes him and the others no difference; victory was their *only* option.

She could see that her duty was to be the leader that Cain could believe in; so that he doesn't feel any more alone than he already does. She had to be up to the task. Though her mind was spinning and she had a lump in her throat, Alron Driax spoke with a robust authority. **"I understand my servant. Your orders are clear: destroy them. Dear Antonius, you are needed. You are not expendable; none of your troops are. My orders of destroying the siders efficiently has not changed. There is much work to be done my dear Oculari."**

A smile crossed over Nick's face. He laughed at his boss. **"God, you are such a *girl*. You are just like the old man said; don't worry my sweet chancellor. I said that I couldn't wait for you to come to the beach. That obviously means I expect us to *win*."** Now she was pissed, **"you ass!!! You cheated, you used my feelings against me! Jesus, you're really good. I am going to get you back Nick; oh you are going to pay!!! Get off my damn monitor. Here I am about to cry and you think this stuff is funny. Kush's files said that you are trixie; I can't believe I fell for it! I will be there when you are done. Good-bye you jerk."** *Dammit, he got me*, thought the chancellor. He got the chancellor to laugh and smile in the most ridiculous time. Kush said that he had a sick sense of humor. But he is right;Cain needs people ready to do the unthinkable; that's why he didn't want the IGF/Alliance there. The uncommitted will be a distraction.

Michael had been spending a great deal of time with his aunt and the rest of the Altarian command ever since he dared her to kill him. Because of Michael's unique physiology, he was stronger than any Altarian soldier. Even the strongest warriors of the Gondronian Federation were not much of a match in physical strength. Alvarnari was also impressed with the relationship that he had developed with the humans. Humans always had the reputation as being selfish and destructive in the Altarian Federation; well all of them accept for Cain. The Queen was pleasantly surprised to learn different. Alvarnari had found a kindred spirit in Kira. The monarch was more than pleased. She was walking with Michael as he was showing her his home; the mighty Alpha Centauri. She had many things to discuss with him, because of her impending demise, but she really only wanted to talk of one thing in particular.

She squeezed his arm as he led her past the training dojo. They saw Cain sitting in a seated position of meditation. She spoke slowly, but deliberately. **"Michael, I am so glad that Antonius found you on that planet. You have no idea how I have dreamed of killing that bastard Atlas. Oh I am sorry, I didn't mean,"** Michael, kissing his aunt's hand and cut her off. **"No need Alvarnari; no need at all. I of all people know what he was. But most importantly, I know what Antonius *is*."** The leader of the Altarian Federation clarified. **"No, that isn't what I meant. I am glad that Antonius found you because I wouldn't have been as kind. Being honest, I always knew that you existed. Atlas' adjutant informed me of your birth and said that he was willing to smuggle you out of the empire and deliver you to the Rioans and then they could have brought you to me. But I was so filled with anger that I declined. I knew that if I had seen you, I would have probably killed you."** She began to cry and fell at Michael's feet. Michael picked her up and kissed her face several times as he cried also. He spoke softly. **"I know. I am not angry because I would have done the same thing if I were in your position. I guess Father is *a lot* smarter than both of us."**

At this point, AC is completing her evening jog; it is a way for her to clear mind. She is so focused, she barely noticed the two of them. Michael motions for her to come and join the conversation. He is especially proud of his human mother; she will always be welcome in his presence. **"Lady Alvarnari, I apologize; I know you want to be alone. Besides, I have to take a shower."** The Altarian warrior queen kisses AC on both of her flushed cheeks; an Altarian sign of greetings and good will. **"No dearest AC, I want you to be here. How does Antonius say it? 'God doesn't do random.' I need to say thank you from the bottom of my heart. You raised Michael as your own; he has so much of you in him. I am proud."** AC blushed at the gesture of gratitude; Altarians are known for the graciousness and honesty. **"No need. When I saw him all those years ago, I just fell in love."** The queen continued. **"And I must also say thank you for observing are leadership customs. Your mother, Aya, told me of the protocols you followed for Michael; it must have been difficult watching Antonius provoke Michael into combat the way that he did."**

At this point, both Michael and AC were both confused by Alvarnari's statement. **"What customs are you speaking of?"** The first lady smiled. **"Why the Altarian custom of male leadership of course. If the male heir to the throne is born outside of the kingdom, he is to be raised by someone who is not of his blood. To test his worthiness, the current monarch is not supposed to see or speak to him for the first seventeen years of his life. Then the King is to test the prince in combat, to take his measure; to find him worthy of the throne. If he was found wanting, he was to be killed by the King and the process would begin again. I know that this is a brutal process; in our history, this is happened only twice before. This happens when the bloodlines were broken because their was no heir to the throne. I must say that Michael is more than my people could have ever hoped. Congo informed me that Antonius knew of this custom and told him that he had respected Altarian culture. I know that humans bond with their children quickly but he didn't even *touch* him until they first met in combat. It must have been a magnificent encounter to see in person. What, you didn't know?"**

Both AC and Michael were both speechless. The lady continued. **"I guess Cain's reputation is completely justified. He is the Apex Predator after all,"** AC was steamed; *why didn't you tell us Nick,* she fumed. The lady smiled and began to laugh. **"I guess I should start calling your father Nick huh Michael? I knew he was smart, but how did he find out about our customs of royalty? I mean, we are on the other side of the quadrant? Then again, he is the Master Oculari; they always know things that they shouldn't know."** Michael smiled. **"She doesn't know Dad, right Mother?"** The young king was glad that his aunt was willing to call his father by his birth name; that meant the Altarian Queen was of the belief that she was a member of their family. AC finally laughed at the absurd rationality of Nick's mind. **"You have no idea."** AC kissed them both and took off to take a shower. Once again, Cain showed why he is Cain.

Since the battle was inevitable and should be history altering, the warriors of all the free peoples of the Milky Way, met on Earth for relaxation and meditation. For many warriors, this is was a time for excruciating anxiety. For Michael and his father, this is a perfect time to meditate on the events that will transpire and preparation for the future of the Milky Way, their home. In deep meditation, Nicolas is so relaxed, that he actually falls asleep and begins to snore. His son wakes him. **"Dad!! Wake up!! You are snoring."** The mighty Paladin doesn't move, he is on chill mode.

Admiral Kira Darius, the beautiful commander of the United Earth Forces enters the room. Not surprised by what she sees. **"He is snoring isn't he? He always does that. In such a relaxed state, he falls asleep. Cracks me up every time I see that."** The young king responds to his surrogate sibling. **"I don't see how he can do that. I guess he has been through so many battles, he is oblivious to it."** The sister touches her little brother's face; warmly and comfortably. **"Not at all. To him, all war is different. He is at peace because he knows that is serving a higher cause. To him, that and the people he is charged with protecting, including us is his only concern. But not really."**

The boy-king inquires further. **"Why is that?"** Kira, now sitting in a meditative position herself. **"Because he has prepared for this as best as he can. The rest is out of our hands; it's up to God. Your father says that once you've given Him the best of your endeavors, the rest is not up to you. My master believes that the word impossible is something that humans say far too often. Nothing is impossible if you have faith and prepare. We are prepared, now we just have to believe. Get some rest little brother; you will need it."**

Even though he was asleep, Kima could tap into Cain's subconscious. She wanted answers to why Erik and her brother were excited about showing whose power was stronger between the light of the Paladins and the Dark Sider Assassins. She thought to Nick that he still hadn't answered her original query. *Okay Kima I will answer you,* thought the Alpha.

Two Hundred Seventy rotations ago, Erik and Nick were tasked with destroying a Dark-Sider research facility in Faxcillan Galaxy. There, in that galaxy, the Dark Physician had been working on a more efficient drone creation process. Erik and Nick had been tasked by Kima and Kira's grandfather, Danyzer, with destroying it. This was the same facility that Lt. Colonel Elisma, Nick's mother, had been ordered to destroy and failed. What they didn't know was that the Physician was being protected by the Assassin. They killed everyone there and had set a series of ion bombs for detonation. The research survived but the Dark Physician didn't; Nex escaped with the data and they have been using the drones to fight ever since.

Nick and Erik killed the Sider medical scientist and seven of his protectors, but there were nine in the facility. Nex was the last warrior there. The Dark King was angered at the fact that the siders lost 8 important members of their royal house, but it couldn't be avoided. This is the first time that the Dark-Sider nation became aware of the Alpha Paladin. Nick didn't get a chance to fight him because the destruction of the facility was the objective.

Erik's escape route had been cut off before Nick could reach Nex. He couldn't let Red be hurt just so Cain could get a crack at the Assassin. Even though Cain hates loose ends, the thought of loosing Erik was unacceptable. When Erik and Nick left the Faxcillan Galaxy, they were ambushed by the Kurgax on the way back to Alliance space. In the midst of the sneak attack, the two were separated. Erik's ship had crash landed on a planet in the Kurgan system and had been left for dead. Cain had been given orders to continue back to headquarters, but he thought that his wingman was still alive. He was a Paladin; they *never* leave their friends.

The Alpha Paladin found Red's locator beacon was still active and went after his friend. It was the first time that he disobeyed a direct edict. His friend, his partner came first. When being debriefed about it, Nick stated that Erik's life was more valuable because the war hadn't begun yet. He was not an asset that Cain could afford to not have with him during the rough period ahead. He was given a commendation for original thinking. Erik has been in his corner ever since.

Up until this set of events had occurred, Erik the Red had been thought to be the Paladins most capable warrior. Nick had come so far so quickly, he had made the other Paladins nervous. They knew that he had been trained by the Oculari. Paladins had been taught to despise everything that the Oculari stood for and the best Paladin was working with the best Oculari. Erik thought that Nick was too unpredictable and was apprehensive about fighting alongside him. The Oculari are known for sacrificing their own to reach an objective, while the Paladins would never leave a friend in trouble; they would nobly sacrifice themselves first. After the Faxcillan assignment, they became a legendary dynamic duo.

The Paladins never got a chance to settle the debate of whose power was greater. Until now. Erik's father was the only other person to survive the original encounter with the Assassin. This time, we will find out whose faith is the strongest; either the light or the darkness. Red likes to say that the dark may consume the light but never extinguish it; time to prove that theory correct. *Are you sure that he can be stopped*, thought the little sister, fearing for her brother. *Erik and Mother are afraid and so is Petamauck; is there another way to beat him?* When having this conversation a smile crossed his face. What many are not aware of is Cain's incredible ability to both tune everything out around him, while at the same time seem totally engaged in what is happening in front of him. No one has the mental ability to handle so many conflicting mental faculties simultaneously like him. *Even if there was another way, I have no intention of using it*, thought the Alpha. *Have a little faith baby*, thought the brother. Kima smiled.

The Kronos is a beautiful construct of art, but it also a deadly piece of technology. From its bow to its engines, it is a marvel, that rivals any Alliance, Rioan, or Federation based technology. Its original design concepts come from Antonius' creative mind. He gave those plans to Emily before she left for Earth, stating, **"you will know what to do when it is time."** If there was ever a way to show how far the Earth humans have come, this would be it. This mighty warship alone is proof of the three levels of galactic growth by Earth. Its fusion modules will rival any efficient power system by any Terran manufacturer and its antimatter/nuclear arsenal are one of a kind. Dr. Martinez, Dr. Igeleke, Dr. Aleksandra Nikitin and her colleague, Dr. Siblya Moreau was instrumental in developing the technology that makes this marvel possible. There was a time, in the short past, that these magnificent scientists would not have dared to work together, but by putting their differences and short-sightedness behind them, these brilliant people have made a dreadnaught that will make the continuation of the planet Earth's population a strong possibility.

Dr. Martinez, a proud son of Mexican descent, shares a word with Emily, now second in command of the mighty warship, ready to fight for the rights of all peoples in the galaxy. It was the right course of action to put Kira in command of the fleet; that kind of humility has always stood out to all the humans from Earth, especially the good doctor. As strong as her skills are in the realm of administration and management, Emily willfully cedes her command to Kira, the finest combat strategist short of Cain in the entire fleet.

No one is better suited to lead this contingent into such a deadly and unpredictable set of circumstances. The beautiful Admiral has the ability to render the mostly novice group of patriots calm in the midst of battle. Many of them know that it is a strong possibility that they may not return; this part of the fleet is ready to represent the best of what the Earth's humans can be. Cain always says that pride is useless if it gets in the way of the primary objective. That edict is the primary reason that Cain's warriors are the best in the known universe.

It is dusk in the Pacific ocean, the ship floats on the ocean with the two Terrans, one from Earth and one from the Terran Alliance, are sharing a drink and a quiet conversation. **"Commander Uchida, I would like to say thank you to the Paladins for coming here; we wouldn't have a chance if you hadn't come."** The wise and beautiful leader sighed and smiled sweetly at the handsome doctor. **"You are us and we are you. No doctor, we had to come; Earth is *our* home."** The man of science interrupted her. **"No, that isn't what I meant; you saved *us from us.* We had many of the resources to grow and become great assets to our planet. We had paradise and threw it away, well almost. God really does believe in second chances. To think that I was so full of pride, how all of us were. Think of how far we have come. I am glad to be living in such dark times. You gave us a chance to be a beacon, to be better. Thank you."** Emily smiled, wiping away a tear. **"Thank me when this is over. Chancellor Driax has always said that it was our duty to be charitable because someone else was charitable to us. I never thought that it would be to my own kinsman. My master will make sure that we have something to celebrate tomorrow."**

It is daybreak and the sunshine is gleaming off the bow of the Centauri. Many of the varied races have gathered. Some of these people have been enemies longer than they have been comrades. All of that has changed now. Words of encouragement have been spoken to races that have never had anything but hostility and mistrust. This is the most pivotal moment in the most pivotal time perhaps in the history of the entire Virgo Super Cluster.

A brother and sister, brought together by fate are speaking quietly. Vice Admiral Kira Darius, leader of the United Earth Naval Group and her little brother, Michael, heir to both the Altarian and Gondronian Federations walk quietly towards their respective star ships. Michael speaks first. **"No speeches huh? I guess there is nothing else to say. Dad doesn't believe in that stuff Kira?"** She smiles and shoves her brother lovingly. **"You act like you just met Nick. This isn't the movies little brother!! In all the fighting we have ever done, I don't think he has ever said more than 'let's go.' We are Janitors, this is what we do. You are not one of us; remember that."**

Michael stopped walking when she said that. He didn't know whether he should have been hurt or offended. Kira isn't known for using a lot of words, but she could see that he was confused by the statement. **"Michael all I am saying is that Janitors have a single purpose, while you have been trained to be more than that. You may be a fantastic warrior, but that is just one aspect of your duties, you are also a future king. You will be something that your father can never be."** Michael began to walk again with his sister; she put her arm inside of his. **"What is that Kira?"** She smiled sweetly and kissed his cheek, something she rarely does. **"A visionary. We are Janitors, the most terrifying of servants. You will be a visionary, a leader. Our job is to protect democracy, not practice it. Little brother, your job will be to both *protect* it and *practice* it. You will be responsible for building a better world, while our job is to protect it. I admire you. When we kill the siders, your work will begin. Be strong; be stronger than all of us; good luck. I love you Mikey."** With that, the siblings depart. What Michael didn't see was his sister's tears. *God please watch over my brother, he is just a baby.* After reaching her quarters on the Kronos, the commanding officer saw an encrypted message log from Lady Alvarnari. It was designated eyes only for her, but not to open until after the offensive was complete.

The hour is upon them. The fleet is ready. Everyone has moved into their attack positions. The queen of the Altarian race, Alvarnari, is now escorting the good Dr. Martinez, who fine tuned the energy signature system that Jaylun Harris and Nathan the Magnificent created to find their elusive prey. The flagship of the Altarian Federation, the Avis, waits quietly as the monster that is the Dark Sider Armada goes past the sun. A source of warmth to the humans, but a source of annoyance for the siders, the monstrous fleet passed by the sun. Moving at the speed of light, slower than the optimal warp speed that it possessed, the ship would take more than four hours to reach the Earth, in part because the bright yellow sun has reduced its efficiency.

As the ship entered the solar system, the phalanx's sensitive instruments, barely able to keep from melting in the vast expanse of the sun didn't notice the Avis. The demon was located; but the Altarian's communication system was damaged. The long range system, which could easily have relayed the message were it not for the radiation from the sun, their protector but now their hindrance. A decision has to be made. The shielding has been damaged and the long range communication antenna array has been destroyed. This is a time for legends to be born. Alvarnari has a conversation with the scientist. **"What is the best case scenario doctor? How close do we have to be in order for us to communicate our discovery?"** The doctor grimly stated the obvious. **"I don't think that we can. We can try to beam the Intel directly to Jaylun once we are in Earth orbit but it won't do us any good. We may have to paint the target and hope that they can see it. But what can we paint that ship with?"** The queen smiled and said with kindness and conviction. **"Us."** They raced at the best possible speed to their quarry, hoping that when they arrive, it is not too late.

As the mighty war machine bears down on the planet Earth, the fearless warriors of Terra, with the help of some valuable friends decided that now is the time to stop this beast, hopefully for the last time. **"Any word from the Avis?"** Nicolas knew that his troops were out of time; it was time to go to work. Major Faris sends word. **"None. What would you like to do?"** Cain makes his decision. **"Admial, send word for Jaylun to head to Earth, he needs to continue final modifications of the system to his ship. We go to plan B. We will have to kill them the hard way."** At that point, the mighty Kronos moves into position. Kira Darius, the commanding officer gives the word. The Kronos uses its antimatter weaponry to fire upon armada. Nothing happened.

The Dark-Sider ship was bigger than originally reported; the math was wrong. Even though it was only traveling the speed of light, the formation was still traveling too fast to make an impact. That is when two destroyers, the Daedalus and the Koga decided on their own to act. The Koga activating its warp engines, overloaded its antimatter armaments, and went straight towards the armada, port side. At the same time the Daedalus attacked from the starboard side, with the same intention. The crash was catastrophic. The overloading of the warp engines, coupled with the anti matter artillery cracked the armada. The momentum had been slowed. The remaining Earth warships, coupled with the Gondronian destroyer fleet fired their most powerful weapons all at once. The blast was so powerful that the Earth's moon tilted seven degrees from the shock wave. But the job was done; the sider monster not only stopped dead in its tracks, but several thousand miles of it was also destroyed. The phalanx was originally more than 20 thousand miles in length, was now 500 thousand warships, ranging from ninety meters to four thousand meters. The job was done, Antonius gave word. **"Attack. Top kill eats first and,"** Nathan chimed in. **"Low kill has to clean up, it won't be me!!"**

Their opposition was prepared for such an incursion. One million ships of Milky Way and sider origin went to battle. In an instant, the Alpha Centauri destroyed eight thousand warships with its massive energy turrets. The claws of the mightiest warship ever conceived had finally come out. However something unexpected happened; the ships reassembled into smaller ships, ranging from eight to 30 meters. Another one hundred twenty thousand ships were created. *They had scouted us well* thought the commander. The commander knew that in order to capitalize on the enthusiasm of his fleet it was time for the Janitors to unleash the entirety of their resources. It was a scary proposition, but if ever was there a time to attack with everything that the Janitors had, it would be it. Cain also knew that because of the proximity of Earth to the fighting, there was a possibility that they could accidentally destroy the planet. He looked at his beautiful home world and smiled. *Forgive me*, he thought.

Cain was so certain that he was right that he then made a message over the comlink. **"Any suggestions?"** Michael, his son and comrade in arms replied, **"It is time to misbehave. Use the good stuff; the *real* stuff. We need to go all in. I am sick of these Dark-Sider assholes Commander. United Earth attack from the port flank; the**

Gondronians and Altarians will attack from the starboard flank. The Janitors attack from the bow and stern; and fear no darkness!! Today is a good day to die!!!" Kira said with joy, **"he's his Daddy's boy."** Cain smiled. The attacked continued. Seven hours had passed and the Milky Way had given no quarter to their dangerous foes. Undaunted, the siders pressed on, knowing that their fleet could outlast the brave warriors of the Virgo. A sider missile attack had crippled the starboard flank. The siders attempted to reassemble in their phalanx; the Aires, another mighty Earth destroyer sacrificed itself to stop it from forming, ramming itself into a section of star ships, forcing the siders to resume unpleasantries with their noble enemies.

Seven more hours have passed and the Avis, barely able to function finally reached Earth. The shockwave from the Kronos first attack knocked them severely off course. Finally they were in transmission range of the Earth; but another issue had occurred. The Gondronian flagship, the Roa, was under siege. Fourteen sider star destroyers were preparing to destroy it as it had sustained heavy damage. Nicolas was on the other end of the mosh pit; the father didn't see his son in jeopardy. But Michael's aunt did. The crew of the Avis, desperately transmitting the vital information that would help the galaxy's cause was left with a desperate, but inevitable decision. A man of science who learned the value of using his gifts for the betterment of others and a terminally ill Altarian Queen Aunt, who had lost so much in her life, was not prepared to lose what was last of her family.

Calling the bulk of the starships that were of Altarian descent to Michael's aid, eighteen ships including the Avis had descended upon the sider ships, crashing into all of them. Michael, realizing what his beloved aunt had done screamed in agony. He then ordered his solar powered cannons to fire upon a cluster of two hundred ninety sider ships and the most amazing thing happened; the ships were totally incapacitated. An anti-matter missile then destroyed all the ships. Eureka. He then got on the comlink to all the ships to inform the brave defenders of liberty that the siders cannot handle the light. For the first time, in the conflict, the standstill finally began to tip in the favor of the United Fleet.

At this point, nearly 34 hours into the conflict, Nicolas saw the opening he was looking for. He contacted Jaylun, who was following his orders at Earth command. **"Jaylun. Activate the 'Show Stopper.' Aim them at these coordinates on my mark. Fire!!!"** A weapon that had been prepared as a defensive weapon on Earth fired into the section where almost thirty thousand sider ships had been patrolling. In an instant, these ships were incapacitated. Lance then fired a tactical nuclear missile, destroying the whole section of sider ships. *Guess I won't be low kill today,* he mused joyously. The weapon, a solar powered energy cannon based upon ancient Arcadian technology, used up its entire energy reserves to damage the Dark-Sider Armada. Alvarnari and Dr. Martinez's sacrifice was not in vain.

Jaylun received the communication of how to find the hiding command ship. He raced to his star fighter with full intentions of lighting up the sky with the ship. Erik the Red saw Jaylun's fighter rocket from Earth and figured out that Jaylun had the information that was needed to locate Nex; he told the young human that he would be his wingman, protecting him as they made their way to the target. **"Commander, follow this signal; it is time to hunt our prey!!!"**

Nicolas then reached the Centauri, who had just destroyed another thirteen hundred ships, to pick up AC, and Petamauck. The mighty Wing Alpha would now be replaced with a Delta Raider, the fastest short-range transport ship in the fleet. As they zeroed in on Jaylun's signal, the mighty Terran gave a warning to his grizzled comrade. **"Whatever you do, don't engage the target until we get there. Do you hear me? Erik!! Red!!"** *Dammit,* he thought. *He is going to get himself killed.* Jaylun's ship was damaged in route to getting to the hiding star ship, but Erik was able to pick him up in space before he fell. Then Jaylun took control of Erik's fighter because he knew the way. Confused, Erik said to his newest partner in crime. **"How the Hell do you know where you are going?"** Jaylun replied simply **"I have no idea; but I just know."** Dr. Chandler also received the communication and relayed this information to Kima, whose telepathic power provided a link to both Jaylun and Nicolas as to where to find their mutual prize. *God bless you baby sis,* thought a smiling Nicolas. Then it appeared; the prize that the veteran Paladins and a baby Earthling star pilot had been searching for.

The star ship was unremarkable; it didn't have any impressive weapons or defensive armaments. It was designed to allow the Dark-Sider commander to hide in plain sight. Erik the Red jumped out of his fighter and landed on the launch platform, with Nick, AC, and Petamauck all following right behind. The explosions of the other sider and United Fleet ships seemed further away. There was the reason; the ship had a damping field. But because of how the space was warped around it, Jaylun could find it, the information that so many people had died for. A few minutes later, the antimatter armaments had been calibrated to the dark matter energy signature thanks to Jaylun's smart thinking and the remainder of the sider fleet had been decimated. Every time a ship was destroyed, another group of missiles fired again to make sure the ship couldn't be reconfigured. The explosions literally lit up the night, almost like fireworks. The only ship that remained was the Dark-Sider command ship. With the remaining Fleet all pointed at the one dark sider ship, it wasn't going anywhere. Now all the warriors not on that ship could do was wait and see if their champion could actually stop this deadly assassin of the Dark Sider Royal House.

As the four warriors walked towards their date with destiny, a sense of calm had washed over Antonius. This is what all the lives that he had had taken, that all of his family had taken, was for; preparation for this moment. He knew that killing the Assassin was vital; Nex would be among the hardest of the royal house to kill. He knew more about death than Nick did. In fact, he knew more about death than all of them put together. But if there was ever a time, he wished that the old Petamauck was not instead of *Old Petamauck*, this would be the time. While still a formidable warrior, he was still older. Erik was even older than Petamauck was. AC however is as deadly as ever. She is at least Kira's equal with daggers and AC is also as agile as anyone who has ever been a warrior of the Order of Paladins. AC, who recently tied her luxurious hair in a bun, is ready to die if necessary for this task to be completed. As is Petamauck and also Erik, no matter what has happened these last 45 hours, none of that will matter if they fail to kill the Assassin. If they don't, he will just keep returning; the plan unfolds, this is what Cain meant by stopping the siders cold.

A royal member of the Dark siders, when faced with what they consider a worthy opponent, will never run. They will stand and fight, even die if the foe they face is deemed worthy in their eyes. The rest of the royal house is watching as these events unfold. It is the first time that they have ever had the opportunity to see the mighty Paladins against one of the deadliest of the Royal House; Nick was of particular interest to them. Nick was the one that killed the Physician, which was no easy task indeed. No one really knows how Cain did it and he wouldn't tell anyone either. But the Dark-Siders knew what Cain did; they were eager to see if that was a fluke. The last time that they faced warriors from the Virgo Super Cluster, the siders were cheated in the fact the Rioans had to use a genocidal weapon to stop them. This time, no weapon will deny these proud warriors the opportunity to fight in hand to hand combat, as they believe that only the bravest and deadliest would ever do.

This is a unique set of circumstances for the Alpha Paladin and Erik the Red. Usually when they have to take out a target of this kind of magnitude, these two warriors deal with it on their own. It has been a long time since this duo has had the opportunity to take down an opponent of Nex's reputation and now they have help. AC and Petamauck haven't been in a combat situation of this level of peril. In the past, Red has always known when to back off and let Nick do his thing. His job is to watch Nick's back and take care of people that he misses; which is rare. The others have never truly seen Cain in combat. That being said, Cain is unaware if the Dark Assassin is actually the real deal.

As Nick was walking with his friends towards their date with death, Nick allowed himself a moment to contemplate what was about to be done. *We can stop this assassin*, he thought. *Is this it? Is this what I am?* In the Assassin, Nick saw a version of himself. To defeat the Physician, Cain tapped into the deepest, darkest parts of his soul. It was darkness fighting even more darkness, but that was a long time ago. He had changed; he was better. He was more whole. As an Oculari, he had been in many situations where he and his fellow assassins knew that this could be the end for one of them, if not all of them. This was different; he loved the people he was going into battle with.

The problem with this situation was that he is a different person now. Yes, he is just as deadly as ever, but he is a better person at this point in his life. Nick never talked of how he felt about doing all these terrible things before. He didn't even let Kima get into his head like that. In the past, he would never let AC or Petamauck be involved in a conflict of this level, but this is different. He has been fighting his entire life. He is tired and weary. So many people have died in the last 45 hours and even if they prevail, many more will have to die before this conflict is over. Nick likes to believe that God doesn't put burdens on people that they cannot bare; but the strain does wear on him from time to time. This is the price he has to pay for being both an Oculari and a Paladin; the schools bottom lines conflict each other.

If he was handing this situation with his fellow Oculari, he would have never worried about the potential loss of life. The Oculari know in every fight that their comrades are more than likely going to die. The fact that these operators know the likely outcome and perform those tasks anyway bonds them on a level the few families will ever know. For the Commander, this is different because he is going into an important mission with loved ones. He has never been in this situation where everyone he is involved with is a person that he is committed to. For the first time ever, he is afraid of letting them down. Most Oculari don't even know each other's name, but he knows everyone in this fight intimately.

The four warriors enter the control room with only one figure waiting in only one seat. AC speaks to the other three. **"Either he sent the rest of the crew away or he controlled the entire conflict by himself. What do you think?"** Erik replied, **"It doesn't matter. He is going to die today! I don't care what intel they have acquired about who we are or how we fight. They were stopped cold today. Killing this bastard will be icing on the cake. Right Nick?"** Cain continued walking forward, either unaware of the banter by his friends or he doesn't care; his target is right where he wants him. The Dark-Sider warrior is about the same size as the rest of them; a little more than two meters. His uniform is completely black, save a yellow sheath. He only has a couple of swords. The blade of the weapons seem to resemble a material that looks similar to gold that is found on Earth, is the material that it seems to be made of. Once they are upon their folly, the only things that they see are red eyes. He is masked save those eyes. He hasn't said a word. In this kind of confrontation, he doesn't need to.

The Paladins all began to take off their restrictive clothing and put their blasters down. This is as old school as it gets. AC pulls out her two daggers; Petamauck and Erik pull out their respective double bladed staff and twin swords respectively. The Alpha Paladin pulls out his dangerous Katana. All of the warriors have stretched and prepared. The Paladins, the greatest warriors that Terra has to offer the universe; the deadliest of the Virgo Super Cluster have surrounded their foe.

They attacked the assassin; he then somersaulted over all of them. When he jumped, Petamauck jumped with him. Steel to steel, blade to blade; all of the Paladins locked in combat with the murderer from nearly fifty-three billion light years away from Earth. AC attacked from the left, Erik from the right, and Petamauck the middle. Nicolas was already fighting him in the center of the action. The speed of all five warriors was almost incomprehensible to the untrained eyes. Then the thing that they had never seen happen to Cain happened. He was cut. He was cut deeply. Shocked, the other Paladins hesitated and then Nex took advantage. He kicked Erik in the face while stabbing AC in the shoulder, causing her to drop one of her daggers. Petamauck then was able to knock the warrior down, kicking him away from the skirmish.

Nex, barely fazed by the action, got back into his combat stance. It took a few moments for the Paladins to gather themselves, each of them assuring the other that they were all able to continue. Cain ran at the patient and confident warrior in a full sprint, turning back flips with incredible speed, landing right in front of the warrior continuing the action, with his fellow Paladins following his lead, he then cut the mighty dark warrior, causing black blood to fly from his uniform. Angered by the cut, he kicked Cain with tremendous force, cracking his ribs, causing Nick to spit up blood. AC then stabbed the warrior in the area where a human kidney would be found and Erik then cut his legs, causing him to fall; Petamauck then stabbed the warrior in the throat, only for the mighty opponent to spin kick all of his opponents, knocking all of them in various directions.

Frustrated at the fact that the mighty Paladins would not back down, he pulled out his second sword. Spinning in a counter clockwise motion at high speed, the warrior then cut his foes down. All of the Paladins were in extreme pain; but Cain recovered from his wounds and was ready to resume his deadly march with the dark champion. He leaped over the combatant, kicking him in the face as he went by. Then Petamauck tripped him and then AC stabbed him in the chest with both blades, rolling off of him as she did it. Erik, leaping almost 20 meters into the air, came down on him with tremendous force, creating a crater, while stabbing the warrior in the stomach. All the warriors started nursing their wounds, figuring that they had finally defeated their competent opposition.

The warrior, now angered beyond measure, finally spoke to his adversaries. **"Now you die."** The warrior then began to pulse with dark energy. His aura was as black as possible. He ran at Nicolas, knocking him down. Nex then picked Cain up and then broke Nicolas' back by dropping him on his knee. He then kicked Erik the Red in the sternum, cracking it in two. Then Nex grabbed AC by the throat and threw her against the walls of his ship creating a huge dent in the hull. Kicking Petamauck in the stomach, the warrior then quickly punched the aged warrior in the eye, then using his own blade, had the warrior fall on it. As he laid there dying, Erik the Red attacked the sider with all he had, but it was in vain. The warrior laughed at Erik's futile efforts to protect his friend. Nex then broke Erik's right arm, at the same kicking him with such force, he also broke the Paladin's knee cap. He finished him by ripping the proud warrior's throat out.

Nick saw his mentor and most experienced partner fall. He was beyond angry when he saw Erik's body. He screamed and ran at the Assassin. This was unexpected because Nick never makes noise when he fights. He ran straight at Nex, who stabbed him with both of his swords, but it didn't matter. Nick punched him with such force that the dark warrior flew back more than 40 feet. He reached his friend and then he told the others to get out while they still could. AC and Petamauck refused stating that they were going to finish this together. The dark warrior was now furious; he grabbed Nick and separated his left shoulder and his right hip and slung him into the adjacent corridor. He then kicked Petamauck, breaking his tibia. As he kicked him, AC stabbed Nex in his left lung cavity; he elbowed her in her stomach, knocking her down. She fell with such force that she broke four of ribs on her right side. He then kicked her right out of the room. As she fell from the kick, her left hip was cracked nearly in two. As she screamed from the pain, the dark lord said sweetly, **"beautiful."**

Again, Nick recovered to protect his friends from his monstrous foe; but this time, the beast struck Nick in his heart. Gutting him like a fish; Nex literally cut the Alpha Paladin's heart in two. Nick for the first time, fell like a regular human. He was motionless and unconscious. Petamauck, bleeding and broken legged, with all his wisdom and intensity, knew he was powerless against this foe. He knew that if he didn't act his dearest friends, AC and Nick would be just like his close friend Erik, who died just a few meters away from him. He realized that his friends were in service of something higher. Why else should they continue to fight? He attacked Nex with Erik's blade, it was a pointless venture, but it was a true sacrifice from the soul; he had in that instant, been vindicated and redeemed for his previous transgressions of madness and arrogance.

When Michael saw Nick fall on the video monitor, he screamed. He tried to take off running for a Delta Raider. Kira and Kima stopped him. He was trying to leave, Kira grabbed him. Screaming at her to let him go, that he would not watch his father die; his aunt's death was already more than his heart could bare. Kima hugged him as he cried in agony. Kira slapped him so that he would snap out of his hysteria and spoke to him sharply. **"How dare you! You think you are the only who feels like going there? We would only be getting in the way!"** Kima spoke calmly to both of them. **"I will talk to him now. Wait little brother; your Father always gets up. That monster will be dead shortly. Big brother always gets up. Besides Mother is there."** Kira did something unexpected; she kissed her little brother and spoke softly. **"Remember, you are the son of the Alpha Paladin. Your troops can never see you act like this. Your father taught you how to be a king; it's time to start acting like it. I love them too. We serve the wishes of God first and foremost. You still have *much* to learn little brother."**

While he was lying there, Cain also heard a voice in his head. It was Kima. These two had such an intimate connection, going all the way back to when she was a little kid. Nick's body had been beaten in ways that it had never been beaten before. She was so emotionally connected to him that she could actually hear his heart stop beating. His safeguards that kept her out of the deepest parts of his soul had now been released. Kima could feel her brother being pulled away, but not because he couldn't fight back, but rather because he was tired. If she was to bring him back to her, she was going to have to have to go and get him. The youngest Darius child just realized that her brother needed her again in a way that only she could help.

As she entered the deeper parts of Cain's soul, she saw memories of pain and agony. Each memory was an instance whereas she witnessed her brother give so much to others while at the same time; lose the people that he held so dear over and over. Kima was able to see things from Nick's point of view. *Oh Nick, I am so sorry.* She was crying as she watched him see Quenas die in his arms and the pain of having to kill Petamauck. Kima felt his pain of leaving Arielle for the last time. She wanted to turn away from the pain, but knew that she was going to have to go further if she was going to reach her brother. Kima was frantically searching for a good enough reason to convince Nick to come back to the land of the living. Back to the pain; for him to return to the madness.

As she moved through Nick's mind, she also saw his joy. She saw a memory of when Maya played with him when he was a boy. Kima heard Nick actually giggle, but not a sadistic giggle, rather a child's joy. She saw a memory of Quenas and Nick in love; she felt his happiness. Kima also saw a memory of Arielle sleeping in his arms, the love he felt for her. She saw the joy of him teaching both Kira and Michael. She saw his deep affection for her mother and grandmother. She could also see the deep admiration for Kush and his even deeper love for Driax. The thing that stood out the most was seeing how Nick felt about God. How he was so desperate to please the Father; that he saw himself as doing the Lord's work. It was so much; it was too much. Kima knew what she had to say to get Nick to return and become what he was meant to be.

Kima realized that this moment was the tipping point for her brother. Yes, he was truly a deadly agent of the Alliance and the Federation but it wasn't enough. She saw all the concern that he had for the other part of Cain's rogue's gallery that he never discussed. How the foes that the Janitors and the others would have to face in the future concerned him. She realized that the opposition that they had faced was merely the tip of the iceberg. She grasped that he was concerned that in his present state, he would not be enough to defeat all these enemies; that Nick was going to have to become more than what he already was. That proposition concerned him a great deal. Antonius was not certain that he wanted to embrace everything that he was meant to be because of the cost that he had already paid. He saw how much his teacher, Danyzer, lost to become the Khan and that scared Cain. What else would he have to give up? How much would he have to give for the good of others? There were many queries, but only one answer.

At this point in her journey, she finally found Nick, or at least a version of him. He seemed young, not much older than 25 Earth years old. It was a memory of when the Ocularian Commandant told him what he was destined to become, the first human Khan. Her brother was overwhelmed by the responsibility. He reluctantly took the mantle, but had never truly embraced what that meant. Yes, he was powerful, but he still didn't want to do it. It wasn't fair. OC said fair had nothing to do with it; this is who you are. *God has chosen well*, he said. *But what if I fail*, he said to his mother, Aya. She said *you won't my son*. Kima had never seen fear in her brother before, it was difficult for her to accept. Even still, it comforted her though, because it made him seem more human. To know that even he had doubts and reluctance.

The son trusted his parents. His biological parents died within minutes of his birth, these two would be his new parents. They would guide him through the ages, helping him stay on the path. That the Cause was the most important thing in the universe. Nick would be *God's* Assassin. He knelt before Aya and the Commandant, with tears and blood streaming from his eyes. She told him that his life would be a terrible privilege, but he was ready. **"Only when you embrace what you are totally will you become everything that God intended or we will have to start over. And if that is the case, all the good people of the both the IGF and the Terran Alliance will fall. It's up to you son, commit to being the Khan. You will kill without hesitation and love without fear. We need you to make those who worship darkness learn what fear truly is; for them to fear the light. Be transformed into Khan Antonius and become whole and powerful; convert into the most devastating tool of the Father dear, sweet child."** Both Aya and the Commandant kissed him gently. His father then gave him his katana. The sword was made with a metal only for the most worthy; the material is only used to forge a Khan's weapon. It would be a symbol of this covenant; of Khan Antonius' charge. *That's what I must do*, thought Kima. *I have to get him to accept the truth.*

At this point, she came upon Nick himself. He was lying on the ground. Kima spoke to her brother in a quiet, yet intense tone. She felt his pain, his weariness. She spoke to her brother with a resolve she never knew that she possessed. **"Hello Nicky. I have gotten to know you better. You have been holding out on me."** Nick smiled at his sister and responded sweetly. **"Ah yes, I guess I am too tired to keep you out. It's been a good run. It wasn't meant to be."** Kima yelled at him. **"I don't care what has happened; you don't have the right to quit! You don't have the right to be so selfish. You have been given a gift that only *you* can use. Yes, your pain has been awful and I am hurt for you, but at this point, it doesn't matter. You have more power than you have displayed and the foes that you have to face will become even more dangerous than the one that is standing before you now. I see now why you have been hesitating. You are afraid of what you might become aren't you? You haven't accepted the truth."**

Kima was sobbing deeply and then she wiped her face. Her tone changed immediately. She held Nick's head in her lap and spoke sternly. **"You don't have the right to question whether God chose the right man for the job. He has chosen the *only* man for the job. With all that has happened, you still think that God's grace is sufficient. Who else amongst us would take that position? My dear Khan Antonius, I need you to accept the fact that you are the last Elisma, because you are *best* Elisma. Remember your charge brother: kill without hesitation and love without fear. I need you to do so right now or else Mother is going to die."** He looked sad. **"Yes I know; she won't be the only one either. I have to go back don't I?"** At this point, she understood Nick's issue. He never felt that he had a choice. This is not only just his burden; she had to remind him that it was also his blessing.

Kima cradled her brother's head and rubbed his neck, much like Maya did when he was a toddler. Nick remembered what it felt like and began to cry. She smiled and kissed him. **"No. You don't have to go back and you don't have to be Khan Antonius anymore. I can't make you; you have to choose. Its always been your choice. God needs you to choose; He isn't forcing you. Yes, it's both a burden and a blessing. This is the most terrible of privileges. That choice is solely up to you. I *want you to want to* go back. No more running brother. I need you to allow God to use you completely. Stop holding back Nicky; I want you to become everything that He intended. By the way, I also need you to get up and kick the shit out of Nex. He has lived far too long, don't you think?"** At this point, she stood up; she realized that she was out of time. **"I don't have the right to ask, but I need you to come back and I need you to come back now. *Let's get this done.*"**

At this point, she faded out of his mind. Nick had some decisions to make. His birth caused his mother's death. He had failed to save Maya, he was too late. He had failed to save Quenas and his child, it was not meant to be. But not lying 4 meters from him was AC; he was not going to lose her also. All she ever wanted to do was be there; all she ever wanted to do was love him and protect him. He hadn't let them love him. That had to change.

All the Alpha had to do was get up and do what he was trained to do; protect the innocent. There was no reason for her to die. Cain realized that he could no longer wage war out of obligation; he must fight for a higher cause; that's what Michael, Alvarnari, AC, Erik, and Petamauck have done. *No more running from who I am; no more running from what I am*, the warrior pondered.

Arielle was right; Antonius did have a choice and it was time to make it. He had mastered the skill of killing without hesitation but he had yet to master the ability to love without fear. *That is why I failed before*, he thought. In all the times that Cain had spoken of the Cause, this was the first time that the words really resonated with him. *Forgive me Father, I did not see*, he prayed. *I am your blade my Lord; you have my love and my answer. I am Khan only because you willed it; thank you for trusting me. Amen.*

Khan Antonius learned in that moment that everything wasn't always a reckoning, which sometimes it is best to act simply out of love. He realized in that instance what it meant to kill without hesitation and love without fear. He understood the level of sacrifice that his beloved Quenas had performed. Her love was not selfish, but rather it was selfless. She was so certain that Cain would destroy the Unori and make the universe a better place, that a sacrifice of that level would be required. This is a similar time. Petamauck, Erik, and AC knew that they could die fighting along Cain's side and they went anyway. Those three loved him so much, that they didn't want him to face such a horrible task alone. He understood everything so much more clearly. It was time for Nex to die. A smile came across his face. He thought to Kima only one statement; *thank you for coming after me*. His heart began to beat.

AC, the noble Rioan warrior looked at her beloved Antonius. *This was not it*, she thought. *He is going to get up, he always gets up*. Then a thought entered her mind that she did not put there. *It's a matter of time mother, he will get up*. Kima was trying to keep her mother encouraged in such a desperate time. She was certain that he wasn't dead, but at the same time, he had never taken so long to recover before. Maybe she ws wrong and that he had died. After all that Nick had been through, maybe this was his reward, to finally be at peace. Then again, she pondered, the *Dark Siders are inequities that need to be rectified*, thought the mighty warrior. *I just need to give him time to get up. I need to stall. Besides that, Nick would not let anything happen to me, he won't let Nex win.*

Then the Assassin pointed his anger towards AC, the noble Rioan warrior. He walked into the area where he had kicked her; she was in tremendous pain with cracked ribs and a torn ligament in her knee. She had crawled towards her dearest friends, unable to fight much longer.

She picked up Erik's sword and used Petamauck's staff to stand and fight again. This angered the dark champion even further. He then reached her and had her by the neck, gloating as prepared to finish the last of his victims. **"Why do you stand? You cannot win. I have killed your friends; I have killed your master, why do you still fight?"**

At this point, AC heard a voice in her head; it was Kima. *Keep stalling mother; it's going to be alright.* AC was in such pain, it was becoming harder for her to not go into shock. She mustered all the rage that she had in her soul; she had to keep her blood flowing before she passed out. The proud warrior laughed and smiled at her opponent. **"You can't be the best that the siders have? The secret is out, you're hilariously over-rated. I know what you are; you're nothing but a loose end. You are so very stupid; you want to know why we are fighting? Open your eyes! The rest of the universe saw us not only stand up to you, but we obliterated your fleet! This was just a sample of our navy. Wait until the whole armada is unleashed. Your people are all on Cain's shit list; and you should know that it's *never* a long list."**

At this point, the Assassin grabs AC by her throat. He is inspecting her, almost perturbed at her confidence at his inevitable demise. What does she know? She laughs at the warrior sarcastically. **"You have no idea what is about to happen do you? I am going to enjoy watching you die. Your king did you a tremendous dis-service. If he thought that you were going to win, don't you think he would have come with you? The fight hasn't even started. We were just stalling. Who in the Hell does your intelligence? All you did was gut Antonius' heart; that's all you did? You could gut his heart, shoot him, burn him, and drown him; you could do your worst and it won't matter. You are NOTHING. You have no idea what you are dealing with do you? By the way, you should know this; *I am a Rioan, we don't bluff.* Before you ask me how I know that is true, you can ask him. Nicky, please close his fucking eyes."**

Before Nex could turn around he heard a familiar sound, a gun was being cocked and loaded. The barrel was placed behind his ear, next to the base of his skull. He heard a twisted giggle and then the words, **"this is going to hurt motherfu..."** He never heard the statement because of the blast. Nex knew that the blast wasn't going to kill him, but it certainly hurt like hell. The bigger issue for him was how Cain got close enough to him to fire without him noticing it. That had never happened to the Assassin before. Nick hadn't shot the sider with an ordinary pistol. The ordinance had the equivalent of an anti-matter mine. The blast sent his dear friend sprawling into the air with no way to control her fall. Antonius caught AC in mid air and kissed her. He yawned and said sweetly, **"stay here Sugar. Be right back."**

AC could barely get her mind around what she had just witnessed. A part of her never truly thought that Nick was going to get up from his wounds and now he seemed different. The room had been cold and dark, but now it seemed warmer. The air had been damp; she could see the waves of heat, like she was in a desert. Nick looked at his prey and smiled slowly. Cracking his knuckles, he spoke to the deadly sider assassin. **"Good evening. I must introduce myself. I know that you are the Assassin. I am Khan Antonius. I am the *Alpha* Paladin; I am the *Master* Oculari. I am the last of the House of Elisma. And I will be your executioner this evening."** The thing that made the circumstances even more arduous was the fact that the dark warrior radiated a power that was derived from darkness itself. Cain smiled. **"You can radiate that dark bull shit all you want; it doesn't make me any difference. You have no power over me, because I serve the *light*. This can be the easy way or the hard way, the choice is yours. *Let your next move be your best move.*"**

Nex tried to punch Nick in the face, but Cain blocked his punch and then proceeded to head-but the Dark-Sider. After the first counter attack, Nick then bent down on one knee and proceeded to punch Nex in his left knee with a well placed strike and that made him bend over in pain. Once he did, Nick elbowed him in the sternum. It was violent, efficient, and most of all, sudden. The warriors that were watching Cain were shocked; how was he *this* good?

Both of the men then returned to their feet, with the Assassin noticeably limping. Nex punched Cain in the ribs and then kicked him behind his ear. He then punched Nick in the jaw with tremendous force. Nick sarcastically spit blood from his mouth and smiled. The dark warrior tried a spinning heel kick to Cain's face, but this time Cain dodged it by bending down. He then grabbed Nex's leg and punched him in the thigh. Nick lifted the dark warrior and threw him through the supporting wall of the ship's hull. As he pressed his head against the hull, Cain then proceeded to drag the Assassin's face against the steel frame. Then that awful whistling that AC hated but secretly loved began. The song was *A Minute to Pray and a Second to Die*. Michael winced in pain after he saw Nex's face dragged against the steel. *Make him pay* thought Kima. *Make an example of him.*

It looked like Cain was going to end him right on the spot and the sider used a blade to cut Nick deeply while freeing himself. The assassin ran straight at Cain and attempted to punch Nick several times at point blank range. You could literally hear the air being from his attempts; but all Nex hit was air. He never touched Cain. Cain blocked a punch and in the same motion, hit Nex in the throat. A back-spin kick sent the Dark-Sider sprawling. Nick smiled and said sweetly to the dark champion, **"I love it when they choose the hard way."**

The warrior took off again in full sprint but this time Cain leaped in the air and kicked him in his face. AC cringed at the sound of the sider's nasal bone being crushed. He tried to hit Cain with Petamauck's staff. The Master Oculari in one motion blocked the strike with his right forearm, and the staff shattered. Cain then elbowed Nex in his broken nose, causing blood to spill. As he bent over in pain, Nick then kneed him in the face, knocking the Assassin down. Michael then questioned his sisters. **"Have you ever seen him do that?"** To which an overwhelmed Kira replied, **"I didn't know *anyone* could do that."** Kima smiled at both of them. *Kill him slowly brother; make them all see*, she thought to Nick. A warm smile crossed his face. *Don't worry sister, watch this*, he thought back.

Antonius motioned for the beast to get up. Nex picked up his sword and Cain picked up his Katana. The swords clashed at high speed. The energy of both combatants was on display; sparks of dark light and sparks of yellow golden light radiate with every blow. Cain sliced the tendons on Nex's hand, forcing him to drop his weapon. Nick smiled and then said, **"all too easy."** In the same motion of dropping his blade, Nick used a beautiful spinning roundhouse kick to the assassin's abdomen. Black blood flew from the warrior's mouth.

Nex was on the ground looking up at the mighty Ocularian, realizing that he was in over his head. He tried to stop the onslaught. **"Look I was mistaken. I have information that you may find useful to your campaign. I am only a soldier. I follow orders. Just like you."** The Alpha Paladin was angered by his words. **"You were just following orders huh? I hate when you cock suckers say that. You still don't get it? Why do you think that we came to see you? I don't need you** dummy; I already have your ship. Everything that I need is in your data files. My soldiers has already hacked into your system. I am going to beat you to death, because I *can*. You never understood the truth of your situation. *I was never stuck in here with you. You were always stuck in here, with me."*

As the Dark-Sider began to assess the fact that the fight was not going to go his way, he resorted to more desperate tactics. He grabbed Erik's heavy cannon and began to shoot at Nick. Nick ran around the corridor of the area where they had been fighting. Nick began knocking out all of the lights in that area. Cain pulled out both of AC's daggers. *Want to watch him bleed Kima*, he thought. Kima giggled. Nick whispered to the warrior, **"so disappointing."** Nex couldn't see him, but Nick could see him though. Nick disguised his scent and moved so lightly on his feet that the assassin couldn't detect him until it was too late. AC then thought to Kima, *did you know that he could do that too?* Kima smiled and thought back, *yeah I did. My brother has all kinds of wonderful toys*, she mused.

In the dark all you could hear was Nex heavy breathing. In the dark, there was an eerie whisper. **"I seeee you."** Nex threw a punch and missed; then Nick stabbed him at the base of his left shoulder blade. When he turned, Nick stabbed him behind his right knee. The Assassin yelled and threw another punch and missed him again. The Alpha Paladin then elbowed his prey in the temple with tremendous force and the warrior groaned. Nick then stabbed him between his left sixth and seventh ribs, separating them. Nex desperately swung a punch, but the pain was excruciating. Cain then cut off his right ear. The warrior finally struck Nick, but it was by design. Cain whispered, **"I don't mind taking a punch to get close punk."** Nick dodged the second attempt and then proceeded to cut off his left thumb. Nick smiled and said, **"this little piggy went to market."** As he groaned, Nick then stabbed him in the mouth, removing some of the Dark-Sider's tongue, some teeth, and gum cavity. *Come on Nicky, I can't see*, thought Kima. *Oh yeah, I was having too much fun in the dark,* thought her brother.

Finally Cain grabbed the warrior by the leg and begun dragging him back into the light while he was humming a tune, *The Itsy Bitsy Spider*. Unexpectedly, he let the Assassin go, as if he was stringing out the beating that he was administering. Nex then tried to shoot Cain but missed, in part because Nick had made both of hands useless. His right hand tendons were severed and he had also cut off Nex left thumb. This futile attempt seemingly angered Nick; his body wasn't regenerating fast enough. Cain spoke quietly again. **"So obvious."** All needed to be witness to this ass whipping. Nex limped and picked up his two blades; the mighty Khan motioned for him to continue. Cain spoke with a sense of relief. **"Finally. Come get some."**

As he stood there waiting on Nex, Commander Cain began to radiate an aura of every light within the known spectrum. The Master Oculari didn't even pick up his katana. The Dark-Side champion attacked with his swords; he couldn't even touch the mighty Khan. He kicked the dark warrior in the face, shattering Nex's jawbone. The Alpha's attack resembled a gymnast performing a floor exercise, except the final results were deadly. Every punch and kick radiated with light, sparks were seen everywhere Antonius struck the warrior. Nex then realized the true combat abilities of this monster; him being able to use his body in ways no other human can. In this moment, the Assassin realized why AC smiled and told him that the fight hadn't even begun yet.

The mighty Khan is unpredictable in combat because of his understanding of multiple human and other alien martial arts. He knew the anatomy of his foe; most of the Assassin's original wounds were healed enough for Nick to be satisfied taking him apart again. Antonius kicked him in the ribs, while also grabbing and eventually rupturing the dark warrior's left Achilles tendon; combining Ocularian efficiency with Rioan agility. The Ocularian then removed Nex's left humorous bone and stabbed him in his right shoulder and then his left lung cavity. Antonius then kicked the assassin in his right femur with such force that it was split in half; creating a compound fracture. Then Antonius removed the exposed bone and then he jabbed it into Nex's liver.

It was brutal, primal, and intimate; it was Cain at his best. His performance was both psychotic and seductive. AC and the rest of the United Fleet were witnessing an artist at the peak of his powers. He was literally rearranging the sider's skeleton. Nex's body would become a masterpiece of the macabre. Every movement was ruthlessly economic. *Arielle would have been proud of this abstract art,* thought the apex predator. As he continued his destruction of Nex, he shook his head and whispered in a caustic tone, **"amateur."**

The fight was being broadcast to all the warriors from the defense directorate. The leaders of the Alliance and Federation were also being beamed this broadcast. The Commandant was thoroughly enjoying the display. He has finally accepted the truth. *He is perfect,* thought the Ocularian mentor. His mother, Senator Aya, saw it and thought, *finally, he has stopped holding himself back; excellent.* Michael and the rest of the fleet who had never seen Nick in action were completely speechless. *My God, he could have done that to me,* thought the young king. Lance said to Nathan, **"Nick is worse than any foe we have ever faced."** To which Nathan replied, **"a different kind of evil, man; a worse kind."**

Alron Driax was also ecstatic. She wanted everyone to know just how far Cain was above everyone else and this was the best display of those abilities. He is a sadistically efficient monster of a man. For the enemies of humanity and her allies, he is without one once of mercy. Kira and Emily both smiled as they saw Cain in his truest form. There was something exquisite in what they saw. Something extraordinary in his movements, it is almost indescribable.

AC was witness to this destruction in person. She understood why she was so needed; she saw Nick with his humanity stripped away. The Paladin was close to the action, but it seemed so far away. Nick's power exuded warmth, but she couldn't feel it. Her pain was excruciating; she was still trying to fight off shock. She felt a chill that she had never felt before. Nick seemed so different to her, even his voice was different. She was uncertain if she felt that without Cain's humanity was he truly evil or not. Or was he something else entirely? Perhaps something *worse* than evil. She was no longer certain. He *is* the spook story. If anything, the words used to describe Cain, never did him justice. This is Cain representing the epitome of the phrase *being the very best at being the very worst.* For the first time in her life, she was truly afraid of Nicolas Cain. What if he can't turn this off? *My God, why did you make him like this,* she wondered. Kima eased her feelings. *He is still our Nicky Mother.*

Even though Cain beat the mighty dark sider without mercy, he didn't seem in a rush to kill him. Aya once said that if her son were really annoyed with someone, he would take his time. Cain had essentially broken the Assassin's face in half. He made the Dark-Sider champion bleed from places that no one even knew that they were capable of bleeding from. Nex couldn't walk and seemed to barely be holding on for his life. But Nick wasn't done with his masterpiece for one reason: Nex hadn't yielded yet. **"I see you for what you are. You are NOTHING. You are not a predator, you are prey. You are not a monster, you are** a little pig. Weak. Pathetic. A coward. A pig. You owe me a sound. You can't scream because I just took your jaw so how about a squeal? I am thinking of a squeal, how does that sound? I want to hear you squeal like a pig. I will bet that when this battle began, that you never figured that your end would come like this did it?"

If anyone else would have asked that question, AC would have believed they were being curt. Not Cain. He then used his power in a way that no one could have predicted; he channeled the whole of his being, all the light and joy and faith in his soul into a single point, he punched Nex with such force that literally disintegrated, squealing like a pig in the process. The Executioner smiled and then quietly looked into the view monitor and spoke to the entire Dark Sider Empire.

Commander Cain is one of the few people in the Virgo Star Cluster that actually knows their enemy's native tongue. **"Good evening. To make sure that you understand me, I will speak in your language, so there is no doubt about my words."** AC and most of the United Fleet had never heard the auditory language of their enemies. He spoke with a quietly hostile tone. His comrades didn't know what he said, but they could imagine, it wasn't very nice. **"He might have been the Nex the Assassin, but *I am the Dark-Sider's Assassin*; you are all finished. I serve the *Light* and my master demands that your darkness be extinguished. I intend to meet this mandate. Your people are on the shit list; and you know it's never a *long* list."**

After Antonius had destroyed the view monitor, he looked at his dearest friend AC. She was still trying to get her mind around what she had seen the mighty warrior become. He was still emanatinga spectrum of light at the time. He noticed that she was actually frightened of him. He smiled. He turned away from her and he ceased glowing. AC was still stunned. He smiled at her sweetly and said **"are you okay? Do I need to carry you to the ship or can you walk?"** She tried to stand but couldn't. He reached over to help her and she started to pull back, but stopped. He smiled. He picked her up and kissed her on the cheek. **"Don't worry it's me AC. I am still Nick. Thank you. I have never used it in a positive way before. But it is me sweetie."** She was stunned. **"Used what? What are you?"** He smiled, whispered to her softly and said, **"I am the APEX Predator. You have no idea what that means do you?"** His dear friend finally passed out from shock.

A funny thing happened as Nick was finishing off the last Dark Sider. There was a spike in his energy signature. Antonius has always had this incredible physical and mental strength but this was different. Faris said that the kinetic energy from Nick was beyond anything that he had seen before. Apparently the Assassin was hit with a punch that had the equivalency of the Earth's magnetic field being disrupted. Nex was literally hit with the *planet* in one single point. *No wonder he disintegrated*, thought Faris. *I better not tell anyone else about this. First off, they won't believe it. Second of all, I saw the readings and I don't believe it.* Just what the Hell happened to Nick?

On planet Acre, a Rioan general knows what happened to Nick. The best of worse case scenarios. Aya, the top human representative in the IGF walked into the solarium to speak to her husband and tell him what had just occurred. She didn't have to; Danyzer already knew what had happened. It was something that he knew was possible but he had secretly hoped that it had never happened. Aya is AC's mother. She knows her husband well enough to know that he is really afraid. The worst of worse case scenarios has just become a reality. Just then, a knock came at the door. It was the Ocularian Commandant with a huge smile on his face. He spoke with such glee. **"We need to talk don't we? Are we going to tell her? Or do you want to keep the secret a little longer? I can't wait to see what happens."**

Federation Log: Danyzer

General's Log: The Blood Knights have done it once again; made the improbable a reality. When I heard of Cain's plans for destroying the armada, I must admit that I was among those that were incredibly concerned. Not because I thought that his plan wasn't sound, but rather because it was *so sound*. If anyone else had been in charge under those conditions, I am not certain that anyone else could have pulled off such an impressive feat. Sometimes I do not think that neither the Alliance nor the IGF realizes just how amazing he truly is and how no matter the abilities of our combined military strength, that he provides an incredibly distinctive advantage in combat. Our strategic advantage begins and ends with *him*.

When we defeated the Dark-Siders so many rotations ago, they completely underestimated our resolve to vanquish them. My guess is that the Strategist figured that only the Iconians had the resolve necessary to face them and not fold. If they had been more concerned with our military strength, they would have sent a much better equipped force to defeat the warriors of the Andromeda Galaxy. Even still, they almost wiped us out anyway. As much as I hated Atlas and wanted his death to become a reality, we needed him. I was forced to negotiate with that psychotic animal. We had to leave this part of the quadrant just to ensure that the pending war we had with the Gondronians would not continue if we were fortunate enough to defeat the siders. Just think of it, Nick killed him *before* the war had even started with the Dark-Siders..

It was not that our forces wanted to work with Atlas; I wanted him dead more than almost anyone. I never got over the Rioan hierarchy asking me to put my emotions aside for the greater good. That bastard killed my son; he killed my boy. Nick didn't even consider killing Atlas a waste of experience or organic capital; he considered all the Gondronians save one hybrid child expendable to his campaign. He never even considered them part of any compromise. I knew that the Gondronian would have been a match for me, the fight could have gone either way.

But with Cain? He took him out in moments. He is a greater warrior than I ever was. In fact, his *mother* was a greater warrior than I ever was.

I know that the decisions that I made were done under the most perilous of conditions; it was the only play that I had with such an awful hand. We had to nearly destroy everything in the Andromeda just to stop the siders; once. It was so full of life; we had to sacrifice so many. It haunts me to this day. When I saw the Terrans, I was certain that they may have been able to do what we could not and that was defeat the Gondronians. I had hoped that Erika was going to be strong enough to stop them. I had been training her and pushing her as hard as I could because so many fates were riding on her shoulders; it was unfair. For Nick? Atlas was just another obstacle to the main objective; history has given us Nick's pathology for dealing with obstacles.

The Milky Way and the Andromeda were destined to collide anyway; I felt that synergy was also going to occur between our peoples as well. The Rioans and the Terrans would be able to one day stand together in friendship and that our unified strength could defeat Atlas; I was mistaken. I felt that Erika and I would be able to take down Atlas once and for all and then we would be able to stop the Dark-Siders, with whom we could match power for power. The Federation could return to its original home galaxy and begin anew. None of my original plans had ever come to fruition and more than likely, they never will.

When I look at Cain, I see his mother. She was such a sweet, precious soul. Never the less, she was an Elisma. The House of Elisma were the greatest warriors of Terran blood; they were heroes My dear, sweet Erika was the most powerful of them all. I knew that she was not a warrior, but she was so gifted. I see all of her potency, all of her character. After she died, I thought that all hope was lost. Then I find out that she had a son. I dispatched Petamauck and AC as soon as I found out. Don't you see, it was a race to get to Nick first. If I knew about Erika's son, I already knew that the Oculari already had a head start. Fortunately, Rioan technology is better than Ocularian tech. Or Nick's entire narrative could have been different. We dodged that bullet; at least temporarily.

When I first saw him, he was a child. He had no idea of what his purpose was or maybe he did and was already plotting how he was going to kill me. I was never certain about which was more of the truth. I don't see any of her weaknesses though and that is what scares me about Nick. Nick was better than his mother by the time he was twenty; remarkable.

Our weaknesses give us something to keep us humble, something to constantly strive to improve. He has no such motivations, no true Achilles heel. His motivations are from his wish to serve the Cause in its purest form. That he is truly a tool of God. The price that all of us pay for those actions are incredibly high.

He was so strong, he was so angry, he was so intelligent. I knew that after a quarter of a rotation that we didn't have the skills needed to train him to his fullest potential. My wife and friend told me that he knew the truth. I was the reason that his mother left the Alliance. If he resents me for my actions, he doesn't say and I don't ask. At this particular point, it doesn't matter. With all the enemies, all the monsters at our doorstep, I knew that the Paladins would not be able to handle all of these problems. I knew that the Federation did have the one group that could bring out the best of the worst in who he is. We couldn't keep fighting all these bastards. We needed to start getting rid of them. The Oculari were probably better trained than the Paladins, but the Paladins were probably better equipped.

As a much wiser leader now, I realize my mistake. I should have crossed the isle. I should have combined the best of what I knew with the best of what they knew. I let my pride get in the way. That we didn't need them. It was going to be so perfect. Like my mentor, Nicolas Cain, says. Pride only hurts, it never helps. My total lack of humility may have cost hundreds of trillions of lives and I must live with that the rest of my life. I am glad that God is so much smarter than I am or else we would have lost to the siders, to Atlas, and to countless other groups that Nick has dispatched since he was given to us.

Cain became the bridge, to make us all one. It doesn't matter that the Federation and Alliance are governed by two different groups because we have thing in common: KHAN Antonius. I must admit, the Oculari did a wonderful job with him. They brought out the *very best of the very worst*. He didn't cheat the process but at the same time he modified it to fit his immense ability. No one has ever completed the program faster; no one else was as deadly an operative. I know what she did, it took courage that I don't think anyone else in our ranks had. To make a rational transaction of that level. She always was so good at Economics; it was her favorite subject. God, she taught him well. Better than she had ever been taught I think.

I have consulted with Driax and she is of the same mindset. If we have to choose between the Cimms and the siders, I would rather deal with the siders. I don't want to think of the possibility of the Cimms and the siders joining forces to attack us from both sides of the star cluster; it's bad enough that the Altarians and the United Earth Fleet is going to have their hands full with those other guys who are sneaking in from the Haggishaw Quadrant. Nick can't be everywhere at once. This is going to be one wild night.

The IGF is quite pleased as well as the Terran Alliance at the outcome of this last conflict. This marked the first time ever that a Dark-Sider invasion has been stopped without a significant amount of collateral damage. Even though many will praise this victory, we know the truth. There was little faith that Cain and the rest would be able to claim victory. Deep down, I know why Nick didn't want the Alliance and IGF deeply involved in this encounter. He knew that we didn't truly believe that we could win. Nick says that to be humbled before God is to be willing to make a fool of yourself. To be thought of as mad. He needed people who were crazy enough to believe. That is why even though he has more than 100 trillion troops at his disposal, he hardly ever uses anyone but the Janitors. It is remarkable that he is committed to the Cause to this level. I often wonder that when Thomas implemented the Cause, did he have a vision of Nick in mind.

My family has devoted their lives to being in the service of the Alliance and the Federation. I have done terrible things to them and I have had to do horrible things for what would be considered a greater good. In my time of command, I have ordered some of the most cruel actions that would rival some of our most vile enemies, All in the name of a greater good. At least that is what we have told ourselves over the eons. Countless species have serious issues with my choices and that includes my wife's son. I know that before I die, Cain and I are going to have some *serious* words.

The funny thing is, that most of the citizens of the IGF consider me to be their greatest hero and Antonius is some Terran scoundrel. These people couldn't be more wrong in their assessment. He may not consider himself a hero, but I certainly am not. Most of the people of the IGF thought that my tenure was a time of prosperity but that isn't accurate. My troops just did a good job of keeping the violence away; that was until the Unori showed up. Then Nick destroyed them; all of them. At that point, I knew my tenure as Khan was complete.

The IGF made me hero of the Unori war and also the hero of the Federation/Tronic conflict. In actuality, Nick was the most responsible for our success. He just didn't give a damn enough to set the record straight. I am no hero; now everyone looks at me as some elder statesman. Its strangely ironic; the warrior responsible for more death than anyone else is the hero. History is funny like that. I have ordered countless people slaughtered and star systems completely obliterated. I hate going to sleep. Unless Aya is near me, my mind reminds me of all the awful actions that I have sanctioned. I made my best friend give up his name. In spite of all of it, I know that what I have done was right and that will have to be enough. This is what my wife, my best friend, and my student taught me.

The Commandant told me of when Nick showed up at the Ocular Theta. Antonius had every right to demand my life and the life of his adopted father, maybe even his adopted mother too. At a time when he should have been inconsolable, Antonius allowed us to live. I have no idea why he did. I don't know if he actually forgave us, but I am not going to ask; I don't want to push the issue. We are alive, that's enough for now. Nick has had everything taken from him that should have been reason to kill us all and leave the Alliance and Federation to our collective fates. He could have been selfish or took the small view of what had happened. His mother faked her own death to get away from me and some of my people will never forgive me for the loss of their loved ones. He could have easily came to Acre and killed me, right after he killed him. I am glad that she was his teacher and not me; obviously her approach was more effective. The Cause matters above all, even love. I would have never thought to say that.

CHAPTER 9

The Deep Breath

The feelings of the joy over the dealing the Dark-Sider Armada was short-lived to say the least. A familiar face has come to Earth to send the great Khan Antonius his next improbable mission. A threat from the abyss has become a priority and no matter the need to eliminate the Dark-Siders, this ancient threat must be dealt with as soon as the Centauri is ready to depart.

The impossible happened; the motley crew that had been put together by Commander Nicolas Cain has succeeded in the task of destroying the Dark-Sider Armada. The warriors know, however, that retribution for these actions will be coming sooner than later. The entire Virgo Super Cluster, while relieved that the siders were beaten are now holding its collective breath at what kind of fallout from this defeat will be. Furthermore, the Earthlings have let the entire section of space know that they will not go down without a fight and the Altarians/Gondronians are now their trusted and committed allies.

The Earthlings are now part of bi-galactic association of more than 900 races of people connected with the Earth as one of the primary hubs of this network. This part of the universe just became a whole lot more interesting. Several other star systems with species that had been afraid were now willing to join up with the United Earth Fleet and the Altarian Federation. The Terran Alliance and the IGF will have to make a whole ew set of relationships in this sector of the quadrant, including becoming acquainted with their kin. Once again Cain showed why he is Nicolas Cain. These warriors are now legends. How few stood against many and how the light overcame the dark.

On Eden, the capital planet of the Terran Alliance, a conversation between three of the most important people in the Quadrant is taking place. Chancellor Driax, the Commandant of the Oculari, and the mighty general turned statesman Danyzer are discussing the greatness that is Nicolas Cain and how this incredible warrior has surpassed their expectations once again. **"Did you see what he did? He is so hideous! I love it!! Antonius has become so much more than we could have expected Chancellor,"** the Commandant exclaimed. **"I knew that he was capable, but not *this* capable."**

Danyzer looked at both of his colleagues with a pensive stare. He finally spoke about what they were witness to. **"Neither one of you have any idea what kind of danger we are truly in; we have just jumped into the deep end of the pool. Driax, his skills and abilities are far greater than I expected. I never thought that he would be able to do so much in such a short period of time. I knew that sending him to the Commandant was a gamble, but he is far superior to any of the others. We had three anomalies, including his mother, and he would literally wipe the floor with all of them combined. That is significant Chancellor. He is so much more than we could have ever anticipated and that might be the problem."** Driax, the capable, visionary leader of humanity smiled. Cain was exactly as she had hoped. He was even more than she had desired; he was more than what Kush had expected as well. Kush wrote in his journals that Cain would have no limitations, because God had no limitations; that men would truly fear him and that despite their concerns, that she shouldn't be afraid.

Driax then inquired as to why Danyzer was so fearful and why the Commandant was so joyous about this set of circumstances. The Federation statesman responded to her inquiry. **"He is the hybrid of the Paladins and the Oculari. I only wanted him to gain some of the skills that the Oculari had, I never intended for him to *become* an Oculari madam. He was supposed to have been exposed to some of the training and then return to the Paladins. There is a belief that my Ocularian comrades kept him longer than could have been anticipated; actually that isn't true. It was just that his capacity for growth was even greater than we could have foreseen. There is power and then there is *Cain's* power. I have made many mistakes over my life and I have done many things right also. I am unsure which one is an accurate assessment at this point. There has never been an operator so beautifully sadistic. No human, not even Cain, should have survived the Ocularian Killing Academy. Then he executes everyone else faster than anyone else in the history of the Oculari.**

Cain's mother was a mistake; what we did to her was totally unfair. We all should be beyond afraid Driax; we should be truly terrified. Now we have *him*."

Danyzer spoke with a sense of dread that he has never spoken with. He has faced the siders, dealt with Atlas, and fought countless campaigns during his career. Never has he sounded *this* concerned. **"He is so much more than we could have forecasted. None of our analysis concluded that this was remotely possible. His brain shouldn't have this level of capacity; he should be at *least* psychotic. I have a question for you. *What do you do when the craziest person you know is actually sane?* I don't know the answer to that either. The only thing that can stop him from doing anything that he wants to do is Cain himself. He doesn't have any reason to comply with us and there is no way to stop him or deter him if he goes rogue. There is no counter measure for that. Never in my wildest dreams could I have imagined that he was capable of this. There was a one in seven *Centillion* chance that he reached this level of power. He hit the Dark Assassin with the power of a *planet*. A planet Driax!! What have we unleashed upon the universe Chancellor?"**

The Ocularian Commandant, Nick's adopted father, spoke again. However, this time, he was truly annoyed. **"Once again, you are acting like them. You are not; even if you would like to be. Stop over-reacting. It is not like you haven't seen Nick do this before or have you forgotten about the Tronic Reconciliation?"** The Chancellor's eyes began to widen. She had heard of that, but had never received a straight answer on what had happened. The files were incredibly vague. Now she knows why. The father defends his son. **"He has done this before and if need be, he will do this again; and *again*. He didn't do this out of anger. He did this out of joy. Remember, he will kill without hesitation and love without fear, or have your forgotten the oath? He radiated *positive* colors from the spectrum. It is a gift from his very soul. Wouldn't you agree Alron?"**

Driax again smiled at her two comrades. **"Danyzer, you are such a *girl*. I think that is wonderful. He keeps us accountable, not the other way around. My friends, I have no doubts about Cain at all; his belief in the Cause is our greatest deterrent. He will follow whatever he believes God's will to be. As powerful as he may become, I am not worried because Nick believes that God is *greater*. I have no doubts** at all; Nicky will *never* stray from the light. My dear Cain is the epitome of the phrase 'how awful goodness is.' His best friend got out of line and he killed him; he'd slaughter any of us if he needed to. He is *Khan* Antonius; you act like you don't know what that means? You of all people should know better. Our dear Gaius Nicholas Cain is the best of the very worst. That is why he is the *Apex* predator."

The Commandant smiled and laughed at this conversation. He agrees with the Chancellor, Cain could have killed him and didn't do it. He is on easy street as far as he is concerned. Driax continued making her point. **"And believe me, God help the those who would try to hurt the innocent, much less a loved one. I dare not think of that situation. The term *Extreme Prejudice* doesn't it justice. If he was going to go rogue, he would have already. If he was going to usurp us, he would have already. I have known him the least amount of time and I love and trust him the most; maybe you should also. It is easy to forget that he is our side Danyzer, but he is. Besides, it would appear that if he harbored any resentment, you would have known about it. *He hates loose ends.*"** Then the stunning woman leaned back in her chair, crossing her legs, she said, **"I am not afraid of my dear Nicolas for one reason; he doesn't crave power. *He uses it.*"**

As the ships began to land on Earth, Commander Emily Uchida was eager to speak with Khan Antonius. Many events had transpired throughout the time that he had been in the Gondronian Federation's territory. She had a full report to make and did not want to waste any time. Even though she had been a member of the Blood Knights, she was a relatively new member. What she didn't know was that Faris handles the logistical reports for the Centauri and the Alliance; he has no use of such matters. Lance spoke to her quickly and quietly before she angered her commanding officer. **"Look Commander, I know that you want to talk to Nick about the reports, but take this advice: let it go. It can hold off until later. You know our tradition; the Blood Knights always share a meal commemorating the fact that we returned and mourn those who are gone. Because he left you in charge of Earth, you will be expected to speak of our circumstances. Worry about that."**

AC slowly began to stir; she was in the trauma section of the transport ship. The medicine had begun to take effect but her knee was ravaged and would need surgery. She began to cry and screamed for Nick who was just placing the bodies of his dear comrades in the cold storage section in the aft part of the ship. Cain had begun to make preparations for departure from the star ship that transported the Assassin, he had downloaded the vital information from the ship's data unit and had set the explosive ordinances on a timer. There would be nothing left of the ship when they departed. He was so busy in thought that he didn't hear AC's voice. He reached her and kissed her on the forehead. **"Sorry Admiral, I didn't hear you. Are you hungry? The medicine usually gives you the munchies."** He was pleasant, almost as if nothing had happened. She hates how quickly Nick moves from issue to issue. AC was ready for answers.

She couldn't move because of the pain in her knee and her ribs. Her other injuries had begun to heal but she was going to need more attention. Nick started the ship and put it on auto pilot and then returned to attend to his friend. He began to feed her soup and she was fussy; she hated Nick taking care of her. She loved him taking care of her. She snapped. **"That's hot!! Blow on it Nicky."** He smirked at her. **"Really? God you suck!! You're going to act like this all the way home aren't you?"** AC looked at him and began to cry while he fed her. She was feeling euphoric as it was a side effect of the medicine. **"We aren't going to talk about what happened are we? What happened to you?"** Nick smiled as he blew on his fussy patient's soup. **"What is there to talk about? Mission complete. We lost two people but the job is done. Got the intel we needed and the ship is about to be destroyed in once we enter the atmosphere. No worries."**

AC knows that even though he isn't really speaking on the subject, she knows that both Petamauck and Erik's death has affected Nick deeply. She knows that if not for extraordinary circumstances, he could have lost her as well. She pressed the issue. **"Is that why you didn't want us to come; why you didn't want *me* to come? What did they do to you?"** She began to yawn. She put her head in his lap, Cain began to eat the soup, since he was hungry also. His abilities are hyper metabolic; so much is taken out of him when he fights. **"Yeah, that's part of it."** He began to leave the room; she inquired again while dosing off. **"You didn't answer me. What happened to you?"** He kissed her again and whispered. **"Something wonderful."** With that, the ship was shaking because the primary ship of the Dark-Sider Armada had just exploded thanks to Jaylun's anti-matter ordinances. *Kima's beloved is so smart; she picked well*, he thought while smiling.

As the victorious warriors began slowly arriving back, the Delta Raider carrying Nick, AC, and the bodies of Erik and Petamauck finally arrived. When they landed, both Kira and Kima were there to greet their mother and Michael was there to greet his father. The entire family embraced, both old and new. Nick normally mourns alone when he thinks about his lost friends, but he realized that too many had lost too much. Michael had just lost his aunt and was now going to be monarch of more than 50 percent of the galaxy in the course of the last few hours. Nick had lost two of his dearest and oldest friends. Many of the different peoples had lost a tremendous amount just to win that day. They were all surprised when there were more than one million people inside the primary hanger and countless others all across the planet waiting for their mighty champion to return. It was time to mourn the dead and celebrate the living; to celebrate the victory.

Commander Uchida, the leader of the Earth Defense Project, was nursing a broken foot and she walked up to the podium with a cane that Dr. Parker Igeleke had made for her. She raised her glass and spoke with an authority that belied her age. **"Greetings to all. I want to honor the brave that sacrificed so much so that so many could have a chance to exist in this star cluster and the rest of the universe. Thank you to our kin who fought and died for a cause that was greater than we could possibly imagine. To our newest comrades in arms, we salute you. This bond of fellowship shall not end today. This is not the beginning to the end, but rather the end of the beginning. To Lord Michael, the son of our great Khan; we are bonded both in friendship and in blood, but most importantly, we are bonded in love. To our fearless and selfless Commander, thank you for believing in us and thank you once again teaching us that the Cause matters above all else. Cheers."** Tears rolled down many faces within the crowd. With that said, Emily continued. **"Let us celebrate this victory and the lives lived in glorious service. Dr. Chandler if you would please."** Turns out that Dr. Chandler was an excellent musician and put together quite a band. Kira, the tough leader of the Earth Defense turns out has an incredible singing voice. The warriors sang and danced throughout the night.

As the celebration continued a lonely figure was standing in the observation tower. He was enjoying himself yes but he was still in mourning of his two friends. Emily's words spoke directly to the commander's heart. *God, I miss you both; thanks for being there.* Nick has always been so focused and strong minded. So much has happened. He sat alone in the tower chair, with his hands touching his chin, massaging his beard stubble. He smiled because he knew that Erik would have complained that he was a Paladin and not a hoodlum. That made him laugh as a few tears rolled down his face.

To his surprise, he was not alone. There she was; Sho's niece. His novice project director, someone who he required to grow up so fast, had done well. Emily walked into the observation deck and sat next to him. She leaned her head on his shoulder while he put his arm around her. She sobbed quietly, overwhelmed at what had just occurred. Nick then did something that he isn't known for; he hummed Erik's favorite song, *The Storm is Passing Over.* She sobbed hard; the tears began to flow from her eyes. He spoke quietly as she cried, **"it's okay Emily. Tears are always a strength; never a weakness. Well done."** There was so much to feel sad about and so much to celebrate; it was too much. The young apprentice said to her master, **"How the Hell do you do it?"** Nick smiled said to her sweetly, **"that was an excellent report by the way. Just perfect."**

Uchida was flustered at the fact that Cain was so seemingly okay with the madness that is the life of a Paladin. She had not been a Paladin very long, but in a very short period, she has gone from a graduate of the Paladin Academy to being the leader of the Earth Project to now being the de-facto leader of the planet Earth itself. These changes, coupled with a devastating, but successful encounter with the Dark-Sider Armada has left the young leader emotionally spent and confused. Why wasn't Antonius as freaked out as she was? She had a query for the Alpha. **"Why did you pick me for all of this? What if I had failed? What if we had failed because of me making a bad decision? This doesn't make sense. How could someone as wise as you make such a gamble? You had endless options Commander; Hell,** *I wouldn't have picked me.* **You picked me for a task that I wasn't equipped to do. Based on the craziness of what we've endured, there is no way you could've known. Why?"**

When listening to Commander Uchida speak about her emotional state, Cain almost laughed. *She is so young,* he thought. Emily is more gifted than he originally thought; she's almost ready. Nick looked at her sympathetically. **"That's a silly question Emily. You still don't know?**

You were ready. I studied you; I've watched your growth. I am an Oculari; I always know things that I shouldn't know." He then kissed her on the forehead and smiled. Much like her first encounter, he revealed himself to his apt pupil.

They both listened to the band and watched as Michael was teaching Lance an Altarian dance step; Lance had found a beautiful Altarian pilot that he needed to impress before Nathan got to her. Laughing at the site, he continued, **"Look at what you did little one. Under your leadership, Earth reached FTL, binary fusion, and developed a defense force capable of defeating the siders. I think that your track record speaks for itself. And like you said, this is the end of the beginning. Humans prepare a lifetime for a single moment, a single opportunity; then one day, it is tomorrow. I thought you would have figured that out by now. Just wait until you find out your *next* assignment."**

Emily was still trying to get her mind around everything that was accomplished. She was proud of her friends and her kin; they accomplished everything that had been mandated from them. It does seem that Cain picked the right person to the lead the Earth through such a difficult time and it would seem she is the right person to lead the Earth for the immediate future. Their troubles have really just begun. Nick smiled and said to his young comrade. **"Always remember Commander, if you don't learn anything else from me. God doesn't always call the equipped. *He always equips the called.*"** Emily, satisfied with her commander's answers, asked quietly **"Nick can we stay here for awhile?"** The mighty Khan smiled and responded, **"of course. As long as you want."** She asked one final question, **"How do you sleep after days like this?"** Nick yawned and closed his eyes, **"like a baby."**

As the Festival of Life was commencing, two dear friends were away from the organized confusion speaking quietly in the trauma center. AC was getting her knee repaired. Her appendage reconstruction was taking longer because of her complicated Rioan/Terran physiology. Lt. Colonel Sayied Faris was waiting by her bed quietly. He has been her friend for many years; both have served Cain on the Centauri longer than either would like to confess. AC began to slowly stir, she was having a nightmare. **"No Nick!! Stop it! That's enough,"** Sayied woke her from her ordeal. **"AC! Wake up, you are dreaming."** The beautiful superior officer woke up and saw her dear comrade. She was relieved to know that what she was witnessing didn't actually happen. However, the reality of what she had actually been witness to was far more frightening.

"How long was I out? I had the most awful dream. That Nick wasn't what they told us that he was." Sayied touched her hand. **"No my friend, what you saw actually happened. I saw what Nick did. In fact, we all saw what Nick did to the Assassin. I was monitoring his vitals; it was unlike anything that I had ever seen. I erased it from the archival logs. A planet AC. He hit him with a *planet*."** Both of these dear friends began to piece together what they had been witness to. They had to re-evaluate all the actions of Cain. Just how did he destroy the *entire* Unori system? What really happened during the Tronic Reconciliation? Those were just a few of many incidents that intrigued them both. The man that they had always loved and followed into battle seemed to be a being of power that was beyond their limited comprehension. No wonder they were hardly ever shown a vid-link of Nick in action. How long has he been this good? How long has he been this deadly?

Another figure walked into the room with a large bouquet of flowers. It was the Ocularian Commandant. He was smiling. Both of these veteran Paladin officers had enough history with the cunning leader to know that he is always up to something. However, that didn't mean that he didn't have information. **"Hello beautiful. You look more like your mother every day."** AC has known the Ocularian Commandant her entire life. Her children refer to him as "Uncle" and she also refers to him as such. He is such a deadly and unpredictable operative. She knows that her relationship with him has to be positive because her mother adores him and he is Nick's adopted father. Even her father begrudgingly recognizes OC as his best friend.

The lt. colonel did not share the same level of sentiment. Sayied was clearly displeased with him; Faris has never forgiven the Commandant for his hand in Nick's development. **"You have some nerve for showing up you bastard! Get out before I kill you where you stand. How in the Hell did you get in here past security?"** The Ocularian mentor smiled. **"Security? Really? You think that security could keep me out? I think that you should put your gun away Colonel Faris. You might want to look down at your crotch. My sniper doesn't take kindly to threats to my life. And how are you feeling today pretty girl?"** He then reached over and kissed AC on both of her flushed cheeks.

AC smiled. She knows what the Commandant means to Nick. She knows that Nick for whatever reason, truly adores him. She also knows that because she is Aya's daughter, the Ocularian will not lie to her if she asks a legitimate question. The Commandant is a master of DIP (Dis-Information Protocol), which is partly why Faris hates him. People have been trying to kill this crafty leader for eons, but he always escapes with his life.

No one within the Federation or the Alliance has as much information about the leadership. Every dirty little secret and questionable behavior is in the files of the Oculari. It is better to leave the Commandant alone. Nick affectionately refers to his father as "The Nastiest Rat in The Shit House." The Commandant is one of the few who actually knows where all the bodies are buried; in part because he is responsible for a majority of them. Her "Uncle" is one the few that Cain greets warmly whenever he sees him. He doesn't even do that for Kima. When AC asked him why, Cain told her it was because he may be evil, but he is a necessary evil. The Commandant knows his place in the universe and Nick has always admired that.

AC, the alluring daughter of Aya, asked the master of espionage a direct question. **"What does the term *Apex Predator* mean to you Uncle?"** The veteran mentor of Cain responded sweetly. **"You saw my son in action didn't you? Isn't he the most beautiful monster that you have ever seen? Which color was he? Red, Blue, Yellow, Black, Green, Purple, Orange, or White? Or better yet, did he continue to change colors? My monitor couldn't keep up with his changes. It doesn't matter. I love them all. I am surprised that you haven't seen him in action before. Ah yes, he was always with Erik wasn't he? Just wait, he is going to perform a magic trick that you will *never* forget."**

AC then leaped from her bed and grabbed the head of the Oculari; both she and Faris had grown tired of the games. **"Answer me."** Faris began to cock his pistol. The Commandant smiled again and spoke with a pleasant demeanor. **"So disappointing. You have learned nothing from my son. You think you've got me? Please. You are two of the mightiest Paladins but you wouldn't last a *day* in the Killing Academy. Being one step ahead of someone like you is for amateurs. So obvious. You see professionals like my son and I have beaten you before you even *know* that there is a conflict. Who do you think trained Nick in the *Art* of *War*?"**

A knock on the door occurred and someone opened the door. AC's mother came inside. She was not happy with the picture that she saw. **"AC, will you unhand my friend please? And Sayied please put your gun away before they kill you."** Faris was confused and inquired, **"who? No one is in here."** At that point, a blade was placed near his throat. There were four Ocularian assassins that had been in the room the entire time. The Commandant laughed. **"You forget, I am an Oculari; we can be *anywhere and we are everywhere.* Never send a Paladin to do an Oculari's job. Aya, your daughter and her friend wanted to ask me a question, but maybe you are better equipped to answer it. They want to know what the *Apex Predator* means to me. Should I tell them? Or should *you*?"** Aya then smiled at both of the confused Paladins. **"Sit down."**

After the destruction of the Dark Sider Armada, many different species descended upon Earth. Many of these peoples were members of the IGF, several were not. The leadership of the Terran Alliance, the Gondronian and Altarian Federations which had become one, and the Earth warriors welcomed all of these different groups had come to give thanks to what had been lost. More than four hundred seventy million people of more than 120 species had died to protect the entire star cluster. A relatively small number until consider who died. Many were of the system's dearest blood. Erik, Alvarnari, Dr. Martinez and Petamauck were among that dearest blood. Emily gave words of strength, comfort, and greetings. Earth was introduced to the rest of the universe in a mighty way. Of the thirty million Earthlings, only seventeen million remained. However, the transaction of life did make this part of the star cluster that much more secure; which was Cain's goal all along.

Even though the most deadly adversary of the star cluster had been dealt with for the time being, that did not mean that all was well within this region of the universe. Much like when Antonius spoke to those recent graduates back on Arcadia, the universe is a dirty place, full of tyrants, would be despots and vicious predators. It was time that these enemies of liberty in this part of the Virgo know that those behaviors would no longer be tolerated. The Knights and the Altarians were now making preparations to deal with those persecutors with extreme prejudice. That being said, it was time to upgrade the various components of the war machine that would be responsible for waging a crusade against these new and unknown, unpredictable rouges gallery.

For the unified forces, their troubles have just begun. As far as Antonius is concerned, the mandate of the Knights hasn't changed; they are *still* the hit squad of the Alliance and the Federation. The warrior's elite. They are the lethal, the adaptive, and the exceptional. Being in the Milky Way doesn't change anything. It doesn't change anything at all.

Several allies had undergone changes in their circumstances. Since there were no more Gondronians technically, the great young king Michael took his grandfather's name to become officially, Avis V, the new leader of the Altarian Federation. His people would remain split in both the near and far sides of the Milky Way, ready to protect the innocent against tyranny in all its forms. The new King made the allianceofficial with the United Earth Command, which would be the combined forces of the Earth Knights, the Wig Splitter Fighter Squadron, armored infantry, and Mega Assault Squadrons. The entire Earth military force would be led by the newly promoted Commander Kira Darius. She became the second youngest combat commander in history after her friend and comrade in arms, Emily Uchida. Her second in command will be the newly promoted Colonel Jamie Harris, a hero from the Dark-Sider War.

The planet Earth would also have a new official leader as well. Commander Emily Uchida, the capable project manager of all the planet's endeavors would now have a new title: Regent of Terra. Even though the Earth's entrance into the Terran Alliance has never been made official, a presence of Paladins and Terran Military will be on Earth none the less. She is the first Regent in the history of the Alliance who is also a Paladin, a reflection of the current realities in this part of the Virgo Super Cluster. Regent Uchida, with the help of Lord Congo of the Altarian Federation, re-wrote the Genesis Accord. Its policies now reflect a new reality, a new Earth. A permanent treaty of friendship and cooperation would be established between these two mighty armies bent on freedom and peace; in no small part because the Gondronian/Altarian hybrid king's father is the greatest warrior in the history of humanity.

Earth would be declared neutral territory for all the Terran Alliance; no one has claim, but all have claim to the home world. The only official population would be the seventeen million Earthlings who had endured so much to exist in this new universe. It would serve as a training ground for new Paladins, as a second Paladin academy would be established there. The Blood Knights have been officially split; each unit receiving a new set of troops for both Commander Kira Darius and Khan Antonius to lead into their never ending campaign against the cruel and unjust. The Earth Knights will be larger than the Blood Knights, with a number north of fifteen thousand. With new troops coming from the second Paladin Academy that will actually be based on Earth, the Terrans will have an endless supply of human capital for their charge. Kira will now lead a contingent, the Earth Knights, guardians of Terra, the Milky Way and beyond. A permanent presence will be maintained in this section of the Virgo Super Cluster. All enemies of freedom be warned.

The battle mecha of the unified forces took on a different appeal after enduring such an exhaustive ordeal with the Dark-Sider Armada. Even though the united forces emerged victorious, the price was high in terms of damaged or destroyed equipment. It was time to upgrade the Blood Knights, the Earth Knights, the Altarians/Gondronians, and the United Earth Fleet. Combining the total knowledge and brain power of some of the most creative minds of this group yielding incredible results. The intellect of Congo, Dr. Igeleke's staff, Jaylun, Nathan, Lance, AC, and a certain Khan were able to create a war machine that combined the various skills of these parties.

The Blood/Earth Knights' Delta Wing Raptors were the first to be updated. By using the Altarian energy system, the fusion engines were able to reach a capacity that would enable the raptors to operate at the 5th level of the Tachyon Pulse Drive. The Gondronians had an alloy that allowed the tremendous heat to be dissipated; allowing for a greater energy output. The Altarians had never had a star fighter squadron; thanks to collaboration with the other groups, they do now. The fighters were similar to Earth ships, resembling Eagles. These were first look; first kill star fighters of immense acclaim.

The Earth Star Destroyers were now much sturdier and had defensive armaments such as ray shielding similar to the Gondronian energy shields. All of these battle groups were now capable of utilizing solar energy based upon the Alliance technology that Antonius had created; none of the shared technology was proprietary. The Wig Splitter Squadron was decimated in the war; they have been completely upgraded to Rioan levels; AC's gift to her kinsman. Dr. Chandler, along with the medical teams from these various groups were able to make the Earthlings' bodies as sturdy as their fellow Terran counterparts, so that in an issue of hand to hand combat, the natives would have a chance. They still were no match for the Paladins, because no one in the universe is, but they wouldn't be bullied either. The anti-matter technology and nuclear arsenals would now be common throughout the quadrant, as well as utilization of microwave and electromagnetic pulse weaponry.

The star destroyers of all the groups couldn't use the Pulse Drive because that technology was Rioan, which would be in violation of the treaty. However, Nathan, Lord Congo and the Igeleke science group had developed a warp speed drive that was so much more efficient and powerful. This drive was now referred as an Ultra Warp Drive. It was a Trans-dimensional propulsion system that was at least in the ball park of 1/150 of level One of the Tachyon Pulse Drive. Traversing the Inter galactic neighborhood would never be a problem; distance to any issues in this area of the universe would never be a concern. This speed would allow the combined forces of the United Earth Fleet decided benefits over many of their potential opposition. These kinds of technological collaborations allowed the warriors of this galactic neighborhood to maintain significant tactical advantages over those who would bring tyranny to others.

The alloy that these collaborative groups created is something that is certainly beyond comprehension. The anti-matter and gravity technology now allowed the Centauri's Pulse Drive to literally have no limitations. The reason that the drive only had five levels of speed was because the energy generated was not allowed to dissipate. With the anti-gravity/anti-matter system combined with Earthling cold fusion technology ensured that there would be no true imperfection of the Alpha Centauri. This energy was now recycled into the ships operating systems; the faster the ship travels, the ship's operating efficiency also increases. Congo also gave the Alpha Centauri the means to create a fusion based anti-element that made sure that the vessel would never have any energy concerns again. It was the adjutant's gift to his master. Super Tachyon Pulse had been created. All the Deltas, either Raptor or Raider, would now have it; Wing Alpha, in Nick's hands was even deadlier than before. The toys have all been upgraded beyond comprehension; all Milky Way Certified.

The most glaring changes had been to Antonius himself. When he laid there on the floor of the dark assassin's ship, his heart actually stopped beating, but his brain was still functioning. He understood the value that his friend's sacrifice was. Erik, Petamauck, and AC knew that they could not handle the warrior, yet they continued to press on. His friends on the Avis knew that by entering the fight against the siders would mean certain death, but yet they pressed on. Several different warships sacrificed themselves to stop the phalanx, even if that lead to their deaths, yet they pressed on. All of these instances, these comrades in arms, fought and died for something greater than them. Then the Alpha thought of something in the bible that always stuck with him. *The path of the righteous man is beset on all sides by the iniquities of the selfish and the tyranny of evil men. Blessed is he that shepherds the weak through the valley of darkness for he is surely his brother's keeper and the finder of lost children.*

All of his comrades that faced Nex had been shepherds of *him*. AC and Petamauck saved him from that miserable life on Earth and Erik had helped make him the man that he had become. All that charity for a boy that none of them had even known. How his life could have turned out if they hadn't intervened. He realized how blessed he was in that instant, how joyous his life has been. It is time to repay that kindness. Kima told AC that their love restarted his heart. His heart began to beat and the amount of adrenaline flowed throughout his entire body couldn't be quantified. There was a fire in his soul, a joy that had always been there but now has to come out.

The Khan has been truly born. In that moment, Nicolas Cain would never be the same person again. No one really spoke about the physiological changes to him, but Danyzer and the Commandant did mention that he was a quarter meter taller than before. His musculature seemed even more defined than before also. His voice was heavier, but his laugh, the sound that AC wished she heard more often was also richer in sound. Michael also mentioned that when he touched his father, he literally felt his power. His eyes were a rich mahogany, now seemed lighter. As if in the light, they were bright, but in the dark they were even more luminescent. Kira and Kima mentioned that his skin seemed stronger than before as well. The part that really seemed to make both Regent Uchida and Alron Driax feel at ease was the fact that Cain seemed wiser; as if a burden had been lifted. To Kima, Aya, and her Uncle, they knew that is exactly what has happened.

As Cain began to introduce himself to the leadership of the other races within this part of the quadrant, many were truly impressed. There was a new strength, a passion for helping his fellow citizen. Many of the sovereign powers, both royal and political, commented to Chancellor Driax that he was nothing like the rumors. *That's because he is worse than the rumors*, she commented. She and Regent Uchida made it clear that this would more than likely be the last time that any of them would ever have contact with the mighty Khan. He was not going to go to diplomatic functions; he is a warrior. He protects democracy, he doesn't practice it. However, he did make the people of this part of the super cluster just as comfortable as the other end. He considered all of these species family. And when his loved ones needed him, Cain's warriors would give their last breaths to defend any of them.. He no longer did these things out of a sense of obligation; he now did these things out of love.

At this point in his life, Khan Antonius finally understood his oath. He will kill the enemies of liberty without any hesitation. Any of the enemies of his people are now an endangered species. He will love without fear. He no longer hesitates to do the right thing, even if that means that he will be in conflict with his superiors or even his loved ones. The Terran people are not his primary priority; all the people who are suffering are. He and his warriors will shepherd the weak through the darkness. They are truly their brother's keeper and the finders of lost children. The siders or anyone else who tries to prey upon the weak will have to deal with the good shepherd. And he is not forgiving. Even in these dark times, the light will always prevail. He is not Antonius because he is obligated to be, he is the mighty Khan because he chooses to be. *God is so much smarter than I*, thought the mighty commander.

After the festivities had subsided, a conversation occurred between the Khan, the Chancellor, and a representative of the Federation Military Liaison. He was a familiar face. A Rioan with which the Alpha Paladin is most warmly acquainted. Danyzer was part of the Federation contingent that had come to see Earth. This is the closest he had been to his home in the Andromeda Galaxy in eons. He lamented at the fact that while he was glad that Nick had emerged triumphant, but was saddened at the fact that to defeat the Dark-Siders, the powerful general had to make the Andromeda nearly uninhabitable. Danyzer spoke to his apt pupil. **"Nick congratulations on what you have done. You and your warriors did what my warriors and I could not; you stopped them without destroying your home to do it. Well done."** Nick responded to his venerable mentor and addressed his chancellor as well. **"Greetings mistress, I trust that you are pleased with the outcome. My Lord Danyzer, I need you to know that if you hadn't been such a good** teacher, we wouldn't have won this day. I followed your example, but I wanted to use a less populated area. We know so much more now than you knew back then. It was the dark matter issue. If you hadn't been in such a dark matter infested area, it wouldn't have damaged such a significant portion of the galaxy. Under the circumstances, I would have done the same."

The chancellor seeing the opportunity to lighten the mood did just that. **"Lord Danyzer tell the Commander why you have come. It is excellent news. I believe that you should be the one to tell him."** Danyzer, taking the lead from his comrade moved the conversation forward. **"Lord Antonius, we have found them. You have a new assignment. They are about 76 billion light years away. They have to be stopped. I am sorry but the Dark-Siders are going to have to wait. Here is the code card. We have to deal with them once and for all. We know where the Cimminorks are. Our time has come. This code card contains the easiest route to find their empire. The last thing that we can afford is for the Dark-Siders and the Cimms becoming allies via mutual hatred. I am sorry that we must keep having you clean up our old messes, but you know how it is. I know that the siders are a priority, but this is a Federation/Alliance Priority Alpha Tasker."**

Nick looked at his chancellor and his former commanding officer. In that instant, whatever feelings that he had about running down the Dark-Siders would have to be tabled for another time. The Cimms would now have to be a new priority. The work of the Khan is never done. The chancellor smiled at him and spoke gently to her victorious warrior. **"Antonius, it is time. I will have Admiral Kun coordinate with the Federation military to strengthen our borders because I know that the siders are still going to be a problem. I wouldn't have you take up this charge if I wasn't certain that the Cimms were not the greater of two evils. Remember what I told you. All of our enemies are coming to our doorstep. We cannot afford for the Cimms to plan a sneak attack on us from deep space."**

This has been a long time coming. The Cimminorks were former allies to the IGF before "The Grudge." They are now located in the Halicon Super Cluster after they have been in the Yotslot Super Cluster. The problem is that Halicon Super Cluster is incredibly difficult to reach. It is in a region of space that is further out than the Leo Super Cluster; it is almost 20 billion light years further than the Leo. These guys are worse than the Dark-Siders, depending on your vantage point. The siders are more parasitic, but the Cimms are just conquerors; really nasty people. Nick knew that as much as he wanted to finish off the siders, the Cimms are a bigger problem. This celebratory feeling would have to end early. Nick looked at Danyzer and Driax with confidence. It was time. **"As you wish. They will be swept out of the universe as soon as possible. They will not escape this time."**

As the Federation and Alliance leaders continue to converse with their most trusted and deadly agent, three figures enter the conference area. One of them is a beautiful human, the newest Regent Uchida, the second is the weapon maker, AC, Danyzer's alluring daughter, and finally the giant boy-king of the Altarian Federation. Normally no one would ever dare enter a conversation that would be occurring between people of such importance, but this is a different set of scenarios. Michael is the newest ally to the Federation and the Alliance, while Emily is the representative of the Alliance in this region of the Virgo Super Cluster, and finally AC is both Nick's executive officer and also she is the daughter of the great Federation General. All three based upon their relationships with the people in the room knew that something is terribly wrong.

Michael speaks first. **"Greetings Father, I know that we have much to mourn and also much to celebrate, why do you look like that? What has happened?"** Nick looks at his son, his powerful noble son. He knows that as much as the new king understands, there is so much that he does not know. It is time to make him aware. **"My son, I have to leave earlier than I expected. I need you to work with Emily; we have a lot of problems that have to be addressed. Lady Uchida, the Earth Knights are at your disposal; use them well. Hopefully, we will see each other again. Where we are going, you cannot follow. You have a bigger job. The army assembled here will be dissipated among this galactic region. AC, tell Faris, that we will leave within the next 240 minutes. Here is the code card; tell Jaylun to map out our course and be ready to go. Our celebration time is over and we've got a job to do. This is an Alliance/Federation Priority Alpha Tasker."** All of these three people understand that a Priority Alpha Tasker is the highest tasker that can be undertaken. This means that the Centauri will go into deep space and will remain there until their task is completed. The last time that the Centauri went on a similar task, more than seventy trillion beings were slaughtered; to put it in context, Driax's great great great grandparents hadn't been born yet. This is as serious as it gets.

Away from the group of people who were just speaking about the issue at hand, two figures wait to speak to their noble, deadly adopted son. Aya and the Commandant didn't want to get in the way of Nick's affairs with the rest of the contingent, but there was one more vital loose end that needed to be addressed. This conversation would not be interrupted by anyone. It is a well-known fact that when Cain speaks to Aya and the Commandant, territorial maps of star systems tend to be remade. Not Alron Driax, AC, or Danyzer are privy to that conversation.

Lady Aya always knows something that she shouldn't know; she is a lot like the Oculari in that regard. The senator always knows more about Nick's intentions and emotional state than either her daughter or her husband and that has always been disjointing. The familial arrangement has always made everyone within the Federation uncomfortable to say the least. AC knows that Cain loves her dearly, but he will never let her completely inside; not even Kima can get that deep. For whatever reason, Nick has allowed her mother and the Commandant in. There is certain jealously there; Aya had Nick's love, in spite of all they've done to him. AC and the others just don't get it; it is always about God's work. His mother and father are just better assets. It's an Oculari thing, they wouldn't understand.

The son smiles and speaks warmly to his father and kisses his mother. **"Greetings father. Hello dearest mother, I trust that you approve. The armada has been destroyed. The Cimms are now on the *shit list*; they won't be there very much longer. The plan is moving according to schedule. Have you made contact with Congo yet?"** The Commandant speaks first. **"My son, I am pleased with the outcome. I am sorry about Erik; he was a good soldier. We will depart for Alta Major as soon as we end this conversation. I am delighted that you have made this decision. I can't wait to get started."** His mother chimes in. **"Something funny happened recently. AC demanded to know what the term 'Apex Predator' meant. She and Faris tried to strong arm your father. It was hilarious!"** Nick began to laugh. **"What?! Really? What did you tell them?"** The father giggled. **"I told them everything; I'm kidding. I told them nothing: half-truths, and confusion; the usual. Ramifications, end of the galaxy, blah, blah, etc."** Nick smiled. **"They bought it?"** Aya grinned as she spoke. **"Of course. You know** that your father is the best at Dis Information Protocols. I followed his lead; left them with a story that will keep their minds occupied for awhile. Your mother can be convincing. They know nothing. By the way, is Lord Congo bright? This doesn't work if he is not bright my son." Nick kissed her softly. "Not as bright as you mother."

As AC watches her mother and dear Uncle prepare to depart from Earth, she is joined by the leader of the Terran Alliance. Chancellor Driax and Admiral AC have many things in common beyond the fact that both work diligently for a better tomorrow. They both have been taught extremely well by a brutal, yet loving set of teachers. Aya and Nick are not cold at all, but rather they are hard. The mother and son understand that their job isn't easy on those that love them and they can sometimes appear cruel but that is not the case at all. Both of these women reach a similar level of acceptance. "I think that you need to try and talk to Aya before she leaves; your mother hasn't left AC. I know that look. I am *ordering* you to talk to her. Oh I see now. You must have tried to ask about how Nick, her and the Commandant are bonded?"

The relationship between Nick and Aya has always been an extremely frustrating thing for the Admiral. Every time she is given an answer from her mother, it just seems to lead to more questions. AC wipes a tear away from her face. "Yes. I know that what they do is necessary, but God it is such a difficult thing to accept. Those two live in a bubble don't they? It can wear on you sometimes. Aya and Uncle seem to be cut from the same cloth; the Cause matters more than anything. Love, peace, and joy mean little to them. They find comfort in fulfilling their duty. Nick is worse than *both* of them; that's what worries all of us. That's why those three work so well together." The youthful chancellor touches her soldier's shoulder. "I know. Nicky is *something* isn't he? She must have really been special."

At first AC is annoyed, then puzzled. AC hates when the Alron knows more than her when it comes to Cain; then Driax starts to sound like Aya, which pisses her off a great deal. Does Nick have a beloved that she hasn't met; unacceptable. What woman is she referring to? AC looked puzzled. "Who Alron?" Driax smiled. "Quenas. She is the only person that really understood him wasn't she? Your father once told me why the Alpha Paladin picked Aya to be his mother. It really gave me a deeper insight into my dearest Oculari. I will tell you only if you think that it will bring you comfort. It is your choice." AC turned and looked at the chancellor slowly. **"Okay my Lady Driax; why?"** Driax wiped the tears from her eyes. **"You really don't know do you? Because Aya reminds him of *her.*"**

Aya reminds Nick of Quenas. That statement shook AC in her very soul. Her mother understands Nick in a way that no one else does and he loved Quenas like no other. These issues have always been tremendous sources of frustration. *It's time to find out why*, thought the daughter. The soldier takes the advice of her Alron and runs down her mother; AC finally has the chance to talk to Aya alone. She doesn't have much time. Within the next 180 minutes, there is a strong possibility that the child will never see her mother again. Of all the times that the Alpha Centauri has gone into deep space, this is the furthest from known civilization that they will go. The daughter has many questions for her mother, but she only has time to really ask her one.

AC greets her mother with a kiss and speaks sweetly. **"Hello Mother. We are leaving soon. Father says that we have found the last known location of the Cimms. That we are assigned to stay out in deep space until they are completely wiped out. I am going to miss you and father. I am even certain that Nick is going to miss you as well."** Aya smiles. **"How has human motherhood grabbed a hold of you? It gets in the way of your duty sometimes doesn't it? Both Kira and Michael are staying here aren't they? Does it pain you to leave them?"** AC said coolly. **"Doesn't Nick, myself and Kima leaving bother you? Sometimes I don't understand you, Nick, or Uncle at all. When you three are together, you really frighten me; you really frighten all of us. I know that you will miss us all, but doesn't it bother you that once again you and your colleagues are asking more of Nick than you've ever asked of any other Paladin?"** That is the kind of question can truly anger Aya. Now she has no choice but to respond the best way she knows how; directly.

Whenever AC asks her some question like the one she just proposed, it takes everything in the senator's soul not to lash out in anger. Sometimes Lady Aya believes that her daughter doesn't know her at all. Like she has a monopoly on caring about Nick. The Terran Senator recognizes that her daughter can be selfish when it comes to Cain. It was time to bring perspective to her emotional state. Aya responds in a cold, calculating manner consistent with her reputation. **"No sweet child, it doesn't. Nick isn't my property; he is my child, but not really. Nick** is really God's child. I am just a steward of him; just like you are of your children. You are such a beautiful, but naïve child. Sometimes I believe that you forget who you are and whom you belong to. We belong to God; we are doing His will. Someone has to; it might as well be us. If you remembered that, we wouldn't be having this needless conversation. You get that useless compassion from your father."

At this point, AC is both confused and annoyed with her mother. Aya always speaks as if her husband is not as bright as she is. That Danyzer's warmth and compassion are somehow weaknesses. **"Why are you so cold? And why do you belittle father this way? And why do you speak as if your children are not important to you? We love you dearly mother; you have never shown the same love to anyone but Nick, not even me."** Aya's face and her tone of voice softened. It was in that instance that she realized that AC doesn't know as much as she had been given credit for. That she was truly unaware of what her mother meant by that statement and many others. Aya knows that Rioans are known for their extreme compassion. That compassion, while a deeply expressive trait can sometimes hinder a Rioan officer from completing their primary objectives. When articulating that statement, she was not belittling Danyzer, but rather an honest critique.

Aya's eyes moistened and she smiled; she is absolutely stunning. She grabbed her only daughter and hugged her with all that she was and kissed her sweetly. **"My child, is that what you think? I am so sorry. Sometimes I forget that you are not as smart as Nick is. I fail to remember that I need to sometimes tell you what I am thinking. With your brother, he always tells me *what I am thinking.* Please understand that I love you and your father with all my heart and soul; I love your children, and that includes Michael, with all that I am as well."** She was stroking her daughter's beautiful hair. Even though AC is a mother, she is still Aya's beautiful little girl. She smiles and continues speaking about her other child; the *monster.* **"My relationship with Nick is just different honey. You see, I have to love him differently, because he is *different.* Sometimes you forget just how brilliant and complicated that he is; how truly terrifying he can be. You forget sometimes what he is. He may be my son, he may be your brother; but he is and will always be a monster. I have to always take into account that he is *Khan Antonius*; the gifted, the deadly, and the** necessary. He was the Khan the day that he was born; he was never really a child, darling. Every moment of pain, of tragedy, was merely training him for these dark times. Now he has truly accepted the truth and look at how magnificent the truth is. He is a devastating tool, a servant of God's will."

AC was surprised by such a display of emotion from her mother. Aya has always been about the Cause ever since AC could remember. Service to the Alliance and Federation and most importantly, service to the people were constants in her life growing up. Danyzer wanted AC to become a politician like Aya; it was her mother that introduced her to Elisma. That meeting changed the course of many lives that day. She touched her daughter's face and whispered to her. "**I just love Nick; I don't own Nick. Too many parents try to hold their children's lives hostage by their expectations.** *I don't do that.* **He belongs to God. Nick understands this better than everyone. You are lucky to be a Rioan. Humans are so stupid when it comes to following God's will. If it were up to me, I would protect you, your father, the girls, and Michael from all the evil in the universe. I would selfishly put you all ahead of everyone else. That is truly how much I love you. If it were my choice to make. Your brother's very existence from his birth to right now, is a constant reminder that it isn't.**" AC had never received such an open declaration of her mother's love. How Aya wanted to be selfish with that love and just how important her mother's family meant to her. She was completely caught off guard by this near spontaneous announcement.

Aya continued speaking about the love that is in her soul for AC's father, her dearest husband. "**Your father believes in a better today and tomorrow; that is why I love him so. Even after all the terrible sacrifices and awful decisions, he finds a reason to smile. It is the most beautiful thing about him; it makes me fall in love with him all over again;** *every single day.* **The problem is that he thinks he has more control over things than he actually does and that is a very human trait. In many ways, your father is more human than I am; that can be a problem. From time to time, his humanity can blind him and that gets in Nick's way. My job, Driax's job, and your Uncle's job is to make sure that** *nothing* **gets in Nick's way. Cleaning up evil has nothing to do with a sunny day; you know that my beautiful child. Being a Senator does create a conflict in my soul; to** send those that I love deeply into the abyss and pray that they return. As long as Nick is with you and Kima, I never doubt that you will succeed."

The mother stands up and looks at the Alpha Centauri, the mighty starship's reflection shimmering against the Mediterranean Sea; it is being bathed in moonlight. "If it were up to me, I would protect your father's heart; he has suffered so much trying to do the right thing. If it were up to me, I would try to make it up to Nick, his mother, and his father. The thing is baby, my son *doesn't want it changed*; he believes that everything has happened exactly the way it is supposed to happen. That's so *remarkable*. That's so *awful*."

Aya realizes that by talking about Nick, she is letting her daughter see her in a way that few have ever seen. She is usually so confident, but now she is so vulnerable. This is so unexpected to AC, who is having difficulty with dealing with this different side to her parent. There is much that she doesn't know. Aya continues. "Nick once told me why he doesn't question God. He said that he is fully aware of the dreadful existence that the Elisma family has had; *and he doesn't give a shit*. Did you know that they were all among the first Paladins? They literally had no other profession; the killers elite. Three other Elisma kinsmen, including his mother ran from their obligations in one shape or another; Nick *ran to* those expectations. And every one of his ancestry died in service of the Terran Alliance. *Every. Single. One.* An entire family dedicated to following the Cause, to following God. Their reward was death. In a universe with more than 11 trillion humans, he is literally the *last* of his bloodline. He has no relatives. His mother was an only child and so was his father. There are no long lost Earth relatives either. The Earth global-war and the Erixan occupation took care of that. He has no one waiting for him at night, hoping and praying for his safe return. He said that he is humbled by the responsibility that has been placed at his feet. He said that he hopes to be the steward that God believes him to be."

Aya then revealed part of the operational plan that AC and the others were not privy to. A secret conversation that neither Danyzer or Driax had been informed about. He told both his father and mother that he needed to split the unit because Cain knew that if he had gone to Earth, he might not have been able to complete the mission. He would have killed every Erixian on Earth, and he wouldn't have stopped. He would have literally cleansed the whole galaxy on principle. He would have killed everyone on Earth because of what they did to each other. Cain knew that if he had done that, he would have no longer been useful to God's plan because he used his gifts for his own interest. That he placed his own pain above the needs of the many. That was not how he had been trained. Nick couldn't put that need for vengeance ahead of God's agenda. Every member of the Cain family on Earth had died either by Erixian or human hands. The Commandant and Aya were both devastated at the prospect that Nick was truly alone.

The mother continues educating the daughter with the most sensitive of information. **"They all died in service of God; every last one of them. Cain doesn't care; as far as he is concerned, God doesn't owe him an explanation. Don't you see? We are his family; his responsibility. The whole race; the whole quadrant. The whole universe. He has neither fear nor distractions; he possesses the unique ability to let that which does not matter truly slide. To my beautiful son, this suffering and sacrifice is merely a means to an end. Your sweet brother once said to me 'Too much sunshine is a desert and too much rain is a flood. You need rain and sunshine for fruit to grow. God is in the sunshine and everyone loves that. But I love the fact that God is in the *rain*.' Even if it was in my power to change everything, my son wouldn't let me. *I hate that*."**

In this moment, AC began to truly understand the pain that being Nick's mother causes Aya. She turns away from her stunned daughter and wipes the tears from her gorgeous face. She lets out a deep sigh. It never occurs to AC that her mother could feel so deeply about anything, much less her adopted son. She has always been so under control, this was a rare display of raw uncompromising emotion. Aya gathers herself and continues. **"You have no idea at all baby. I was so angry at God when it came to Nick. Why do he and his family deserve so much pain? Have you ever imagined how your *commander* looks at it? How your *friend* looks at life? How your *brother* looks at love? As far as Nicky is concerned, it is always about God; never let feelings or anything else get in the way. When you spend time with him, you tend to start looking at things the way he does. I am so glad that he has you and Kima. He asked me and my friend to be his parents because it makes *strategic* sense to him."**

The Senator realizes that her daughter is both shocked and confused by everything that her mother has told her. The mother knows that her only daughter needs to be comforted at this point. Her adopted brother is such a loving but deadly soul. She kisses her daughter and AC leans her head against Aya's shoulder. **"Don't get me wrong, Antonius loves us dearly in his own way, but there is always an objective in his actions that few would have ever considered. That's the thing with my son, there is *always* an objective. No matter how disturbing the objective may be, it makes perfect sense; you have to learn how to live with that. Some of his choices frighten me. Child, everyone is afraid of me and my friend; but he *terrifies* us. You have no idea how disturbing his mind really is; so much peace and so much turmoil in one soul. As much as he loves me, as much as he loves us, we are all still expendable."**

In the case of being deeply involved with Cain, AC is beginning to realize that she has merely scratched the surface of the commitment of being involved with the Alpha Paladin. Everyone wants to be in the Janitors, until they are there. Then a warrior realizes the relentless madness of the Janitor's life. Once someone joins this unit, they can *never* get out. The only people who are not with the Janitors are on assignments, such as Emily and Kira that Cain considers vital to whatever objective that make sense to him. The only thing more emotionally taxing is being in his inner circle.

AC now realizes that her mother and the Commandant are strained beyond measure when you have entered the world of Nick. It is madness that exceeds comprehension. They have to meet his expectations at all costs; at all times. There is a strong possibility that failure could lead to their deaths. Is she ready for this? **"What happened was incredibly special when he saved you because you were a loved one in danger. Not a comrade or a mission; but a loved one. That's what caused him to respond that way. Erik's father once served with his mother; she saved his life. Erik had been the only one to see what you had seen. He was the only one that he ever trusted. That was growth on his part; the development of trust. Now he has *you*. You know that Erik was named for his mother didn't you? You want to know what will happen when he has vanquished another foe? That's right; nothing. Antonius will just go and hunt down *another* foe. *There is always another foe baby*. Remember, we all operate at one speed; his speed.**

You and Kima are the ones that he trusts now. You will be in danger on a level that I cannot imagine, but that is your job. To keep Nick from being *himself*."

Aya continued letting her in to the inner sanctum. Is AC truly prepared to deal with the true mechanisms of Nick's mind? Aya knows that by speaking this deeply about Nick's heart, there is a true danger. She is dangerously close to breaking the covenant of the Oculari. Aya's life could be in jeopardy but she feels that this is a conversation that must be had. Where they are going, AC will be the sole voice of reason that her dearest Nicolas may have in his ear. If he goes too far, there will be no one but her and Kima to stop him. The other Knights don't have enough influence with Cain; they will follow him into Hell. At least Kima and AC have been given the right to ask him why.

AC then realizes a most terrible set of realities. The Oculari are deadly assassins and exceptional spies; but the most *gifted* killers in the entire Virgo Super Cluster are members of her crew. The Janitors are the most blood thirsty unit that has ever been in either the Federation or Alliance Military. They kill everything that is put in front of them and never ask questions; Cain's orders are completely trusted. Many of the Blood Knights are orphans or from single children homes. Their psychological reports all indicate a certain moral ambiguity necessary for such destructive means. Loyalty is also a consistency among their profiles. These warriors were always among the most brutal in their graduating classes. Everyone of the Paladin and Special Ops operatives on the ship had been given that label coming out of training. Everyone but two people; her and Kima.

The Alpha Centauri is a warship that was created with one purpose: to kill every species that has been put in front of it. The Alpha Centauri is the only ship in the entire universe with its kind of propulsion system. The (fuck you) nova cannon is easily the most destructive weapon in the known universe and Wing Alpha should have *never* been built. It never occurred to her that her home was a starship built solely for the purpose of wiping out entire star systems. No matter how many ships the Alpha Centauri has faced, never has the crew truly felt overmatched.

The Wing Fighters are so destructive that very seldom is the entire fleet ever dispatched to deal with any problems. The Wing fighters' arsenal is so powerful that one ship has the fire power of an entire battle group. It never occurred to her that it is highly unusual for one star fighter should have so much power. These ships have one central purpose: to completely obliterate their opposition. The pilots have been trained to deal with these ships' incredible operating systems. Wing Alpha is even more deadly than the other ships, in no small part because Nick is the Alpha Paladin.

She also realized that the Alpha Centauri wasn't even really involved in the battle against the armada. Nick was proving a point to the rest of the United Fleet. If the Centauri had been activated, the battle wouldn't have taken nearly as long. Cain wanted to build the confidence of his allies. It was an analysis of the most deadly purpose. Only Cain would have done what he did. At the instant realization of his actions, she couldn't breathe. No one but Cain would have gambled on his people like that. Except that it wasn't a gamble. She deduced that Cain considered all of those lives lost as acceptable *before* the battle had begun. Her Uncle always said that he would never play any game with Nick because he had already figured out the outcome. Nick liked to say wars are won in both the will and the mind. That's why he wasn't surprised; at *anything*.

Rear Admiral AC then realized that she had been tested and also had been given opportunities to leave the Centauri the entire time. Paul didn't have the stomach for the viciousness of the assignments that the Centauri had been sent on. He knew what the Centaur had been built for; Cain had just been waiting for a crew with the proper resolve. It was Cain who decided to promote Paul. That was why Darius had been given the command of the Polaris. Aya had warned her daughter that she had to make a choice. A part of Aya hoped that she had chosen to be with her fiancé, but she chose to stay with Cain. The Senator couldn't be biased, because Nick wouldn't allow her to be biased. Aya secretly hoped that Nick did not take Kima with him, but it was to no avail.

Both Aya and OC had hopes that Faris would become a good influence on Nick, but the opposite happened; Faris is almost as dangerous and sadistic as Cain is. Cain somehow turned a pacifist into another blood thirsty killer. Faris will show no mercy and might be at his most dangerous when cornered. There is no one left but her and Kima. Michael has already seen what his father is and Nick has a special training for his son that makes sense to only the Alpha Paladin. Aya and OC have no choice but to obey his marching orders. Only now does AC understand that her mother had been trying to protect her all along from Cain's hyper *madness* and more importantly, his hyper *sanity*.

To make matters worse is Nick's relationship with the Oculari. Yes, her uncle might be their commandant, but Nick is their *master*. The clan is everywhere and anywhere. As a point of fact, these assassins are all over the super cluster. They will kill for Cain in a moment's notice. They will kill anyone, including Aya and OC if he instructs them to. If anyone ever tries to harm the Terran Chancellor, Lady Uchida, or his son and one hair is misplaced, they will all have to answer to Cain. The Oculari know that is a fate far worse than death. To Khan Antonius, only an assassin is smart enough to protect both Driax and the IGF High Command. Just because no one thinks that they are there doesn't that the Oculari aren't there, much like their master.

This is why Aya is having this conversation; because Driax has ordered her to. That being said, she knows where the order *really* comes from. The senator continues. **"He was ready to give that responsibility to Petamauck and then he was forced to kill his mentor, his friend; his brother. Imagine the emotional toll that took on him. He put that aside to do what was needed; imagine killing a loved one for a greater good. We are lucky that we got Petamauck back. If Nick knew that Petamauck had been born under the Riddle of the Sphinx, he doesn't say. Most of us, including your father, are afraid to ask. When I asked him about his actions once before, he said that he didn't care. Petamauck got himself on your brother's shit list and it is *never* a long list. Your father thinks that he is on the list; Nick told me that he was never on it, but I could never tell your father. He likes keeping Danyzer on edge; keeps him accountable. The IGF Security Council can't stop him either. It was a test of both my and OC's loyalty. Imagine that; he tested his parent's loyalty. It stretch's you emotionally and cognitively to be loved by Nick. You can't tell your father either. Don't worry child, Nick knows about this conversation already."**

AC was puzzled. **"How?"** Aya smiled and kissed her lovingly. **"Who do you think had the conversation with Driax to get this course of events to happen? He suggested it to her who suggested it to you. He said that he would do it directly, but didn't think you were ready for it."** AC again was stumped. **"For what Mother?"** She smiled. **"Everything."**

At this point, AC is finally aware of why she and Kima are so vital in the grand scheme of things. Their job is to keep the Apex Predator human. Their mere existence is a disincentive for Nick to devolve into some state of mind that is beyond madness. Cain has a rationality that is disturbing because of his clarity; the ability to truly focus on the objective beyond self interest. Aya concludes her thesis. **"Everything Nick does is based upon the fact that God is smarter than him. He doesn't need any other reason to do these incredible, often terrible things; he chose me to be his mother because I believe the same thing. We are the out cost of liberty and charity my child. Our duty is to protect those who cannot protect themselves. Make no mistake child, Nick doesn't work for us;** *we work for him.* **Our job, including yours, is to make his job easier to complete. Nick is answer to the riddle '***who truly scares the boogey man?***' He is the gifted, the deadly, and the necessary; that's who he is. That is what he is.** *That is why he is* **baby. Why else would he be immortal? With him, there is just a beginning; there is no end. He will outlive us all. It's almost time to start getting our replacements ready and he has already chosen them. He won't ever stop and now, you can't either. Only death can end your obligation. We all have parts to play little one. Driax, I and OC have learned to just enjoy playing ours. Perhaps you should learn to love it like we do."** With that final statement, the daughter hugs and kisses the mother. **"Forgive me mother, I did not see."** AC headed towards the Centauri with a better understanding of who the *Apex Predator* truly is.

For the first time in a long time, Nick and his adopted son Michael will not be in close contact with one another. Both of these powerful men have found something in their bond; something that is beyond being both comrades in arms and also being father and son. Nick has asked a great deal from his troops and a great deal from himself over the course of his life. Now he has to ask a great deal from his son. Before fate intervened in each other's lives, they were both prisoners, both orphans. In spite of all the bloodshed and tears of loved ones, they have always known that each other is going through something similar. Michael has gotten used to being loved and adored by his father and the father has grown incredibly found of the son. Now Cain has to depart and he leaves with the knowledge that Michael Cain has been trained well. One final lesson for his son before he departs for the unknown.

As Nick and Michael share a quiet moment, they are interrupted by Michael's surrogate mother, AC. The Alpha Paladin doesn't mind that because in many ways this may be more difficult for her than it will be for him. Cain could have just arranged for a nanny for Michael, but he felt that his dear friend should have the opportunity to experience the ups and downs of motherhood, even if it was for just a short period. Because of her tremendous sacrifices, she never got to know her own children until they were older. She spent most of the first 17 years of Michael's life bonding with and nurturing him. When he cried as a baby, she was the one who rocked him to sleep and sang to him. When he did well in his studies, AC was the first person to encourage him and she was the first person that Michael can remember to kiss him. That is a lot to be giving up. The mother and the father are leaving the son to rule well and protect this part of the universe. Kira will be there and support the mighty king and he will support the Terrans that he has come to know and love as family.

"**You know what I was thinking about son?**" The mighty father spoke in whimsical tone; a warm breeze always makes him feel joy. "**I never told you about my favorite parable.**" Both AC and Michael looked at Nick in an inquisitive fashion. "**Parable? No you never have Dad.**" At this point AC also chimed in the banter. "**Nick, I have never heard you mention a parable ever. Almost everything you say is awful so we are used to that, I understand, but you've never mentioned a parable you liked. Please tell us.**" Nick smiled and spoke. "**Well there was once a rich man that lived on Earth, he was quite mad. He believed that he could go around the world in one day. He tried everything; he used cars, used horses, boats, planes, and balloons. Never could accomplish the task. He spent his whole life and a great deal of his fortune on this venture. Every day he failed, every day he attempted to do it again. He'd look at the sun and give it the finger; stating that the sun was 'no-good, cheatin', son-of-a-bitch.' Spending resources, his money and his time on such a crazy goal.**" At this point, Nick was in tears, laughing at the absurdity of such a notion. His loved ones were confused.

Nick was laughing to the point that he fell to ground in joy. The type of joy that a kid feels when he has seen something incredibly hysterical. They didn't understand why he found this story so funny. He then explained his joy. "**You don't get it? He always cursed the *equipment*. He was always bitching about the car, the boat, or the plane. He literally believed that the sun was *cheating*. It never crossed his mind that what he wanted to do was *impossible*. I admire that.**"

Michael and AC now understood why he found so much joy in that set of circumstances. **"Michael, every time we are out fighting and protecting the universe, the situation seems impossible. It is just** *improbable.* **We are out flanked, we are outgunned. It doesn't matter. As long as God is with us, nothing is impossible. You will be a wise ruler and great king; I may not be with you, but God is always with you. Impossible is a word that humans say far too often."** With that, he kissed his son, his noble, courageous son good-bye. Michael knew that he would see his father as soon as the job was done. The young monarch also realized that his job was just beginning.

AC, the beautiful second in command of the Alpha Centauri sent notification to Faris and the Blood Knights began to make preparations for the "Deep Breath," the term used for when the soldiers who follow Antonius into the deep dark reaches of space. Usually by the time that they return, many things in the lives of their friends and comrades have changed. It is difficult for many of these warriors to keep close relationships outside of the Knights because these warriors are always gone on the most clandestine, search and destroy missions.

"The Deep Breath" is exactly the reason that Commander Nicolas Cain almost never gets involved in the normalcy of Terran life. Most of the people that are under his care have never been out of many of their own star systems. Even with the vast advances in technology accessible in Terran society, there is still immense distances between these systems. The majority of the Terran people are blissfully unaware of their true protectors. These men and women who serve under Cain are always aware that the lives of their loved ones will inevitably be different when they return. These men and women miss out on the lives of generations of their kin; a truly noble sacrifice. The leadership of the Alliance have their aging process slowed considerably, but the Paladins aging process is slowed even further. Very few Paladins actually live to the end of their life cycles; their lives are so dangerous that it is an inevitability that they will all die in combat. Not many people are truly aware of how old Nick is because it's not really that important. He has traveled through at least 7 of the twenty-nine known galactic super star clusters, encompassing more than 130 billion light years; the Halicon Super Cluster will make *eight*. Time means little to someone who constantly travels it. God's work is the only thing that matters to Cain and his acolytes.

AC speaks to her father, her oldest daughter, Kira, and also her youngest daughter Kima. Also her son, Michael is spending time with his adopted family. Danyzer is impressed with his adopted grandchild; he makes sure that he knows that whenever Michael needs him, he will be there for him. This is a seemingly complicated proposition but not really; it is custom in Rioan culture to develop familial bonds regardless of blood. To a Rioan, a person's actions make them worthy of love. Being Nick's son will cede a difficult road. Even though Michael is a new king, he will still need counsel and Congo cannot do it all by himself. This family is totally dedicated to the Cause; this is the cost of that devotion. They never have a chance to spend time together, but that is job of a Paladin under Nick's command. Familial bonds are a luxury many cannot have; this family is fortunate to share these moments before departing from each other.

As Antonius and Driax go on their final consult, she marvels at the natural beauty of their native planet. The white sand feels good under her feet. The sunlight kisses her face and the morning breeze is welcomed. *How could this planet be so warm with just one sun*, the Alron mused. Amazing. Tired moments find the chancellor a delightful treat. In these next few minutes, she once again has to get Nick to do the improbable but not the impossible. They sit together on the beach quietly. Driax's arm is in Nick's. She finally speaks. **"It is so pretty here. I think that this place is nicer than Mu, maybe even Aquilonia. You were right; I love walking on the sand here. AC tells me that you plan on building a house here; a safe haven for when you finally retire huh? I can't wait to visit. By the way, your son has a lot of you in him. He is handsome; he even has some of your sweet side."**

This will be last time for the immediate future that she has the opportunity to have a face to face conversation with her dear monster. Nick will only break one order if a greater issue persists that will force him to leave his campaign against the Cimms. It has happened before; the results were beyond bone chilling. A sweet side? The last statement brings a smile to the Alpha Paladin's chiseled face. **"I have a sweet side? That's a good one my chancellor. I never knew you had such a sense of humor."** She responded demurely. **"Yes you do. I have always thought that your sweet side was your best side; I just happen to be one of the fortunate people who have ever seen it. And just think I am not even a red head."** Nick smirks at his boss. **"That's funny** madam. What would you request of me?" She pauses, and then speaks sternly. "**I want you to return. Wipe out the Cimms; all of them. This time, don't return until that task is complete. Do it as quickly and efficiently as possible. The siders are not vanquished, just defeated. By the time you return, they will be your priority. I know what you want of me; Michael and the Altarian Federation will be a great ally to us. He will have access to both Danyzer and me whenever he needs us. Now go my monster. Be the *very best at the very worst*.**" Nick smiles and kisses her on her cheek and then he bows to her. "**As you wish.**"

On planet Alta Major, three beings of immense intelligence, a Terran Senator, the Commandant of the Oculari, and the Adjutant of the Altarian Federation are in consult with one another. The Terran Senator, Aya, adopted mother of Antonius speaks first to the others. "**Congo, have all the arrangements been made? My son wanted me to go over the plans with you and his father once more. The timing has to be perfect. Have you gotten confirmation from the Altarian Leadership Council?**" Congo, the brilliant administrator responded as she sipped her Ynarian Fire Tea. "**Yes Senator. They are all in agreement with my master. This has to be done for the good of all in the Star Cluster. By the way, that tea smells incredible. He is only a boy; do you believe that he will be up to the task?**"

In this instant, both Aya and OC both come to the realization that their extended family under Nick has just grown by one more. They are aware of why Antonius put them in proximity of Congo. He is both a kindred spirit and he is also aware that failing his master is not in the best interests of either. Congo is also aware that whatever plans that Cain has for his son is intertwined with everything that has occurred in this part of the super cluster. Killing Atlas and installing both Michael as king and Congo as steward are both essential pieces to this puzzle. When Aya realizes the level of intelligence that Congo possesses coupled with his level of devotion to his duty reaffirms her deep rooted belief that her son never does anything without a plan. *Well played Nicky*, she mused.

At this point, the Ocularian Commandant chimed in. "**It doesn't matter what we think, Antonius says that he is going to do this. Only God can change his mind once Nick chooses a plan of action. Our son's plan is coming along nicely. People tend to believe that he is crazy and he isn't. His insanity is far too rational. It is so incredible.**

What happened to the Altarians will not happen *twice* that I promise you. Michael has no idea the greatness that is within his soul. We shall all see. Danyzer is not going to approve." The senator smiles. "He *never* approves of our fun my friend. It doesn't matter what my husband says. *We don't work for him.* Either the king will come back to his people an Oculari, or *he won't come back at all.*"

As the Khan once said to the Terran Regency, things are in motion that cannot be stopped. There is no time for him and his fleet to stop and ponder all that has been lost and more importantly, all that has been gained. The crew of this ship had made all its repairs and restocked its supplies. Innovations and improvements to the Centauri's primary weapon systems and sensor array have been completed by the newest member of the crew, Jaylun Harris. His brother Jamie will serve as Kira's right hand in combat. Another example of the Earthlings showing themselves approved. Because of his sacrifice and service in the fight with Nex, the Alliance got an unexpected bonus; their original bridge officer is back. However, the people in the Milky Way will need him more than the Centauri will.

This time, the greatest teacher of logic and reason will enthusiastically follow his master's mandate. For what lies ahead of the newest leaders in the Milky Way and for the troubles that lie in the future, they will need him. Both Michael and Emily will need his counsel, love, and expertise. It is night time and the moon is shining against the sea. Petamauck ponders how fortunate both the Alliance and the IGF are that this Khan is the most prepared warrior to meet the incomprehensible task of wiping out the Cimms. He is also humbled at the fact that God has again chosen him to aid in the growth of his people's mightiest protectors. He watches as the Centauri rises from the sea and prepares to head off into the unknown and says his good-byes. *Be careful brother*, he thought.

The Alpha Centauri is a magnificent sight to behold. Many of the children of Terra, both young and old, watch in silence as the ship heads off into space. Then it happened; in less than the blink of an eye, it was gone. In less than one second, she traversed the Milky Way Galaxy. In fifteen seconds, it had passed through the Andromeda Galaxy. Within the first minute, it was beyond the local group. An hour had past and the ship was already 40 million light years from Earth. Like Sayied had once said, it could move beyond the speed of thought. However, that description may not be accurate. That assessment was made *before* Super Tachyon Pulse Drive.

Colonel Faris went to the ready room. Three figures sat in a stance of meditation; two gray-eyed beauties and a monster, a man, a super Paladin, and a Khan who usually snores when he relaxes. The colonel looked at the sight and smiled. *No need to disturb them*, he thought. **"Mr. Harris, take us to level 6. Let's see what she can *really* do."** The Dark-Sider Empire is on borrowed time. As the Centauri rocketed off into the abyss, Regent Uchida, Danyzer, and Chancellor Driax shared a drink, toasting the end of the Cimms. A search and destroy mission to eliminate the Cimminork Empire from the known universe is the new assignment for the Alpha Centauri and their mighty commander. After cleansing the universe of the Cimms, then he can finally get to the Dark-Siders. Happy Hunting Antonius, happy hunting.

APPENDIX

The Secret File

The following is an excerpt from the file on Nicolas Cain. This file is classified as **ABOVE TOP SECRET.** Only a select few of the Paladin Order, Terran Alliance, and a few select Chancellors of the Terran Alliance have actually seen this file. It is incomplete on purpose. Only a few of his abilities are actually recorded and his strength measurement was done only once and that was more than 40 tons in Earth gravity; that was done more than 5 million years ago. His powers from his ascension haven't been measured either. History about his biological family and significant other(s), save one, has also been left out of this file as well.

Khan Antonius

Real Name: *Gaius Nicolas Cain*
Eye Color: Brown
Hair Color: Black
Height: 6'3"
Weight: 215
Earth Age: 33
Aliases: Jaden Campbell, Logan Cain, Nicolas Constantine
Known Associates: Rear Admiral AC, Colonel Sayied Faris, Regent Emily Uchida, Dr. Kima Darius, Commander Kira Darius, Petamauck, Erik the Red

Abilities
1. Immortality
2. Total Night Vision

3. Perfect Reflexes
4. Complete Control over Body (From Electrons, Body Tissue, and Organs)
5. 90 percent Brain Function
6. Super Human Strength (Ability to lift up to 40 tons in Earth Gravity)
7. Super Human Speed
8. Knowledge of all forms of Terran Martial Arts and Several Iconian/Rioan/Oculari Combat Techniques
9. Super Human Agility
10. Rapid Regeneration
11. Genius Level Intellect (Equivalency of 1500 IQ)
12. Super Human Stamina
13. Genius Level Strategist
14. Limited Ability to be in 2 Places at Once
15. Can disguise body Heat and Scent

Appearance: Nicolas tends to keep his head shaved, much like his ancient Carthaginianancestors. When he is in uniform, he tends to wear the colors of red and black in some combination, because those are his two favorite colors. He has a scar over his left eye socket; the result of combat on one of his missions. Even though he has the ability to both regenerate and has complete control of his organs, his dear friend, Kima, thought the scar made him look handsome. He doesn't wear any jewelry save one item; a child that he saved on Mu system's capital planet gave him a woven bracelet that she made as a token of her appreciation for saving her and her family. That child *was Kima*. He only removes it to bathe and he tends to rub it when he becomes agitated. When he is not in combat, he tends to wear a long denim coat, mostly to cover the two hand weapons, a hand held Gatling gun and a miniature pulse cannon that he almost always wears. Even though he shaves his head, he tends to have facial hair, primarily a well manicured goatee. He has no piercings or tattoos. His reasoning is that if he died in combat, he didn't want any distinguishable marks on his body. A nameless corpse because he felt the Cause always mattered more than he ever did.

Personality: Nicolas Cain (KHAN ANTONIUS) is a complex man. He is incredibly misunderstood. Nick is thought to be vicious and cruel, even sadistic. He is none of those things. The thing about him is that he is capable of those actions, but only because those actions are necessary. He is feared by many, but he is adored by all who have ever served with him or under his command. For his loved ones, he would easily kill and never think twice about it. He is capable of incredible kindness and caring, rarely does he ever show it to anyone that he doesn't consider important.

Because of his time on Earth, he developed an incredible faith in God. He reads the Epistles of the New Testament for guidance and the Gospels for strength. He does all this for the kingdom of God. He does not just look at Christ as a deity, but he is a follower of his teachings. He also has great affinity for both David and Job of the Old Testament and Paul of the New. He has seen many things that should have shaken his faith, but instead it has strengthened it. He believes he is following a just cause and his actions are reflective of that believe.

As a child, he developed a tremendous sense of justice and is tolerant of others' ideas and beliefs. He makes decisions both decisively and sensibly. He says that the Cause matters the most, but he will protect his fellow Paladins above all. He is kind to children, hostile towards the self important, and respectful of those who seek enlightenment. He is firmly committed to AC, in part because he knows that she will stand by his side as he wages battle after glorious battle

Even for a person whose past was filled with such cruelty and his future could be considered grim, he is remarkably upbeat. In his mind, God never puts burdens on humans that they cannot bare and if He believes that Nicolas Cain is up to the task, then so be it. If difficult decisions have to be made, he makes them, even if that puts him in conflict with his closest of allies. Once he was forced to kill a version of Petamauck who had taken the Regis of Mu prisoner and threatened to kill her. When faced with killing his friend for a higher cause, he didn't hesitate to do it. He mourned his friend and mentor and was saddened by doing what was necessary; when asked by AC if he would do it again he replied, **"In a heartbeat. If necessary, I would kill you also."** He then found out that this incident was one of the tests to prepare him for the long dark road ahead. He is almost joyous in combat; willing to let opponents believe they have a chance. He will also eliminate all potential threats, believing in total destruction of his opponent/enemy. He often dotes upon Kima and laughs at any joke Sayied says.

Before every battle he prays to God, often while massaging the charm that Kima gave him when she was a girl. To those that he doesn't consider important, he does not smile often and can appear both sullen and pensive; however to his troops, they know him to be funny and full of joy. He tends to laugh and smile before, during, and even after combat. This is in part because he loves his job, crushing the enemy. He will sometimes taunt his opponent, in particular if he feels they have been arrogant before combat. The only person that can get him to laugh or even smile in public consistently is Kima. No one really knows why; Sayied and someone else can tell the same joke and Nicolas will only laugh at Sy's joke.

He could remove the scar he gained from saving Kima, but she asked him to keep it because it makes him look handsome and every time she sees it, she is reminded of Nicolas' vast abilities. She often kisses it; she is the only person allowed to even *touch* it. He is also an accomplished artist, who draws landscapes of the various planets he has visited. Some of the works are hanging in the Museum of Arcadia, where many of the great artistic works reside in the Terran Alliance. His art teacher said that he was the best student that she had ever had even though he only had one lesson. He is humble because he says that he is just a tool. God could have chosen anyone, but he is humbled by the fact God chose him.

Cain's Allies: Because of Commander Cain's multiple and sometimes conflicting bottom lines, he does not share all the details of all missions. His primary confidant is AC, who is not human. She is a hybrid, the mighty Rioan General, Danyzer, married her mother, a human, Aya. She is a quantum traveler, capable of understanding and seeing multiple futures and pasts. She has seen Cain's future and knows what he must do. These multiple responsibilities of Cain cause him to leave Earth and deal with conflicts throughout not just Terran space, but all of the IGF. AC is both respected and feared both inside and outside of the Terran Alliance.

AC has only admitted hatred of one person in her life, that individual happened to be Quenas, Nick's first wife. Once she learned that Quenas was a natural redhead, she immediately dyed her hair back to its original color. Cain was supposed to begin his combat training under Erik the Red and Sho; but she is of the belief that Quenas arranged for Nick's ship to be damaged and eventually diverted to Ocular Theta, but she could never actually prove it. She and her father worked hard along with

Petamauck to get Cain back, but it was too late; once a person starts the academy, they have to complete it. This was particularly disturbing to AC because she knew that Nick was essentially a child. His humanity was still in the process of being formed.

The Oculari are a dead race, but their traditions of manipulation, murder, and destruction live on through the Killing Academy. While AC, Danyzer, and Petamauck were glad that Nick had completed the academy, they were angered further to learn that he had been placed under Quenas' command within the Killing Unit. They were all aware of the kinds of assignments that these people were sent on and what was the expectation. When Nick finally returned, he was even deadlier than before. He was dangerous to both friend and foe. It took a lot of care and affection to attempt to break the conditioning that Quenas had given Cain. Needless to say, those attempts are still considered to be work in progress.

Once at a conference, a Brunan knight tried to accost AC; they are known for their crass behavior. Nick did not like that one bit. When the Brunan became aggressive AC put the knight on his ass; he thought that was foreplay. That was a *huge* mistake. His friend had tried to hit AC from behind with his gun and then Nick acted. Not because she needed his help, but more out of principle. The Brunan Delegation was two members short in a span of 12 seconds. Nick punched the first warrior in the chest, removing part of his sternum and then using it as a stabbing weapon on the other one. The entire delegation was shocked; he killed them so fast that the video monitors couldn't catch him doing it. When asked about this incident, Nick simply stated the obvious; no one can ever *touch* AC without her permission. Whoever does will not only die but the person next to them would die as well. Still, it took eight Earth years for AC to have permission to touch Nick and almost 10 years for her to kiss him; she has been in his personal space ever since.

Once Cain became a Paladin, he became the protégé of Erik the Red. Before Cain became a Paladin, Erik was considered the greatest warrior of the Order. Erik taught Cain several combat techniques, but within a matter of one Earth month, Cain became Erik's superior in combat. However, Nick was so respectful of Erik because of his experience. Erik and Nick were actually a tremendous duo for almost six hundred Earth years, gaining in reputation and stature throughout the Terran Alliance and also the IGF. During the conflict with Hunians, Erik discovered the nature of Cain; the monstrous ability in combat. The Hunian Prince kidnapped AC and two members of the Chancellor's cabinet. Erik and Nick were sent; there were twenty warriors from the Hunari race waiting for them. Nick killed 18 of them within 90 seconds, but he ripped out the spine of the prince and kept him alive for almost 40 hours; all because the prince had the *nerve to kidnap* AC. Erik realized then and there two things; one Nick was not to be trifled with and two, AC is a priority to Cain.

Two rotations later while on assignment, Erik had crash landed on a planet in Kurgan territory. He was considered expendable, but not to Cain. That was the first time that Nicolas went against direct orders from a chancellor; he was not going to leave someone he loved out there to die knowing full well that if the situations were reversed, Erik would do the same thing. Cain retrieved him alone; five hundred Kurgans tried to capture Erik. Because of Cain, there were 500 less Kurgans in the universe. Erik was unconscious during the conflict; he awoke back on the Centauri in the trauma center. The one thing that he remembered was that he thought he heard Nick whistling (Time is on My Side). Erik was glad that this monster was on his side. Yes he is.

Sayied Faris was Nicolas Cain's original wingman in star fighter combat. In the academy, Sayied was considered the only person who was as serious about the Cause as Nick. Sayied originally was studying to be a cleric at the Corinthian University of Theology. He was considered the best student in the university; his thesis on faith and favor was considered to be a masterpiece. Nick actually enjoyed talking to Sayied, which is rare. Compared to Nick, even the brightest of the world of academia in the Alliance is considered stupid. Nick and Faris had several thousand deep conversations, often about second chances and redemption. Cain always respected his point of view, even if they sometimes were in conflict. Faris was on a base in the IGF territory that was the first to be attacked by the Dark-Sider Armada. Sayied took one of the fighter jets that hadn't been destroyed and went into action. In that moment, the pacifist would never be the same again. Cain also went into action in Wing Alpha, destroying several thousand. Encouraged by Faris' action in combat, he was recruited into the Paladin Order. On their first mission together, Sayied made a corny joke before racing into combat; it was so stupid that Nick had to laugh. It was the first time that anyone had heard Cain laugh; ever. He has been laughing in combat ever sense.

The future leader of the Terran Alliance is also among the Paladins of Earth. Her name is Emily and she is both a great communicator and also a capable warrior. She is from New Venice and also has roots with the Carthaginian people who are related to Nicolas which he likes very much. In many ways, she reminds him of what his mother might have been like. For she has the gift of discernment, she has also plans for Commander Cain. She knows that for Nicolas, personal feelings are not as important as the Cause. She has a longer life span than Kira, but that makes Cain little difference. She is a brunette, a red flag for being a lover of Cain. No one really knows why Nick only likes red heads and AC tells everyone that it is not in anyone's best interest to really ask. Nick is a complicated man. The people closest to him understand his motivations for the Cause but not much else; but the beautiful part is that they don't have to. The worst case scenario about asking him a question is that he might actually answer you.

Quenas and Nick: The Oculari are a mystery to everyone within the Terran Alliance and also the IGF. Yes the IGF does have a standard military; infantry, star fighters, and destroyers, but their greatest strength is the Ocularian Assassination Unit. These warriors are the most devious and dangerous. No one within the IGF truly trusts them; in fact no one is quite sure how they are selected, much less trained. Furthermore, no one is sure of just how many have been made or how many are still left alive. They kill their own if necessary and completing their tasks are more important than their own lives. These warriors will sacrifice their loved ones, their planets, and their entire race to complete their jobs. Their understanding of the Cause is probably the most pure of all groups of people within this part of the universe. They are monsters; the vicious, the deadly, the gifted, the necessary. And these people have had their eyes on a certain Earthling since the day they found out that he existed. They create a life for their warriors that seems like a version of Hell itself on Ocular Theta. This is where Nick finds a home.

Nick's combat training is unlike any Paladin before or sense because of a purposeful accident. When Nick had completed his academic training on Arcadia with Petamauck, he was supposed to begin his combat training with Erik the Red. Instead, fate intervened in that set of circumstances when instead of meeting Erik at first, his transport ship had been attacked randomly by an unknown vessel, severely damaging it.

The closest outpost to him was in IGF territory on planet Ocular Theta. Here was the training ground of the Oculari, the deadliest assassins that the IGF had at their disposal. Since he had been deemed a strong candidate for the training, Nicolas was admitted to the Ocularian Killing Academy. It was the cruelest tutelage that any humans in this part of the universe could have ever been given. Rumor has it that this was no accident and that the Oculari had their eyes on this Terran ever since his presence had been made known; this purposeful accident put Nick on his path.

The Ocularian Killing Academy has one goal: to create the deadliest assassins that the Inter Galactic Federation has to offer. These warriors don't know fear; they don't have any remorse or pity. They will stop at nothing to accomplish their tasks and will kill anyone or anything that tries to stop them from completing those tasks. Every class begins with 500 students, but there is *only one* graduate. For the equivalent of 90 Earth years a warrior is trained and put through every kind of physical, emotional, psychological, and spiritual cruelty that could be imagined by the mind. The Oculari purify their students by having them kill and betray each other. The student's pain, be it emotional or physical, would be turned into a deadly addition to their arsenal. All of these students are locked in combat, using whatever means are at their disposal to achieve success, which means that a graduate must kill and/or manipulate the deaths of the other 499 students. Only once all the other students have been vanquished can the final student graduate the Killing Academy.

Nick's Kaepa, or teacher, was considered the cruelest of all Ocularian task masters. She was powerful and manipulative on a level that few humans could ever comprehend. Quenas was stunningly beautiful; even more beautiful than AC (Which is saying A LOT) and deadlier than anyone from the Killing Academy up to this point. It was her job to mold Nick into an efficient, devious, panic inducing killer. She was more than just his trainer, she was his first love. She made Nick fall in love with her intention only to completely crush his heart; it would be a valuable lesson, that all weapons are useful in combat. Emotional weapons are sometimes the most valuable. She used that scenario of her loving Nick as a training exercise. Under her manipulation and subterfuge, he was able to use his mind as a weapon on levels that his fellow Paladins or Ocularian warriors could not conceive. She encouraged him to use his aggression and power to their fullest destructive potential; to dance between wisdom and psychosis.

Over the next 30 Earth years, he killed many of his fellow students in the cruelest of ways. He also used their strengths against them, taking advantage of their fears, their pride, and their own intelligence. He would become an expert in the emotional condition; how to use it against his fellow warrior, how to use it against his fellow allies. After he had killed the 499th student during his campaign of carnage, he met up with his love, his kaepa. After spending the night together, he did the unthinkable. He stabbed her in the heart, killing her. As the Commandant of the Academy inquired about his choice to kill his teacher, he replied that she had been mispronouncing the word the entire time he had been a student.

He concluded that either she was a student or there was some other treachery; either way, she had to die. The academy leadership had no idea that Cain spoke perfect Ocularian; he learned the complex language in less than 60 hours. He knew that the way that she had been using it was incorrect; it gave her away. Cain patiently waited until the right opportunity presented itself and that was when he decided to strike. He received the highest honor ever bestowed upon a student; he was a master assassin as soon as he completed the training. He was correct, there was no such thing as an Ocularian kaepa, but he was incorrect about Quenas loving him; she did. And she still does. He killed her clone; she concluded that once Nick killed the last warrior, that he would probably kill her also. When she realized that she had mispronounced the word, she knew that it was a matter of time before Nick did something about it. After all, she is one of the few people who know just how brilliant Nick is. No explanation that she could give would be sufficient. Her logic saved her life.

Of all the graduates of the Oculari Killing Academy, Cain was by far the most unique. The Paladins and Oculari have always had very different views of what a warrior is and how that warrior should be trained. The Oculari use their emotional pain to fuel their rage and aggression. These warriors don't know fear, in part because these agents have often felt an emotional torture that is normally beyond the pain of their assignments. They have betrayed friends, killed lovers, and manipulated the deaths of people that they might have cared about to become what they are. This was all *before* they graduated. Paladins are nothing like that.

While most Oculari use rage and strength as weapons of choice, Nick was different; he used intellect. He was stronger than any other Ocularian, ever. He was stronger emotionally, physically, and spiritually than all his counterparts. However, he was also the most intelligent Ocularian, ever. There was no strategic or intellectual discourse that he was not completely prepared for. This combination made him something to both behold and fear. He used fear in a way that his peers never did; but if his opposition was not afraid, that was no problem either. He was more than proficient in deadly force on so many other levels. His Paladin abilities just added to the arsenal. A perfect assassin, a perfect knight; a perfect operator.

After completing this training, he was assigned to his lover's command unit. In the 19 rotations that he served, he was involved in more than 12,500 assassinations. He had the highest success rate of anyone within Ocularian Assassination Unit; he never failed to eliminate a target or complete any assignment. He toppled governments, destroyed terrorist groups from within, and destabilized entire star systems with his abilities. Here, he was able to develop the ability to use more than 90 percent of his brain capacity. His intelligence, coupled with his incredible physical ability made him an apex predator; a warrior with no known exploitable weaknesses. He is the only Terran to ever complete the Ocularian Killing Academy; in fact he is the only Terran to ever *attempt* to complete the Ocularian Killing Academy.

On his final assignment with the Assassins, he lost his love. Quenas had been captured by the Unori, a race of Dark-Sider worshipers. They wanted to sacrifice the heart of an assassin of the highest renown, believing that Quenas had the power to cheat death. Little did they know that her beloved Cain was actually the assassin that they needed to sacrifice. The Unori had no idea that when they sacrificed her that they were also killing Cain's unborn child. Nick found the planet where the ceremony was taking place; he killed more than 800 Unori with his katana before reaching his beloved Quenas. By the time that Nick had reached her she was dying. He arrived just in time for her to die in his arms; and then they were gone. And his unborn child, a gift that he given to her, was taken away. He mourned his dearest love for three Earth months, and then he decided that the Unori should join his love in the after-life.

Cain went on a tactical campaign to destroy the entire Unori race. Over the course of two rotations, he manipulated, damaged and destroyed more than one trillion Unori. He killed them all in the cruelest of fashion. He used every skill that he had acquired in the both the Paladin and Oculari academies. He used an electromagnetic propulsion weapon to destabilize their primary star and then he sterilized their race, making it impossible for them to reproduce. He created a neurotoxin that forced the Unori to kill each other in mass panic. He poisoned their water supply and finally destroyed their economy. After Cain had essentially destroyed everything about the Unori race, he did the ultimate. He used a gravity destabilizing weapon to force the planets and moons of the Unori star system collide with each other. These celestial bodies continued crashing into each other over and over until only fine dust particles were left.

Upon hearing the destruction that the Alpha Paladin had caused an entire race, the Terran Chancellor, Alron Zhou, contacted the leader of the IGF; stating that these methods were too severe. The Federation Senator in charge of Clandestine Services, Aya, at the time simply replied, **"He doesn't work for you."** The actual effect on the rest of the quadrant was quite clear; the Ocularian Assassination Unit had an operative capable of destroying an entire system if they felt it necessary. The Commandant of the Oculari was quite pleased. After the carnage, Antonius was told that the Unori had been a thorn in the side of the IGF for eons. No one had been able to stop them until Cain had come along. Danyzer, who had arrived to transport Cain after the final assignment asked him how he was going to sleep that night after killing so many. Cain smiled and replied, **"Like a baby."**

Quenas' entire race save a few here and there was slaughtered by the Unori. She swore revenge upon those people that had destroyed her loved ones. Quenas had served with Nick's mother for a time in the past. The Ocularian knew that if Erika had children, they would be a potential asset to Quenas completing her assignment. She had been on the search for Nick when he was a child, feeling that he had the necessary skill and physical ability to bring about the destruction of the Unori race. Unfortunately, AC and Petamauck had reached him on Earth before she could. She would have to wait to finally get her hands on this deadly creature. Then a funny thing happened, something that she did not expect, she fell in love. She had never felt any sense of love or comfort until she met Nick. So here is the dilemma: fight by Nick's side forever as his wife or continue with the original plan; to use him to get rid of the Unori.

Her rage and lust for vengeance was indeed greater than her love for Nick. She decided that his destructive ability was more valuable to the Terrans and IGF. To her, the math was simple and rational; her life and the life of their unborn child for countless innocents. Cain would understand, she thought. Quenas knew that Cain was the only person capable of bringing about the Unori's destruction but she knew that he would need a catalyst for that kind of aggression. Once he saw himself capable of destroying an entire race to prove his point or for a greater good, he would never have qualms about it again. She let herself get captured, in order to bring about the events that led to the destruction of the Unori. It was a final lesson for the greatest teacher that Nicolas Cain had ever known. The Cause matters more than anything, even love; even his great love and his unborn child. It may have seemed like a terrible price to pay but the message was received.

Danyzer/Paladins/Oculari Relationship: Danyzer was Nick's first commander in the Paladin Command Unit. He was never a Paladin, because he is a Rioan. He is the mighty general who was deemed a Khan, a high protector within the known universe. He was the primary trainer of Nick's mother, Erika Elisma, one of the most deadly Paladins to have ever lived. It had always been Danyzer's hope and wish that Erika would eventually become the next Khan after Danyzer; she was *that* good. She was so good that Danyzer considered having her enter the Ocularian Killing Academy, she was *that* deadly.

Erika was Danyzer's protégé; she was the reason that AC decided to join the Paladin Corps instead of going into a career in politics, which was what Danyzer and his wife, Aya, actually wanted for their daughter. The reason that they were interested in AC going into politics was because of the Unori Massacre. Most of Danyzer's first family had been killed in the service of the Federation and the emerging Terran Alliance more than 925 rotations ago. Aya was a delegate from the Terran Alliance; she had worked with the mighty Rioan General on developmental procedures for the Terran Alliance. They both believed in a better tomorrow; a better and stronger Terran Alliance meant a better and more secure IGF.

They believed that the futures of both groups lied together and worked very hard to make that future a reality. These two driven people eventually fell in love and had a child. Danyzer's relationship with his other children, in particularly his oldest daughter, would never be the same. They felt that he had spent too much time with the humans and not enough time preparing for the upcoming war with the Unori and eventually with the Dark-Siders. His daughter felt his apparent lack of preparation was because her father was letting love interfere with their way of duty. When AC was born, Danyzer seemed even more sidetracked. The mighty Rioan Warriors were going to pay dearly for their Khan's distraction.

The Rioans had been the primary peacekeepers of the Federation and the primary trainers of the Paladins. When the Unori attacked the Federation/Alliance border, many of the remaining Rioan warriors went into battle, they were slaughtered. The majority of the Rioan Khan's family, including his father, three sons, and another of his daughters had been among the warriors who had fallen to the Unori onslaught. When the smoke had finally cleared, the Unori were defeated, but the Rioan race had been almost completely decimated.

The remaining warriors who had served the Federation were furious with their general, feeling that he had been neglectful in his duties as Khan over all the forces. That his vanity project, the Paladins, had taken up far too much of his time from preparations with the Unori. Danyzer's own daughter was beyond incensed at her father's perceived distraction. Even though the Unori had been defeated, many of the remaining Rioans had vowed revenge upon this race, that no matter the personal cost to the Rioans who were left alive, that the Unori would pay. There was a split among the Federation military on whether they should become a more active and far more aggressive unit; whether they should settle issues with other races before they become a problem or continue with the philosophy of defense first. A vote among the board of governors stated that going after the Unori, especially with such depleted numbers was not a prudent decision. Perhaps the Oculari, a near extinct race of warriors, thieves and assassins had it right after all that aggression was more prudent than patience.

When assessing the losses of the Rioan race, it was discovered that more than 88 million males and nearly eighty million females of the Rioans had died in the battle. Because of the countless wars that had occurred over the eons, between the Gondronians, the Unori. The Maogo, and the Kurgax among others had left the mighty Rioan corps depleted. The Rioans gave way to the Terrans, who it was hoped would become the primary peacekeeper force. This did not sit well with the Rioans who remained, many of these warriors' dearest blood had died in the service of the Federation and helped train many warriors including members of the Alliance. They were not pleased with how these actions had occurred and were prepared to go much further than the Federation and the Alliance were.

The Oculari had also been wiped over the years as well, but there was a plan to keep their secret espionage and assassination clan from being completely becoming extinct. An academy created from the most deadly warriors of the Federation was created. The mandate was simple: create a group of spies and assassins who could carry out clandestine missions designed to make the Federation and the Alliance a more secure place. This is where many of the remaining Rioans had been rumored to go. Because of the clandestine nature of the Oculari, no one is really certain how many Rioans joined this group. The results though speak for themselves: Of the remaining 890 million Rioans, over the next 25 rotations, more than 100 million had perished in the most peculiar of ways.

It was decided that two Rioans would be in charge of the Oculari and also the Paladins; Danyzer would lead one contingent's development and another unknown Rioan would lead the Oculari. There was a rumor that the Commandant was both Iconian and Rioan or that he had been raised by one the high priestess of the last house of the Oculari, no one really knew for sure. In fact some were certain that he doesn't really exist. That was the power of the Oculari, it was impossible to dispel rumor from fact, which was how they wanted it. It would also be a school devoted to the preservation of freedom by death and subterfuge, an interesting contrast to say the least. Danyzer's oldest daughter was rumored to have joined the Oculari before AC had been born; after a fight between daughter and father, no one in the family had seen or heard from her since. It is a strong possibility that she was among those 100 million Rioans that died over the eons; if Danyzer knows the truth, he hasn't ever said one word in public about her since that day.

If the loss of his first daughter to the secrecy and madness of the Oculari was a terrible proposition, then being the Kaepa to mighty Erika

Elisma made up for that disappointment. Rumor has it that this young woman from planet Thessalonia was the most gifted Paladin perhaps in the history of the order. There was no physical task that she had not been up to nor was there any foe that she had not been able to best in combat. There had been several incredible battles that she had been a part of, many of her dearest friends had died before her very eyes. For more than 50 rotations, she had fought and conquered everything that her mentor Danyzer had given her. She had been given a legendary standing amongst the humans and even the races of the Federation had become impressed by her exploits. There was a certain girl with gray eyes who had been impressed by her service to the Cause that she gave up on a possible career in politics to be a member of the famed Paladin corps; to be like Erika.

There was a problem though: Erika was tired of being Erika. She bottomed out completely. One mission in particular left her particularly jaded; every member of her mission team died but her and a young Paladin named Seth. She said that the life of a Paladin had a price that was too high for her to pay any longer. With the help of Ryxadrona, the originator of the Paladin process, she attempted the *agroge*, the purge of all her powers. It had always been a theoretical project than an actual one because no one had ever wanted to have their powers purged. She faked her own death and headed to Earth. Danyzer was devastated that another one of his "children" had left him. However, the mighty Khan had no idea that she was alive or had left the system. She assumed the identity of dead baby and began her life as a normal human. There was one problem: the process didn't hold. The longer she was on Earth, the more unstable her powers had become. *This lead to the birth of the Alpha Paladin.*

Once Nick was a member of the Paladins, Danyzer realized that the way that he was being trained was not adequate for the long, dark road ahead. He was constantly being held back by the methods of the Paladin; he wasn't tapping into the fury and focus that he truly possessed. He was a child born from the most painful of circumstances. He had been a prisoner in some form or fashion his entire life. He never had anything close to normal childhood. Nick would never trust any of them at this rate. Nick was beyond angry, he was borderline psychotic. He knew almost nothing of his parents and he was forced to trust a group of people who needed him beyond any reasonable measure. He was smarter than the teachers that he had and was already stronger than almost every other Paladin by the time that he was eighteen. Danzyer's daughter, AC, had been charged with trying to build up his humanity; every interaction that he had for the majority of his life had been hostile, cruel or disappointing to say the least. Danyzer was deliberately thwarting her every attempt to build it up. He had other plans for the young Paladin.

Nick had killed more people by the age of twelve than some of his counter parts had as members of the military. He was terrifying in the combat trials and most of the people who had come in contact with him, were beyond petrified. The Federation was interested in him getting in the field as quickly as possible, while AC and Petamauck were constantly fighting Danyzer that his humanity was necessary. At this point in his life, he had no reason to care about anyone or invest in anything. That no one had the right to ask so much from such a young boy who had no family. He was needed, but not loved. He was feared, never comforted. *It was exactly how Danyzer wanted it.*

Danyzer went to Ocular Theta and spoke with old acquaintances; they hadn't had pleasantries in a long time. He knew what they had become; the vicious, the gifted, the deadly, the necessary. The Darksiders were still a problem, as well as the Unori, the Kurgax, and the Gondronians among others. The Oculari had done many incredible things, many horrible things to make the quadrant more secure. The Paladins had done many incredible things to help make the quadrant secure as well. Neither group was going to be strong enough as currently constructed to thwart the danger that would be coming from the furthest reaches of space as well as the problems that were going to be present in their back yard. Danyzer had been trying to train a warrior that could lead both the Federation and Alliance forces into battle after glorious battle with their endless hoards of foes. He was certain that Cain was up to the challenge. He was certain that the Paladins alone couldn't complete the job of training him. He would be the connecting piece in this complicated puzzle.

A decision was made between the Oculari and the Khan of the Federation who was moonlighting with the humans. It would be the cruelest decision that could have been made. Danyzer would act as if he had no knowledge of these actions; he knew that if the Paladins believed that he was in on this, they would never trust him again and his daughter would never forgive him, but this had to be done. Danyzer's wife was annoyed because she suggested that he should have never been a Paladin in the first place; he was already stronger than any of them and Nick was definitely smarter than all of them. The Paladins were a waste of time as far as she was concerned. Cain's life was filled with so much pain and suffering. That being said, there was no student who understood the Cause better than he did. He believed that God never put more on his people that they could bare. It was obvious from his birth that he could shoulder a tremendous charge if necessary. Nicolas Cain was about to become an Oculari. He would be the first Terran Oculari and more importantly, he would be the first human KHAN. May God forgive them for what they have done.

The Terran Issue

The following is an excerpt from the Genesis Archives about the history of humanity in the stars completed by the records keeper, Nari the Wise. This document will hopefully shed insight into why the Earth issue is such an emotional situation for many of the citizens of the Terran Alliance. On one hand, the Alliance has thrived as a fully vested people in the universe, both capable from a diplomatic standpoint and also a military standpoint. That being said, the Earth is the home planet of humanity, the home of both Jesus and the home of Paul; these two issues make the thought of leaving Earth to its fate without Alliance protection either too much to bear or that humanity has moved on.

History: The Rioans, beings from the Andromeda Galaxy began taking note of human development sometime between 7,000 and 5,000 BC and were marveling at the progress that was being made by several ethnic groups simultaneously. The Rioans also were intrigued by the human capacity for war and bloodshed. After their encounter with the Dark-Siders and various other insidious races, the Rioans were a depleted race of warriors; many of the other peoples of their galaxy did not have the resolve to continue fighting at such a proficient rate. To the Federation, the humans of Earth were the people who could not only stand against any foe but would be prepared to destroy themselves to achieve victory. So a decision was made that humanity's introduction to the rest of the universe would have to come sooner than later. Many races were already aware of the human race and knew that it would be a matter of time before they would be able to defend themselves. Coupled with the resources that Earth possessed, it would be a prime target for stronger opposition. The Rioans believed that those actions were unfair and would sponsor humanity's development, much like the Iconians had once sponsored theirs.

Between the years of 4,000 BC and 400 AD, with an occasional incursion after that time period, the Rioans began to seed the quadrant with humans. The decision was to take the best of what the planet had to offer in terms of science, art, and the humanities. The Rioans selected the Aztecs, Mayans and Incans of South America because of their ability to recognize the concept of zero, the value placement of the absence of value, and also their ability to create pyramids and develop architecture. The Africans, in particularly the Egyptians, Ethiopian, Carthaginians and the people of Kush in particular for their ability to develop large scale construction projects such as pyramids, medicine breakthroughs, and also the development of the first institutions of higher learning, such as a university and also libraries.

The Greeks and Romans were also taken as well the several groups of people from the continent of Asia. The native North Americans and Greeks were important because of their development of democratic means of governance and resource allocation. The Asians understood war strategy and espionage as well as perfected hand to hand combat. In addition, the Romans and Asians had discovered the means folding both iron and steel into weapons, coupled with the ability to create gas powered weapons. These groups of people in particular were all advanced for their time; the Rioans considered these groups better prepared for the long journey ahead for making humanity a viable race within the universe.

It was also important that over time the Rioans would be able to select scholars who had studied under the best of humanity in several fields. The best students of the theologians, mathematicians, astronomers, and politics had been also picked over time. The thought process was to introduce these new concepts to the humans gradually while at the same time speeding up their development. The Rioans, while formidable in combat, knew that they had to be careful. If other planetary systems caught wind of their plan, they could be overwhelmed and humanity could very well be destroyed before it has an opportunity to truly begin. Since time works differently in different parts of the universe, the humans had the chance to develop space travel, fusion technology, deal with economic and also religious issues amongst themselves. The benefactors of the Terrans were also interested in the humans being unified by the cause of freedom and protection of the innocent. The helpless would never be preyed upon. Danyzer began to implement the second part of the plan

With most races who have been "sponsored", a decision is usually made early in its existence of what kind of people they were going to be. The humans were different because they were capable of being many things at the same time. The farmer could at any time take up arms to protect his family, the scholar could also be a servant, the mother could become a warrior, the cleric could become an educator; these varied skills always intrigued the Rioans. The Rioans however decided that there would be at least one group dedicated solely to the protection of the innocent in all forms; that all tyranny and oppression would be dealt with swiftly and efficiently. The Paladins were born.

The Paladins were created with the thought of a swift acting defense force that would eventually be the primary protectors of both humanity and also the newly formed Inter Galactic Federation. Many sentient peoples were not strong enough on their own to last in the universe. The universe operates much like the law of the jungle; the strongest shall rule the weakest. Whoever was at the top of the food chain shall rule over the others. The only way to combat such a savage proposition was to be in collaboration with others and hope that combined strength was better than standing alone and being wiped out. Many races of people never get the chance to fully develop because of enslavement or outright destruction. As large as the universe is, only a relative few planets can naturally sustain complex life. People like the Rioans tried to ensure that this would not happen to all recent developing races. The Paladin Project was a way to make sure that the humans would not fall to that kind of fate.

Over the years of the human development, the issue of religion was always a hot button issue. With so many different kinds of people, there was an abundance of religions to say the least. However, the religion that eventually won out was that of Christianity. The Greek, Roman, Africans, and Arabians who had grown up in the universe all had an affinity towards it. Many of the warriors from around the Mediterranean Sea had been exposed to it by Paul. Several of his students had been taken off planet Earth and had continued to preach the gospel according to him. A great many conflicts ensued over the course of time but because of the sheer number of believers, they eventually won out.

Because of the viciousness of the combat over religion, Danyzer eventually had to find scholars from the end of the second AD millennium to help bring some sort of sanity. Eventually science and religion became another issue and it finally took a cleric who had both a science background and was a well-trained theologian to stop the humans from killing each other. The order of clerics who prescribe to this merging of science and religion call themselves the Order of Saint Thomas, named after the cleric who saved humanity. Thomas was instrumental in the development of binary fusion technology as well as someone who was trained in theology at the University of Eden. Other religions exist within the Terran Alliance but the dominant one is Christianity.

As the Paladins began to develop, the Rioans realized that the humans while well trained were not physically strong enough to handle all the threats to the IGF and the Alliance. A young female Rioan scientist, Ryxadrona, developed a physical and neurological process that would make the humans strong enough and smart enough to be able to fight against any foe and not only be capable of standing a chance in hand to hand combat but would more than likely be stronger than most of their opposition. The biological process has been kept secret accept to small number of people, both human and Rioan over the eons. The process had been modified over time. The first "new" Paladins were borderline psychotic; the next couldn't control their emotional equilibrium. They had too much power and too little understanding. It was only after Thomas suggested that conditioning of spiritual and emotional content was essential to the being of a Paladin was the right mix created. That is when the Cause was created.

The Cause is the essential principle that all Paladins adhere to. It is simply that all these warriors are tools of God. That these warriors' purpose is to protect the innocent and helpless; to make those that would prey upon others become preyed upon. That service to others and being a good steward were the premises under which a Paladin must operate. That dying in the service of God and their fellow human was the ultimate gift of charity. All other groups of people throughout the universe had a similar version of the Cause; this would be the connecting line between humanity and the rest of its brethren of the IGF.

After spending so much time in development with each other and the agreement that Earth would be allowed to develop without their interference has left many humans jaded about their home world. Many of them while not always in agreement about issues of policy, religion, economics, and other issues would never have acted in the way that their ancestors have behaved. Many are truly disturbed at the actions of what they like to call the natives or the "savage landers." When several of the Nubian and Indian humans went to Earth to visit in secret, it took a military strike to rescue them from the planet. Intolerance, paranoia, racial prejudice, and sexism were consistent factors that were discovered on these pilgrimages. Chancellor Apollo finally decreed that visitation of the home world was prohibited; stating that it was unfair to hold their brethren accountable for what millions of years' worth of development did for the Terran Alliance. Most of the humans there had never even left the planet, much less left their own countries. It was too dangerous to do so.

Since the planet was deemed too dangerous for the Terran Alliance to visit, many humans developed contempt, if not outright hatred for their fellow man. Earth was always considered a part of the Alliance technically because it was the ancestral home of the humans. It was never mentioned as more than a passing thought by the clerics, stating that was where Jesus and Paul had come from. However, it was always a point of hostility because both of them were killed. Men like Cain believe that the events on Earth were and are central to the development of humanity in the universe and it should always be protected. That one day God will make Earth the center of humanity; this does not sit well with many people within the Alliance. There is a contingent that believes that Earth will eventually become too much of a hassle to continue protecting it. A damping field has been placed over the entire Solar System to protect it from predatory groups.

Several eons ago, the Earth's damping field was destroyed accidentally by a rogue planetoid. A parasitic race, the Poluux, had discovered a planet with water. Since their planet was a dry desert, they felt that the water should be theirs. A contingent of humans, led by Vice Alron Dannica Halima went to try and negotiate a peace accord and with promises of helping the Poluux obtain water from another source. The Poluux felt that this negotiation was from a position of weakness and destroyed the contingent. Chancellor Castor sent the Paladins, led by a young Captain named Nicolas to deal with the Poluux. In one hundred seventy-two hours, the damping field had been restored. There also were no Poluux left in the universe; all 380 billion of them werepurged. The young officer led a search and destroy mission to eliminate the entire race. When asked about his course of action, he stated that fear of Paladin retribution would be a deterrent from ever bothering the Earthlings if they were discovered. It was the simplest solution to a complicated problem.